NO
PLACE
TO
HIDE

NO
PLACE
TO
HIDE

JS MONROE

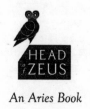

An Aries Book

Head of Zeus Ltd
First Floor East
5–8 Hardwick Street
London EC1R 4RG

WWW.HEADOFZEUS.COM

For Hilary, Felix, Maya and Jago

FAUSTUS: For the vain pleasure of four and twenty
years hath Faustus lost eternal joy and felicity. I writ
them a bill with mine own blood. The date is expired.
This is the time. And he will fetch me.

—Christopher Marlowe, *Doctor Faustus*

The new camera appeared last week. Perched high above the platform in Wiltshire, it watches the early morning commuters like a heron waiting for fish. Patient, predatory. Two women hurry past, unaware they're being observed, keen to secure seats on the London train. Behind them, a late-runner jumps on board between the closing doors. He slumps down by the window, breathless, sweaty, staring back at the receding camera.

Up in south-east London, a helicopter arcs across a grey sky, the clatter of its blades cutting through the din of rush hour traffic. Effortlessly, it banks back towards a busy junction, losing height as it approaches. A woman taps on her steering wheel, checks her baby daughter in the car seat beside her, smiles at her son in the rearview mirror. She glances up at the traffic lights, but it's the helicopter that has her attention, hovering in front of her like a behemoth, a sleek camera slung beneath its belly.

Further south, in Lewisham, a courier driver is already running behind with important medical supplies for the hospital. It's a temperature-controlled delivery and he hopes he's not too late. A dashcam points towards the road ahead. Another is angled back at his face. Keen to make up time, he accelerates, brakes too suddenly, cursing the car in front of him – and the AI technology that will slash his pay.

Meanwhile, over in Cambridge, a student locks up his bike, chatting with a female friend. He seems relaxed, almost carefree, as he strides across the college courtyard, catching

*at spilled anatomy lecture notes. Outside the porters' lodge,
a CCTV camera, fixed to the ancient wall like a giant insect,
clocks their arrival. His friend walks inside but he hesitates,
studying the camera. Deep within its lens, a tiny red light
pulses impassively.*

1

What's the time, Mr Wolf? Adam counts to twenty paces before he glances up at the security camera. Yesterday he barely managed ten. When he was a child, he used to love the thrill of the stop-start steps, the mounting tension. *Dinner time!* But he's not playing games now. If only his life were so simple. The camera appeared a month ago, at the bottom of his road, impaled on a thirty-foot steel pole. Sometimes the lens moves, angling its Orwellian gaze on the local youths who gather below. Every time Adam leaves the house, he tries to ignore it, walk past without looking up, counting his paces like a child, but he can't. He has to stop, convinced that the camera's started to watch him too, which is ridiculous. He's a law-abiding citizen. Makes sick children better. Not exactly a crack dealer.

'I'm tired,' Freddie, his five-year-old son says, tugging at Adam's sleeve.

'Tired?' Adam says. 'How can you possibly be tired, monkey? We've barely made it out the front door.'

Earlier, Freddie announced that he wanted to walk to the park today, but now he wishes to be carried. And who is Adam to refuse? He scoops Freddie up onto his shoulders, at the same time wedging one foot under their jogging pram's back wheel to stop it rolling down Maze Hill. He knows he's a soft touch. Too soft, according to his wife, Tania.

'I've got it,' Adam says, as Tania offers to take the pram. Their six-month-old daughter, Tilly, has finally given in to sleep after a busy night.

Tania lifts up her hands in mock surrender. She's exhausted, tired to the core. Tilly's still breastfeeding and Freddie's been playing up all week.

'Sorry,' Adam says, letting her take the pram. Freddie buries his hands deep in his dad's hair, kneading it like Play-Doh. Adam tries to do everything at weekends, which only seems to make things worse.

'How I manage without you is a mystery,' Tania says as they continue down the road in the spring sunshine. A gentle breeze is blowing in from the south. Before they had children, Saturday mornings used to be a highlight of their week. Lie-ins and lovemaking followed by runs along the towpath, moseying around the market, drinks at the Cutty Sark Inn. Now it's the playground in Greenwich Park. The soft-play area on Creek Road if it's raining.

'The camera's doing a good job,' Adam says, looking up at its menacing dark glass. He hasn't told Tania that he thinks it's filming him. 'No trouble.'

'The guy in the corner shop says it's not a police camera,' Tania says as they turn off into the park. It's true: there's no official sign, nothing to say who actually erected it. 'MI5, apparently,' she adds.

'He would say that.'

Adam has to listen to a new conspiracy theory every time he pops in for a pint of milk. But he still can't resist another glance back at the camera after he lowers Freddie to the ground. Has it moved, changed angle? It's no good. He should seek proper help. Accept how bad things have become: that he's convinced he's being observed every hour of every day. Filmed. Last week, he even asked a colleague in psychiatry about it.

'Scopophobia – a fear of being watched,' his colleague said, rather pompously. 'Own it and become an actor. Actors love being watched.'

That's the irony. Adam was an actor once, when he was a medical student. But he couldn't tell the psychiatrist that university was where it all began. He's never been able to tell anyone.

Five minutes later, on the bench together with a couple of coffees, they watch Freddie run about the playground. Tilly is still asleep in the pram beside them, which doesn't bode well for later. At least it gives Tania a break. Adam's desperate to launch Freddie skywards on the swings, spin him dizzy on the roundabouts, but he knows that Tania wants to talk.

'I think I'll go down to Mum and Dad's this afternoon,' she says, tucking a strand of her long, light brown hair behind an ear. 'They haven't seen the kids for weeks.'

'Today?' Adam says, failing to hide his disappointment. The plan had been for her to go on Monday, but he doesn't want another row with Tania. There have been enough of those in recent weeks.

'Of course, that's fine,' he adds, feeling sick. He so wants Tania to be happy, but it's as if a light has gone out in her life and he doesn't know how to switch it back on. 'If you're not too tired. I could drive you down, take the train back?'

'I'm fine,' she says.

They sit in silence, watching a group of women jog past. When he and Tania used to go running together, they synced their Bluetooth headphones to the same playlist. It felt like they were in a movie – in a good way.

'I just need some time,' she says quietly, sipping on her coffee. 'You always say that you want me to be happy, but you also don't want our kids to be brought up by strangers.'

'Tania, that's—'

'I just miss my job, that's all,' she says, interrupting him.

Tania was a successful GP before she had children. A professional, independent woman.

'And you're better with the kids than I am,' she adds.

Before he can answer, Adam spots someone on the far side of the playground filming him on his phone. His mouth dries, pulse starts to quicken. Could it be him? Instinctively, he stands up, considers his options. The man is in his forties and Adam's sure he recognises him from university.

'What is it?' Tania asks, looking up at him.

Perhaps he's imagining it. 'Nothing,' Adam says, about to sit down.

The man turns to walk away, but then he stops and holds his phone up in their direction again. It *is* him.

'Won't be a moment.' Adam sets off at a brisk pace through the playground, focused on the man, clenching and unclenching his fists, trying to ignore the adrenaline sluicing through his body. He manages to smile at a fellow dad by the swings as he passes, keen not to create a scene.

The man with the phone is dressed in a black T-shirt and black jeans. Adam's sure it's him. The familiar hawkish face and sickly pallor. The same unmistakeable air of menace.

'Excuse me,' Adam says as he approaches. The man is lost

in his phone, half turned away from him, and hasn't seen Adam. 'Were you filming me just now? When I was over there?'

'You what?' The man looks up.

It's not him. Shit. Adam knows at once he's made a terrible mistake.

'I'm so sorry.' Adam surveys the playground. A little boy runs over from the sandpit and wraps his arms around the man's legs. 'Forgive me, I thought you were someone else.'

The man gives him a derisive look and walks off with the child, glancing over his shoulder as if Adam's a madman. He was filming his own son.

2

'Are you going on a run, Daddy?' Freddie asks as Adam stretches his calf muscles. Adam glances across at Tania, still sitting on the park bench. She gives him a tired smile.

'Just a quick one, a little scamper around the park with Tilly,' he says, 'to keep her asleep.'

'Can I come?' Freddie squints up at Adam in the sunshine.

'You stay here with Mummy.'

'But I want to come with you.'

Adam crouches down until he's at eye level with Freddie. 'I know you do, and I want to go running with you too – if I can keep up. What have you got in those trainers of yours? Secret jet-powered rockets?'

'Don't be silly, Daddy. Why can't I come?'

He checks on Tania and lowers his voice. 'Because right now Mummy's a little bit tired – your sister here seems to like being awake at night and asleep during the day. Topsy-Turvy Tilly – I think that's what we should call her from now on, don't you? So I want you to look after Mummy while I go for a quick run. And then you and I will speed around the park later.'

Adam turns away. No they won't. Tania's taking Freddie and Tilly to her parents this afternoon. He wishes she'd go on

Monday, after they've all had a happy weekend together. Like a normal family.

'OK,' Freddie says reluctantly, hanging on to the second syllable.

Adam looks across at Tania, who's cupping her coffee, staring into the middle distance. 'Back in ten minutes,' he calls out, but they both ignore him.

He tells himself he's looking after Tilly as he strides off across the bottom of the park. Giving Tania a proper break. In truth he just wants to run, release some of the pent-up tension of recent weeks. At the top of the park, where he and Tania once gathered for the London Marathon, Tilly begins to cry. They couldn't be further away from her mother's milk, if hunger is the problem. Taking her out of the pram, he rests her against his shoulder, holding her tiny body in his big hands to shield her from the breeze, gusting now from the south-west. His dad taught him how to read the wind when he was learning to sail as a child, beating across Mount's Bay in an old National 12 dinghy.

'It's OK,' he whispers, cradling her head as he starts to sing.

'Hush, little baby, don't say a word,
Mama's going to buy you a mockingbird.'

They are the only words he knows of the lullaby, but he repeats them a few times before laying her back down gently in the pram. It seems to have done the trick. His dad never got to see his grandchildren, never knew his son had left Cornwall to become a doctor in London.

'You available for babysitting?' a jogger asks as she runs past them.

He grins back at her. 'Fully booked, I'm afraid.'

'No surprise there,' she calls out over her shoulder.

The exchange makes him feel better after the hideous scene with the man and his phone. He's such a fool, needs to chill out. He sets off down the steep Maze Hill side of the park towards the playground, big feet pounding beneath him. Against all odds, Tilly is still asleep as he slides the pram through the playground gate.

Up ahead, he can see Tania on one of the benches and, to judge from her listing body, she is asleep too. A burst of panic, like gunfire. Where's Freddie?

He glances over at the swings, the rocky sandpit area, the roundabout. Freddie's nowhere to be seen.

'Tania!' he calls out, still twenty yards away. 'Tania?' he shouts, louder now. This time she sits up and looks around. 'Where's Freddie?'

'Shit, I'm sorry,' she says, standing as Adam jogs up to her. 'He was just over there, playing in the sand. He can't have gone far.'

'He's not there any more.' Adam tries hard not to sound accusatory. 'Freddie?' he shouts, half-heartedly at first, as if he's calling him in from their garden. 'Freddie? Freddie!' He's bellowing now.

People stop and turn.

'We're looking for our son. Five years old? About this high?' He gestures with his hand. He can hear the tremor in his own voice, which scares him even more. 'Red T-shirt, blue shorts. White trainers.' With secret jet-powered rockets.

'Oh God, I'm so sorry, Adam.' Tania stares out at the park. 'He can't have gone far.'

'It's OK,' Adam says. 'It's not your fault. I shouldn't have gone for a run.'

Tilly starts to cry. Tania leans down into the pram and picks her up. 'She needs feeding,' she says.

'You stay here. I'll have one more look around and then call the police.'

Adam sets off, heart thumping like a drum. The playground is a large area, enclosed by wrought-iron fencing. If Freddie's no longer inside it, he must have gone out through one of the two gates, which swing shut automatically. It's not like him. Adam starts at one end, where, beyond the gate, a large shallow lake is used for paddling. A quick glance at the water. Relax. Freddie knows not to go anywhere near it. He works his way around to the other side of the playground, scanning the grassy slope beyond.

He's about to ring the police when he sees a woman in the distance, walking towards him, diagonally down the hill. In her arms, a boy in a red T-shirt and blue shorts. Freddie, no question. Adam lets out an involuntary sigh of relief.

'It's OK, he's here!' he calls across to Tania, who's struggling to feed Tilly on the bench in the playground. Tilly is still crying. 'He's safe.'

He starts to jog towards the woman. Freddie is balling his knuckles in his eyes – the way he does when he's trying not to cry – but his face lights up as he sees Adam. 'Daddy!' he yells.

The woman lets him down. She's still twenty yards away and Adam hasn't taken her in. He's more interested in Freddie, who runs down the slope and hugs him.

'Where have you been, you little monster?' he says, lifting Freddie up in his arms.

'I found him over there,' the woman says, turning to look back up the hill as she comes over to join them. 'He seemed lost, so I was bringing him back down to the playground, where he said his mother was.'

Adam swallows. He knows that voice, even though he hasn't heard it for more than twenty years. He would recognise it anywhere, its raspy, textured tone shot through with the faintest of French accents. For a second he avoids looking up, but then he lifts his gaze.

It's Clio, the woman who broke his heart at Cambridge and has haunted his dreams ever since. Older, of course, but just as he remembers her: short, cropped hair, high cheekbones and such big eyes, black as the leather jacket she's wearing.

'Adam?' she says, seemingly as surprised as he is. 'Oh my God, it *is* you.'

'Clio?' Adam clutches Freddie's hand a little tighter. 'What on earth are you doing here?'

'Just passing through,' she says, her voice returning to a lazy drawl. 'Friends in Blackheath, you know? How about you?'

'I live here – over there.' He waves in the direction of their house on Maze Hill. He remembers the frisson of danger he used to feel whenever he was in the same room as Clio. He feels it again now: fear mixed with something else, more adrenaline than excitement, as if her empowered sexuality is some kind of primal challenge. *Call yourself a man?*

'How incredible,' she says. 'Freddie's a lovely little boy. Now I know why.'

Adam shakes his head in disbelief, a blur of unfaithful emotions coursing through him. Is Clio married? Has she got children herself? Where's she been all these years? He checks himself.

'You must come and meet my wife, Tania,' he says, glancing guiltily at her left hand. No wedding ring. 'She'll be so pleased to meet you. To thank you for finding Freddie.'

3

Cambridge,
May 1998

The big news is that the last night went well. Despite my intense misgivings – as already confided to these pages – I didn't fluff any of my lines and even Clio seemed impressed. The audience too. There was a stunned silence at the end of the play, when Doctor Faustus is dragged down to hell by demons. No forgiveness, no redemption for a man fired by hubris and his lust for limitless knowledge. Just a brutal, shocking conclusion to the deal he'd struck with the devil: a lifetime of power and pleasure in return for his soul. *Lucifer and Mephistopheles… I gave them my soul for my cunning.*

As ever, though, my mind went blank when Clio came round for a chat afterwards in the dressing room. I'd just spent two hours on stage, exchanging some of the most memorable lines in English literature with her Mephistopheles – *Was this the face that launched a thousand ships/And burnt the topless towers of Ilium?* – but when the curtain came down, I was tongue-tied. Again. Couldn't string two bloody words together. Articulate on stage as Doctor Faustus, a mumbling wreck as aspiring Doctor Adam the moment I came off. Am I really so awkward around women that I can't even talk? I thought acting might help make me more confident. Medicine, too. After all, surgeons and actors have a lot in common – big egos, both work in a 'theatre', boom-boom.

Anyway, there I was in the ADC Bar tonight for the after-show, feeling out of my depth surrounded by aspiring thesps, not to mention the ghosts of all those famous ADC alumni – Ian McKellen, Derek Jacobi, Simon Russell Beale, the Monty Python set. Given such a high hit rate, there's a fair chance that some of the people who were at the party this evening will be the famous names of tomorrow. Not me, that's for sure. That sense of anticipation, of career expectation, causes too much looking over people's shoulders for my liking. Having said that, I know we'll see Clio's name in lights one day, maybe in film rather than theatre. Everyone thinks so, not just me.

It was pretty raucous at the bar. The Deptford Society, who produced the play, was paying for drinks, and people were filling their boots. Clio was further down the bar and, emboldened by the free beer, I couldn't take my eyes off her. You'd have thought I'd have done enough of that on stage, sharing nearly all my scenes with her, but no. I've never seen anyone like Clio, her blatant femininity, the heightened sense of intimacy you feel in her company, the way she leans in close to you when she speaks, as if you're the only person who matters to her. Though that probably says more about my limited love-life back home in Cornwall. She seems so at ease with her own body, comfortable in her skin without ever appearing vain.

'Your tongue will fall off if it hangs out any further.'

It was Louis, standing next to me at the bar and dressed from head to toe in black: black T-shirt, battered long black leather jacket and torn black jeans. He's a bit of a star is Louis, a mature student already hailed as a groundbreaking director at uni – an auteur, the next big thing in film. He's certainly got something, an aura of creativity that draws people into his circle, including Clio. Money too. There's little evidence that Louis has ever had to suffer for his art. Eton-educated, he's one of those people who go out of their way to cover up their privilege. Take the yellow-stitch Doc Martens boots he always wears: scuffed, unpolished, a calculated rejection of the shiny brogues he no doubt sported at school. He even had the luxury of choosing where to do his PhD: Oxford and Cambridge both made him offers, apparently. Rumour has it he tossed a coin.

He looked from my face to hers and back again. I'd seen him around with Clio, exchanged occasional nods, but we'd never actually spoken to each other before and I blushed, taking refuge in my pint of Doom Bar.

'That obvious?' I managed to say.

It was a toss-up between walking away or fessing up to my embarrassing infatuation. Was my tongue really hanging out? Ouch. I wanted the ground to swallow me up, particularly as I've always suspected that he and Clio might be an item.

'You're in good company.'

Louis raised a small camcorder to his eye. A Sony Handycam. I watched him pan it across the crowded bar, as if it was the most natural thing in the world to do. No one appeared to react or even notice – Louis was seldom seen without his camcorder – but then the camera settled on Clio. Instinctively, she seemed to know. She turned and scowled, eyes narrowing, chin raised in smouldering defiance.

'She's a natural in front of the camera, isn't she?' Louis

whispered, still looking through the lens. 'The best movie stars never blink.'

I couldn't think of what to say, mesmerised by Clio's response to the camera, the way she stared back at Louis. Her gaze was fixed – unblinking, just as he said. After a few seconds, he lowered the camcorder and ordered a vodka and lime. Clio turned away, as if in victory. Louis wasn't a member of the cast or crew and had to pay for his drink. Technically, he shouldn't have been there at all, as it was a private party, but I assumed Clio had invited him. Most hosts would let him in anyway, just to add a bit of cred to their party. I had time to look at him properly as he waited for his vodka. His pale face was sharp-edged and angular, like a bird of prey's, his lips almost feminine, defined by a pronounced Cupid's bow.

'You were good tonight,' he said, after his vodka had arrived. 'Very good.'

'Thanks,' I said. 'Clio was the star.'

'Isn't she always?' He pulled out a bag of tobacco. 'It's a great play. One day I'd like to shoot the film. A modern take on the original Faustian pact. Not literal, you understand, and without any of the low comedy scenes.'

'No boxing popes round the ear, then?'

'Just the important bits.'

'Which are…?'

I was keen to hear his take on *Doctor Faustus*. Our version stuck pretty closely to Marlowe's text, but the story is so rich in human insight, it's ripe for reinterpretation. Faustus, an ambitious but frustrated academic, craves a deeper knowledge of the universe, turns to magic – necromancy – and conjures up the demon Mephistopheles, Lucifer's agent. They strike a deal: Faustus can have infinite knowledge and power in return for giving his soul to Lucifer – in twenty-four years' time. The way I played it, Faustus doesn't really believe that the devil will come calling: the date of reckoning is just too far ahead to be of concern. Ironically, though, he's unsure what to do with his new-found power, frittering it away on practical jokes on the pope and lusting after Helen of Troy. But when the date finally approaches, he panics at the prospect of eternal damnation. The incessant pain! He doesn't repent, though, despite being given every opportunity, and when he calls out to Christ to save him, it's too late. By the end of the play, he's certainly discovered more about the world and himself: human pride comes at a hideous price, limitless power is overrated, and free will is illusory. In true Calvinist fashion, Faustus was damned from the day he was born.

I watched Louis lick a Rizla paper and finish rolling his ciggy. He didn't seem in a hurry to offer his own interpretation.

'I first heard of the play as a child,' I said, filling the silence. 'When I spotted "Doctor Faustus" carved into one of the concrete seats at the Minack, an open-air theatre not far from Land's End.'

'The Minack?' Louis said, looking up. 'Know it well.'

'You do?' I was surprised. 'My dad took me there far too young to watch *King Lear*. It's where I caught the acting bug.'

Louis smiled. 'A good place for Lear to rage in a storm. And Doctor Faustus.'

'Nineteen sixty-seven – that was the date of the performance on the seat.'

I didn't add that when I was a tearaway teenager returning to port after a week of fishing at sea I used to see the evening lights of the theatre shining out into the night sky from the cliffs and fantasise about being on stage rather than on deck.

'It's a play about the folly of human ambition,' Louis said, cutting into my memories. 'In many ways, Faustus was the ultimate over-reacher – and prepared to do anything, even sign away his own soul, to achieve his goals, to gratify his desires.' He lit up. 'We all make them, you know, in our different ways,' he continued, throwing back his head to exhale. 'Deals with the devil to get what we want, shameful trade-offs that come back to bite us. Faustian pacts.' He held my eye. 'Every day we wrestle with good and bad impulses. And at the end of our lives, the ledger of our actions, the decisions we've taken, must balance, as Doctor Faustus discovered.'

I was about to show off, say something about the clash of Renaissance and Medieval world views, when a student squeezed past and kissed Louis on the cheek. I moved aside awkwardly as the two men chatted, Louis' back to me. And then another student approached the bar. He had distinctive auburn hair and a light dusting of freckles, but he was not someone I recognised. For a second, I flattered myself that he had been waiting to congratulate me on my performance as Doctor Faustus. But he seemed nervous, shooting a furtive glance in Louis' direction. I could hardly hear his voice above the noise of the crowd, but his words were audible enough to shock me.

'Don't have anything to do with that guy or his films,' he said. 'Trust me, I mean it. He's not just a bad person.' He looked around the bar again and leant in close. 'He's evil.'

4

'So you were at uni with Adam,' Tania says as she blends a fruit smoothie in their new, brushed-metal and marble kitchen. She insisted on inviting Clio back to the house, wanted to thank her for finding Freddie, and they have already exchanged numbers. Adam can't think of a less likely liaison, but they seem to have hit it off. It's as if Clio's arrival in the house has energised Tania, woken her up from her stupor in the park. Maybe it's just him who's the problem.

'We didn't know each other very well,' Clio says. Not for want of trying on Adam's part. She is outside the open back door, smoking a cigarette. Is she playing down their relationship at uni, to avoid any awkwardness with Tania? 'Until my last term,' she adds, glancing at Adam, who's still in his running gear.

Tania hates cigarette smoke, particularly when the children are around, but for some reason it doesn't seem to be a problem today. Freddie is upstairs in his room and Tilly is asleep in her pram in the hallway. It wouldn't surprise Adam if she even had a drag of Clio's cigarette.

'I was an aspiring actor in those days,' Adam says, fixing Clio a black coffee – she turned down a healthy smoothie.

'Played a rather bad Doctor Faustus opposite Clio's wildly acclaimed Mephistopheles.'

'Hey, you were great.' Clio exhales theatrically.

'Hardly,' Adam says. The reviews, which he can still remember word for word, were OK – *a workmanlike, perfectly serviceable Faustus* – but it was Clio who stole the show with her modern Mephistopheles. Clad in black leather trousers and jacket, she made a very good servant to Lucifer, doing the devil's work as she realised Faustus's increasingly frivolous wishes. *Another Cambridge star is born.*

'I thought Mephistopheles was a man,' Tania says.

'We were ahead of our time,' Adam replies, relaxing a little. 'It was a very gender-fluid production.'

'I've never liked the use of gender and fluid together in that phrase,' Clio says, stubbing out her cigarette. She walks back into the kitchen, staring at one of Tania's rotas stuck on the fridge door. 'Takes things in the wrong direction.'

Oh God. Adam concentrates on making the coffee. Tania won't enjoy this conversation if Clio gets earthy. Tania's world is clean, like their kitchen. Efficient and wholesome. Maybe that's been the problem. She hasn't given in to the mayhem of motherhood, waved a white flag and let chaos reign. Easy enough for him to say. He's always been messy, drives Tania mad with his piles of stuff left around the house. At work, he's more organised, which irritates Tania even more.

'I've never thought of it like that,' Tania says, laughing as she opens the fridge door.

'Whoa, what are those?' Clio asks, peering inside the fridge. Adam looks over at the two women. Tania must be a good foot taller. Clio points to a row of plastic boxes arranged neatly on two shelves, each one labelled with a different food item: 'Strawberries', 'Cucumbers', 'Apples', 'Snacks'.

'They're for Freddie's lunchbox.' Tania holds the door open. 'He chooses his own food – a sort of DIY Meal Deal. Better chance of him eating it all – at least that's the theory. Adam thinks I've lost it.'

'Not true,' Adam says. They've learnt to demarcate their roles in the kitchen and Freddie's lunchbox has always been her domain, despite it involving children and food. He's the foodie, and early on in their marriage they agreed that he would do all the cooking if she washed up. He used to try and clean up afterwards too – he's a good but spectacularly messy cook – but always fell short of her impeccable standards.

'That's so cool,' Clio says, looking at the labelled boxes. 'My mother used to spoil me with dark chocolate truffles.'

Outside on the street, after they've finished their smoothies and coffee, Tania waves Clio goodbye and thanks her again for retrieving Freddie.

'Let's go for a walk in the park, next time you're visiting your friends in Blackheath,' Tania adds. 'Text me.'

'Sure,' Clio says. 'I'd like that.'

Adam tries not to shake his head in disbelief.

'I'll just walk Clio down to the station. Back in a bit,' he says, failing to sound casual. His mind is still buzzing, trying to process Clio's arrival today. And work out why the hell his wife is being so nice to her. Topsy-Turvy Tania.

'How have you been keeping, anyway?' he asks Clio as they head down Maze Hill. 'Still acting?'

'Sometimes,' Clio says, turning away.

He's surprised. When she left uni in 1998, the internet was

in its infancy: Friends Reunited and Facebook had yet to be invented. He searched online everywhere for Clio – all he had was a postal address in France – and regularly trawled the expanding internet in the years that followed, expecting to see her name in Hollywood, but he couldn't find her. Not a trace. Girlfriends came and went, but it was only when he met Tania that he finally accepted that Clio had gone, the dull ache for what might have been replaced by a more realistic nostalgia.

'I went back to live in France with my mother,' Clio continues. 'She was... unwell, needed looking after. We're very close. When she was better, I travelled the world for a while before returning to France to be her full-time carer. She's not ill, just old, needs help around the house. I promised myself she'd never go into a care home, even though she can afford it. Sometimes we get a helper when I come over to the UK.' She pauses. 'To see friends.'

It's not the path Adam expected Clio to follow, but he's impressed by her filial devotion. She could have done anything in life. Born to an English mother who wrote literary novels and an often absent French father who was a successful stage actor, she grew up in a bright, bohemian world. The Lycée International school in Paris was followed by Cambridge, where she'd been a brilliant actor herself and sailed through her English degree.

'I tried to stay in touch,' he says, 'wrote you a few letters.'

At least twenty, maybe more.

'I know.'

'You got them?' he asks, blushing as he tries to recall what he wrote. The bad love poems. The quotations from *Doctor Faustus* comparing Clio to Helen of Troy: *Here will I dwell, for heaven be in these lips.* Oh God. He stopped writing to her when he met Tania.

She nods. 'I read them too.'

And never replied to any of them. Clio was always out of his league, but for a few days in the spring of her last year at Cambridge she had allowed him to dream. He takes a deep breath, not sure whether to ask his next question.

'Did you ever patch things up with Louis?'

It's the first time he's mentioned Louis' name in years and the sound of it sends a shiver through him. He's spent half his life trying to forget the man. To this day, Adam doesn't know the exact nature of the relationship between Louis and Clio. Some said they were a couple, others that they were just good friends. Soulmates. They certainly slept with each other, but it wasn't an exclusive arrangement. All Adam knows is that for a while there was something between them, a strange, fiery bond that seemed too combustible to last. Sure enough, they fell out spectacularly in her final term, which Adam found reassuring. It always upset him that Clio could love a man like Louis.

'Louis?' Clio almost spits out the word. 'You must be kidding.'

5

'What are you studying?' Louis asked me, glancing around the bar, a rollie bobbing at his lips.

I took another long draught of my beer, trying to process what had just been said to me by the guy with red hair. 'Evil' is a strong word by anyone's standards, but the man could have had any number of reasons for bad-mouthing Louis. The ADC Bar is a snake pit, full of petty rivalries and jealousies, far removed from the camaraderie of the Swordfish back home. What I wouldn't give for a pint or three in somewhere like the Swordy, but there's no pub up here that comes even close. Cambridge isn't Newlyn, that's for sure. Maybe the redhead was a spurned lover. I looked up at Louis, trying to forget what I had heard.

Louis' face was now close to mine – it was hard to hear each other above the din of drunken actors – and I was struck again by how ill he looked. It wasn't just the sallow skin, with telltale patches of what looked like atopic dermatitis, or eczema. It was his eyes, bloodshot and watery. Hay fever? Maybe a corneal abrasion? Or just too many rollies.

'I'm a medic,' I said. 'First year.'

He raised his eyebrows and seemed to adjust himself, stand a little taller. I've noticed this a lot in people recently, as if I might somehow be able to sense, as a future doctor, whether they are hungover or have eaten something unhealthy. At least he didn't ask me about some ailment or other, which is what people also do when they meet a medic. My choice of degree appeared to genuinely pique his interest. What I thought would be a quick bar chat turned into a discussion about my hopes and ambitions, my plan to become a consultant general paediatrician in London and then one day move back to Cornwall, and about the long journey I've embarked on: two years of pre-clinical studies, one year of intercalation, followed by three years of clinical training in hospitals and then a further eight years of training before, all being well, becoming a consultant.

'Maybe our paths will cross again,' Louis said. 'My parents have a house in Cornwall. I go there often with my brother.'

'I'm amazed we've not met before,' I said. In truth I wasn't surprised at all. 'Let me guess… Rock?' Where most of the moneyed second-homers end up.

He smiled. 'Polzeath, actually.'

Near enough. It was never going to be Camborne.

'I should be a keen surfer, shouldn't I?' he said.

I couldn't think of a less likely candidate.

'But the sea's not for me. I prefer the moors.'

'And the Minack,' I added.

'And the Minack, of course.'

Louis' speech was educated and cut-glass, despite the occasional dropped consonant, which made me more self-conscious of my own Cornish lilt. He was charming too, at ease with conversation, those sculpted lips often breaking into a pinched, twitchy smile.

'Six years here is a big investment,' he said, changing the subject as he looked around the crowded bar. 'I imagine you have to keep your nose pretty clean.'

'How do you mean?' I asked, still surprised that this apparent star of the arts scene was talking to me.

'Aren't they very strict about that sort of thing – the powers that be? "Do no harm" and all that.'

Louis was right, even if 'do no harm' was not actually in the original Hippocratic Oath. It was the first thing our director of studies explained to us when we arrived in college. As medical students, we have to go 'above and beyond' – to work harder than other students and behave better, which is ironic, given that most medics are animals, partying the hardest, drinking the most. A police caution – for anything from fare evasion to possession of illegal drugs, drink-driving to violence – can scupper a medical career before it's even started. '"Your behaviour at all times, both in the clinical environment and outside of your studies, must justify the confidence that patients and the public place in you as a future member of the medical profession,"' Professor Beale told us, quoting from the General Medical Council's official guidance for students.

'I have to be doubly careful,' I said. 'As a medic who wants to work with children. How about you?'

'An expensive drug habit's de rigueur if you wish to make it in the film world,' Louis said, smiling.

I laughed. 'Is that what you're studying – film?' I knew the answer but didn't want to appear sycophantic.

He nodded. 'I'm doing a PhD. The first of four happy years, if they don't chuck me out.'

'What's it about?' I asked, trying to sound interested. In truth, I wasn't too bothered, but my scheming brain was working overtime, already calculating that he might be able to help me see more of Clio.

'The aesthetics of evil in modern cinema.'

I nodded as intelligently as I could. It's a skill you learn quickly here. '*Psycho*?' I offered, naming the first film that came into my head.

'That sort of thing.' He paused. 'But right now I'm working on another project – looking for people to help me, in fact. As I say, your performance was impressive tonight. Accomplished. I was wondering whether you might want to appear in a small film of mine?'

Appear in a small film of his? Accomplished? I stood a little more upright, tried to stay cool. Maybe my Doctor Faustus wasn't so bad after all.

6

Adam and Clio arrive at the station. It feels weird for him to be with her again, as if no time at all has passed. He glances at a camera further down the platform. Was it always pointing in their direction? He needs to get a grip, focus on reality, not the weird machinations of his overactive mind. According to the platform indicator, a train to Blackfriars is due in one minute.

'It's been nice seeing you again,' he says. 'What are the chances, eh?'

Clio looks at him and he can't help but notice that her eyes, heavily lined with kohl, have changed in some imperceptible way. She glances down the platform – at the camera? – and back at him again.

'I was thinking,' she says, her voice even more husky, 'it would be great to catch up – when you have a bit more time, maybe. I haven't seen anyone from uni for years. And I'm sorry how it all ended, you know? Wish it could have been different.'

Adam swallows. He doesn't want to think about Clio's last few months at uni. He's been over it all in his head a thousand times. Clio was an innocent party, caught up in something beyond her control. Louis was the cause of it all and he disappeared off the face of the earth too.

'You OK?' Clio asks.

He nods, still confused by her sudden appearance in his life again. She's the same but somehow different. Is it her eyes? Or the way she angles her face upwards by a few degrees when she talks? She didn't use to do that except on stage, a tic she adopted to transform herself into the animated, threatening Mephistopheles.

Adam checks up and down the platform, making sure no one is within earshot.

'Can I ask you something?' he says, thrusting his hands deep into the pockets of his exercise hoodie.

'Sure,' she replies.

He takes a deep breath. 'Was it really a coincidence – you being in the park today?'

She pulls back from him, a quizzical expression on her face, as if she can't quite believe what he's just said. And then she cocks her head to one side to check that she's heard him correctly. He remembers that mannerism. Like a blackbird listening for worms.

'A coincidence?' she asks. 'Of course it was a coincidence. What else could it have been? I had no idea you lived in Greenwich. If I'd known, I'd have come knocking at your door. What a strange question.'

She laughs, staring at the ground as she dabs at a puddle with her foot.

He needed to know, to hear her say the words, but he's still embarrassed. He's deluding himself again, just as he did at uni. Of course Clio hadn't come to Greenwich to seek him out. Who's he kidding? She was passing through, their meeting was pure chance. Serendipity.

'A catch-up would be great,' he says, keen to move on. 'How long has it been?'

She hesitates before answering, glancing down the platform again. 'Must be more than twenty years.'

'If you say so.' He's never been very good on graduation dates. They only overlapped for a year as undergraduates. Adam stayed on for another two years and then did a further three years of clinical training.

'Here comes my train,' she says. Adam turns to see it nosing around the bend. 'How about tonight? A drink in town.'

A drink? His immediate impulse is to say no – Saturdays are movie nights at home with Tania, Tilly permitting – but then he remembers that Tania will be away. Clio continues before he can say anything.

'Bring Tania along too, if you can get a babysitter.'

'She's going away this afternoon,' he says. 'To stay with her parents.'

He didn't need to tell her that. She holds his gaze. Again, those eyes. What is it about them?

'Oh, OK,' she says with a Gallic shrug. 'So text me if *you* fancy a drink. Tania's got my number.'

'I'm on call tonight,' he lies. 'Maybe another time, when you're back in the area. We can all meet up.'

But Clio's already boarded the train, disappearing from his world as quickly as she entered it. Will he ever see her again? Should he? And then he realises what it was about her eyes. Like the best movie stars, she didn't blink.

7

'It sounds interesting,' I said, throwing a glance down the bar. Clio looked over in my direction and smiled. Was Louis' film project her doing? Had she put in a word on my behalf? 'What exactly do I have to do?'

'Just be yourself,' Louis said. 'I'm doing a series of *A Life in the Day of...* shorts. Nothing to trouble the jury at Cannes, just a slice of old-school cinéma-vérité. You go about your normal day. I follow you around with my camera. Simple as that.' As if to demonstrate, he lifted his camcorder to his eye and started to film people at the bar again. 'And then I'll present you with a copy of the finished article when we're done.' He lowered the camera. 'Something to keep for posterity, to remind you of your time here when you're rich and famous. I imagine consultant paediatricians earn a fortune.'

'I've no idea,' I said. Medical students are notoriously ambitious, myself included, but I know I'm not studying medicine for the money. 'Believe me, my life is so boring,' I added. 'This play is the first extra-curricular thing I've done since I arrived. And it might get me thrown off the course if my grades drop. It's all lectures, lectures and more lectures in my world. Throw in some practical classes and supervisions

32

and that's the extent of my life. We do so much science in the pre-clinical years compared to other medical schools. I can't see my life here making a film. Honestly, it would send people into a coma.'

He turned away and I wondered if I'd offended him. Who knew, maybe my mundane world could be made to look interesting in his expert hands?

'That's just what I'm after,' Louis said. 'Snapshots of student life. Vignettes of actualité. We're all here to work, after all. In the last film I made, I even managed to make an aspiring accountant's life seem interesting. Medicine must be more exciting than that.'

'Possibly,' I said. 'Maybe you should film me in my third year, what we call intercalation – "the piss-up year". Allegedly. We're encouraged to study something to broaden our horizons – history of art, that kind of thing. My life might be a little more interesting by then.'

I was bluffing. Much as I'd like to study the Newlyn School of painters, I've already decided that I'll do a natural science topic for my third year, something like physiology, development and neuroscience (PDN). I can't afford to waste my time here on a non-medicine-related subject. I owe it to others. To Mum and Dad.

'Events might be a little manipulated in the film,' Louis said. 'Curated.'

'OK... How do you mean?'

'I've always felt Jean Rouch's "docufiction" is the best way to get to the truth. Perhaps we can ask Clio to be involved. Arrange for you to bump into her for a coffee.'

I blushed again, glancing over at Clio, who was deep in conversation with another woman. I wish I didn't blush so easily – an overactive sympathetic nervous system, I guess. Just like Dad, who could blush for Britain. My ears started to burn too.

'That's not really part of my normal day,' I said. 'Or hers.' Much as I'd like it to be.

'I quite understand if you don't want to participate.' He drained his vodka as if in readiness to leave.

'No, it sounds intriguing,' I said, trying to forget what the red-haired student had said about Louis and his films. Anything to keep in touch with Clio now that the play was finished.

'She's more interested in you than you think,' he added.

I stared at him. 'Really?' I despised the eagerness in my voice, but it was impossible to hide. Clio interested in me?

'She's never met anyone like you before,' Louis said. 'She's curious.'

The feeling was mutual.

'Despite – or maybe because of – her extrovert nature, she's drawn to quiet people.'

I was her man then. I could do quiet all day.

'I'll drop by,' he said. 'You're at St Thomas's, right?'

'Yes,' I replied.

Most people just call it Tom's, but Louis seems very proper, possibly even a pedant, keen to get the little things right. Apparently he did his undergraduate degree in Classics at Oxford. And then I realised that I hadn't told him which college I was at. Which struck me as odd, but maybe he'd read the play's programme, which included a small biography about each of us. Or perhaps Clio had told him.

I looked over to where she'd been at the bar, but she was gone. Louis left a moment later. The place was still jumping, but I didn't want to stay late. Too much work to catch up on. And then, as I was about to leave, I saw the student again, the one who had warned me about Louis. He was over by the door, on his way out. I drained my pint and set off in pursuit.

'Hey,' I said, outside on the street.

He was twenty yards away, walking quickly. He turned to look back at me and carried on, almost breaking into a run, head down. I glanced up and down the empty road and jogged after him.

'Wait,' I said. 'I just want to ask you about what you said back there. About Louis.'

'I can't say anything else,' he said, hurrying ahead of me. 'I shouldn't have talked to you. Please, leave me alone.'

'Why did you call him evil?'

He stopped and turned to face me. 'You should know,' he said. 'You of all people.'

'How do you mean?'

'After tonight. The play. The pact Faustus made with Lucifer. Stay away from Louis. And stay away from me. If he sees me talking to you, he'll…'

'He'll what?' I was shocked by the fear in his eyes.

'I've got to go. Please, never speak to me again. You promise?'

I watched him run off into the Cambridge night.

'OK,' I said sarcastically to myself. 'I promise.'

8

'She was nice,' Tania says, when Adam returns from the station. 'I can't believe you've never mentioned her before.'

Tania is wiping down the kitchen surfaces, Tilly hooked over one hip. She's awake and not crying, which is a bonus. Freddie is pushing a toy car across the floor at her feet. He's obsessed with cars. And Tania seems animated, which could go either way.

'Daddy!' Freddie says, driving the car up his trouser leg.

'Hello, you.' Adam picks him up. Freddie continues to steer the car over his head and down the other side of his arm.

'Hey, that tickles!' Adam says, and starts to tickle Freddie back until he's laughing uncontrollably.

'He'll wet himself if you're not careful,' Tania says, as Freddie begs Adam to stop.

Freddie escapes and runs off to another room, driving his car across the walls, leaving tyre marks. It was a mistake to have had the house painted, but Tania insisted. New baby, new coat of paint. Thank God they didn't have twins – the walls would still be wet with the second coat.

'I thought I'd mentioned her,' Adam says. He's only stayed in touch with a handful of people he met at Cambridge.

Medics mostly. And Ji Ma, of course. Godfather to Tilly. A computer science student from China, Ji became a close if unlikely friend at Cambridge, almost persuading him of the joys of videogames. Almost.

Tania shakes her head. 'Did you go out together?' she asks.

'Not exactly,' he says, wrong-footed by her directness. He shouldn't be. Tania has always been straight-talking, never one to tiptoe around issues.

'But you wished you had,' she says. 'I mean, which man wouldn't?'

Adam feels uncomfortable talking about his past relationships, unlike Tania, who is happy to chat about her previous partners – she had had one long-term relationship before she met Adam. He's never gone into much detail about his own modest love-life. The art student who worked Saturdays at the Tate in St Ives and used to let him in after hours to wander the empty galleries together; an older barmaid at the Swordy in Newlyn, who followed him down to the cellar one day and kissed him as he was changing barrels.

'Come on, she's gorgeous,' she says. 'That chopped pixie cut, the leather jacket, rock-chick skirt. And what a voice! You couldn't make it up. If I was a man... I could never pull off a look like that.'

It's true. Tania couldn't be less like Clio. If Clio smoulders, Tania is pure sunshine, a difference heightened by their contrasting physiques. Tania is tall, blonde and athletic, Clio short, dark and petite. It was one reason he fell for Tania. Meeting her was like a release, a chance to break free from the past, from his increasingly delusional memories of university life. Of Clio.

'OK, so I wanted to go out with her, after we'd acted in

Doctor Faustus together – it's the only reason I applied for the part. She just came up to me one day, started to flirt and told me to audition for the play. How could I refuse? But...'

He pauses, long enough for Tania to prompt him with raised eyebrows. Long enough for an unwelcome memory to return. 'I wasn't the only one interested in her. And she certainly wasn't interested in me. Not in that way. We were friends.'

'Did you sleep together?'

'No!' Adam protests, trying to laugh it off, but he feels better for being honest with her. Christ, it's not as if he hasn't wondered what it would be like to sleep with Clio. And the conversation at the station had unnerved him. 'There was a time when I thought we might, but I was never really in the frame. She had this weird on-off relationship with another bloke. An older man.' He can't bring himself to say Louis' name.

'Nothing wrong with older men.' She smiles seductively at him. When they first met, at Charing Cross Hospital, she was a junior doctor and he was a registrar, five years her senior. 'We should hang out with more people like her,' Tania says. 'Get out of our comfort zone. We're in a social rut – it's not good for us.'

It's true, most of their London friends are middle-class south London medics.

'I'm not sure how happy Clio is,' Adam says. He had the same feeling at uni, that Clio was unfulfilled, dissatisfied, a deep melancholia running like a buried stream beneath the wild, party-girl facade. 'And I'm amazed she's still alive, to be honest. Still smoking like a chimney.'

She used to take a lot of drugs too. He wonders if she still does.

'She seemed fun to me,' Tania says. 'Maybe that's what we need. A bit more fun in our lives. Once I've caught up on five years' sleep.'

Now seems as good a time as any to mention Clio's offer.

'She asked if we both wanted to meet for a drink in town tonight,' he says, focusing a little too hard on loading the dishwasher.

'That's a shame. I've told Mum and Dad I'll be down there by 5 p.m. – in time for Freddie's tea.'

'I said that you were going away and' – Adam swallows, feeling guilty – 'that I was busy. I don't even have her number.'

He detects the faintest hesitation before Tania speaks, her voice artificially upbeat, as if she's making an effort to be cheerful.

'You should go – have a drink with her,' she says, straightening a tea towel on the oven rail. She trusts him and in that moment he loves her more than ever. Her openness. There's never any side to Tania, no hidden agenda. She is what she is and she expects others to be similarly straightforward, which often leads to disappointment. 'You're not on call tonight, are you?' she continues. 'It'll be a chance to chat about old times. And she gave me her number.' She reaches for her phone and shares the contact. Adam's phone pings accusingly in his pocket. 'You don't see anyone from uni these days.'

And Tania thinks she understands why. Adam has given her the bare bones of what happened towards the end of his first year, but he has never told her why he thinks he's being watched, filmed. Or the real reason he still has nightmares.

9

Louis kept to his word and dropped by my room this
morning, asking if I was still up for taking part in his short
film. He explained that he often spends up to a week shooting
enough material to edit down into someone's typical day and
he wants to get started sooner rather than later. Once again I
protested that twenty-four hours of my sad student existence
is unlikely to win him any Oscars, even if it is a collection
of spliced-together 'highlights' from an entire week, but he
also came with a card. I recognised Clio's handwriting on the
envelope and put it in my pocket, to be read later, but Louis
insisted that I open it there and then.

*Are you free for lunch? I need to debrief about the play
and feel we've hardly talked. Which is crazy, given the
amount of time we've spent together in recent weeks. I've
booked a table at Sweeney Todd's for 1.30 p.m. tomorrow.
On me.*

Clio xx

*P.S. This has nothing to do with Louis and his shitty
little* A Life in the Day of… *If he asks if he can film us,
please tell him to fuck off, politely of course.*

'Well?' Louis asked.

'Clio wants to meet for lunch,' I said. 'Tomorrow. Did you arrange this? Say something to her?'

Louis held up his hands in mock protest. 'Of course not.' He smiled. 'You cannot tell Clio what to do. I might have told her she has a new admirer, but that's all. More importantly, we have our opening scene.'

'But—'

'She asked that I don't film you?' he interrupted.

I nodded, more confused than ever by their relationship, whatever that is. The longer I looked at Louis' matchstick figure, the more unwell he seemed. Maybe he'd just had a particularly heavy night – he made no secret of his drug taking. His eczema had flared up around his eye sockets like red goggles, which didn't help, but there was also a miasma of ill health about him that I couldn't fathom. Whatever Clio's drawn to, it's not his wholesomeness.

'Relax,' he said. 'Neither of you will know I'm there.'

'I really don't think she wants to be filmed,' I said. 'She was quite... adamant.'

'Let me guess – she told me to fuck off.' He glanced down as I slid the card into my pocket. 'It's OK. She often does that. She won't know I'm there. Tell her you passed on her message and I went off in a sulk.'

'Will she believe me?'

'Of course. I often sulk. Runs in the family. My brother Gabe is a world-class sulker.'

I desperately wanted to ask if he and Clio were an item, but I chose not to pry. I was, though, having misgivings about the whole film project, but Louis seemed to anticipate my concerns.

41

'We can make something special here, I promise you,' he said.

'Honestly, my days are spent reading, going to lectures. And then more reading.'

'And is that how you *want* to spend your time at Cambridge?'

'I don't have a choice.'

I've been playing catch-up from the moment I arrived here, less prepared than other students whose parents are doctors, who've been immersed in the medical world since they were kids. And the stakes are high. Medical students are chucked out if we fail our first-year exams. And I really don't want to be chucked out. Wouldn't be able to look Mum in the eye or walk the streets of Newlyn. A whole community would be disappointed.

'See this film as wish fulfilment,' Louis said. 'A chance to live the life you'd like to lead at Cambridge.'

'You don't understand. Playing Faustus was a massive gamble, given my workload. I can't risk doing anything else now apart from studying.'

'I do understand,' he said, glancing at his watch. 'You can work today, but tomorrow we must film. Lunch and then punting.'

'Punting! I don't have time for bloody punting!' Louis really had no idea of how much work I had to do. 'And isn't that a bit, you know, hackneyed?'

'You sound like the American who complains there are too many clichés in Shakespeare. Punting *is* Cambridge. And so is getting drunk in Grantchester Meadows. Clio's always wanted to go there.'

I've heard about the posh drinking societies that gather on the banks of the Cam near Grantchester – members get so inebriated that ambulances have to take them away. It's the sort of thing I expect Louis to have done, but I was pleased and surprised to learn that Clio hasn't indulged.

'Are you sure she's not involved in all this?' I asked.

'Not unless you want her to be. I'm just saying that if you offered to punt her to Grantchester with a bottle of vodka and some grapefruit juice, she might not say no. Personally, I can't think of anything worse. The tree pollen at this time of year is unbearable.'

I glanced at his bloodshot eyes, satisfied by my hay fever diagnosis: seasonal allergic rhinitis. I stood there, torn between my books, spread out on my desk, and the thought of spending the day getting drunk with Clio. Drinking vodka with grapefruit is one of the quickest ways to get alcohol into the human body, short of injecting an eyeball. She's obviously used to being corralled into Louis' PhD projects – her defiant response last night to being filmed at the bar has stayed with me – but it sounded like she'd had enough, for now at least. I was beginning to feel the same way.

'I will gladly meet Clio for lunch tomorrow, but I really don't think you should film us,' I said. 'She's specifically asked that you don't. And I can't take the afternoon off to go punting. Jesus, if only you knew.' I turned to my overflowing desk. 'By all means film me here and cycling over to the Medical School, but I'll have to check if you can film inside. I seriously doubt it. Honestly, I won't be offended if you decide there's not enough interesting material for your film.'

But Louis seemed far from troubled. In fact, he wasn't at

all surprised by my increasing reluctance, maybe because he had a plan that I'd find hard to refuse.

'I almost forgot,' he said. 'I'm having a party on Wednesday night. At my house. Mortimer Road. The usual suspects, I'm afraid, but you're very welcome to join us.' The usual suspects meant all the university's top actors and directors. The elite arts set. Not the sort of party I'd ever be invited to. And then, almost as an afterthought, he added, 'Clio will be there, of course. But you might have had enough of her by then.'

The idea that I might ever have had enough of Clio was too absurd to contemplate.

'If I can get all my work done, I'll try to come along,' I said, trying to sound casual. I'd just been invited to Louis' party, and Clio would be there.

'Please do. It would be great to see you. We can film for the first twenty minutes or so – discreetly, of course – but then we'll down tools. There are some things that shouldn't be caught on camera.'

He gave me a wink and I thought of Clio again, whether we'd hang out at the party, what I'd say to her, but then the words of warning from the student at the ADC Bar came crashing back. *He's not just a bad person. He's evil.*

I'm generally a good judge of people – at least I think I am – but nothing about my own encounters with Louis so far have rung any alarm bells. Apart from his state of health, but that's just me being a medic. He's bumptious and arrogant, of course, in a typically private school sort of way. No idea how the other half live. Not a bloody clue. He's pushy about the filming too. And if it weren't for his connection with Clio, the access to her that he might afford, I wouldn't choose to spend time with him, despite his growing reputation as an auteur. But evil? I can't see it. Maybe the student was high? He seemed more scared than stoned. Or perhaps he's just jealous of Louis. A lot of people are.

10

Adam reaches across to fasten Freddie into the back of their VW Touran. Tania is already behind the wheel, eager to leave. Tilly is in her baby seat, asleep next to Freddie.

'If she sleeps the whole way, you're going to be up all—'

'I know that, Adam,' Tania says, interrupting him. 'But it's a deal I'm prepared to sign up for right now. Have you ever tried driving with Tilly crying?'

He has. How can he ever forget? Six hours of pure hell when they drove down with Tilly to show her to his mum in Cornwall. But it was worth it, just to see the happiness in his mum's watery eyes. For a while it had been touch and go whether she'd live to see any grandchildren. Adam jumped onto her medical case as soon as he qualified, established that she'd been put on the wrong drugs 'for her nerves'. The improvement was startling. If only he'd been able to do the same for his dad.

'I can come with you, take the train back,' he offers again.

'It's OK,' Tania says.

They are both on best behaviour in front of Freddie, who is listening intently to their exchange.

'Please can Daddy come,' Freddie says, showing the first

signs of grouchiness. 'I don't want to go to Granny and Gramps'.'

'Oh yes you do,' Adam says, spinning his head round so his face is upside down in the open window. 'You're just being topsy-turvy, like Tilly,' he says, 'and speaking in opposites.'

Tania turns, hushing him as Freddie starts to laugh. Adam leans in to kiss him on the forehead. 'Better not wake your sister,' he whispers. 'Got the Ferrari?'

Freddie holds up a red model car, grinning from ear to ear. Some children get attached to teddies. Others to comfort blankets. Their son's fixated with a Ferrari 412 P, made in the 1960s. Admittedly it's a Scalextric racing car. A real one costs $45 million, but this one was £40 on eBay – worth it alone for the working front and rear lights. Adam's not really into cars, but he plays along, bought it for Freddie last Christmas. An elaborate Scalextric racing track is ready and waiting in Grandpa's garage.

Adam closes the door gently and walks round to the driver's door.

'Go carefully,' he says, leaning in to kiss Tania. 'And please come back,' he adds, more quietly.

'I think you're better off without me when I'm in this state,' she says. 'I'm sorry. I'm just finding it all so hard.'

'I know you are. I get that. Send them my love.'

He waves as they drive off down Maze Hill onto Trafalgar Road, past the camera, and then he disappears back into the house. He wants to go straight up into the attic, but he waits. Despite her awesome powers of organisation, it's not uncommon for Tania to forget something when she's tired and drive back to collect it.

After waiting for fifteen minutes, he rests the loft ladder

against the hatch, climbs up and feels for the light switch. Rows of boxes disappear into the darkness, but it's the one nearest him that he's most interested in. A memory box from his university days: a diary documenting the whole horrendous drama, graduation photo, college rugby shirt, May Ball ticket, well-thumbed copy of *Doctor Faustus* with his acting notes. And a video. He lifts the box down, puts it onto the bed and climbs back up into the attic. The old video player should have gone to the dump years ago, but he finds it wedged beneath the eaves in a corner and brings it out, blowing off the dust. He's about to take it down when something else catches his eye in the memory box. A brown barn owl feather with darker bands. He pulls it out, turning it in his hand before returning it to the box. Clio gave it to him the last time they ever talked to each other at Cambridge, said it was a symbol of protection.

Two minutes later, he's on the edge of the bed, watching the TV screen in the corner of their bedroom. It's an old set, given to them as a wedding present. There he is, sitting on his own at a quiet table in Sweeney Todd's – the opening shot of Louis' *A Life in the Day of...* film. How young he looks, so much thinner around the face. More hair too. And so naive, his innocent eyes full of expectation. Little did his younger self know what lay ahead of him. The film was meant to be a record of one Cambridge student's gilded life. If only.

Louis had lied to him. There was meant to be no filming in the restaurant, but somehow he'd managed. Adam watches, transfixed, as Clio appears, joining him at the table. His stomach lurches. It's years since he's seen this film. He thought that time might have healed the wounds, but he stops the tape. He can't bear to watch what happens next.

11

'Am I late?' Clio asked, sitting down opposite me in Sweeney Todd's. She was sporting a strappy red slip dress, white canvas pumps, and a slick of clear lip gloss.

I glanced around the restaurant, not because I wanted other diners to see that my date had finally showed up and was drop-dead gorgeous – OK, there might have been an element of that – but mainly because I couldn't quite believe that I was having lunch with Clio. Ever since receiving her unlikely invitation yesterday, I'd been playing out various versions in my head of what might transpire today and kept returning to a no-show. This sort of thing just didn't happen in my life: the bursary boy from Cornwall didn't have lunch with people like Clio.

'Not at all, only just got here myself,' I said, as breezily as possible.

She glanced at the half-empty jug of drinking water, the remains of a roll on my side plate and smiled. It was so obviously a lie that I blushed.

'Is he here?' she asked, scanning the restaurant.

There were a few diners on other tables, including a family of four, and a group of six students in the far corner, beyond the old water wheel – a legacy of when the building was a working mill house. Rowers, I guessed, based on their physique and the size of the pizzas they were consuming.

'Louis?' I said. 'Not as far as I know.'

I'd already had a good look around and decided that he wasn't there, unless he was hiding in the kitchen. I'd also checked outside. Sweeney Todd's overlooks a millpond on a tributary of the River Cam that runs through Coe Fen, a peaceful nature reserve. If he was out there somewhere, stalking the riverbank with a zoom lens, I hadn't seen him.

'I passed on the message – politely but firmly,' I said.

'Sometimes he can be such a jerk.' Clio poured herself a glass of water.

Again, I wanted to ask what, if anything, was between them, but I checked myself. None of my business. Another version of what I thought might play out today was that Clio had only invited me to lunch because Louis had asked her to, and the whole occasion would feel contrived, a set-up for his film. Wish fulfilment, as Louis had put it. Capturing my wannabe dream life as a Cambridge student on camera. But Clio seemed to be there on her own accord rather than at Louis' behest. I need to stop being so down on myself.

'Does he film you a lot?' I asked. 'I saw him the other night, at the bar—'

'All the time. He is obsessed. Not with me, but with filming "life".' She made air quotes with her fingers. 'He needs to grow up, stop being so pretentious.'

'Am I making a mistake, then?' I asked. 'Agreeing to be filmed?'

'It's your life. Louis and I aren't talking, so I'm biased.

Of course, he is a brilliant filmmaker. Truly gifted, though it pains me to say it. Why not?'

'He didn't ask you to have lunch with me, then? For his film?'

I regretted the question as soon as I'd asked it, remembering Louis' words.

'Of course not,' she said, laughing. 'Nobody tells me who to date.'

A date. We were on a date. 'I'm sorry, I didn't mean to imply—'

'Please, let's not talk about Louis and his films,' she said. 'Not today, not here.'

She dabbed the corner of her full lips with a napkin. Instinctively, I picked up my napkin too and wiped unnecessarily at my own mouth, just as a young boy started to cry at the neighbouring table. I glanced across at him and pulled the napkin up over my face for a second, lowering it with a mock frown. He stopped crying and looked at me with a mix of bafflement and terror. The dad turned around and we smiled at each other.

Clio watched the exchange and leant forwards across the table. 'Do you want to have children?' she asked, glancing over at the boy, who was smiling now. Her voice was even more intimate when she spoke quietly, her breath warm and sweet. She knew the question was loaded and I blushed again, less so this time.

'I do, yes,' I said.

The sensation of falling in love with Clio was so physical, I worried she could actually see me tumbling and plummeting. There was nothing I could do in her presence, nothing any grown man could do, but give in and admit defeat. I felt so powerless, emasculated, such an idiot, it was embarrassing. She's not my type, never will be, but I was unable to resist. *He that loves pleasure must for pleasure fall*, as the Good Angel said to Faustus, hoping to steer him away from his pact with Lucifer.

'I seem to get along with them,' I said, raising my eyebrows at the boy again. 'Maybe that's why I plan to become a paediatrician. I always thought I'd go into neurosurgery, but I think it's paediatrics for me.'

'You have your whole life mapped out already,' she said, lighting a cigarette as she looked at the menu. 'Have you always wanted to be a doctor?'

I turned away, wondering how much to tell her. 'I wasn't one of those young kids who played doctors and nurses, wrapping bandages around my teddies, if that's what you mean,' I said. 'It happened a bit later for me, after my dad died. I was fifteen years old and he'd been ill for a while. Brain tumour the size of a satsuma. I desperately wanted to make him better, but I didn't know how.'

'And now you do?'

'Not quite. I was too late for him, but I hope that one day I'll be able to help others, if that doesn't sound too worthy.'

I knew it did but she didn't seem to mind.

'My mum's not in the best of health right now,' I continued. 'She had me late – in her early forties – and Dad's death has aged her terribly. I felt so helpless watching him get ill. I never want to have that feeling again.'

She rested a hand on mine. Her touch was warm, electrifying. 'I'm sorry about your father,' she said. 'It must have been hard.'

'Even harder for my mum. She adored him. Everyone

did. He worked as a fisherman out of Newlyn, first on the trawlers and then on an inshore day boat, hand-lining bass and mackerel, but he should have been a full-time artist. He could paint beautifully – two of his pictures are in the Tate at St Ives.' (But his very best one is here, with me right now, hanging above my desk as I write this. Dad's stormy abstract rendering of Cape Cornwall is my favourite. Mum insisted on me having it, and its shades of blue, grey and burnt orange keep me grounded whenever I'm missing her, him, Cornwall.) 'He was an avid reader too,' I added.

She seemed impressed. 'He would be so proud that his son is studying medicine at Cambridge.'

I swallowed hard, tears welling. It's one of my biggest regrets that Dad never knew I'd made it to Cambridge. He would have been the proudest man in Cornwall, and that's saying something. 'He was always telling me to get a good education, a proper job. He gave me a copy of *Moby Dick* for my twelfth birthday.'

'Did you read it?'

'Cover to cover. And Hemingway. And Conrad. One year Dad gave me *Youth* for Christmas. "Pass the bottle" – we always laughed at that line.'

'You weren't tempted to follow him into the fishing trade then?' She smiled. I could see she was joking, and I was almost afraid to tell her the truth. It didn't exactly show me in the best academic light.

'Actually, I was. When he died, I dropped out of school and started work on a sixty-foot fishing vessel, a gill-netter, crewed by a bunch of young nutters. When we weren't out at sea trying to catch turbot, we were off our faces in the pub. Dad would have been ashamed of how badly I went off the rails. I'd been good at school, everyone expected me to go on to university. But I was also angry with Dad for dying, even angrier with myself.'

'For not being able to make him better?'

I nodded. 'I blamed myself.'

'It wasn't your fault,' she said.

'It won't happen again.'

'Because here you are, training to be a doctor.'

'Here I am,' I said, glancing around the restaurant.

Clio smiled sympathetically, encouraging me to continue. And then her bare foot started to rub against my ankle. She must have slipped off her shoes. I was about to move my foot away, but I kept it there.

'What made you change your mind?' she asked.

'It was Mum,' I said. 'I came home drunk one night with a plastic bag of John Dory – Mum's favourite fish – and she was just staring out the window like she couldn't even look at me. I remember her words exactly: "I went to the hospital today. Seen by this lovely young man, just a few years older than you. Born in St Austell, studied at Bristol University. And as I sat there, looking at his smart white coat and nice haircut, I thought he could be you in a few years." And then she turned to face me, tapped the plastic bag, and said, "Thank you for this, Adam, but I don't want you bringing me fresh fish any more."'

'Ouch,' Clio said.

'I was so angry, stormed out the house, but I knew she was right. I quit the fishing job the next day and signed up to night school. For the next two years, I studied for the necessary A-levels, did some work experience at the hospital in Truro, and applied to read medicine here.'

'That's amazing,' she said, her toes working their way up my leg.

'Not your normal route to doing medicine at Oxbridge,' I continued. 'I'm what they call a first-gen medic, which is still quite unusual. Medicine tends to run in families – like fishing. Most of my fellow students' fathers and grandfathers were doctors.'

'Like acting too,' she said. It was her turn to look away.

'Is that right?' I asked, sensing the swell of emotion in her voice.

'My father was an actor,' she continued. 'Quite famous in France.'

'Is he still acting?'

She stared down at the table. 'He died,' she said quietly.

I waited for her to say more, to elaborate, but she didn't.

'Shall we have some champagne?' she asked, switching back to her normal theatrical self. I hadn't drunk champagne since my mum bought a bottle from the Co-op in Newlyn to celebrate my getting into Cambridge. 'Drink to Doctor Faustus and his pact with the devil?'

'Why not?' I said. I wasn't used to all this emotional sharing. Our date needed to lighten up.

12

Adam paces up and down the kitchen of their Greenwich home. Tania's not away very often, but when she is, Adam reverts to bachelor mode. He wanders around the house in boxer shorts and T-shirt, eats too many chocolate digestives, too much peanut-butter toast, watches all those violent movies she doesn't like and buys oven chips from the corner shop. But tonight he can't settle. Not since getting the video down from the attic. Not since Clio's appearance in the park. To meet like that after twenty-odd years could have been a coincidence. Just about. But for Freddie to have gone missing and be found by her of all people – it's too much.

He sits down at the kitchen island and searches for 'Clio Baudin'. It feels strange, wrong. It always does. He tells himself it's different this time, legitimate. Nothing. He types in 'Louis Farr'. Again, nothing, even when he adds 'Cornwall' and 'Polzeath'. He trawls Instagram, Facebook, Twitter, LinkedIn. Not a trace. It's as if they both never existed. Did they change their names after leaving Cambridge? He adds 'the aesthetics of evil in modern cinema' into the mix, searches for everything he can possibly think of. So much for

Louis being the next big thing in cinema. Unless he's become an underground filmmaker and taken it literally.

He glances at his watch. Tania will be putting Freddie to bed any minute. A thankless task. He's sure to have slept in the car, like Tilly. He will be excited to see his grandparents too, despite his earlier protests. They adore him. A minute later, he's chatting to Tania, asking about the drive down, how her parents are.

'Can I have a quick word with Freddie?' he says. 'I need to ask him something.'

'I've only just put him to bed, Adam.' She sounds tired, even more than usual. And she knows he has form when it comes to revving up Freddie before bedtime.

'I'm guessing he's not asleep, having slept the entire way,' he says.

'Anyone would think you work with kids. At least it was a peaceful journey. I'll take the phone up now. But please don't over-excite him. What do you want to ask him anyway?'

'It's a secret. Someone important's got a birthday very soon.'

Tania will be a year closer to forty next week. Something else that won't help.

'I was trying to forget,' she says. 'Here he is.'

'Daddy!' Freddie shouts, so loud that Adam has to hold the phone away.

'Hello, monkey. I hope you're being good.'

Freddie gives him a rapid-fire, nonsensical account of what he's done since their arrival, and then he stops as suddenly as he started. 'Mummy's sad.'

Adam doesn't want to picture her face if she's still in the room with Freddie. 'Is she with you now?'

'Gone downstairs.'

'Are you looking after her for me? Like I asked?'

'When are you coming?'

Adam closes his eyes. 'You know in the park today, when that nice lady, Clio, found you?'

'Yes,' Freddie says, distractedly.

'Were you a long way from Mummy?'

'Hmmm, I was in the sandpit, where Mummy told me to stay.'

Adam sits up, adjusting the phone in his hand.

'In the sandpit? But I found you up on the hill, outside the playground.'

'She wanted to show me a puppy.'

'A puppy?' Adam's stomach goes into freefall. Freddie's been desperate to have a puppy, ever since his friend got one. 'And she took you from the sandpit, out of the playground, to show you this puppy?'

Silence.

'Freddie?'

'I'm tired.'

Adam hasn't got long. 'I know you are, monkey. Did Clio have a puppy with her?'

He definitely didn't see her with one in the park.

'No. She said it had gone away.'

'Was that why you were sad? When I found you. Because the puppy had gone?'

'Will she have one next time?'

'I don't know,' Adam said, his mind racing. *Next time? What does he mean? Did Clio say she would be back?* 'Do you want to go downstairs now, give the phone back to Mummy?'

'OK.'

'And I'll see you very soon. We mustn't forget Mummy's birthday present.'

'Can she have a puppy?'

Dear God. It's only a matter of time before they give in and get a dog. Maybe it's what Tania needs. Maybe not.

'Not this birthday. You are getting her those special bubbles for her bath, remember?' And a promise not to climb in with her when she's trying to relax. 'Can you take the phone down to Mummy?'

'I was going to get the phone from him, rather than him come back downstairs again,' Tania says, irritated, a few moments later.

Adam listens as she tells Freddie to go back to bed. 'Sorry. I wanted to check something with you. Has Freddie mentioned anything about a puppy today?'

'No more than usual. I thought we were trying not to mention the P-word.'

'We are, but did he say anything about Clio having a puppy?'

'Clio? I don't think so. She didn't have one, did she? Unless it was hidden in her handbag. You know, one of those posh little Parisian pooches.'

'Freddie said that Clio found him in the sandpit, that she had a puppy to show him.'

'But I thought you found Freddie with her outside the playground?'

'I know. I did.'

'Maybe Freddie's confused. You know what he's like.'

'It doesn't add up.' He doesn't want to worry Tania unnecessarily. 'I think I'm going to see her tonight. For that drink. Ask her where she found Freddie.'

'OK.' A pause. 'You don't need to make excuses to see an old girlfriend from uni, Adam. If you want to go for a drink with her, just say you're going for a drink. That's fine. We're all adults.'

Adam closes his eyes. Her tone has changed again, hardened.

'I'm not making excuses,' he says. 'And she was never my girlfriend. It doesn't make any sense, that's all. Her turning up in the park today like that. After all these years.' Silence on the line. 'Are you still there?'

'I've got to go,' Tania says. 'Tilly's crying.'

She hangs up and he leaves the phone by his ear for a second. And then the front doorbell rings. It's almost 7 p.m., too late for a delivery. He walks into the hall and peers through the eyehole.

It's Clio.

13

'It's nice to meet like this,' Clio said, once the champagne had arrived and we had ordered our pizzas from Sweeney Todd's jokey, lavishly illustrated menu: a 'Home Computer' for her ('bits of ham, chips of pineapple, discs of salami') and 'Another Season of *Dallas*' for me (pepperoni, pimentos and chillies). Clio ordered a 'preposterous' side portion of chips too. Sadly there were rumours that the restaurant, something of a Cambridge institution, was about to be swallowed up and become a Bella Pasta. She insisted lunch was on her, as a thank you for putting up with her for the past month. It was also a reminder that we were on completely different budgets at uni. I never ate out like this. Or drank champagne.

'As I said in my card, I feel we've hardly spoken,' she said. 'Which is insane, given what we've just been through together.'

'Same,' I said, worried that I was beginning to lose the power of speech. We were in new territory, speaking our own lines rather than Marlowe's, but I hoped the alcohol would help. 'Do *you* see yourself having children one day?' I managed to ask.

'Are you out of your fucking mind?' she said, laughing.

I glanced around at the family of four, the two young children, hoping they'd accept my smile as an apology for the sweary language.

'I would make a terrible mother,' Clio continued. 'Can you imagine?'

I could, as it happened, but I didn't say anything. One of the actors joked the other day that I should ditch the degree and become a house husband. Just because I seem to have a way with children and can cook meals that don't come in a tin. Mum would have been proud if she'd overheard – all my domestic skills come from her – but she'd also know I wouldn't be brave enough. Too steeped in patriarchal traditions, though she would never put it like that. She would have been disappointed too. Dad worked himself to the bone on his boat, leaving at dawn and returning late at night, while Mum brought me up. The least I could do was go out and get a decent job in return.

'I've seen what motherhood does to women,' Clio continued. 'What happens to them.'

'Physically, you mean?'

'How others behave towards them.'

I was about to ask her what she meant, but she changed the subject.

'It would be nice to hang out more like this,' she said, sipping on her champagne.

Her foot had come to rest on my ankle. For the first time, Clio's dark eyes locked onto mine and we held each other's gaze. I drank deeply from my own glass, felt the alcohol melt away my inhibitions. Our director had asked us not to socialise outside rehearsals. He was keen to 'curate the chemistry' between us, insisting that we remain in character while we were all together, and we had largely abided by his request.

'Are you and Louis an item, then?' I asked, before I could stop the words from tumbling out of my mouth. I needed to know.

'An "item"?' she asked, cocking her head to one side as if I'd just used an unknown, foreign word. Or had I made a hideous faux pas? 'Sometimes we sleep together, if that's what you mean, but not so much recently. He calls me his muse, which I used to find flattering, but now it's just annoying. I think we are coming to the end of our relationship. He's got a lot of issues, shall we say.'

'Like what?'

'He's from a rich family but has no money. His father cut him off when he refused to enter the family wine business and pursued his film studies instead.'

'My heart bleeds.'

'And he...' Clio faltered, glancing around the restaurant.

I raised my eyebrows, encouraging her to continue.

'He's got a younger brother.' She hesitated. 'The prodigal son, as far as his parents are concerned. Gabe can do no wrong, unlike Louis. Parents shouldn't have favourites.'

'Are they close?' I asked. 'Louis and Gabe?'

It's an unusual name. Short for Gabriel, presumably.

'Like twins,' she said. 'Louis is very protective of him – Gabe's not well right now.' She thought for a moment. 'Maybe it's Louis' way of getting back at his parents, I don't know. It must infuriate them that their perfect son gets on so well with his bohemian brother. Do you have siblings?'

'I'm an only child.' Although I sometimes wish I had a

brother or sister, right then it felt good to have something in common with Clio. 'What's wrong with his brother?' The medic in me was curious.

'I don't know, exactly. Depression, I think.'

'The pressures of being a prodigal son. Disappointing your parents.'

'Where are you from, by the way?' she asked, changing the subject again. 'I've been meaning to ask. That cute accent. Is it Bristol?'

'Cornwall,' I replied. Cute? Nobody's ever said that about my accent before. I was about to elaborate, tell her about Newlyn, its medieval harbour and modern fish market. How the Swordy feels like an extension of the sea, a place where fishermen adjust to life on land after weeks on a fishing vessel; the unique smell of diesel and pilchards that hangs over the town like an invisible cloud; the articulated lorries waiting to take hake and turbot upcountry; the way young people move away for work or uni but never quite leave, drawn back by family and an unfathomable sense of belonging. But before I could speak, I saw Louis outside, lens pressed to the restaurant window.

My eyes must have widened because Clio spun round in her chair and was up and out of the restaurant before I knew it. I watched in disbelief as she argued in her bare feet with Louis beside the millpond. I couldn't hear what she was saying, but I could guess as she pushed him backwards in the chest, gesticulating wildly, until he walked away.

Two minutes later, she was back in her seat opposite me, unembarrassed, despite her cheeks still flaming with anger. I've never met anyone with such passion before.

'Sorry about that,' she said, tucking into her 'Home

Computer' pizza, which had arrived in her absence. 'Sometimes he thinks he owns me.'

'What did you say to him?' I said, glancing around the restaurant. Everyone had seen what had happened, but she didn't seem to care.

'I told him I wanted some privacy and that he can shoot his shitty film later.' I loved the way she said 'shitty', pronouncing it like 'sheety'. She raised a glass to mine and leant in towards me. 'Sometimes it's nice to be off camera, don't you think?'

14

'Oops, I rang the wrong bell,' Clio says, standing outside the front door. It's pouring. Hard, spring rain. 'In fact, I rang two front doors before yours,' she adds, pointing at the houses either side. She is soaked to the skin, her hair flattened, raincoat dripping.

Adam glances down Maze Hill – they live halfway up on the left-hand side – and waves at Lynda, a neighbour, who is pretending to tidy a tub of lavender under her porch. Is the camera down by the station pointing towards them again?

'Sorry again,' Clio calls over to Lynda. And then to Adam, in a whisper, 'She wasn't very happy when I disturbed her. It's not that late, is it? What time do you people go to bed in England?'

'What are you doing here?' Adam asks, trying to calculate the harm Clio has already caused to his reputation, the collateral damage in the neighbourhood. Of all the doorbells to ring, she chose Lynda's. A retired librarian, she doesn't miss a thing in the street. She will text Tania, text everyone in south London about Clio's arrival.

'I came back to see my friends in Blackheath,' Clio says. 'I'm meant to be staying there tonight – but they're not home yet. So I thought I would drop by, except I couldn't remember which house is yours. I've brought some champagne.'

She holds up a bottle. Her expensive tastes haven't changed.

'You'd better come in,' Adam says, wishing she'd stop waving the champagne around as he ushers her through the door. 'It's chucking it down.'

He hesitates, then calls across to Lynda. 'Just an old friend of Tania's,' he says. 'From university.' He knows it's a futile gesture. Glancing up and down the street, he's about to go inside when he looks again at the camera. The lens is definitely angled up the road, towards him. He pushes the thought away and heads into the hall, closing the door behind him.

Clio hands him the champagne – chilled, of course – and he shows her through to the kitchen. It felt awkward enough when she was here earlier in the day, but at least Tania was in the house. This time it feels far worse, wrong on so many levels. As soon as the rain stops, he'll ask her to leave. They can chat in the kitchen, where everyone met before, where Tania made her feel welcome, gave Clio her blessing. As long as they stay somewhere well lit, it should be fine. And he needs to ask her something. It's why he was going to text her to meet for a drink tonight. He wants to know about Freddie and his puppy-in-the-park story.

'Where shall I put this?' she asks, taking off her raincoat.

'Anywhere,' Adam says, avoiding direct eye contact. Soaked to the bone, Clio looks even more beautiful than she did earlier, her wet clothes accentuating the natural swells of her body. He's such a typical man, his responses so predictable. 'On the back of the chair.'

He places the champagne in the middle of the table, as if it's contaminated, in some sort of quarantine. Does she remember what happened the last time they drank champagne together? He can't drink the bottle tonight with her. Not just the two of them, in his home. Tania's home.

She seems to sense his reluctance. 'It's not going to open itself,' she says, nodding at the bottle.

Relax. He just needs to play for time. And if it takes a drink, so be it. It still doesn't feel right though as he places two champagne flutes on the polished granite island.

'And do you have a towel?' she asks.

'In the bathroom.' He points through to the hall. 'First left at the top of the stairs.'

He watches her leave the kitchen. Events are spiralling out of control. She shouldn't be using their bathroom. Shouldn't be here at all. But what else could he have done? Not let her into the house?

He's about to text Tania when Clio reappears.

'I have a confession to make,' she says, a towel around her shoulders as if she's arriving poolside. It would have to be one of Tania's special White Company fluffy towels. She leans against the sideboard and pats her face with it.

'You do?' he asks, curious.

He starts to prise off the champagne cork. Is everything about to become clear – her arrival in his life after so many years? She has unfinished business, made a mistake at uni, wants to pick up where they left off. Sorry, it's too late. He's a happily married man.

'I admit, it wasn't a total coincidence that we met in the park today.'

The cork pops.

'It wasn't?' His heart thrums. He pours the champagne, trying to stop his hand from shaking. 'How do you mean?'

He's still struggling to look her in the eye. Doesn't trust himself.

'Are you nervous?' she asks, laughing, as he overfills a glass.

'Nervous? Why should I be nervous?' He passes it to her. Eye contact. Christ, she looks good. He needs to get her out of the house as fast as possible.

'A long time ago, I read an interview with you in a newspaper,' she says, wandering over to the fridge. She peers inside again at Freddie's lunchbox arrangements. The snack boxes are empty. Adam was hungry earlier and it had seemed a shame to waste it all, given Freddie was away. 'You said how you liked to run in the park on a Saturday morning.'

He remembers the article, a favour for a journalist friend who was writing about people running the London Marathon for the first time: 'Marathon Virgins', to coincide with the new sponsor. He and Tania were a case study. Had Clio spent the years after uni trawling the internet for him too?

'So when I was coming to meet my friends in Blackheath today,' she says, towelling the back of her hair, 'I decided to take the train to Greenwich instead and walk through the park, in the hope that you might be there.'

'And I was,' Adam says. 'Still running on Saturdays – just with a jogging pram these days.'

So it wasn't such a complete coincidence after all. She wanted to see him, engineered an encounter. But what about Freddie? Finding him was too much of a chance. She's not telling the whole truth. Freddie's only five, makes up stories all the time, but he wouldn't just say something like that about Clio and the puppy. Should he ask her now? He watches, bides his time as she takes a tour of the kitchen, looking at the pictures drawn by Freddie on the pinboard beside the fridge. Puppies, the lot of them.

'Will Tania mind that I am here?' she asks quietly, her back still to him.

He swallows hard. Will Tania mind? Of course she will, even though she trusts him. 'Why should she?' he asks, failing to sound casual.

Tania's initial encouragement to have a drink with Clio had felt forced. And she wouldn't have imagined that the drink would be a bottle of champagne in their own home, while she was away with the children. He would mind if the situation was reversed. Mind terribly.

Clio turns and shrugs. 'Some women might have a problem with it.' She looks at a photo of Tania on the kitchen dresser. 'I like her. You're very lucky. She's beautiful.'

'I know. Very beautiful.'

Clio's phone pings and she glances at a text. A moment of respite, time out.

What is she really doing here? He takes a long draught of champagne. A part of him wants to drink the bottle with Clio and see what happens. But an alarm bell is also ringing in his head, so loudly and insistently that only a fool would ignore it. And he's not a fool any more. He was once, at university, a naive young man, but not now. He's a successful consultant paediatrician, married with two children. And he's learnt to avoid women like Clio, knows their game. Except he doesn't know Clio's.

'Would she mind if I stayed the night?' she asks, putting down her phone.

'*The night?*' Adam repeats, almost choking on his champagne.

A flash of lightning, followed by a crack of thunder. It's as if they are back on stage together, all those years ago. Lines from *Doctor Faustus* pop into his head out of nowhere.

Now that the gloomy shadow of the earth,
Longing to view Orion's drizzling look,
Leaps from the Antarctic world unto the sky,
And dims the welkin with her pitchy breath,
Faustus, begin thine incantations

It's the first time Doctor Faustus has conjured evil spirits, the beginning of his journey to hell. Adam's brain was a sponge back then, soaking up Marlowe's lines in between memorising endocrinology mnemonics. These days he can hardly remember his own name.

'That sounded close,' he says, glancing outside.

Clio seems unmoved by the dramatic weather, the pathetic fallacy. 'My friends in Blackheath,' she says, glancing at her phone again, 'they're not coming back until very late now. They want me to join them, but my crazy clubbing days are over.'

What has he done to deserve this? His life has been going along well, particularly at work, where he's flying. He and Tania have been arguing, but it's nothing major, just the usual bickering of a married couple with two children under five. Trying to balance their lives and careers. Not a lot of sex, admittedly, but that's fine too, given the circumstances. And now this. How have things gone from a chance meeting in a park with a friend from uni to her wanting to stay the night? Not just any old friend either. He could ask her to leave, walk the streets of Greenwich in the rain. Or he could suggest that she join her clubbing friends. Neither sounds very charitable.

'You can wait here in the kitchen until they get back,' he says, trying to set a practical, no-nonsense course of action. The kitchen is a safe place.

'I am so tired,' she says, stretching as she peers into the sitting room. 'I don't mind sleeping on the sofa. I have an early train to Paris in the morning. Can I charge my phone?'

He nods, watching her walk over to her bag and pull out a charger.

'Freddie's drawings are so cute,' she says as she plugs in the phone beside the pinboard.

Why is she doing this to him? An image of them in bed together comes and goes. He needs to stick to the script, ask her about Freddie, where she found him, but her arrival at his front door has thrown him. It would have been so much more manageable if they had met in town for a drink, on neutral territory.

'Do you need to ring Tania?' she asks. Is his confusion that obvious? 'Check she's OK with this? I don't mind speaking with her.'

'No, it's fine.' Christ, the last thing he wants is Tania to talk with Clio. It was confusing enough when they got on so well earlier.

'Consent is very important,' she says, coming over to him. She places the palm of her hand on his chest, as if she's listening for his heartbeat. Holding her champagne in the other hand, she looks up into his eyes. 'I always told Louis when I was going to sleep with someone else.'

15

We were both drunk by the time we climbed into the punt. Stuffed too, after our meal at Sweeney Todd's. We'd made the mistake of ordering a 'Rupture Rapture' to share for dessert – 'a perverse landslide of six flavours of ice cream, whipped cream, cherries, peaches, nuts, wafers and chocolate flakes' – and wanted to walk it off with a stroll along the river. When I suggested that we head back the way we'd come and take a punt to Grantchester Meadows, she leapt at the opportunity, as Louis had predicted, particularly when I produced from my rucksack a small bottle of vodka and a carton of grapefruit juice.

Clio had forgotten about Louis, having emphatically told him to keep away, but I was sure that he was around somewhere, filming us from afar as we set off in our punt. It was his original idea, after all, to go punting; his idea too to ply Clio with vodka. He wouldn't pass up the chance to shoot something so filmic as two young students making their merry way upriver to Grantchester.

'Do you want a go?' I asked as I pushed us along the Backs, past King's College and its sloping lawns running up to the

73

famous chapel, and on towards Silver Street Bridge. A gentle wind was blowing in from the south.

'I like watching you do it,' she said, reclining in the bottom of the punt.

She was sitting on a bed of cushions with her back to our direction of travel, facing me, her legs barely covered by her red slip dress. It was hard to know where to look. I enjoyed being back on the water again, even if it was a far cry from the sea. I'd not been in a punt since I took Mum down the Cam in my first few weeks here. Mum beamed the whole way, so proud to be in Cambridge, on a punt propelled by me, her medical student son. The sun shone and the fresh autumn air had seemed to do her fragile health the power of good.

The outdoors suited Clio too. Her cheeks were pink, a light breeze ruffling her dark, lustrous hair. I was about to bend down and kiss her, unable to resist any longer, when I heard the unmistakeable noise of someone nearby falling into the water. My hands froze on the punt pole. *The sound of the splash that the corpse soon made as it struck the sea –* Melville's words still haunted me as much as the noise itself.

'You OK?' Clio asked. 'Look like you've seen a ghost.' She'd sat up to see what was going on – a sodden student was being hauled back into a punt by his laughing mates – but she was now eyeing me with concern.

I flashed her a smile that quickly faded, chased away by a stab of emotion – and that sickening noise in my head again. I could still hear the splash so clearly.

'It's nothing,' I said quickly and started to punt again.

But I couldn't get the sound out of my head: not just the splash, but everything that had led up to it. The banter inside the pub, the sudden silence when the strangers walked in, their jeers on the North Pier later. It was all coming back now, the horror of what had happened next.

'You can tell me,' she said, leaning forward to squeeze my leg.

'It reminds me of a night in Newlyn, that's all,' I said hesitantly. 'When some posh idiots chucked a friend of mine into the harbour. He couldn't swim.'

'What reminds you?'

'That sound.' I gestured in the direction of the nearby punt, where the drunken student was now safely on board again.

She looked across the water and back at me. 'Was he OK? Your friend?'

I shook my head and turned away.

'You don't have to tell me,' she said.

'I'm sorry,' I said, concentrating on the river, shocked by how raw it still felt, how difficult it was proving to explain.

'It's OK,' she added. 'Sometimes it's better we don't share everything.'

I looked at her, turned away again.

It was as we were approaching Queens' College that I saw him, recognised his distinctive red hair. The same student who'd told me in the ADC Bar that Louis was evil. He was walking across Mathematical Bridge, its complex lattice of woodwork bleached pale in the dazzling May sunlight, and hadn't seen our punt. As I watched him, a woman came running up from behind, finally drawing level with him, and they talked for a few seconds.

'Hey, Clio, do you know that guy?' I asked, as casually as I could. We were thirty yards away and the couple now appeared to be arguing.

She sat up in the bottom of the boat a little too quickly.

'Whoa, I'm seeing stars.' She lay back down again. 'Who?' she asked, staring at the sky.

'Up ahead,' I said, pointing.

'I've no idea,' she said, still lying down.

I watched, transfixed, as the student brushed the woman off, leaving her alone on the bridge.

'Try again? Slowly?' I said to Clio. 'The red-haired guy on the bank.'

She pulled herself up and turned for a second, before reclining again. 'Aldous – can you believe it?' she said.

'What?'

'He's called Aldous. That's his name.'

'As in the novelist? You know him?'

'I had a drink with him once. At the ADC Bar, I think.'

'When?'

'Last term. Crazy name, cute guy.'

I looked again at Aldous as he disappeared into the modern complex of Queens' College buildings on the far side of the Cam. What did he know about Louis that I didn't? And why couldn't he tell me?

We glided under the bridge, where the woman was now leaning over the side. Her head was turned away, but it was obvious that she was crying.

'Does he know Louis?' I asked, wondering what had passed between the two students.

'I've no idea,' she said. 'And I don't care. Why?'

'He told me to be wary of Louis. At the after-show the other night.'

At first, Clio didn't seem interested, but then she shielded her eyes and lifted her head a little. 'What did he say?'

Even though the encounter was stuck in my head, I didn't

want to repeat Aldous's words when I knew nothing about his reason for saying them, so I downplayed the warning. 'Just told me to stay away from him, that's all.'

'Sounds like good advice,' she said. 'Louis is *un abruti*, as we say in France. A fool.'

16

May 1998

I realised it was going to take almost two hours to reach Grantchester, and that I would never have a better opportunity to talk to Clio on my own, get to know her better. But we were drunk and she was soon asleep in the bottom of the punt. To be honest, I can't recall much about the early part of the journey either. I was still shocked by my reaction to the sound of the student falling into the water, my inability to tell Clio what had happened in Newlyn. I know we passed the Newnham Riverbank Club and an elderly woman swimming naked, and Skaters' Meadow, with its solitary 1920s lamppost from back when the whole area used to freeze over in winter. Beyond that, I can't remember.

When Clio finally stirred, I wanted to ask more about her parents, particularly her father, but I'd sensed a reluctance earlier and so I tried a different approach: shameless flattery.

'Was it your dad then who taught you how to act so well?' I asked.

She smiled. Sleep still hung heavy on her eyes.

'He could hold an audience's attention, I'll give him that,' she said. 'The critics loved him. We used to go and watch him on stage in Paris, when I was younger. At Le Théâtre du Châtelet.'

'Were you close?'

'Close?' She looked up at me, one hand shielding the sun from her eyes. 'I worshipped him – until I realised he didn't just act on stage. He pretended to love my mother for twenty years.'

'I'm sorry.'

'Don't be. He wasn't. He put her through hell.'

Her words shocked me. 'Why? What did he do?'

She didn't answer. Not immediately. Instead, she turned away, watched the world drift past.

'He was jealous, couldn't bear to see his wife love someone other than him. Their child. He was used to being the centre of attention.'

'But he never… made life hell for you?'

She shook her head, tears coming. 'He adored me. That was the irony. It was OK for him to love me but not for my mother.'

We floated on through the idyllic countryside, passed the occasional punt travelling in the opposite direction. I sensed she wanted to tell me more but it was up to her now. I'd pried too much already.

'Do you know what he did to her once?' she eventually said, her voice quiet with reflection. 'When he came back from a long tour?'

I shook my head, fearing what she might say.

'He told her to fetch a good bottle of wine from the cellar in the outbuildings. Said it was her choice – it was the least he could do after being away for so long. "*Ma chérie*, you choose tonight – anything you like." He had a lot of special bottles and my mother... she liked her wine in those days. I had gone to bed but I couldn't sleep. I must have been ten at the time. My mother has a very beautiful voice – it used to soothe me at night when she was talking to friends on the phone – but I was worried that I hadn't heard it for a while. I went downstairs and she wasn't there. My father had passed out in front of the TV. He was overweight and drank too much – his doctor was always warning him. I didn't try to wake him – he had a terrible temper – so I looked around the house, searching everywhere for my mother. And that's when I heard the noise. A distant thumping sound. I went to the outbuildings and eventually managed to lift the cellar door. My mother had been locked down there for hours.'

'That's awful.' I stopped punting, let the pole trail in the water as I took in what she'd just told me.

'She suffers from claustrophobia and thought she was going to spend the whole night in there. She was in a terrible state, her whole body shaking.' Clio bit her lip. 'Even worse, she tried to make excuses for him. Said it had been an accident, that he was tired after weeks of touring, must have fallen asleep. She was trying to protect me – from the horror of my own father.'

Her tears were flowing freely now and I slipped the pole into the punt and moved down to be beside her.

'Why didn't she leave him?' I asked, cradling her in my arms. 'Report him to the police?'

She didn't reply. I tried to comfort her, stroked her hair, held her close, but it took a long while for her sobs to subside.

'She was sent to the cellar quite often after that to "choose a good bottle of wine". I hated the look she used to give as she walked past me – a mix of terror and maternal reassurance. Later I found out that he had threatened to kill her if she ever tried to leave him,' she said, resting her head on my shoulder. 'She was frightened of him. We both were. It was a mercy when he died.'

Half an hour later, we finally reached Grantchester. Clio had stayed beside me in the punt, leaning against my legs as I'd pushed our way along the Cam. Once we'd moored up on a secluded stretch of riverbank, we lay side by side in the late-afternoon sunshine and watched the shimmering willow trees, their branches hanging down like curtains over enticing pools of dark, slow-flowing water. A warm zephyr had swung round to the west. We had changed too. There was a new intimacy between us, after what she'd confided in me about her parents' relationship.

I hooked one leg over hers as we looked out over the meadow. It was here that Virginia Woolf and Rupert Brooke used to skinny-dip before retreating to the shade of the Orchard Tea Garden. Today, our only company was a herd of cows in the distance, and an occasional cyclist on the footpath on the far side of the meadow, taking a more direct route into town than the meandering river. There must have been others enjoying the Cam – passing kayakers, punters, swimmers – but we were blissfully unaware of them.

I asked her if she wanted to swim. She turned to smile at me with such seduction in her eyes that I assumed she knew all about the history of the place. It wasn't just Woolf and her neo-pagan set who liked to swim naked there. Lord Byron used to take a dip a little further upstream. But then her smile faded. We lay in silence, our bodies slowing to the rhythm of the river. A flash of blue as a kingfisher darted downstream. The startled alarm of a moorhen.

'What are you thinking?' she asked, our heads close as we watched white clouds scud across the big Fenland sky.

'That's it's so sad, about your father.'

'Forget about him.'

'I'm also thinking that Louis might be watching us,' I said. The footpath would be an obvious place for him to film us from. I rolled over to check but couldn't see anyone.

'He's not,' Clio said. 'I told him I'd never let him film me again if he followed us.'

'And he does what you say?'

'Always.'

A small part of me was disappointed. I wasn't so bothered if he was filming us, perched in the boughs of a nearby willow with a zoom lens. The footage would be empirical evidence that today actually happened, in case I wake up tomorrow and it feels like a dream. I have to admit that I'd begun to feel oddly emboldened by the thought of being filmed. It wasn't the same sort of transformation that I experienced on stage, but I definitely seemed to be more confident and articulate than my usual jabbering self.

'You are thinking something else, I can feel it,' she said, her voice quiet now.

'I think that I'm falling in love with you,' I said, and I leant over to kiss her, eyes closed, heart skipping.

Clio kissed me back, opening her soft lips to let me in, and I felt her body begin to stir, pressing against mine. If the world had ended in that moment, I'd have died happy. It was what student life was meant to be about. The sun beat down on the meadow and our heads spun with champagne and vodka as we started to explore each other's bodies.

And then Clio stopped.

'We mustn't do this,' she whispered, lying back on the riverbank. 'I'm so sorry.'

'How do you mean?' I asked, propping myself up on one elbow.

'I'm not good for you.'

'You're the best thing that's ever happened to me.'

I rested a hand on her stomach.

'You don't understand,' she said, putting her hand on mine.

'I'm trying to.'

'I should never have invited you to lunch.'

'So why did you?'

'To warn you.'

I sat up properly now and gazed down at her. 'About what?'

She turned her head away. My heart started to race again.

'About Louis?' I asked, thinking of the student at the bar. Aldous.

She turned to look up at me, her limpid eyes burning into mine. A lone tear rolled down her cheek.

'About me. It's better you stay away, steer clear.'

'I'm not sure I can.'

I bent down to kiss her again, but this time her lips were unresponsive. I pulled back.

'Please don't come to Louis' party tomorrow night,' she said, still staring up at the sky.

'Why not?' Did she know that I'd been invited?

'Because bad things always happen at his parties.'

'What sort of things?'

She shrugged and said nothing.

'Why are you going then?' I asked.

'Why? Because I am a bad person.'

'I don't believe you are. Not for a second.'

It was a long while before she answered. 'I'm not the person you think I am, Adam. Believe me.' She paused. 'I've done some terrible things in my life. Today we've had fun. You are kind and I have behaved myself. But I'm not a good human being. I'm not always kind to others. You want to settle down one day, have a big family, lots of kids. I am restless, always will be. And I never, ever want to be a mother.'

'That's so sad,' I said. I knew that not all women wanted to have children, of course, but I was biased. I also sensed that she wasn't being entirely honest with me about her reasons.

'Why's it sad?' she asked, sitting up now. Her voice was more animated as she picked at blades of grass. 'It suits me. You have a plan for your life, to become a doctor. Mine is to experience this world in every way that's ever been invented, to wring every sensation out of it, even if it kills me. I want to travel, not stay in one place. Or stay with one man, or with one woman or with one family.' She studied the blade of grass in her hand, let it fall. 'I'm sorry if I've misled you. But I saw something in your eyes, the way you looked at me just now, and I wanted to warn you. I tried to stay strong today, but I am weak and you are...' – she reached up and stroked the side of my face with the back of her fingers – '... you are one of the good guys. Too good for me.'

More tears started to roll down her cheeks. I held her in my arms and she hugged me until the sobbing subsided. I didn't know what to think or do. My shoulder was damp with her tears. I kept on saying to her that it was OK, that I understood, but I didn't understand. I didn't understand at all.

17

'We need to talk,' Adam says, removing Clio's hand from his chest and walking over to the kitchen island. He tops up his glass, hoping to draw strength from somewhere, and turns to face Clio, glad of the physical space that's opened up between them. Her hand had felt soft and enticing.

'With Tania?'

'Not with Tania, no,' he says, suddenly irritated by Clio and her reappearance in his life.

The rain intensifies outside, hammering down on the glass roof of the kitchen extension.

'OK,' she says. 'I'm sorry. Can I smoke in here?'

'I'd rather you didn't.'

'It's raining outside.'

'I had noticed. Can you stand in the front porch?'

But Clio has already opened the back door and is lighting up.

His sudden irritation with her makes it easier to switch the focus of their conversation to what he wants to talk about. He takes a deep breath.

'When Freddie went missing today...' He stops. It's not

as easy as he thought. He's about to cross a line, effectively accuse Clio of kidnapping their son.

'It must have been very worrying for you both,' she says, exhaling smoke into the rainy night air.

'Where exactly did you find him?'

'Near where we met.' She turns to look at him. 'Why?'

'Did he say anything to you about a puppy? Freddie?'

'Not that I remember.' She nods at the drawings on the pinboard. 'Looks like he wants one.'

Perhaps Adam has got this wrong. But then, out of the mouth of babes... He doesn't know what to think. Freddie can also tell lies, as he knows only too well.

'Freddie said something about you showing him a puppy,' he says.

'Oh, I remember now. When I found him, he was crying. There was a family nearby with a puppy, so I tried to distract him by taking him over to meet it.'

Odd that she hadn't mentioned the encounter when he'd first asked. But it might just be true.

'You should get one. Why not?' she adds.

Because they can barely cope with the mess of two children, that's why. A crapping dog might tip them over the edge. And he knows who'll end up walking it. Before he can reply more politely, his phone rings. It's Tania.

'Who's my old friend from university, then?' she asks.

'What?'

Tania's voice is tense, laden with sarcasm. 'Lynda just texted me. Said you were in a bit of a state but that I wasn't to worry as you'd told her you were just "letting in an old friend of mine from university".'

Adam signals to Clio that he won't be a moment and walks into the sitting room, closing the door behind him.

'It's Clio,' he says, looking at a photo of Tania and a baby Freddie on the mantelpiece. It was taken a couple of weeks after he was born. Tania appears tired but happy. The honeymoon period. Friends and family offering to help, delivering meals. Grandparents dropping by. It didn't happen with Tilly. Everyone thinks you can cope on your own with the second child.

'Clio?' Tania says.

'Who came today. Found Freddie in the park. Apparently.'

'I know who bloody Clio is. I just don't remember going to university with her. And what the fuck's she doing in our house?'

Adam winces, his embarrassment only marginally softened by the champagne. Hadn't Tania liked Clio a few hours earlier, suggested they should hang out with her? 'She just turned up.'

'Just turned up?' He knows how it must sound. 'Presumably because you'd sent her a text message asking if she wanted to come round for a drink. At our house. Women don't just turn up on your doorstep, Adam, however much you'd like to think they do.'

That was unfair. This one did. 'She arrived here before I'd had a chance to text her. It was just after you and I had spoken.'

'You don't have to lie to me, Adam.'

'I'm not lying. I'm telling you how it is.' He paces around the sitting room, running a hand through his hair as he glances out of the window onto the wet London street. 'She rang the doorbell seconds after you called – having rung two other bells in the street first. Including Lynda's.'

'Are you pissed?' Her voice is quieter now, a tone of genuine surprise. 'Just how stupid do you think I am?'

He can drink beer all night, but he's always had a light head when it comes to champagne.

'I'm not pissed. I've had two glasses.'

'Glasses? Of what?'

He closes his eyes. There's no point in lying. 'Champagne.'

She punches out a short, dry laugh. 'Well, enjoy your fucking champagne with Clio while I look after the kids, who are both still awake and crying, by the way, and don't expect me to return to London any time soon. Get her out of our home, Adam.'

'Tania, it's not—'

But the line has already gone dead.

18

The punt back to Cambridge was a tiring, joyless affair. It was as if all colour had been drained from the day and with it any sense of fun. The blue sky had turned to pewter, the green of the trees seemed less vibrant, and the water felt ice cold as it dripped off the punting pole onto my bare feet. Even the birds had stopped their singing. It had taken us almost two hours to reach Grantchester. The return journey was quicker, but it still felt long and my arms were aching by the time we slid under Fen Causeway on the western edges of the city. Clio spent the entire trip asleep in the bottom of the punt, but this time she was on her side, knees tucked up in the foetal position, her body tense when before it had been relaxed.

I'm still confused by what she said, the conflicting impulses – to invite me to lunch, drink champagne, punt to Grantchester, tell me about her father; and then the warning to stay away from her. Before today, I'd always felt out of my depth in her company, but I saw a vulnerable side this afternoon, held her while she sobbed like a child. I feel more in control, less in need of being warned off. I can look after myself, decide whether to attend Louis' party tomorrow night. And I still want to go.

The spring sun was slinking away like a thief, stealing the last of the day's heat as we approached Queens' College. I took off my jacket and laid it across Clio's shoulders. And then I kissed her cheek.

'How much further?' she whispered, pulling the jacket up around her neck.

'Not far now,' I said. 'Mathematical Bridge ahoy.'

It was a poor attempt at levity, my heart wasn't in it. I felt depressed, defeated, as if I was returning from battle with a cargo of the wounded.

I punted us on towards Clare Bridge, and then I stopped in mid-flow, my eyes drawn to an incident unfolding to my right. An ambulance had parked up beneath the twin western towers of King's College Chapel. It looked incongruous with its blue flashing lights, at odds with the tranquillity of the setting, the manicured lawns, the neo-classical stateliness of the adjacent Gibbs Building. Police officers were in attendance too, cordoning off an area with tape to keep people away. A small crowd stood at a distance, several of them hugging each other.

'Do you know what's happened?' I asked as we slipped slowly past another punt.

'Suicide,' the student said. 'Jumped off the top of the chapel.'

I closed my eyes. They wouldn't have survived. Catastrophic spinal injuries if they had. Life-changing.

Clio stirred in the bottom of the punt. 'What's happened?' she asked, sitting up on the cushions. Her dress was tangled, revealing a brief flash of nipple. I looked away.

'Someone's jumped off the chapel.' I nodded in the direction of our most famous landmark.

'My God, how awful,' she said, looking across at the scene.

I could see two police cars parked beside the chapel. A second ambulance turned onto the lawns and drew up beside the first one.

The river seemed to flow even slower, if that were possible, punts drifting listlessly as everyone tried to take in the tragedy, process what must have happened only a few minutes ago. The wind had dropped too. Had anyone seen him jump?

'A guy from Queens', apparently,' a student on the riverbank said to no one in particular.

It was one of those moments when you just know something, feel it in the pit of your stomach, even though the odds of being right are stacked against you. There are hundreds of students at Queens', but only one had had a row on a bridge this afternoon, leaving another in tears. Only one had warned me about Louis and run off into the night with fear on his face.

'Do you know who?' I asked.

The student shook his head. But I knew. I was sure of it. A red-haired student called Aldous.

19

Adam holds the phone in his hand, staring at it for a few seconds. He and Tania have had their rows recently, but nothing like that. She was angry. Really angry. *Get her out of our house, Adam.* He would feel exactly the same if an ex of hers turned up one evening with a bottle of champagne when he was away.

He looks around the living room, littered with evidence of the life he's made with Tania. Freddie's scooter in the corner; Tilly's soft toys spilling out of a wooden box; a stack of their favourite Motown vinyl records on a shelf above a vintage record player, bought together in Greenwich Market; a rare painting by his dad, which Tania found online at an auction in Truro and gave him for his fortieth birthday; a glittering Rajasthani throw that they bought in India on their honeymoon for too much money after he managed to haggle the price upwards. He doesn't want to lose this life. Clio is still next door in the kitchen. And it's raining hard outside. He needs to order her a taxi, but where to? She could hang around the Eurostar terminal, wait for her train in the morning. She said it was early. And the station will be safe, well lit.

He opens the door and goes back into the kitchen.

'Christ, what are you doing?' he says, spinning away as if he's just walked into a pane of glass. Clio has stripped down to her underwear and is ironing her dress in the corner of the kitchen, where the ironing board is still standing from earlier. Before Tania left, he'd pressed Freddie's and Tilly's clothes, even one of Tania's dresses, made a special effort. He hadn't put the board away, despite Tania always asking him to. There are limits to his domesticity. Now he wishes he had.

'I'm sorry – my dress was still a bit wet and I couldn't find the tumble-dryer, so I thought I'd iron it.'

'Please, you need to put some clothes on,' he says, rubbing the sides of his forehead with his hands as if he's got a splitting headache.

'Don't be such a prude,' she says, walking over to him. 'Hold this for me – try not to crease it.'

She passes him her dress while she walks back and turns off the iron. He watches as she folds up the ironing board and slips it behind the kitchen door, where it belongs. How did she know? She's in good shape, wearing expensive, skimpy underwear. French, presumably. He tried to buy Tania lingerie once, soon after they met. The red nylon thong didn't go down well.

'Done,' she says, walking back over to him.

He turns and holds out the dress as if, like the champagne, it too is contaminated. They look at each other for a moment. Her eyes seem different again, like they did at the station. She glances across at the garden windows and then back at him. Is she scared of something? He looks over at the windows too.

'You English are so strange,' she says, taking the dress and slipping it on.

'I'm going to order a taxi for you,' he says, walking across to the windows. 'To drive you to King's Cross.'

'But my train's not leaving for another ten hours.'

Not as early as he'd thought.

'You can't stay here,' he says.

He looks out on the garden, the neighbouring houses. He tells himself not to be stupid. There are no cameras out there. No one is watching him. But he draws the curtains just in case. It's darker than usual, because of the storm, but night has yet to fall.

'Your friends didn't leave out a key?' he asks, crossing back over to her. 'Maybe someone else has got one?'

She shakes her head.

'Was Tania unhappy?' she asks.

'That's one way of putting it.'

'I'm sorry.' She disconnects her iPhone from the dresser. He thought she'd plugged it in by the pinboard. 'You're right. I should go.'

She looks him in the eye before turning away. Her words come as an overwhelming relief, but, if he's honest, he's also a tiny bit disappointed. The damage has already been done with Tania and the neighbours. What difference would it make if she stayed over? He checks himself. The champagne has impaired rational thinking, allowed his primal instincts to run the show. He knows it's the right decision for her to go. She should leave now. But he still can't shake off the thought that finding Freddie in the park today was too much of a coincidence.

He's asked all he can about the puppy and she's given him an answer. What more can he do? She found Freddie, who'd wandered off. But had he? *I was in the sandpit, where*

Mummy told me to stay. He has to make decisions all the time at work about whether to believe young children. *Where does it hurt? How long has there been a pain there? Might there be something else that's upsetting you?* It's different when it's your own child. Judgements become blurred. But he's sure Freddie is telling the truth. His son had no reason to lie.

'Let's meet up again, properly, in a bar,' he says. Until he can establish what really happened in the park, he needs to stay in touch with Clio, however risky.

'With Tania too?' she says.

'I'm not sure that'd be a good idea.'

'I'd like to see her again. Apologise for trying to sleep with her man. We do things a little differently in France. I came just before 7 p.m. but maybe you don't have *cinq à sept* here.'

'I have no idea what you're talking about.'

'It's when we have our affairs in France. Our *aventures*. Between work and dinner. I came to the park today hoping to see you. But when we met, and you told me that you would be alone tonight, I thought—'

'Shall I call an Uber?' he asks, keen to stop her from elaborating any further. Why *had* he told her that Tania would be away tonight? He'd also said that he was busy, on call, but she clearly hadn't believed him.

'It's OK,' she says, bringing out her phone.

At least she's being honest with him now, but it still doesn't explain Freddie's version of events. If Clio just came to Greenwich to have an affair with him – flattering but unlikely, particularly after so many years – she could have bumped into him, rather than claimed to have found Freddie.

'I'm sorry,' she says five minutes later, standing on the front doorstep. Her Uber has arrived.

Adam glances both ways to see if anyone is twitching their curtains. A moment later, Lynda from next door walks out onto her porch. Of course she does. Adam gives her a wave, hoping that Clio won't do or say anything else to destroy what remains of his marriage.

'Thanks for dropping by,' he says, loud enough for Lynda to hear, as Clio kisses him on both cheeks. It could be worse.

He watches as the Uber drives her away to her friends' club, where she said she would go. Does he believe her? She's not his problem any more. A blue glow from her mobile is visible in the back of the car. She's texting her clubbing friends. At the bottom of Maze Hill, the new security camera stares down, no doubt clocking the car's number plate as it passes.

He's always wondered what it would be like to be presented with an opportunity to have an affair. Now he knows. A nightmare. Thank God the moment has passed.

His phone rings. It's Tania. He breathes out a sigh of relief as he answers. He can tell her that Clio's gone, that he's got her out of their house, just as she asked. There's a brief moment of silence before she speaks, her voice shaking with emotion.

'Why am I looking at a photo of Clio in her underwear in our kitchen?'

20

I was shattered by the time I got back here, to my room. Clio and I walked over to Magdalene, her college, after we moored the punt. We didn't speak much and I wondered if we'd ever be on our own together again.

'See you around,' she said as she crossed Magdalene Street and entered the main college entrance.

'Maybe tomorrow night,' I called out from the other side of the road. Meaning at Louis' party.

She stopped and turned, as if to say something in reply, but then disappeared through the archway. It was a sad walk back here.

Just strolling into Tom's usually cheers me up – I'm still grateful to be one of the few freshers to have been accommodated here in the historic part of the college, close to the old library, rather than across the river in one of the modern halls of residence. But tonight even the famous view down King's Parade failed to lift my spirits. It was deserted, except for a police car parked up at the far end, outside King's College.

I flopped down onto my bed, still troubled by the tragedy that had unfolded on the Backs. It had upset Clio too. She kept staring at the chapel as we punted past, shaking her head in disbelief. Everyone in college was talking about it. Not only did the student die, but he also critically injured a member of the public who was walking past the chapel when he jumped. The student had yet to be named, but I was convinced that I knew already.

'Hey, Adam, come and look at what I've found.'

Ji was standing by my door, temporarily untethered from his usual position in front of his fluorescent turquoise iMac computer. Since I've known him, I can count on one hand the number of times I've seen him outside his room, let alone outside the college. He sits there day and night, playing videogames and trawling the World Wide Web for the macabre. And sometimes playing poker and drinking whisky with other computer-science students from China.

I rolled off my bed and followed him over to his room, across the corridor.

'You won't believe what I've just seen on rotten.com,' he said.

Words that always make me nervous. It's Ji's favourite website and he's always quoting its tagline: *When hell is full, the dead shall walk the earth – pure evil since 1996.* Personally, I don't get it, why anyone would want to look at photos of recent car crashes, gory dismemberments, fresh amputees and beheadings, the daily fare offered up by rotten.com. I struggle enough with our full-body dissection classes.

'Do I want to see this?' I asked as he sat down in front of his computer.

'Watch,' he said.

And, to my shame, I watched, appalled, as a blurred human body fell past the ancient buttresses of King's College Chapel and smacked into a hapless passer-by on the ground. It was the speed of the body's descent that was so shocking. Like a sack of lead. The exact point of impact was mercifully out of focus.

'Jesus, Ji.' I turned away, thinking I might throw up.

'That's it,' he said. 'What happened here today. Already on rotten.com. Don't you love the World Wide Web?'

'What kind of a sick person would film something like that?' I asked.

'Do you want to see it again?'

'No, I don't, Ji. That's a video of someone dying. Possibly two people. Why are you even watching it?'

The video had been shot from long distance and the images were grainy. In truth, Ji has shown me far more graphic footage in the past, but it was still stomach-churning.

'Curiosity?' Ji said, more thoughtful than usual. 'Or maybe I'm in denial about death. I am immoral!' He grinned, raising both fists in the air like a champion boxer.

'Immortal,' I corrected, although immoral was possibly more apt. I don't feel comfortable pointing out his mistakes – it's not as if I can speak a word of Mandarin, let alone quote any Confucian words of wisdom – but he has asked me to correct him, such is his appetite to improve his English.

'Immortal,' Ji repeated, in his faint American accent. 'I am immortal.' This time he didn't raise his hands but said the words reflectively. 'Seeing something like this' – he gestured at the computer – 'reminds me that death is a reality of life. We all die in the end, some sooner than others.'

I hadn't heard Ji talk like that before. Death is more of a presence in my medical world. Every day we're being taught new ways to postpone it.

I was about to go back to my room when I stopped and turned. 'Can you freeze the footage, when he's falling, and zoom in at all?' I asked.

Ji gave me a conspiratorial smile. 'You wanna see his expression? The face of death?'

'No,' I said, moving over to his desk again as he started to replay the video. 'I just want to see the colour of his hair.'

Ji pivoted to look at me. 'OK,' he said. 'Whatever turns you on.'

'It doesn't turn me on, Ji,' I snapped, but it was no good trying to explain.

I watched as he struggled to enlarge the frozen image. It took him a few attempts and then we were looking at a close-up.

'Hard to say,' Ji said. 'But if I was a gambling man' – everyone in college knows he is – 'I'd say he had red hair.'

It was definitely Aldous. No question.

21

'Adam, you're holding her dress up like the cat that got the cream.'

'I can explain,' Adam says, sighing, relieved that he's finally talking to Tania.

For the past three hours her phone has been going straight to voicemail. And nobody's picking up her parents' landline. He's left four messages with them already – strained, polite, the desperate words of a beleaguered son-in-law. It was hard to convey a sense of urgency without upsetting them or going into lurid details, and he guessed after the first message that Tania would have told them to ignore his calls and go to bed. He can understand her fury, but she needs to let him explain and put her mind at rest. Many times tonight he's contemplated taking a train down to Wiltshire, but if she's not answering his calls, she won't let him into the house. And he doesn't want to create a scene in front of her parents. Or the children.

'You always can explain,' she says.

'But first you need to tell me who sent you the photo,' Adam says. 'Was it Clio?'

'I really don't care who sent the fucking photo.' She's

still cross, more angry than he's ever heard her. 'It wasn't her number, the one she gave me today,' she continues. 'A neighbour, presumably, nose pressed to the window after Lynda told the whole street that you had some fucking floozie from uni staying over in her underwear.'

He thinks back to when Clio was ironing her dress. It was pouring outside. A public footpath runs along one side of their garden. It's fenced off, but there are several places where you can see over. Their neighbours are notoriously nosy, but no one would have gone round into their garden in that weather, would they? He would have seen them.

'Can you send it to me?' he says. 'I need to see where it was taken from.'

'So you can get off on her again?'

'You're being unreasonable, Tania.'

'Me?' Another one of her staccato, bare husks of a laugh. 'I don't think *I'm* the unreasonable one here, Adam.'

'Are you sure it was taken from outside?'

A long pause. Is she looking at the photo again? He doesn't want to picture the image. It can't look good, wherever it was taken from.

'Inside, I think,' Tania eventually says. Her tone sounds marginally less hostile. 'Maybe by the kitchen window, by the dresser.'

The dresser. Where Clio moved her phone earlier to charge it. He was certain it was plugged in by the pinboard when he took Tania's call in the sitting room. By the time he came out again, it was charging by the dresser. Did she take the photo? Set her camera up to record in video mode while he was out of the room and then select a still from the footage later, when she was in the Uber?

'Can you forward it to me?' he says. 'Please?'

'I'm not sending this to anyone.'

Adam takes a deep breath, trying to conceal his frustration. 'Is she looking at me? Or...'

Another long pause. 'She's looking straight at the camera.'

Adam closes his eyes. Clio knew exactly where the phone was. Made sure to stand in her underwear in the right place. Sightlines. An old pro dusting down her acting skills. Christ, he remembers now. At one point she glanced over towards the kitchen window. Or was it the dresser? He thought she was looking at the storm.

'And does it look like it's a still from film footage or is it just an ordinary camera photo? A single image?'

A still from a video would look worse than the actual moving footage, which would show that nothing had happened.

'I really don't care, Adam,' she says. And then, a few seconds later, 'Maybe from a film.'

'I think I should come down to Wiltshire, tonight,' he says, walking over to the kitchen window and staring out into the night.

'You're not invited.'

Adam sighs. What a total car crash this evening has been. He's glad he didn't set off earlier. She definitely wouldn't have let him in. Not in this mood. He's tried to explain in rambling texts and answerphone messages that nothing went on between them, that Clio had arrived soaking wet and ironed her dress when he was out of the room talking to her on the phone, but it all sounded so lame and Tania is understandably suspicious. He needs to speak to her face to face.

'Nothing happened, darling. Please believe me. She wanted it to, but I managed—'

'To resist her charms? Are you actually after praise here? I don't believe this, Adam.'

Silence. Has she hung up? 'Tania?'

22

May 1998

'You look half asleep,' Louis said as I wobbled past him on my old bicycle down King's Parade.

'Because you're working me so hard,' I called out after him. We'd already filmed a short early-morning sequence of me in my room, studying at my desk, and he now wanted a shot of me cycling to lectures. King's Parade wasn't actually on my route. Artistic licence, I guess.

To be fair, Louis didn't look great either. Smoking a roll-up, he seemed more sallow than usual, his black hair thinner too. Maybe to compensate, he'd swapped his regulation black shirt for a flowery one, but he was still wearing his standard black leather jacket, torn black jeans and his I-didn't-go-to-Eton Doc Martens.

I pulled over, waiting for him to catch up. A change to my morning routine wasn't a great start to what I knew would be a testing couple of hours. I've found that walking to the Anatomy Building on the Downing Site, picking up a coffee in Market Square en route, is the best way to prepare for a cadaveric dissection session, but Louis insisted that I cycle. For once, my bike hadn't been stolen. He was continuing to film me with the same gusto as yesterday, but my own enthusiasm was waning.

The dissection classes are getting easier, it's true, now that I've got over the shock of seeing that first cadaver at the beginning of term. The stink of the formaldehyde used to preserve the bodies no longer makes me want to vomit. It does make me incredibly hungry, though – ravenous, just like the second years warned us it would. After two hours of cutting up a human body, we all leave the labs in need of a burger, which doesn't feel right on any level. It's extraordinary, though, how quickly everyone's adapted, become desensitised. Respect is meant to be at the heart of what we do in the classes. We all have to write tributes for the donors' committal services and there's an annual service of thanksgiving. And we do respect those who give their bodies to science, we really do. But medical students are a particular breed, with a very particular sense of humour... In last week's abdo session, two of us were tasked with removing and measuring the small intestine. It just kept on coming, more than six feet of it. Even our anatomy demonstrator struggled to keep a straight face as he watched our reaction. At least we didn't try skipping with it.

'I've got to go,' I said, glancing at my watch as Louis walked up to me. 'My dissection class is about to start.' After three takes of me cycling down King's Parade for him, I was out of time and patience.

'I think we've got the shot,' he said, checking his camera. 'How do you find dissecting a real dead body, by the way?'

'It's OK.'

I'm not sure if it was because of my years of gutting fish – I still remember Dad showing me the intestines, swim bladder and liver – but I was fine with cutting open a human body. Not squeamish at all.

'Do you get to work on the brain?' Louis asked.

'Of course.'

'They're very fragile, I guess. Easily damaged.'

His eyes lingered on mine. I didn't know where he was going with this. 'It's why we have thick skulls,' I said, tapping my own to lighten the mood.

Today's session was to be about the thorax, removing the ribs to get a better look at the heart and lungs. I pored over my dissection manual last night, but I was still a little apprehensive. The human body is complicated inside, messy, not neat and tidy like the anatomy diagrams. And not for the first time I felt out of my depth. But the words of our professor on our first day have stayed with me: 'View your donor as your first patient and your silent teacher.'

'And there's no chance I can film you in there? Discreetly, of course. It would make a stunning sequence.'

I shook my head, alarmed by his morbid enthusiasm. It was the second time he'd asked.

'It's all very tightly controlled,' I said. 'Ever since some medics at another uni posed for pictures with a corpse a few years back. They watch us all like hawks now.'

'How about the seat of the soul – found that yet?' he asked with a smirk.

'The soul?'

'The Mesopotamians thought it was in the liver. Descartes, the pineal gland. Then of course Duncan MacDougall attempted to weigh the human soul in 1907.'

'How do you know all this stuff?' I asked. Not for the first time, I was surprised by Louis' general knowledge, his love of random facts.

'Come on, you have to guess the weight of the soul,' he said, ignoring my question.

'I don't know,' I said, irritated now.

'Twenty-one grams. MacDougall put a dying man and his deathbed on an industrial set of scales and measured the body before and after the exact moment he passed.'

I shifted my bike to one side to make way for a group of approaching cyclists, troubled by the image Louis had painted. As they passed us, I recognised some of them as fellow medics.

'Oi, Adam! Can't keep Colin waiting,' one of them called out to me, grinning.

I smiled back awkwardly.

'Who's Colin?' Louis asked.

'Err, the professor who takes our class.'

In fact, Colin's the name we've given to the cadaver that I've been working on. The one next to mine is called Pamela – she's had breast implants, two incongruous summits in a flaccid landscape of decay. So much for the moral high ground.

'Are you alright today?' Louis asked, once the students had gone. 'You seem a little down.'

I felt more than a little down. The suicide at King's has really shaken me, but, more than that, snapshots of that night in Newlyn keep returning.

Like Louis said, the brain is fragile, and mine must still be processing what happened in Cornwall, even though it's more than a year ago now and I'm hundreds of miles away. I thought I'd dealt with it, or with what I could remember after too many pints. I do remember we'd had a good session in the Swordy, me and the gill-netter boys, who I'd not seen since I'd quit the boat and started night school. It was the usual banter and funny stories, but then a group of braying uni rahs walked in and the mood changed. Everyone knows the Swordy's the roughest pub around, and those blokes were totally out of place, slagging off their holiday let in Mousehole – 'shithole, more like' – and the trashy nightclub they were going on to in Penzance. I could tell there was trouble in the air. They were loud and posturing, completely unaware of how they sounded. And then Tom, good old Tom, never one for subtleties, started to do impressions of them, putting on his posh, Tim-Nice-But-Dim voice. Usually one of us would have told him to pipe down, apologised for his behaviour, maybe explained that he had learning difficulties and tended to misjudge social situations, but this time we left him to it. His impression was spot on – 'What a bloody nice bloke!' – and had us all in stitches.

When I finally left the pub, last one out the door, I saw a crowd gathered up on the North Pier. The rahs were hanging Tom over the harbour wall by his arms and legs, threatening to drop him into the oily water below.

'I can't swim!' Tom was pleading. 'Please let me go. I can't swim!'

I sprinted over to help him, but I only managed to make the situation worse. The splash. The sickening silence.

I wasn't going to tell Louis any of this, though. 'I'm sad about the student who killed himself,' I said, checking that I'd put my dissection manual in the bike's wicker basket.

And it's true, I was. It didn't take long for my suspicions to be proved correct. Aldous was a third-year law student who'd had a row with his girlfriend in the afternoon. I must have witnessed the tail end of it on Mathematical Bridge. She's inconsolable, apparently, but there's talk of other reasons for his sudden decision to end his life. In particular, he was depressed about a recent important job interview. It doesn't add up, but gossip is rife, facts few and far between. And then there was his comment in the bar about Louis, his warning that I should keep away from him and his films. Should I have told someone about that? Confronted Louis?

'Shocking,' he said. 'And the poor woman he landed on. I mean, what are the chances?'

Was there a hint of levity in his voice?

'Someone even filmed it, you know,' I said. 'Posted it on the World Wide Web. One of my college mates showed me last night.'

I studied Louis' pale face for a reaction.

'Filmed it?' He sounded surprised. 'Maybe they were tourists and it happened to be in their shot. You see enough Japanese people with cameras around here, filming the chapel.' He glanced back down King's Parade, towards King's College.

'Who'd put that sort of stuff online, though?' I asked.

'Who'd watch it?' he said, turning to me.

I looked away. Guilty as charged. Ji hadn't forced me to watch the video.

I wanted to ask Louis another question about Aldous – *Why did he tell me to stay away from you and say that you were 'evil'?* – but it was hard to know how to phrase it without causing offence. I also wasn't sure any more if it was relevant. Louis, once again, seemed far from evil. Sickly and hungover, yes, but not exactly the devil incarnate.

'Did you ever come across him?' I asked, unable to let the matter go. 'Aldous?'

'Not that I'm aware of,' Louis said. 'Why?'

'I saw him in the ADC Bar the other night, at the after-show. Wondered if you knew him. Clio thought she'd met him once.'

'Clio? She said that?'

For the first time in our conversation, he seemed troubled. I didn't want to land Clio in it – all she said was that she'd once had a drink with Aldous – so I backed off.

'I'm not sure, maybe I'm confusing things.'

'You had a good time with her, though,' Louis said, happy to move on. 'Yesterday.'

It was the first mention of our date. I still didn't know how much of it he'd managed to film. Had he seen us kissing? Would it even bother me if he had?

'We punted to Grantchester and back,' I said.

'You did?' he asked with pantomime surprise.

'Clio will be mad if you filmed us.' I glanced around, just in case she happened to be nearby. Unlikely, given she said she rarely gets up before midday.

'Mad as hell.' Louis grinned.

He'd definitely filmed us. My mind raced as I tried to imagine where he might have hidden. In another punt? Somewhere on the footpath?

'For the record, it's not Clio's life I'm filming,' he continued. 'It's yours. And you'll have to wait until the final edit. All I'll say is that Grantchester looked fabulous in the spring sunshine.'

I pushed off on my bicycle, shaking my head in mock disbelief.

'Don't forget tonight,' he called out after me. I lifted my hand in a wave. The party. 'Clio's looking forward to seeing you.'

23

'I'm here.'

Tania's voice is quiet. She hasn't hung up on Adam after all. They're still talking, which is something. He'd rather be in Wiltshire with her, but at least channels of communication are open.

'This must have been some sort of twisted act of revenge,' Adam says, pacing around the kitchen. 'It's all I can think of.'

'For denying her your toned body?' she asks.

It's a cruel shot. They both know he's put on weight recently, particularly around the waist. A soft girdle of subcutaneous fat. 'She wouldn't have texted you the photo if she'd got what she wanted.'

'Are you sure it was her who sent it?' she says.

He can't be certain of anything right now. Tonight his worst nightmare has been realised. Ever since the events of Louis' party at university, he's dreaded the thought of being secretly filmed. It's stalked him like an invisible shadow, drawing closer to him in recent months, and now it's actually happened. But not in the way he feared. He wasn't expecting it to coincide with Clio's reappearance in his life after all this time. Or with her apparent attempt to destroy his marriage.

Her behaviour tonight has completely wrong-footed him, made him even more paranoid. If she's done this, what else might she be capable of? He thinks back over what happened today, considering everything in a new light: Freddie's sudden disappearance, how she had appeared out of nowhere in the park with him in her arms, what Freddie had said about a puppy. *Will she have one next time?* A thought hits him like a jackhammer. Christ, what if the whole thing was a dry run? A chance for Clio to build trust with Freddie?

'Where are you?' he asks Tania, his blood running cold. 'In the main house?'

'In my old bedroom. I didn't want my parents to see me crying over a photo of my husband with a half-naked woman who's not his wife.'

He knows she wants to punish him, but he's more concerned about the whereabouts of their son. A terrible train of thought is gaining momentum. 'Can you check on Freddie?'

'So you can rev him up like you usually do at this time of night?'

He does a quick calculation in his head. It takes almost two and a half hours to get from Greenwich to her parents' house in Wiltshire. Clio left three hours ago.

'Tania, please, I just need you to make sure he's… he's safe.'

'Of course he's safe. We're in Wiltshire not Willesden. Why wouldn't he be?'

'I know you're angry. And you've every right to be.'

'I'm glad we agree on that. I think most women would object to being sent a photo of—'

'I don't think Freddie was lying when he said that Clio found him in the sandpit today,' he says, interrupting her.

'It's not going to work,' she says. 'Trying to distract me.

Reminding me that I fell asleep in the playground. You're the one in the dock here, not me.'

'I'm just asking you to look in on Freddie,' Adam says, forcing himself to remain calm.

'OK, OK, I'll check on our son, who I put to bed barely half an hour ago. It's not as if I've got much else to do.'

Adam listens as Tania walks down the corridor in the old stable block that's attached to the main farmhouse, trying to distract himself by picturing her surrounds. Single-storey, no-expense-spared conversion for family and guests. Tania's dad had a very successful career as a brain surgeon – NHS and private – and it's an extensive, late-Georgian property, set in two acres of land. When he first went to stay there, he was put in a separate bedroom and had to creep down the corridor to spend the night with Tania. And creep back to his room the next morning.

He holds his breath as Tania lifts the phone to her ear. 'Adam, he's gone,' she says, her voice shaking with fear. 'The window's open and Freddie's not here.'

24

'How was your day?' Ji asked. He was lingering in his doorway when I returned to my room in the late afternoon.

'I broke a rib,' I said.

'Ouch.'

'Not mine, fortunately. In the anatomy class. I think it hurt me more than it hurt Colin.'

Ji knows all about Colin. I wish I'd never mentioned my cadaver to him as it's stoked an unhealthy interest.

'If only I could come along to one of those,' he said. 'So cool!' What is it about anatomy classes that arouses such curiosity? 'There's some great footage on Rotten. Have you seen the one where the medical student recognises the cadaver as his missing best—'

'I'm not in the mood, Ji,' I said. 'Sorry. I'm tired. How was your day?'

'I found something spicy on rotten.com.'

I raised my eyebrows. Spicy usually meant grotesque.

'No blood. Much more fun. Sony has just released a new camcorder with a "nightshot" infrared feature.'

'And...?'

'It was meant to be for looking at critters at night. But

guess what? It allows you to see through clothes! X-ray vision! They've tried to recall the product – 700,000 have been sold – but it's too late. A Japanese men's magazine has just exposed the mistake. The nightshot function works best with dark clothes in bright lighting. Twelve websites have already posted footage of women in swimming costumes.'

'Including rotten.com,' I said. 'You need to get out more, Ji.'

'OK, no problem,' he said briskly as I walked into my room and closed the door behind me.

I'm very fond of Ji, his loyalty, eccentric mannerisms, mischievous sense of humour and excellent taste in malt whisky, but I sometimes wonder if I'm his only proper friend here. He's at his computer when I leave every morning, and at it still when I return in the evening, but his door is always open, as if he's hoping that someone might drop by, which makes me feel permanently guilty.

It had been a full day of lectures and seminars, but I was looking forward to Louis' party later nonetheless. I wanted to see Clio, and if I'm being really honest, I wanted to experience a slice of that glamorous student life that I keep glimpsing but am never invited to join.

Someone had left a card for me at the Medical School reception. I sat down on my bed and pulled it out of my pocket. It was from Clio.

I meant what I said yesterday. Please don't come to Louis' party tonight, whatever he might have told you about it. I came to your room this morning to talk to you in person, but you'd already left. Yesterday was fun – let's not spoil the memory. xx

What did she mean by not spoiling the memory? And why was she so keen for me not to attend the party? Throughout the anatomy class, I'd kept looking around, just in case Louis had managed to inveigle himself into the lab and film the cadavers. I'd come to realise he wasn't exactly trustworthy, but I still wanted to go to his party. I lay back on my bed, hands behind my head. My plan was to have a quick nap before heading over to Louis' house.

A knock on the door. I could tell at once who it was.

'Yes, Ji?'

'You're not going to believe what else I've just found on rotten.com.'

'I'm not interested in X-ray vision, Ji.'

'It's not that.'

'And I don't want to see another cock-chop video.' He tried to show me one the other night, but I refused, much to his surprise.

'It's not cock chop either. I think it's another video of that kid who jumped. You know, the redhead.'

I sat up on my bed. I didn't want to see more footage of him falling, but I was intrigued by what Ji might have found.

'What's it show?' I asked nervously.

'It's weird, man. Kind of a sex thing. Drugs too. Lots of Bolivian marching powder.'

I'm not sure how old his English tutor is in Shenzhen, but Ji's slang is always very retro, steeped in the world of 1970s movies. A minute later, I was leaning over his shoulder as he played me the video, barely able to believe my eyes. The footage was, as Ji suspected, of Aldous, shot in a dimly lit room with another man. I didn't want to ask how he'd come across it. Both were naked as they snorted coke and started to have sex.

'Jesus, that's a bit explicit,' I said, turning away. All I could think of was the argument I'd witnessed on Mathematical Bridge between Aldous and the female student. And then I remembered the rumours about a job interview. This wasn't exactly a show reel to present his finest legal skills.

'A pinky – that's class,' Ji said.

I hoped that 'pinky' was more retro slang and referred to the rolled-up £50 note that both men had used to snort the coke. Ji played it over again. It was obvious that neither man knew they were being filmed, but it wasn't clear where or how the footage had been shot.

Was this why Aldous had called Louis evil? Because he had secretly filmed him having sex and taking drugs? I tried to think rationally, like a lawyer. There was no proof of Louis' involvement. It was pure conjecture on my part. Both videos – the King's College death and this one – had appeared on the same website, but then again, the website was dedicated to hosting shocking videos. It didn't prove a causal connection in the real world.

'And this has only just appeared on the site?' I asked.

'Couple of minutes ago. I keep an eye on the site so I don't miss anything. Sometimes the best videos get pulled down very quickly.'

'What a shame.'

'Do you want to play a videogame tonight?' Ji asked, still looking at his computer. 'Mortal Kombat 4? It's got great 3D computer graphics. We could get a pizza, maybe—'

'Sorry, Ji, I'm going out tonight. Maybe another evening.'

'OK, no problem.'

His tone was cheerful, but I knew he was disappointed, which made me feel more guilty than usual. Maybe I could have played for a bit before heading out to Louis' party, but I'm not really into computer games. Last week he tried to get me to play *Mario Party* on his Nintendo 64. I'd been at lectures all morning and cutting up dead bodies all afternoon. I was so tired that I fell asleep.

I couldn't stop thinking of the covert footage as I dressed to go out, a process that took longer than usual. Mostly I just chuck on anything I can find, but I wanted to fit in at the party. Casual but stylish, black rather than bright colours. It was the uber-cool arts set, after all. I thought again of the footage as I reverted to my trusty T-shirt and jeans. Would Louis really film something like that? Two people on a punting trip to Grantchester was one thing; a cocaine-fuelled sex session quite another.

'"Dance like somebody's watching,"' Ji said from his doorway as I headed off.

'"Nobody", Ji – it's "dance like nobody's watching".'

But I wondered if Ji's version might be right.

25

'Keep talking to me,' Adam says on his mobile. 'He can't have gone far.'

'He's probably just popped to the loo,' Tania says, reverting to her usual calmness. Adam would be running hysterically through the house by now, calling out Freddie's name.

'Double-check with your parents and then start looking outside,' Adam says, picturing the layout of the property. He can see it all so clearly. The stable block is on one side of the main courtyard, opposite the garages. The windows of the stable block at the back open onto an orchard, bordered by a thick beech hedge. Freddie can't have gone far if he climbed out of the window. It's at ground level, but he's never done anything like that before. Adam has – once. He closes his eyes at the memory. Stupid. So *stupid*. He was reading a story to Freddie at the time. It was about a monster who was scared of children and had climbed out of the window to get away from a little boy. Adam had decided to demonstrate how the monster had done it...

'Where are you?' Adam asks. 'He might have climbed out of the window.' The other option is too awful to contemplate, that Freddie might have been taken by Clio, to see another puppy... 'It's my fault if he's climbed out.' It's his fault too if Clio's taken him. 'I'm sorry, I once—'

'He's here,' Tania says, matter-of-factly, but he suspects she's more relieved than she sounds. 'It's OK, he's safe. He's here.'

'Where?'

'With Dad, in his garage. You've got to stop scaring me like that, Adam. Jesus. Stop being so bloody paranoid all the time. I'll call you back.'

Adam can hear Crispin, Tania's dad, apologising in the background. 'I know it's late, but he couldn't sleep and he loves his Scalextric car,' he is saying.

Tania hangs up before Adam can hear or say any more. He leans against the kitchen island, head bowed, and lets out a sigh of relief too. Thank God Freddie's safe. He probably wandered over to the garages to see Crispin, who couldn't resist an opportunity to show him a new piece of track. The Scalextric set is already huge, but he's always adding to it: a chicane here, pit lane there. Crispin's like that, as all grandfathers should be. Mischievous, untroubled by routine and children's bedtimes. It's just such a shame that he doesn't like Adam. Never has.

Adam wants to take a train down to Wiltshire tonight, to be with them all, but Tania wasn't exactly encouraging. Understandable, given the photo she was sent of him with Clio, but he needs to reassure her in person. It's proved impossible to argue his case in texts and over the phone. He's about to look up train times when something catches his eye on the dresser, where Clio had moved her mobile to charge it. He walks over and picks up a card, propped against a mug. It looks like it could be one of Freddie's, something to help young children learn the alphabet. One side is dark crimson. On the other, written in big black text on a white background, a single capital letter: 'S'. But Freddie's a quick learner and mastered the alphabet a while back.

He pours himself a Talisker whisky and sits down at the table with the card, trying to work out what's happened today, weigh up every possible explanation, eliminate the most unlikely. It's conceivable that the photo could have been sent by a neighbour. Clio had come back into his life seeking an affair, was politely declined, and left, presumably for France to look after her mother. Should he go round and confront Lynda next door? She's surprisingly handy with modern technology. But would she really send a photo to Tania?

He takes a long sip of his whisky, clenching the glass until he can see the whites of his knuckles. Clio knew exactly what she was doing tonight. He walks upstairs, taking the card with him, and retrieves the video player from under their bed. This time he will force himself to watch the whole film. Glass of whisky in hand, he presses play and sits back.

There he is, having lunch with Clio at the restaurant, drinking champagne. Louis had managed to film for quite a while before he was spotted outside. The film cuts away to Grantchester Meadows, panning across the bucolic setting. And then the lens focuses on a distant punt, emerging from the dripping willows into a pool of sunshine. It's him and Clio. Adam shifts in his seat. He'd forgotten how in love he'd felt that day. As if on cue, he is kissing Clio on the riverbank. It's a tasteful, long-range shot, but how the hell did Louis manage it? For a brief moment Clio looks up, staring directly at the camera like she did tonight. Adam freezes the shot.

Had she seen Louis? Was it anger in her eyes? Defiance? Or something else?

He presses play again. Now he's cycling down King's Parade, seemingly without a care in the world. Where was he off to that day? At this point the video is still what it was meant to be: innocent highlights of his life, a typical day in the life of a first-year medical student, give or take a bit of artistic licence. The next shot hints at the darker tone to come. Adam still remembers his surprise when he spotted Louis standing opposite him at the stainless steel dissection table in the Anatomy School, camera lens poking out from under the white coat he'd just picked up. He was only there for a few seconds, before the roll call, but long enough to film the cadaver's exposed heart and lungs. It's been more than twenty years, but Adam would recognise that body anywhere.

'Colin' played an important part in his student experience – the dissection classes were a rite of passage for all first-year medics – but his corpse should never have been filmed. It could have got Adam thrown out of university. But that's nothing compared to the film's finale, what happened that night at Louis' party. Why did he insist on going? Was it just for the glamour? Or was he hoping that some of that effortless Cambridge confidence might wear off on him, the shy boy from Newlyn? Clio had warned him enough times. But still he went.

26

I stopped off at the college bar for a quick pint before heading over to Mortimer Road, where Louis lives. Tim, who's set on becoming a neuroscientist, invited me over to join a group of medics, and the company was good, the banter lively. Medics tend to stick together and my year is a particularly tight bunch, but as the only first-gen, I still don't feel a proper part of the pack. It's more my fault than theirs. They always make me feel welcome, but I find the alpha-male competition difficult to handle at times, particularly Tim's manner. He's full of self-confidence, sure of his own abilities.

They're so different from Clemo, Jori and Morgan back home – typical quiet, artistic Newlyn types, much more my sort of friends. The photographer, the musician and the painter. Sometimes I wish my Cornish mates would shout about themselves a bit more, they're all so damn talented. Smoking less dope might help too. I like how they're just as at home in their own company as in a group. Same with the gill-netter crew; we might have been a team on the boat, but you're also on your own when you're on watch in the wheelhouse at 3 a.m., 150 miles off Land's End. Not that any of that crazy bunch could be described as quiet or artistic.

I miss that, having two very different sets of friends – my attempt, perhaps, to straddle Dad's two worlds of painting and fishing.

'What's this film of your life then, Dosh?' Tim asked.

Tim calls me Dosh because of my surname. Adam Pound sounds fine to me, but Dosh has stuck since freshers' week. Ironic, given how little money I seem to have compared to everyone else.

'Not my idea,' I said, happy to be surrounded by familiar, friendly faces. In a few minutes, I would be at a party where I knew only two people: Louis and Clio. And they were still not talking to each other.

'Sounds like one for the Papworth Sleep Clinic,' Tim said.

'It's going to be action packed, I tell you,' I said. '"He opens his dissection manual, starts to read, falls into a stupor."' I dropped my head to the table.

'It'll be great...' Tim was on his own thing now, tracing a film banner in the air with a finger. 'The name's Pound. Adam Pound. Licensed to kill.'

'Isn't every medical student?' Anil quipped. He's of the few other students in our college who, like me, wants to become an actual doctor who interacts with patients rather than go into academic research.

'I can see it now,' Tim said. 'X-rated, I hope.'

'Talking of which, who was that beautiful creature you went punting with yesterday?' Anil asked.

I blushed, wondering where Anil might have seen us, and took a long sip of my beer.

'She's called Clio. She was in that play I did.' The play that they'd all said they would come along to see, but no one had, of course. 'And I'm about to go partying with her.'

'Get in there, Dosh,' Anil said, clinking his beer glass against mine.

Ten minutes later, I was hovering outside Louis' house on Mortimer Road. I had no trouble finding the place. The music was thunderous, strobes lighting up the night sky like a sparking furnace. Someone was lurking in the shadows on the street, hoodie up, asking students as they arrived if they wanted any gear: Es, acid, weed. I declined and headed towards a group of partygoers who had spilled out into the small front garden, clutching bottles of Beck's in one hand, cigarettes in the other. For some reason they were all wearing sharp black suits, skinny ties and fedoras. One of them was emptying his guts into a flowerbed.

I took a deep breath and walked inside. The smell of weed hit me first, followed by the unmistakeable stench of human sweat. Everyone was dancing – in the hall, in the front room, the kitchen, the living room, in the courtyard out the back. Swaying more than dancing. The music was pulsating techno. The last time I'd heard music like that was when I was gutting turbot on a gill-netter in the Western Approaches. And it didn't take a medic to spot that everyone was off their heads: glazed, staring eyes, all inhibitions gone. I needed to relax, stop analysing people as potential patients, but something else was wrong. What was everyone wearing?

'Adam!' a voice shouted above the music. A tap on my shoulder. I spun round to see Louis and reeled backwards. He had a camcorder in one hand and a silver-tipped walking cane in the other, but it was his face that shocked me, more specifically his eyes. The irises were glowing bright orange.

'You like them?' he said, opening his eyes wider. 'Relax,

they're contacts. My little homage to De Niro in *Angel Heart*. Alan Parker at his best.'

'Was I meant to dress up?' I said, as a sickening realisation swept through me.

I looked from Louis, who had swapped his usual outfit for an immaculate black suit and tie, to everyone else around me. As I suspected, I was the only one who hadn't got the fancy-dress memo. It's one of my worst fears. Of course, the suits outside had been from *The Blues Brothers*. A lot of *Reservoir Dogs* were in there too, what looked like some droogs from *A Clockwork Orange*, one Sheriff Woody, and an Edward Scissorhands in the corner, blades glinting in the flashing lights. And those were just the ones I could identify.

'It's OK, it's not obligatory,' he said. 'If anyone asks, why don't you say you're Nelson from *Flatliners*.'

'Nelson?' I'd seen the film a few years earlier but couldn't remember much – a bunch of medical students exploring the afterlife.

'Kiefer Sutherland,' Louis added.

'I'll take that as a compliment.'

'I need to get a few shots in the can, then we're done,' he said, stepping back to film me with his camcorder.

'Seriously?' I said, blushing.

My failure to dress up had left me feeling more self-conscious than usual. Vulnerable. I tried to pull a cool smile for Louis. His camcorder looked brand new and I remembered what Ji had told me. Was it the latest model, the one with night vision that could see through clothes?

'You need infrared, it's so dark in here,' I said, trying to see if I could read any of the writing on the camcorder.

'Tell me about it.' Louis panned the camera across a group of female partygoers.

Was he ogling their underwear? It wouldn't have surprised me. And then I saw it: the word 'Nightshot' written on the body of the camera. I was about to challenge him when I spotted Clio, on the far side of the sitting room, wearing a long, dark red wig, vintage black strapless dress and matching full-length gloves. She was dancing wildly with Hannibal Lecter, dressed in a blue boilersuit and leather facial restraint.

'Who's Clio come as?' I asked, nodding in her direction. She had her arms wrapped around Lecter's shoulders.

'Clio?' Louis turned the camera towards her. *The nightshot function works best with dark clothes in bright lighting.* 'Can't you tell by the black satin dress? Rita Hayworth, of course. In *Gilda.* You know an image of her in that outfit was put on the first nuclear bomb to be tested after World War Two?'

I looked again at Clio, the way she was dancing in her Rita Hayworth dress, eyes laser-locked on Lecter's in his freakish leather mask. I didn't recognise him, but there was a grotesque choreography about their dancing that made me want to throw up. She was right. I should never have come. But then, as I watched, unable to take my own eyes off her, he seemed to whisper something in her ear, and she abruptly pulled away from him. He stood there in his mask, gimlet eyes widening in surprise, as if he'd been stabbed.

'Go after her,' a voice said behind me, as Clio walked out into the courtyard. It took me a moment to realise it was Louis. I started to turn around. 'Don't look at the camera,' Louis ordered. 'Just walk across the room and find Clio outside.'

I knew Louis was filming me as I made my way across

the crowded room. It was so embarrassing. The party was brimming with the arts set, tomorrow's stars, and there I was, a total fraud, an imposter. Why not point the camera at someone else? Like the guy in the corner in a *Shawshank Redemption* prison outfit, who had already starred in a BBC drama. Hollywood and the West End now beckoned. I was just a boring first-year medic who had scratched an acting itch.

'Go on,' Louis urged as I headed outside to find Clio, necking a bottle of Beck's as I went.

Would she want to talk to me? Not if Louis was filming over my shoulder. If anything, the music was louder out the back. A stack of speakers had been positioned beside open French windows in the courtyard and the sound was bouncing off the brick walls. I walked past, trying not to worry for my cochleas, and saw Clio by the back fence. She was on her own, smoking a cigarette.

I glanced over my shoulder as I approached, sensing that Louis was no longer with me. Sure enough, he'd disappeared, melted into the night. No doubt he was still filming from somewhere, but I was glad that he wasn't visible.

'Rita?' I said to Clio, with mock politeness. 'Rita Hayworth?'

She stared up at me. Her eyes were vacant, bloodshot, and she wasn't smiling as she looked me up and down.

'And you are…?' she asked with barely concealed contempt.

'Kiefer Sutherland,' I said. 'Apparently. You know – Nelson from *Flatliners*?' This charade wasn't working. 'You never told me it was fancy dress.'

'I told you not to come.' She looked back at the house and inhaled deeply on her cigarette.

'I enjoyed our trip to Grantchester,' I said.

'That was yesterday.'

I hadn't experienced Clio in this sort of mood before. I rode the silence for a few seconds, hoping that things might improve. They didn't.

'Are they comfortable?' I asked, nodding at her long gloves, desperately thinking of something to say. They went all the way up to her shoulders, like stockings.

'Better than asking if I come here often, I suppose.'

Why was she being so off with me?

Someone was approaching us. Lecter, the student she'd been dancing with a few minutes earlier. Clio had clocked him too. Mask off now, he was smoothing down his shiny hair, black as wet tar.

'See you around,' she said to me, walking back towards the house.

'Charming,' Lecter said, watching her go. His accent sounded American. Lecter was English in *The Silence of the Lambs*, except when he was impersonating Clarice Starling, so I guessed it was genuine, that he wasn't in character. His eyes lingered on Clio's arse as he took a sip of red wine. 'The biggest cock-tease in Cambridge,' he added, turning to me.

'Is that what you said to her?' I asked. I could feel my blood pressure rising. 'When you were dancing together?'

I surprised myself, speaking to him like that, but I had nothing to lose. The less time we spent chatting, the better for both of us.

'You were watching us?' He raised an amused eyebrow.

'Not exactly. It was hard to miss.'

He laughed sarcastically. 'Do you really want to know what I told her?'

I didn't have time to say no.

'I told her I wanted to fuck her French brains out. Dresses like a whore, what does she expect?'

I closed my eyes, breathed in deeply through my nostrils, tried to shut out Lecter's leery smile, his foul breath, control the anger rising through my limbs like floodwater, but all I could think of was what had happened that night in Newlyn. Images sped through my head. The red mist was descending, just like it had on the North Pier. It was as if I was right there again, hearing Tom moan as they started to swing him by his arms and legs over the edge. I attempted to reason with Tom's tormentors, explain that he couldn't swim, but they weren't listening, told me to 'get back to Bodmin'. I tried to physically intervene, but one of them stopped me. Tom yelled out again. He was desperate now, begging for his life, and that triggered something in me. I'm not a violent man, but I totally lost it with the posh bloke who was holding me back. I managed to break free, pushed him away with a guttural roar, and he slipped and fell. I didn't care. I needed to save Tom.

But I was too late. *The sound of the splash that the corpse soon made as it struck the sea* – followed by a brief, sickening silence. Did they realise that they'd gone too far? For a second, we all just stood there, shocked in our different ways. And then I noticed that the student I'd pushed was still on the ground. Why hadn't he moved? Got up? Had he hit the back of his head on the cobbles when he slipped? I wanted to help him – I was scared by his stillness, the thought that I might be responsible – but then something bobbed to the surface of the sea. Tom. He was floating, face down in the water. I scrambled down the metal ladder on the quayside, managed to drag him onto a ledge, and he spluttered back into life, vomiting oily water.

One of the uni students peered down over the edge of the pier at me. We didn't say anything, just stared at each other, our eyes full of fear. And then a car pulled up and the group lifted their friend to his feet – he was conscious now, thank God – and helped him into it, before speeding off into the night.

I looked up at Lecter, hearing his dismissal of Clio again. *Dresses like a whore, what does she expect?*

'I suggest you keep away from Clio – and me,' I said, flexing my fingers as I walked back into the party.

I'm not a violent man.

27

I wanted to keep on walking, out through Louis' party and into the night, after my encounter with Lecter. My exchange with Clio was bad enough, but I hung pathetically on to her parting words, hoping that I might see her around. It was Lecter who frightened me, the primal anger his words had stirred, feelings that I thought were long dead and buried. I'd moved on, turned my life around and never wanted to go back there. Tonight, in Louis' garden, was the first time since those Newlyn days that I'd felt such emotions and they scared me.

I gave up trying to chat with Clio – whenever I caught her eye she looked away – and forced myself to be sociable, fuelled by too much Beck's. Louis introduced me to some of his less weird friends upstairs on the landing. He seemed to have stopped filming me, which was a relief, but he kept producing white hard-boiled eggs, peeling and eating them, scattering their shells like litter. 'Symbols of the soul,' he said, slipping another smooth egg into his mouth. 'Watch the film.' He also told me to help myself from a drawer in the second-floor bathroom to whatever drugs took my fancy before they ran out – 'just ask me for the key' – but I stuck to the beer.

'Come with me,' he said later, an arm around my shoulders.

It must have been after midnight. I knew where we were going and this time I was too drunk to resist. Once I start on the beer, I can't seem to stop. A legacy of my nights in the Swordy. 'Adam'd drink the piss of a smuggler's donkey,' as one of my fishing mates used to say. Now, somewhere in the back of my head, a voice shouted at me to walk away, but I ignored it. The film of Aldous on rotten.com had nothing to do with Louis. I didn't care about it any more. Far more important was the chance to parade through one of Louis' famed parties with the host. It was a signal to his friends that I was now one of them, a member of his inner circle. That I had arrived. Made my mark on the Cambridge arts scene. Played Doctor Faustus and here I was, guest of honour. A first-gen medical student from Cornwall. I could see a thread running from my dad's abstract paintings through to my late-night reading of Hemingway in my attic room to being a star of this arts party. It all seemed to make sense in my drunken mind. It was meant to be. And my transformation would lead me into the arms of Clio.

People stepped aside as we went up to the second-floor bathroom. Louis locked the door behind us. Pulling out another key, he slid open a wide drawer beneath the sideboard and talked me through the smorgasbord of posh highs on offer: hard-stamped gold-bar Ecstasy pills, Mexican mushrooms, Californian medical weed, Valium and individual pouches of the finest Colombian cocaine. A world away from what we used to get wasted on in Newlyn, where it was mostly weed, and salty weed at that – 'sea hash' that had been thrown overboard by smugglers and was then caught in trawlers' nets. But I wasn't about to start dabbling in hard drugs at Louis' invitation. I've seen too many stressed-out fishermen get hooked on heroin, blowing their minds and hard-earned cash on a quick fix before heading out to sea again. If it wasn't heroin, it was ketamine.

'It's OK,' I said, swallowing. 'I'm fine, really.' An image of a naked Aldous came and went. Some of my fellow medics are into cocaine, having studied its effect on the brain and convinced themselves that, by understanding the underlying chemical processes, they're in some way immune to its dangers. Immortal.

'Shall I leave you to it?' Louis asked. 'Give you some time on your own?'

'It's OK, honestly,' I repeated, but he could see me staring at the drugs.

'Clio's in a mood, isn't she?' he said, sounding almost impressed by the strength of her sulkiness.

'Tell me about it,' I replied. I didn't find it easy talking to Louis about Clio at the best of times, let alone when I was drunk.

'It's usually me who sulks,' he says.

'So you said. Or Gabe.' I was curious about his brother's depression, especially since attending a psychology lecture last week. At present, there are still no biological markers for major depressive disorder.

Louis gave me a strange look, as if I'd been too familiar. 'Actually, I hoped Gabe would come tonight, that you might meet him. He used to love a good party.'

'He's not here?'

He shook his head. 'Not so well.'

I couldn't reveal that I knew it was depression, didn't want to land Clio in trouble for breaching any confidences. 'I'm sorry.'

'Me too,' Louis said.

I stayed silent, gave him the chance to elaborate, but he chose not to.

'Clio's upset because I haven't given her this,' he continued, waving the key in the air like a prize.

'OK,' I said, confused, wondering where our conversation was going.

'She loves her Es. Take it from me, anything can happen when she drops one. But she won't risk them off the street. Had a bad trip once, dodgy pill. Mine are all tested.'

His lips curled into a smile, but I still couldn't stop looking at his orange eyes. And then I watched, transfixed, as he reached for one of the bags of coke, cut two lines with a credit card on the side of the sink, and pulled out a £50 note. A pinky. Was it the same one that Aldous had used? It seemed so unlikely. I glanced around. No cameras in sight. Louis leant forward, snorted one of the lines, and passed the note to me.

For a moment, the nerdy medical student in me was tempted, intrigued by the way cocaine binds to the dopamine transporter and blocks the removal of dopamine from the synapse, causing a build-up that triggers euphoria. Or was I deluding myself and just wanted to be a part of Louis' world?

'I'm OK,' I said. 'Thanks all the same.'

'I'll tell you what I'll do,' he said, sliding the second line of coke back into the bag. 'I'll leave these up here.' He took the jar of Es out of the drawer and placed it on top of the mirrored Indian cupboard above the sink, out of sight. 'Just in case you change your mind.'

I watched him lock the drawer and followed him out of the bathroom onto the landing, where he introduced me to a blonde woman in a flimsy dress made entirely from red rose petals – Angela Hayes, *American Beauty*. Angela was kind enough to say some nice things about my performance as Doctor Faustus. So kind, in fact, that I was beginning to forget about Clio, when someone screamed from down below. A piercing cry that could be heard above the pounding techno. I knew at once that it was Clio. I spun round, so fast that I felt dizzy. God I was pissed.

I peered over the banister of the open landing. Lecter had his hands held up in mock protest as Clio berated him on the floor below. I couldn't hear what she was saying, but I could guess. He'd been whispering sweet offensive nothings into her ear again. And he was swaying like a stick in a storm, barely able to stand on his feet. I glanced over at Louis, who raised his eyebrows at me but didn't move. As far as I could tell, he and Clio had managed to avoid each other for the whole night. And then he produced his camcorder and started to film.

I don't know whether it was the alcohol in my veins or a misguided belief that I was being filmed and was therefore an invincible movie star. Either way, I rushed down one flight of stairs and found myself in Lecter's masked face before either of us knew it, pumped up by a trigger-wash of adrenaline.

'Is he bothering you again?' I asked Clio, short of breath.

'My doctor in shining armour,' she said, hiccupping. 'Or should that be a white coat?' Jesus, she was even more out of it now, completely gone.

'Not you again,' Lecter said, barely able to stand himself. His eyes flitted from side to side.

'What are we going to do with you?' I asked, already weighing up my options. Lecter was light-framed and short, frail as a jockey.

'What are we going to do with *you*?' he replied, jabbing his finger at me. 'Eat your liver with some fava beans and a nice Chianti?'

He raised his glass and poured the last of his red wine through the hole in his mask, dribbling some down his chin.

'Shut him in the bathroom if he's being a pain,' someone said behind me. 'The key's in the door.'

I turned to see Louis walk past. He had stopped filming and was on his way down to the ground floor. I spun back, just as Lecter lunged at Clio, trying to lick her through his mask.

'Get this creep off me, Adam!' Clio shrieked, pushing him away.

Instinctively, I grabbed Lecter from behind and locked my arm around his neck. If it wasn't for the alcohol, it would have been a simple task to haul him up one flight of stairs to the bathroom, as I was so much taller than him. As it was, he kicked at the steps with his heels like a demented Cossack dancer, catching me in the mouth with a flailing arm as I dragged him up to the second floor. People cheered and made way for me as I pulled him through the bathroom doorway.

'Grab me some mandy,' Clio called out from below.

I shoved Lecter up against the bathroom wall. With my other hand, I managed to close the door and lock it. My lip was bleeding and I wiped away the blood on the back of my sleeve.

'Listen very carefully,' I said, my eyes close to his. 'Stay away from Clio, do you hear? Stay away.'

He looked back at me – I noticed his pupils were dilated – and then he spat in my face through his mask. I was back in Newlyn again, brawling on the North Pier. I needed to control myself.

'Haven't you shagged her yet?' he asked, his voice slurred. 'Is that your problem? Must be the only bloke in Cambridge who hasn't.'

He'd crossed a line. I swivelled him around, away from the wall, and manhandled him across the bathroom as if he were a prisoner. I didn't know what my endgame was, but I had a vision of him collapsing into the bath in the corner. And then I pictured the student in Newlyn as he fell backwards, the shock on his face. I stopped.

Lecter turned to look at me and started to collapse. I caught him just before his head smacked onto the floor, propped him up against the wall and took off his mask. He was unconscious but breathing. Had I hit him? Caused him to pass out? Already my own actions were a blur. Time had lost all shape. He was drunk, nothing more. So was I.

I sat down next to him and decided it was the right moment to go home, pleased that I'd checked myself, prevented Lecter from injuring himself. A fresh breeze blew in from the big open sash window, maybe from the south-west, it was hard to tell, filling the gauze curtain like a spinnaker. It was a welcome reminder of a normal world outside that weird party bubble. And then I remembered what Clio had asked me to do. Struggling to my feet, I walked over to the basin and found the jam jar on top of the Indian cupboard. Two pills glistened inside like beady jewels. I looked at the door again and poured them both into my hand.

'Chuck one over,' Lecter said.

His voice made me jump. He was sitting more upright now. I was surprised that he was even conscious.

'You're OK,' he mumbled in his American drawl.

I'd seen this before, someone pinballing between lucidity and unconsciousness, decency and depravity. The cocktail effect: mixing drugs that speed you up with ones that slow you down, ones that turned you into a prize knob with ones that chilled you out. I felt my hand move, ready to lob one of the yellow pills over to him. I stopped myself – what was I thinking? – and slipped them both into my jacket pocket, replacing the empty jar on top of the cupboard.

'All women want it, you know,' Lecter said, his voice still slurred. 'Whatever they say.'

I looked across at him with derision, decided not to deign his words with a response.

'At least Clio makes it easy, she never says no,' he continued, his shoulders rising and falling as he laughed to himself, still slumped against the wall like a park drunk. 'Legs always open for business. She really hasn't let you shag her? Man, that's incredible. Unreal. You don't have to ask, you know. Not with her. Maybe that's where you're going wrong. Too polite. You just have to—'

I couldn't listen to any more. I walked over and lifted Lecter to his feet by the lapels of his boilersuit. The curtain billowed again on the far side of the room.

'Shut up, OK? Just shut the fuck up.' I realised I was shouting. 'And if I ever see you hassling Clio again, I'll break your neck,' I said, quieter now, my face close to his. 'You understand?'

For the first time that night, he seemed to believe me, his eyes creasing with fear as he nodded. I shoved him, harder this time.

'You're a disgrace,' I said as he stumbled backwards across

the bathroom. 'Stay away from Clio if you value your life.' I found myself pushing at his chest with the palms of both hands. 'Understand?' Each time he faltered and almost fell over, I stopped and we looked at each other. But it wasn't Lecter swaying unsteadily in front of me. It was the man in Cornwall again, trying to stop me from reaching Tom. I froze. Lecter stared back at me, eyes wide with raw terror, as the student in Newlyn fell backwards, his skull smashing against the cobbles. Another draught blew in through the open window behind him and I turned away, locking the door behind me.

28

May 1998

I knew something was wrong before I reached the ground floor. It wasn't one scream this time but a chorus, coming from outside. A chilling cacophony of fear. People started to flood into the house, pushing and shoving to get away from something – someone – in the courtyard.

'What is it?' I asked as Louis strode past me from upstairs, moving against the flow of people.

'I don't know,' he said, his voice full of concern. Louis was usually so unflappable. 'But I think you might be needed.'

For my medical skills? Was that what he meant? My head was too muddled by alcohol.

'A guy just jumped out the window,' I heard someone say as we edged our way through the crowd to the courtyard.

The bathroom curtain billowed in my mind.

'Oh my God, oh my God, oh my God,' another woman said, sobbing.

I knew who it was before we were outside. Lecter. And my drunken brain was already shaping the narrative. He had jumped out of the second-floor bathroom because the door had been locked. By me. And the open window had been the only way out – if you were veering from manic lows to euphoric highs. I should have closed the window before I left him.

We found his broken body behind the stack of speakers, an unstrung puppet in a pool of crimson. He must have hit the edge of the top speaker before landing on the brick courtyard, but it wasn't enough to soften his fall. I knew at once that he was dead – his head was at too awkward an angle, neck broken – but I still felt for a pulse, told Louis not to move him in case he was alive.

'Has someone called an ambulance?' I asked.

'Is there any point?' Louis replied, his voice cold and rational as he looked down at the body.

We held each other's gaze for a second. Maybe it was time for him to remove those ridiculous orange contact lenses. Out of respect as much as anything.

'The police, then,' I said. 'Is there a phone in the house?'

'In the kitchen,' he said. 'I'll go.' But before he turned to leave, he grabbed my shoulder and squeezed it, looking at me with his hideous orange eyes. 'We don't mention my drugs drawer to the police, OK?'

'OK,' I said, remembering that I had two Ecstasy pills in my jacket pocket.

'I don't know where he got his from' – he nodded at Lecter's body – 'but it wasn't from me. OK?'

I watched Louis close the French doors behind him, leaving me on my own in the courtyard with Lecter. I knelt down again behind the speaker and double-checked for a pulse, half expecting him to sit up. He had bounced back in the bathroom from unconsciousness, but not this time. I glanced up at the open window, thirty feet above, and looked down at Lecter's body again. *And if I ever see you hassling Clio again, I'll break your neck.* Primary flaccidity had already set in: jaw open, pupils dilated. Pallor mortis would soon begin as blood drained away from the skin's smaller veins. And his body temperature would drop at a rate of 1.5 degrees per hour – algor mortis – until it reached ambient temperature.

Louis would have called the police by now. I felt for the two Ecstasy pills in the inside pocket of my jacket and retrieved one of them. Where was the other? I searched the pocket again. Empty. I had definitely taken two from the jar. A new narrative was already taking root in my fertile mind, sprouting like tendrils. What if I had given him a pill? And he'd jumped as a result? Relax. I needed to stop being so paranoid. Looking around, I was about to hurl the single pill over the back wall of Louis' courtyard when I hesitated. What if a child found it? I shoved it into a flowerpot, burying it deep into the dry soil with my forefinger.

I don't know how long I was with Lecter – long enough to offer up a small prayer – but it felt like an age before the paramedic arrived, followed by two police officers. I stepped aside as the paramedic knelt down beside him, checking for the vital signs of life. There was nothing I could do to save Lecter, but the desire to try still burnt strong.

'No pulse,' I said. 'Pupils are starting to dilate.'

The paramedic glanced up at me. I was only in my first year. What did I know? I turned away, looked back into the house and gasped. Clio was on the other side of the glass, staring back at me like an apparition, her face a ghostly white. We locked eyes and then she was gone.

She was right. Bad things happened at Louis' parties.

29

It was very late by the time I finally got back here, to college. I had to give a statement to the police at the house, along with Louis and a few other guests. The police said they would need to contact me again and, with a heavy heart, I provided them with my college details. It's not the first case of a student jumping out of a window at a party – someone broke their arm just a few weeks earlier in similar circumstances – but it's almost unheard of for someone to die. At least in Cambridge.

Our director of studies' words haunted me the whole walk home, his exhortation to us as medical students to behave. The death wasn't my fault, but I was the last person to see Lecter alive. People don't die at normal student parties. I shouldn't have been there in the first place. The police officer told me that once they've completed their investigation, there'll be a coroner's inquest, to which I'll undoubtedly be called and required to give a witness statement.

Everyone was asleep on my corridor – apart from Ji. I was pleased to see the reassuring spill of light from his half-open door as I came down the passage. It reminded me of the low glow under Mum's crooked bedroom door when I returned home late at night.

'*Falcon 4.0*'s great,' Ji said, coming out of his room as he heard me enter mine. 'North Korea invades South Korea. You wanna play?'

'It's 3.30 a.m., Ji,' I said. I didn't add that I'd just spent the evening with the police because someone died at a party. After I'd locked him into a bathroom and he'd leapt out of the open window.

'Eleven thirty a.m. in Shenzhen,' Ji said. 'Time is relative. Are you OK? You look—'

I sat down on the end of his bed and decided to tell him the whole story from beginning to end, from Clio's warning not to attend to the moment I saw Lecter lying dead behind the stack of speakers. I didn't tell him about the drugs in the bathroom drawer, just as I hadn't told the police.

'Your lady friend stopped by earlier,' Ji said quietly. I could tell he was processing what I'd just told him. He was like that, considered things carefully before he offered measured advice. 'She was standing outside the window,' he added.

'Clio?' I hadn't seen her since the paramedic had arrived. Had the police interviewed her too?

'She passed this through the window,' he continued, handing me an envelope with my name on it. Clio's handwriting.

'How long ago was this?'

'Maybe an hour? Two hours ago?'

'I'm going to get some sleep,' I said, waving the card in his direction as I walked back to my room. 'Thanks, Ji.'

'No problem,' he called out after me. 'I'm here if you wanna talk – or play *Mario Party*.'

Clio's handwriting was as slurred as her speech had been at Louis', but it was just possible to read:

Thank you for protecting me tonight. Whatever happens in the coming months, I will always be grateful, as I have just told the police. Don't blame yourself for his awful death. It wasn't your fault.

I still wish you had heeded my advice and not come to the party, not had to protect me – you can't say I didn't try to deter you. Bad things happen around Louis, worse than you can imagine.

Tonight has changed everything. We weren't speaking at the party, as you probably saw, and after this evening I have no desire to see him again. Ever. He has gone too far this time.

Why am I telling you this? Because I don't want to mislead you. We should not see each other again. Not because I don't like you, but because I like you too much. If that sounds unfair or confusing, I'm sorry. I'm just trying to protect you. One day I might be able to explain, when I am strong enough to choose between Faustus's Good Angel and Bad Angel. To read 'the scriptures' or 'that damned book'.

I must focus on my finals now.
Take care,
Clio xx

30

Adam leans forward and pauses the video player. He had planned to watch the whole film through to the end, fuelled by whisky, but once again he can't bring himself to view the sickening coda, the last thirty seconds. He's watched himself at the party, defending Clio from Lecter in his diabolical mask, mixing with the arts set – why was he so desperate to be a part of that crowd? – but he's not ready to see the ending. Not ready to tell Tania what happened next.

He glances at his watch. Two a.m. He should get some sleep. Although it's a Sunday, he wants to go down to Wiltshire early, hopes that Tania will be willing to see him. He walks back into the kitchen and picks up the card again from the dresser, turning it in his hands like a croupier. Might Clio have left it? But why the letter 'S'? What is its significance? S for son? She found Freddie in the park. S for sex? Not exactly subtle. She always liked to be cryptic, but this is odd, even for her.

He will ask Tania later, check whether it's Freddie's. Again, he wonders if he's got this all wrong; if there's a simple interpretation for what happened today, one that exonerates

Clio from everything apart from a misguided desire to look up an old flame from uni.

He walks over to the kitchen window and stares out into the night. The heavy rain has almost stopped, but it's still drizzling, tiny beads of water dancing in the orange glow of the streetlight above where the public footpath meets the road. What if someone did stand out there tonight in the rain and film him and Clio? He turns away, tries to dismiss the thought, but he can't ignore the feeling in his stomach. It's as if someone has got hold of his small intestine and is measuring it. Skipping with it.

Ten minutes later he's about to go to bed when his phone pings with a text. Tania. No message, just the photo. It takes a second to download and then he's looking at Clio in her underwear, standing next to him in the kitchen. He's holding up her dress and it's not a good look. No wonder Tania assumed the worst. But he's not so interested in the two figures, or the time and date stamp in the corner (19.31 – well past *cinq à sept*), included like court evidence to prove time and place. He's trying to work out where the photo was taken from.

His first thought is that Tania was right and it's a still image taken from a video shot on Clio's phone when it was on the dresser. There's a slight blur to it. But filming through window glass might also distort the image. There's no obvious sign of rain, but the window could have been wiped. Ditto the camera lens.

And then he spots a small, single droplet of rain in the top right-hand corner of the image. A chill of fear ripples through him. The photo was definitely taken from outside.

He goes back downstairs in his boxer shorts and T-shirt,

opens the back door and steps out onto the wet lawn in a pair of slip-on garden shoes. No obvious footprints by the kitchen window, but it's rained continuously since Clio was here. He heads over to where the footpath runs down the side of the garden. A part of the fence that he's been meaning to repair is low enough for an adult (but not Freddie) to climb over. He grabs the post and levers himself up and through the gap to the footpath, jumping down with a squelch into the mud. He looks up the deserted path, checks that Lynda isn't at her window, twitching a curtain. It's too late, even for her. And then something catches his eye by his feet. A fragment, white and fragile. Is it a sliver of plastic? A cigarette butt? It's something more organic. He bends down and picks it up. Eggshell. An image of Louis peeling eggs at his party comes and goes; the way he slipped them into his mouth.

Adam retreats to bed, but sleep eludes him almost until dawn. At 4 a.m. his body is finally at rest, but his brain is busy with housekeeping duties, cleansing itself of toxic waste, storing new information as it enters non-REM sleep. His heart rate and breathing begin to regulate as his temperature drops and he falls into a deep slumber. But it's not for long. Soon his eyes are moving rapidly beneath his eyelids and his body enters a state of temporary paralysis as he starts to dream.

Louis is at the back of the garden, eyes glowing orange in the dark, filming with his old camcorder as the rain pours down. All around him the ground is littered with eggshell. Louis is not alone though. A packed audience sits in rows of plastic chairs on the lawn, bright theatre lights shining in through the window, bathing the kitchen in a warm glow. And everyone is watching him make love to Clio on the kitchen table. They are both naked and his elbows are sore from supporting the weight of his body, but Adam doesn't care. Clio is desperate for him, clawing at his bare back, urging him on as the audience applauds every thrust of his buttocks. Even Lynda is clapping, watching from her window through a pair of opera glasses, her underwear glowing beneath a dark cotton dress. And then the kitchen door swings open and Tania is standing there, holding Tilly on her shoulder, Freddie at her side. They stare at him in silence until the curtain falls.

'Jesus,' Adam says, sitting up in bed, looking around him, relieved that he is on his own.

Breathing fast, he glances at the clock – 8 a.m. – and swings out of bed, pulling back the curtains. The rain has passed, leaving the garden cleansed and shiny. Lynda next door is already up, deadheading roses and removing slugs. He prays she didn't see him out on the footpath last night in his boxer shorts. Or naked in his dream. What the hell was all that about?

He picks up his phone, hoping that there might be a message from Tania, a conciliatory text asking him to join them all for lunch down at her parents'. Crispin has perfected the Sunday roast. Nothing. He considers ringing his mum. Maybe he should head down to Newlyn, stay a night or two in his old attic room, seek refuge in the Swordy, meet up with Clemo, Jori and Morgan. It's been a while, but there will always be someone he knows sitting in the corner of the pub. Ji, his old friend from Cambridge, might be a more practical option. For the last few years he's been living in central London and they are due a catch-up.

He opens the photo that Tania sent again. It was definitely taken from outside. Did Clio know? Or was it chance that she turned to look out the window?

He's about to put the phone down when he looks at the time and date stamp in the corner of the image again. In the early hours he'd only noticed the time, but now he looks at the date: 6 May. He pulls out his memory box from under their bed and finds his student diary, flicking frantically through the pages until he comes across the entry he's searching for. He's right. Louis' fateful party was also on 6 May. He stares out the window, his heart full of dread. There's something else about the date. The party was twenty-four years ago. To the day. He needs no reminding of its significance, or of the lines he spoke all those years ago on the ADC stage: Doctor Faustus had promised his soul to the devil in exchange for twenty-four years of knowledge and power. Now his time was up.

For the vain pleasure of four and twenty years hath Faustus lost eternal joy and felicity. I writ them a bill with mine own blood. The date is expired. This is the time. And he will fetch me.

And there's no place to hide.

31

I woke up at 10 a.m., hungover and scared. Someone died last night. Lecter's was the first dead body that I've seen outside the Anatomy Building. I'd felt surprisingly calm as I watched the paramedic go about his business and knew that I could do his job, deal with the dying or the dead on a daily basis. But I didn't wake up calm today. And I'm far from calm as I write this now.

I can't shake off an all-consuming feeling of dread, as if the sky's going to fall in. My stomach feels bloated, hyperacidic. The last time I felt like this was after I'd lost it on the pier in Newlyn. The next morning I'd found myself phoning Gemma, my nurse friend at the Treliske hospital in Truro, to check if anyone had been admitted overnight with a traumatic brain injury. They hadn't, but I've never forgotten how Gemma read me the riot act, told me that as an aspiring medic I should have made sure the bloke was brought in for a check-up. How a brain injury can manifest slowly, how I should have taken more responsibility. I can hear Gemma's voice now, her anger and disappointment. Still, I convinced myself that the guy must have been alright. And his friends never reported me for what happened to him – an unspoken trade-off, I guess, in exchange for me not reporting them for what they did to Tom.

It's a tragedy that Lecter died, however obnoxious he was, and my thoughts are with his family. Of course they are. I'm sorry for those who saw him jump to his death too. That scene will stay with them forever. But I'm also feeling sorry for myself. I think I might have blown my career in medicine before it's even started. *If you are to succeed as medical students, you must work harder – and behave better – than every other student here at Cambridge...*

What will I say to Mum? It takes all my concentration to be here – socially as well as intellectually – and a small part of me is relieved. I know there'll always be a place for me in a distant corner of Cornwall where I feel safe and surrounded by old friends. But it's only a small part. I used to feel trapped in Newlyn too, held back by others whose ambitions didn't extend beyond the Tamar. I came to Cambridge to succeed, to become a medic, to do right by my parents. To never feel helpless again when someone is sick.

I had to go to the police station again today to give another, more detailed statement. It was clear that I'd had a lot to drink when I spoke to the officer last night, but I was still surprised to be called in again so soon. I was asked to give more details about the party and in particular the hour leading up to Lecter's death and my interaction with him. His real name was Brandon, but I'm sticking with Lecter for the time being – his death is somehow easier to deal with if he remains behind a mask.

'How would you characterise your relationship with the deceased?' the young detective asked. 'Did you talk to him at the party?'

I had to think quickly and clearly. How much had others said? The police were taking statements from lots of students – I'd seen some of the arts set waiting outside the station. I decided that it was simplest and best to be honest. Everyone had watched and cheered when I dragged Lecter upstairs to the bathroom, so there was no point in trying to deny what I'd done.

'He was bothering a friend of mine,' I said.

A headache was rolling in like a dust storm across the base of my skull and I could feel my pulse beating against my eyelids.

The detective consulted his notes. 'Clio?'

I nodded. What exactly had she told the police? I remembered her note, passed to Ji through the window late last night. *Thank you for protecting me tonight. Whatever happens in the coming months, I will always be grateful, as I have just told the police.*

'Yeah, Clio,' I said, trying to sound casual. Innocent.

'And what exactly did you "do" about him?' the detective asked. 'Did you try to stop him "bothering" Clio?'

He knew the answer already. If this was a game, I was going to play it by the rules. 'I took him upstairs to the bathroom to cool off,' I said.

'Took him?'

I closed my eyes, remembering the scene, his flailing arms. Instinctively, I reached up to touch the cut on my lip.

'He was being obnoxious, trying to kiss Clio when she didn't want to be kissed,' I said. My leg had started to bounce and I pressed it hard into the concrete floor of the interview room. 'She asked me to get him off her. "Get this creep off me" I think were her exact words. So I hauled him up the stairs and locked him in the bathroom.'

I fell silent, wondering how much to say. The detective waited, sensing there was more to come.

'Louis, the host, whose house it was, suggested I put him up there.'

The detective scribbled something in his notepad.

Was that OK to say? Had I just landed Louis in it? The police interviewed him last night and would no doubt interview him again today. Would he be honest or say it was my idea to lock him in the bathroom? Last night, we'd agreed not to mention the bathroom stash, but that was all.

'Were there any drugs at the party?' the detective continued.

I managed a wry smile. As Ji had said the other day, 'Do one-legged ducks swim in a circle?'

'It was a student party,' I said. 'I stuck to the Beck's.'

'And you didn't supply any drugs to the deceased?'

I shifted in my seat. In my head I went over what happened in the bathroom again, told myself there was an innocent explanation for the missing Ecstasy pill, that I hadn't given it to Lecter, but the nagging thoughts wouldn't go away.

'I'm not a dealer,' I said, beginning to sweat. I used to know a few in Newlyn but always kept my distance. 'And I'm not a user. I know what these things do to the brain. I'm a medical student. This guy was very intoxicated, as I'm sure the post mortem will reveal. For whatever reason, he jumped out of the window. Some drugs do that to people. Hallucinogens. I was the first on the scene, but there was nothing I could do. He must have died instantly. No vital signs.'

I began to well up, a response that I didn't see coming. For the first time, Lecter's death hit me. I remembered the angle of his neck, the way one arm was slung awkwardly across his body, like an empty sleeve.

'Are you OK?' the detective asked.

'I'm fine,' I said, trying to keep it together. 'Will you be contacting my college?'

'They've been in touch already.' He glanced at his notebook. 'A Professor Andy Beale.'

I bowed my head in shame. Prof Beale, my director of studies, is one of the nicest people I've met this year. An incredible anatomist and a kind, avuncular presence around college and the Medical School. Someone who prefers open-necked shirts and cosy turquoise jumpers to formal jacket and tie. I'm gutted for the damage that might have been done to my medical prospects, but I'm also sad that I've let down someone who looks out for his students with such genuine care. He warned us about the dangers and pitfalls of student life. The need to avoid trouble. And I failed to heed his advice.

32

The police interview shook me, but in truth my nerves were already shredded. Ji could sense that something was wrong and asked if I wanted to talk about anything, which was unlike him. I've always had him down as emotionally repressed, but I realise now that it's me who's had the problem, not him. I didn't want to talk, not yet. Instead, I agreed to play *Gran Turismo* with him for half an hour, to distract myself.

I was getting used to the catastrophising thoughts – I could go back to Cornwall and work on the trawlers if the college threw me out – but something else was bothering me and it took a while to work out exactly what it was.

There had now been two student deaths in as many days – one at Louis' party, one at King's College Chapel – but I was the only person who suspected they might be related in some way. Aldous told me to steer clear of Louis because he was 'evil'. He then took his own life. A day later, at a party hosted by Louis, another student plunged to his death. Odd, by anyone's standards. My problem now was that I didn't know what Aldous's issue was with Louis. Or why Aldous appeared in a video on rotten.com taking drugs and having sex, just a few hours after horrific footage appeared on the same site of him falling to his death.

I have a couple of medic friends in Queens', so I decided after lunch to walk over there to see what else I could discover about Aldous. It wasn't going to be easy as the whole college is of course still in shock. Aldous was a popular guy and his tragic loss is keenly felt. The last thing I wanted to be was disrespectful, but if I could talk to some of his friends, maybe even the woman he'd had the argument with on Mathematical Bridge, I might be able to establish why Aldous thought Louis was evil. And if his suicide was in any way connected.

An hour later, I felt like a tabloid reporter on a death knock as I wandered around Old Court, looking for the right staircase. I'd got a name for Aldous's girlfriend – Grace Anderson – and her room number from a Queens' medic. We've already been told that, as doctors, one of the more difficult aspects of our job will be breaking bad news to relatives. Oddly, it's a side of the role that I feel comfortable with. Maybe because Mum told me so gently when Dad eventually passed away, five years after he was meant to die. 'He couldn't keep going any longer,' she said. 'His candle finally burnt out.' The anger and rage that smouldered inside me afterwards was not directed at her or at Dad but at myself, for my powerlessness, my ignorance, my inability to help him.

'Who is it?' a faint female voice called out when I knocked at what I hoped was Grace's door.

Was this a mistake? Grossly insensitive?

'My name's Adam,' I said through the door. 'I met Aldous in the ADC Bar the other night. I'd really appreciate the chance to talk to you for a minute or two... if that's OK?'

There was a long pause before the door finally swung open. I recognised her at once as the woman on the bridge. Grace managed a smile, which was impressive, given how much she must have been hurting. Her eyes were red, her face bruised with grief. There was something retro about her appearance, a hint of the 1950s in her vintage cardigan and saddle shoes. She reminded me of a photo of Mum when she first met Dad – small and tidy, tortoiseshell glasses – and I held on to this thought for comfort as she ushered me into her room without a word.

'I'm so sorry about Aldous,' I said, accepting her invitation to sit down. I perched awkwardly on the edge of an armchair.

'Me too,' she replied, walking over to her desk. She shuffled some textbooks, her back to me. 'Did you know him well? I think I might have seen you around.'

'I only met him once,' I said, worried that I had intruded on Grace's grief under false pretences. I'd certainly never met Grace before. Her accent was faintly Mancunian.

'He must have made a big impression on you,' she said.

I took in the room: a poster of Audrey Hepburn in *Roman Holiday*, a record player on legs, the rows of books. The space felt old and settled, at peace with itself, as only ancient rooms can. The low afternoon sun slipped in through thick, mullion windows, casting long shadows on the high ceiling. I needed to tread carefully, say nothing that might make things worse for Grace. For all I knew, she was unaware of the video on rotten.com. I decided to focus on my brief exchange with Aldous in the ADC Bar.

'He gave me some advice, actually,' I said. 'I'd just done a performance at the ADC – *Doctor Faustus*.'

'I went to it,' she said, turning round, the first sign of a smile on her thin lips. 'That's where I've seen you before. You were Faustus, right?'

'Yeah,' I said, blushing.

'You were great.' She leant back against the desk, more relaxed now. 'Seriously, I really enjoyed it.'

'You're very kind,' I said. 'Did you see it with Aldous?'

She nodded. 'He liked it too.' It was the first time in our conversation where her voice faltered. 'I'm sorry,' she said, taking a tissue from a box on her desk.

'It's OK,' I said. 'Shall I come back another time?'

'No, please. Stay. It was a great show. Made a big impression on Aldous. On both of us. We talked about it a lot afterwards. What we're prepared to forfeit to succeed in life, whether it's ever really worth it. It's nice that you are here.'

'Did he act?' I asked.

'He wanted to. Never had the confidence to audition. I told him he should...'

She started to sob.

'I should go,' I offered again. 'I'm so sorry. I shouldn't have come.'

'It's fine,' she said. 'It's just all such a shock.'

'Of course it is.' Maybe I wasn't as good in grief's company as I'd thought.

'What sort of advice did he give you?' she asked, beginning to laugh through her tears. 'A bit rich given he never acted himself. Not as far as I know.'

'It wasn't acting advice. It was about someone I was talking to. In the bar.'

Her face seemed to darken, as if a cloud had passed over it. Had I said the wrong thing? Did she know Louis?

'I'm sorry, he was a bit of a gossip,' Grace said. 'We used

to argue about it a lot. He could be quite judgemental about people.'

Maybe she didn't know Louis. 'It was nothing,' I said, lying for the first time in our conversation. 'Just a passing remark. We only talked for a few seconds.'

'Why are you here then?' she asked, her voice suddenly less friendly. 'Who was it?'

'I don't know if it would be fair to say, given what Aldous said about them,' I said.

'In that case, I'm not sure how I can really help you.'

She walked over to the window, her back to me. I breathed in deeply – and took a gamble.

33

'Did Aldous ever have a film made of his life here?' I asked. Grace was still at the window. 'As a student?'

It was the only reason I could think of why Aldous might know Louis. A long shot, but worth a try. Grace turned around, her face full of relief. Mine too.

'He told you about that?' she asked.

'He didn't mention it,' I said, trying to stay calm. It must have been Louis who made the film.

'I'm amazed he didn't,' she said. 'He told everyone – he was so chuffed about it. Highlights of his time here. He did it for his parents, really. Gave me a copy too.' She started to cry again. 'I've been watching it today, actually.'

I was desperate to ask her more, whether Louis had made the film, but she was in pieces now, shielding her face from me as she sobbed at the window.

'Here.' I picked up the box of tissues from the desk and walked over to her.

'Thank you,' she said, taking one. 'I can't seem to stop crying.'

'It's OK,' I said, as she turned and rested her head on my

shoulder. I hesitated and then put an arm around her as she began to sob again.

'Sorry,' she said after a few seconds, her head still on my shoulder.

There was no awkwardness. Bereavement had taken Grace far beyond the borders of embarrassment. We stood side by side, staring out of the window, watching students crisscross the quad below. I knew what she was thinking. Why did everyday life carry on as normal? That's what I couldn't accept when Dad died. The world should have stopped to pay its respects, acknowledge that the sum of humankind was one person fewer. But the *Scillonian* set sail for the Scillies as usual. The beam from the Lizard lighthouse still swept across the bay. And Cornwall's seagulls continued to wheel and cry.

'He used to do this funny little sound, just after he'd fallen asleep,' Grace said, making a pop with her lips. 'Like he was blowing bubbles in his sleep or something.' She made the sound again, exhaling softly. 'I used to watch him do that until it lulled me to sleep.' She paused. 'I didn't sleep at all last night.'

She turned and walked over to her desk, breaking the spell of our sudden intimacy. I was about to follow when a movement below caught my eye. A fleeting, familiar figure in black, moving through the cloisters. Was it Louis? I looked again, but the person had gone.

'Do you happen to know who made the film?' I asked, sitting back down in the armchair. I had to hear her say his name, just to be sure.

'A guy called Louis Farr. Bit too where's-me-baccy-rah for my liking, but Aldous and him got on really well.'

I closed my eyes. It wasn't exactly satisfaction that I felt, but pieces were starting to fall into place. And then it occurred to me that Grace hadn't heard about Louis' party and the death of another student. She must have been living in her own bubble of grief since Aldous died, unaware of anything outside her college. I wasn't sure it was my place to pop it.

'I think Louis is going on to bigger and better things, actually,' she continued. 'Aldous used to joke that a film of his life had been made by a future Oscar winner.'

'And Aldous was studying law, right?' I said. Hearing someone else eulogise about Louis made me feel embarrassed by my own eagerness to be a part of his set.

'We both were,' she said. 'Well, I still am. Trying to. Third year. Not sure what I'll do now, to be honest. Maybe take a year out.'

'Can I ask something? And please say no if it's, you know, inappropriate.'

'Sure,' she said, picking at a speck of dirt on her skirt.

'It's just that Louis is also making a film of my life here, as a first-year medic.'

'No way,' she said. 'That's amazing. You must be so chuffed.'

'Yes and no. I'm not very good being centre stage.'

'Says Doctor Faustus.'

She had a point.

'I wondered if I could see the film about Aldous?' I continued. 'It would be reassuring to watch someone else's. To get an idea of how it might look.'

She thought about it for a second, glancing over to the window as she chewed on a fingernail. 'OK, I don't see why not.'

'Please don't worry if it's a problem,' I said, sensing her reluctance. She hadn't moved from her desk.

'No, it's fine,' she said, as if she'd suddenly seen the light. She walked over to the corner of the room, knelt down and opened a cupboard. Inside was a small TV set. 'But I might have to go out for a walk,' she added, turning on the TV and starting the video player. 'It will set me off again.'

'I could watch it another time,' I said, worried by all the trouble I was causing. 'If it's a problem?'

'It's OK.' She seemed to be in two minds. 'And it's not very long. Maybe I will watch it again.'

I held my breath as the film opened with a shot of Aldous punting along the Backs with Grace, accompanied by Elvis Presley's 'Love Me Tender'. No hidden photography this time. Louis must have been in the punt with them as Aldous and Grace smiled lovingly at each other. The schmaltzy scene faded into a series of short clips: Aldous at a lecture; in his room; cycling along King's Parade. I glanced at Grace, who was still kneeling in front of the screen, like a child.

The next scene made me sit up straight. Aldous was at a corner table of the ADC Bar, laughing with one other man. My eyes widened. It was the same person who was in the rotten.com video, taking drugs and having sex with Aldous. If Ji hadn't shown me that video, would I have suspected that it was anything other than two friends sharing a pint? But I had seen the film and I noticed the lingering glance here, a laugh there. I looked at Grace again. Had she spotted anything? The film cut to the finale: a fancy-dress party in Louis' house, where Aldous was dancing the jitterbug surprisingly well with a drunken Grace. And, in the crowd, Aldous's male lover, looking on.

'It's magical,' I said, feeling increasingly nauseous as the credits rolled. 'He must have been very happy with it.'

'Aldous loved it,' she said as she turned off the TV and closed the cupboard. 'Louis let him throw a big party at his house to end the film. Easier than here in college.' She had a wistful smile on her face now. 'We'd taken dancing lessons specially for that final scene. God, I looked out of it. That was quite an evening – what I can remember of it. Totally disgraced myself.'

'And Louis filmed it all?'

'Just the beginning,' she said, walking over to her desk. 'Aldous told him he didn't want any damaging footage of him getting pissed. You have to be so careful if you want to be a lawyer.'

'It looked OK to me,' I said, thinking of the sex and drugs video again. It was all beginning to make sense. 'Riotously drunken, as all good parties should be.' Had the secret footage been shot at the party? Had Aldous sneaked away with the other man when Grace was too inebriated to notice?

'They hit it off, then – Louis and Aldous?' I asked.

'As far as I know. Chalk and cheese, but they got on fine.' She glanced over at me. 'Why? Are you not getting on with him?'

'So far, so good,' I said.

'Was it Louis who Aldous talked to you about?' she asked. 'In the bar?'

She was too perceptive for me to lie. Too smart. I nodded.

'That's so weird. What did Aldous say?'

'Not much. Just to be careful, I think. He knew I was having a film made of me.'

'But Aldous adored Louis' film.' She looked perplexed. 'Every frame. Liked Louis too.'

'Did Aldous ever say what had upset him?' I asked, thinking of the rotten.com footage, the rumours of a job interview.

She shook her head and started to cry again. 'I told him that whatever it was, he could tell me and I wouldn't mind. Anything. Anything under the sun. But he wouldn't say. He just wouldn't bloody say.'

34

I knocked on Ji's half-open door and walked straight in, as usual, expecting to see him in front of his computer. This time, though, he wasn't at his desk. He was stripped down to his Mickey Mouse boxer shorts, doing press-ups on the floor. At least, he was trying to.

'Everything OK?' I asked, as he lay flat, straining to push his reluctant body upwards.

'Healthy body, healthy mind,' he said, gasping for breath. I watched as his pale torso lifted slowly off the ground – and smacked back down to earth. 'No good,' he said, rolling over onto his knees. 'She will just have to accept me as I am.'

'You should start gently,' I said, wondering who 'she' was. 'When was the last time you did any exercise?'

'The last time? How about the first time?' he said, straightening his glasses.

'You know that film you showed me, the drug-fuelled sex session on rotten.com?' I called out, as he disappeared into his bedroom to change.

He poked his head back around the door with a conspiratorial smile. 'You wanna watch it again?'

There was no point trying to explain why I was interested to see the film for the second time.

Two minutes later, Ji dialled up the modem to connect to the internet. The terrible screeching noise sounded accusatory, as if it disapproved of what we were doing.

'Here we go,' Ji said.

It was definitely Aldous and the guy he'd met at the ADC Bar.

'I just want to see where this one was filmed,' I said. 'Can you stop it there?'

Ji didn't question my flimsy justification for watching the film again and pressed pause. I leant forward, staring at the frozen image. It was impossible to make out the background as the room was dimly lit. Was that the pale outline of a cupboard of some sort? With an Indian mirrorwork design?

'Keep going,' I said to Ji. 'And stop it... there.'

For a brief moment, the cupboard became clearer. Was it the same as the one in Louis' bathroom? Maybe yes, maybe no. It was still little more than a glistening blur. I squinted at the screen like Dad used to do with his canvases when he was painting. If it was the same cupboard, the camera must have been hidden, as there was no sense that either man knew they were being filmed. They weren't putting on a performance for anyone else but themselves. The sex was furtive, rushed. I stared at the smudged image, unable to drag my eyes away from it.

'Are you OK?' Ji asked, turning to look at me.

'Not really,' I said.

I walked back to my room, legs heavy, head spinning. There's not enough evidence to link Louis to the video or to his bathroom – I may have got this all so wrong – but he recently made a film of Aldous's life, hosted a party for him. And now he's making a film of my life and also invited me to his house for a party. Did he secretly film me in the bathroom too? If so, what exactly did I do in there? I didn't consume any drugs – thank God – or have sex with anyone, but I was present when Louis cut a line of cocaine. I also removed two tabs of Ecstasy from the jam jar on top of the cupboard. What if secret footage shows me chucking one across the bathroom to Lecter, shortly before he died? I'm sure I didn't do that, but it would reflect very badly on me if I did. It wouldn't exactly look good for Louis either.

My hand is shaking too much now for me to write legibly here. The possibility that I might have thrown away my time at Cambridge – my medical career – before it's even properly begun is almost too much to bear. Mum might never recover if I'm sent down. Her already fragile nerves would be shattered. I'm not sure I would cope either. Newlyn is my home – it always will be – but I've glimpsed another world. It's not easy being a medical student, far from it, but I have kept my head above water. Proved to myself that I can do this. Until now.

I want to confront Louis, ask him if he has been covertly filming people in his bathroom at parties. And if so, why? But I can't have that conversation without acknowledging what I suspect about Aldous's death. If Louis was in any way responsible, Aldous was right. *He's not just a bad person, he's evil.*

35

Adam makes himself a coffee, thinking back to yesterday morning, when Clio was in the kitchen with Tania. It was so weird, the way they got on together. But not for long, as it turned out. He's already texted Tania a couple of times this morning, suggesting that he take a train down to Wiltshire and join them all for Sunday lunch, but so far no reply. Maybe he should just turn up and surprise them. That way he can talk to Tania face to face.

He's about to check his emails on his laptop at the kitchen table when his phone pings with a text. It's from his boss, Doctor Stephen Goddard, head of the Paediatrics Department. Stephen rarely contacts him at the weekend. He's a family man too, a big believer in separating work from home life. Adam reaches across and reads the message.

Sorry to disturb – are you around for a chat this morning? Maybe a coffee at the Pavilion? Something's come up.

What the hell does that mean? *Something's come up?* Should he call him now? He texts him back.

Call me?

The reply is quick.

Best we talk in person. I'll be at the Pavilion Café in 30 minutes.
See you then?

Adam waits a few seconds before sending an OK thumbs
up. But he feels far from OK. Why does Stephen want to see
him for a coffee on a Sunday morning?

Twenty minutes later, he is washed and changed and
walking past the playground. Stephen lives on Crooms Hill,
on the far side of Greenwich Park, and always likes to meet
at the Pavilion Café, up on the hill by the Royal Observatory.
Adam looks around at the joggers and dog walkers and
remembers yesterday morning, when he went off on his run
with Tilly. He shouldn't have promised to run with Freddie.
He misses them both. Tania too. If only he could wind back
the clock twenty-four hours. They could have taken a walk
down the river instead and not gone to the park, not bumped
into Clio. Unless she'd been watching them. In which case she
would have engineered a different meeting. He still doesn't
know what game she's playing.

Stephen is already at a table outside the café when Adam
arrives. He's an old-school doctor, at least fourth generation,
and ten years older than Adam. West Country private school,
followed by Oxford, and a smooth progression through the
ranks to become a senior consultant in paediatrics. These
days he's most interested in his pension, grumbling about
the freezing of the lifetime allowance, how much more tax

he'll have to pay, and whether he should retire earlier than planned. But he's a decent man, a reassuring presence in a crisis, someone who's seen it all, including most of Britain's golf courses.

'Thanks for coming, Adam,' he says, gesturing at the empty seat opposite him.

Adam sits down and orders a double espresso from a waiter beckoned over by Stephen. It's a reminder of how effortlessly Stephen manages to get people to do things for him, the soft power he wields. Not by barking orders but through gentle persuasion. In another life, he would have been a diplomat.

'Is everything OK?' Adam asks, glancing around. He spots two security cameras, one just inside the café, and one outside, overlooking the entrance.

'I was going to ask you the same thing,' Stephen says, chopping an iced bun into quarters and offering the plate to Adam. Stephen likes anything sweet, the more of it, the better, as his waistline testifies. Not the best advert for doctors.

'I'm OK,' Adam says.

'How's Tania?' Stephen asks. 'And the kids? Freddie and Tilda?'

'Tilly,' Adam says, shifting in his seat. What's this about? Stephen makes a point of knowing the names of everyone's families in the department, but he's not his normal smiling self today. 'They're all down with the in-laws this weekend,' he adds.

'You're not on call, are you?'

Adam shakes his head. 'I'm joining them today,' he says, annoyed now. 'How's Virginia?' he asks, pushing back. It's not the kindest question. Virginia, Stephen's wife, ran off with a rugby-playing junior doctor in Orthopaedics a couple of years back but has now returned.

'You know Virginia,' he says. 'Always busy.'

Often with other men. She's had various affairs in the hospital, not all of them known to Stephen.

'So what's this about then?' Adam asks, keen to cut to the chase. He's suddenly back with Professor Beale, his old director of studies at Cambridge, a meeting he's never forgotten.

Stephen glances around to check that no one is within earshot. A bad sign. Adam looks at the camera above the café entrance. Was it pointing their way before?

'It's a little awkward, actually,' he says. 'We've had a complaint. From the parents of one of your patients.'

Stephen's words are like a punch to the solar plexus, knocking the wind out of him. 'A complaint? Who from?' Adam tries to think of someone, anyone, he might have upset in recent weeks, but no one springs to mind.

'I can't say any more at the moment.'

'You've got to give me something here, Stephen,' Adam says, leaning forward, his leg bouncing under the table. He too glances around to check that they are not being overheard.

'Teenage girl. Seventeen. Says she's received a string of inappropriate texts from you.'

'Inappropriate?'

The word comes out louder than he meant and several customers turn round to look at them.

'That's putting it mildly,' Stephen says, more quietly.

Adam can feel the adrenaline coursing through him. If you work with children, a complaint of inappropriate behaviour, any whiff of child safety having been compromised, is career ending.

'They weren't sent by me,' he says. 'You know they weren't. I don't text any of my patients. I would never do that.'

'That's what I told the GMC. The parents have gone directly to them, I'm afraid. The father's a lawyer. He's complained formally to the trust too.'

Adam looks at Stephen, searching his ageing face for evidence that he believes him, that he is on his side. Stephen offers him nothing.

'You do believe me?' Adam says, his words more of a statement than a question.

Stephen turns away, as if in disappointment. Or is he embarrassed? 'They were sent from your phone, Adam.'

Adam almost wants to laugh. 'You know that's not possible,' he says. 'Someone must have spoofed my number, or whatever they do.'

He has received enough phishing texts himself from numbers purporting to be from his bank.

'I'm sorry.' Stephen dabs at some sugar in the corner of his mouth with a paper napkin. 'The trust thinks it's best, at this stage, if you don't come into work while it carries out its own internal investigation. I've sorted the rota.'

'The rota?' Adam shakes his head in disbelief, running a hand through his hair. 'This is fucking crazy.'

Stephen winces at the expletive, glancing around the nearby tables as if to apologise. 'I suggest you contact the governance team at the Royal College about legal support. At this stage, the police aren't involved—'

'The police?'

A mother and child walk past them, on their way out of the café. The mother looks across at the mention of the police and grabs her son's hand, accelerating away. Adam turns to check the camera above the counter again. A small red light on it has started to wink. Or did he just not notice it before?

'I wouldn't rule it out,' Stephen says. 'This girl's father is like a dog with a bone. He's threatening to take it to the papers too. He knows how successful you are – what a good story it would make. One of the country's best paediatricians—'

'I need to talk to him,' Adam says, interrupting. 'To the girl. At least tell me who it is.'

'You know I can't do that.'

'What did these texts say, for Chrissake?'

'They weren't just texts. They were photos.'

36

May 1998

It didn't take long for me to be summoned by Professor Beale. I was expecting to meet in his panelled rooms, some of the oldest here in the college, but it seems he's aware of how intimidating that can be. And intimidation is not Professor Beale's style, unlike some of the other senior members of the Medical School. Instead, he asked to meet me in Second Court, from where we walked through to the Fellows' Garden, in full spring bloom and one of the most idyllic settings in Cambridge.

'Tell me what happened,' he said. 'At the party.'

For the first time, I noticed that he has a slight limp in one leg. He's in his late sixties, but he's lean and looks after himself, a keen runner.

'And before you go on, it's only fair that you should know, if you don't already, that Louis Farr, the party host, has been suspended from his college with immediate effect. The police found traces of class A drugs in a bathroom drawer.'

'I didn't know,' I said. The news shocked me, but my first thought was whether Clio had been suspended too. 'Anyone else?'

'Not as far as I know,' he said. 'It's important that you are honest with me, Adam. And from what I know of you so far, from our brief but pleasant acquaintance, I have no doubt that you will be.'

And so I told him everything. How Lecter had been harassing Clio; why I'd locked him in the bathroom; how I had been offered but declined a line of cocaine; and how I had tried to save Lecter's life. The only thing I omitted to say was that I had removed two Es from the bathroom. I still can't account for the second one, but right now I'm confident that I didn't give it to Lecter. Every so often I picture the pill arcing across the bathroom, but I try to put that down to my overactive imagination.

'Thank you for being so open with me,' he said as we sat down on a bench at the far end of the garden, in the shade of a mulberry tree.

'I wish I'd never gone to the party,' I said. 'Clio told me not to.'

'She sounds like a wise friend.'

I thought of her face, held close to mine by the river in Grantchester. 'She said that bad things always happen around Louis.'

'He's not been in any trouble in the past,' Professor Beale said. 'I've been talking with his college dean. But Clio was right. These are the sorts of parties that it's best to avoid in your time here. Drugs are everywhere, we are not naive, but when people start dying, the university has to take action. I'm afraid this is going to be all over the newspapers tomorrow. It's why we have to be so careful. The tabloids seldom miss an opportunity to give Cambridge – or Oxford – a good kicking. You've given your statement to the police?'

'Twice.'

'The police investigation will take time and I think it best that you go home until they have completed their inquiries.'

'Go home?' I said. *Go home?* Was it all over?

'We're not formally suspending you as such, nor will you be going before a student fitness-to-practise panel, but it's important that the college – and the Medical School – are seen to act in the wake of such tragic circumstances. And, unfortunately, you were the last person to see this poor fellow alive. I have no doubt you will be cleared by the police, and indeed in the subsequent coroner's inquest. My guess is that the death will be recorded as a drug-related misadventure. They often are. But until that happens you should continue your studies at home. Your place is heavily subsidised by the college and I will do all in my power to ensure that we fund an extra year, should you fail to pass your end-of-year exams. But it's not going to be easy. For any of us.'

Professor Beale's words continued to ring in my ears for a long while afterwards. I went for a walk in town as I mulled them over. What was I going to say to Mum? I kept telling myself that I was innocent until proved guilty as I set off down King's Parade and headed towards St John's and Magdalene. It was university politics; my college being seen to do the right thing, nothing more. Louis' departure felt more serious. He had been formally suspended and would most likely never return. Would that spell the end of his film career? It would probably do the opposite, the whiff of scandal serving only to bolster his reputation. Was I barking up the wrong tree with him and Aldous?

Before I knew it, I was standing outside Clio's college room in Magdalene First Court. I wanted to see her before I left. To say goodbye and to ask her again about Aldous. I was still haunted by her reaction in the punt, when we drifted past King's College Chapel and it became clear what had happened. I knocked on her door and waited. After a bit, I assumed she wasn't in and was about to walk away when the door opened a fraction and Clio's bloodshot eyes peered back at me.

'Can I come in?' I said, disappointed that she hadn't immediately opened the door wider.

'Didn't you get my card?' she asked, still partially hidden by the door. Her voice was faint, weary.

I nodded. The card that said we should not see each other again. 'I've been sent home – from college,' I said.

She closed her eyes, but she still didn't let me in. Was there someone else in the room with her? Louis?

'I'm going away too,' she said, her long eyelashes lifting again, like butterfly wings.

'You've been suspended as well?'

She shook her head. 'Revising at home. With my mother in France. As far away from this place as possible.'

'From Louis?' I didn't care if he was in there, if he could hear me.

She stared back at me. What was it between them?

'He's been suspended,' I added, filling the silence, but I was sure she already knew.

'You should never have come to the party,' she said.

'I know. Bit late now.' I tried a smile, but it failed to lift the mood. She clearly wasn't going to let me in, so I changed tack. I had nothing to lose.

'Aldous, that student who fell from the chapel...' I began. If Louis was in the room, listening from behind the door, so be it. 'I know Louis made a film about him, his life here.'

Clio's eyes seemed to widen a fraction. Maybe I was imagining it.

'At least his parents will have a nice memento,' she said, smiling for the first time.

She was either acting – she was good at that, of course – or knew nothing of what Louis had really filmed. The drug-fuelled sex. Or I was wrong and it wasn't anything to do with Louis?

'Can I ask you something?' I said.

She didn't reply and I didn't expect her to. 'Did Louis film me in the bathroom? At the party?'

'You tell me,' she said, without missing a beat. 'You were both in there long enough together.' I began to believe that Louis wasn't listening, that there was no one else with her. 'Wouldn't you have noticed if he had? It's quite a big camera.'

Again I wondered if I was mistaken about Louis. He might have secretly filmed us at Grantchester, but that didn't mean he had hidden cameras in his bathroom.

We stared at each other. If she had more to tell me, now was the moment, but she stayed silent.

'Will you come back from France?' I asked, hit by a sudden wave of sadness. I was worried that this might be the last time I'd see Clio. 'To sit your finals?'

She nodded. 'I promised my mother.'

It was as much as I was going to get out of her. I was a fool, wasting my time.

'See you then,' I said and started to walk away. I hoped she would call after me, but she didn't. Not until I was almost out of sight.

'Adam?'

I stopped, hesitated. Should I keep walking? I turned around.

'I have something for you,' she said and disappeared into her room.

I went back over to her doorway. She wasn't good for me, but I couldn't help myself.

'Please, take this.' She handed me a brown-patterned feather.

'OK,' I said, surprised. It was a beautiful thing, light coloured with darker bands.

'My mother used to leave ones like this on my pillow when I was younger. It's from a barn owl. Symbol of protection. Owls will do anything to protect their young. She gave me one when I came here too. It's something her own mother used to give her when she was younger. Silly, I know. But maybe one day it will protect you. Those you love.'

I smiled and took the feather.

'Thank you.' I lifted my eyes to hers. 'Protect me from what?'

It was a few seconds before she spoke. 'The past,' she said, glancing at the feather in my hand. 'Be careful, Adam.'

She leant forward and kissed me softly on the lips. 'I'm sorry,' she added. And then the door was closed and she was gone.

37

A low buzzing sound builds in Adam's ears as he walks back across the park to Maze Hill. It's a stress reaction from his junior doctor days that he thought he'd left behind. Stephen told him to contact the governance team at the Royal College of Paediatrics and Child Health, who offer advice to members in the event of complaints, but he's minded to hire his own lawyer as well. The only crumb of comfort that he can take from their conversation is a perverse one. If photos of him were sent to the patient, his innocence can be easily proved.

He and Tania started dating long before sexting became a thing and neither of them, to his knowledge, has ever traded intimate photos with anyone. It's not exactly a consoling thought. Jesus, the whole thing doesn't bear thinking about. He hasn't called Tania yet, doesn't know where to start. She was just beginning to get over the photo of Clio and now this. She knows him well enough to realise that he's being set up, but it still won't be an easy conversation. A part of her will wonder if there's a shred of truth to the allegations, the thought gnawing away at their marriage like a rat beneath the floorboards. And what about those who don't know him so well? Other staff at the hospital. Neighbours. Lynda will spontaneously combust with excitement when she hears. And the tabloids? 'Consultant Caught in Teenage Sexting Scandal' might even make the front page.

Once he's home, he jumps on his bike and sets off for his office at University College Hospital in Lewisham. He will ring Tania later. First he needs to find out what he can about his accuser. It's a twenty-minute ride, maybe quicker on a Sunday, up Royal Hill and onto Lewisham Road. The hospital's at the Catford end of the high street and his office is on the ground floor, beside the Children's Outpatients Unit. After locking his bike, he walks past reception, nodding at the familiar faces behind a glass screen, and heads over to Paediatrics. It's as he approaches the double doors and pulls out his security pass that he senses people might be giving him odd looks. Maybe he's just imagining it. Stephen wouldn't have told anyone. His complaint will be dealt with confidentially – unless the parents have already gone to the press with their allegations.

He touches his pass, swinging from a lanyard around his neck, against the security pad and drops his shoulder into the doors, as he's done a thousand times before, but the doors don't open. He tries his pass again. Nothing. He glances up at the dark dome of a security camera, staring down at him from above the door, and tents his hands against the glass to shield the light. The department's quiet, but an unfamiliar nurse is heading along the corridor towards the doors. He steps back as she comes through and smiles at her. She smiles back, glancing at his lanyard, and he slips inside before the door closes.

He walks swiftly over to his office, which he shares with another consultant, currently away on holiday. His head is in turmoil, thoughts flying past like spinning knives. The fact that his pass doesn't work suggests that he might not have long. He needs to keep calm, focus on what he has to do. Waking up his computer, he opens a file of recent patients. He can access some of this from his laptop at home, but not all of it. Scanning down the names, he keeps an eye on age and sex. A sudden thought occurs to him. Whoever's trying to destroy his career might have scanned through the same list of names, looking for a teenage girl who would fit the bill. He's seen a sharp rise in recent years in adolescents with mental-health problems. The highest prevalence – one in four – is in girls aged between seventeen and nineteen.

He writes down the names of five seventeen-year-old girls he's seen in the past six months. Some he can remember, some he can't. Most he referred on to CAMHS, the Children and Adolescent Mental Health Services. His profession hasn't been great at spotting mental illness in the past, but he's always been mindful of emotional disorders in his patients. He has even helped shape paediatric training within the NHS to promote mental wellbeing in children. But none of that counts for anything now.

'Didn't think you were in today?' a voice says behind him.

Adam spins round. It's Joanna, one of his fellow consultants, leaning against the doorway. She works in Neonatal and is a friend of Tania's, which makes her habit of flirting with him all the more awkward. There's a lot of innocent banter in the office, but Joanna sometimes pushes it too far.

'I had to pick up something,' he says, blushing. He would be a rubbish spy.

'How's Tania?' she asks. At least she doesn't seem to know about the complaint that's been made against him.

'Down with her parents this weekend.'

'Not joining them?' she asks, raising her eyebrows.

'Heading there later,' he says.

'She seemed very tired last time I saw her.'

'That's young kids for you. Why we work with them too is a mystery.'

'Learning the alphabet?' she asks, nodding at his desk.

'What?'

He turns round to see what she's looking at. It's another card, propped up beside a photo of Tania and the kids. He was too preoccupied to notice it before, when he first jumped on the computer. He looks at it now and leans over to pick it up. His fingers are shaking. The card is similar to the 'S' he found on the dresser in the kitchen, only this one is the letter 'O'.

Adam stares at it.

'I could use that when I'm trying to demonstrate a difficult cannulation,' Joanna says. 'Just need another one with "shit" written on it.'

Adam would normally laugh, but all he can do is shake his head. How did it get here? On his desk? It's been placed there deliberately by someone.

'You OK?' Joanna asks.

'Fine,' he says, studying the card for clues as he slips it into his pocket. 'Do you know how this got here?'

'It must be from the Day Care Unit,' she says.

Adam hopes she's right.

'Seen anyone strange around today? Unusual?' he asks.

'Apart from the parents, you mean?'

Adam thinks again of the nurse he passed earlier, the one who inadvertently let him in through the doors. And then he hears a familiar voice from down the corridor. It's his boss,

Stephen. He must have authorised Adam's security pass to be cancelled, doesn't want him in the building. If he sees Adam, suspicions will only grow.

'Got to go,' he says, sending his computer to sleep. 'You haven't seen me.'

Joanna breathes in to let him pass through the narrow doorway, a suggestive expression on her face. She could have stepped away, but instead they brush past each other. 'Don't want Big Daddy to know you're in on a Sunday?' she asks, their faces close.

'Something like that.'

Adam walks down the corridor, away from Joanna and Stephen, as fast as he can without attracting attention. He glances over his shoulder as he exits the building by a side door. No one saw him leave – apart from the solitary CCTV camera above the door. He looks at it for a second, the inscrutable dome of glass, and heads off in search of his bike.

38

May 1998

Ji watched from the doorway of my room as I stuffed my medical books and clothes into the suitcase on the bed. 'You sure you're coming back?' he asked, an unmistakeable note of sadness in his voice.

I fastened the case and hauled another one off the top of the dresser.

'Looks like you're packing for good,' he added.

'I don't know how long I'll be away, Ji,' I said, not looking up at him.

The second case was for the rest of my medical books, which I'd gathered up from the windowsill. It's going to be difficult to continue my studies, but I'm determined to try. Professor Beale has given me a sheaf of lecture notes to read through, and my other tutors have done the same.

'Who's going to play *Quake* with me?' Ji said. 'Or watch rotten.com?'

I dropped *Essentials of Anatomy and Physiology* into the suitcase with the other books.

'Are you busy right now?' I asked, unnecessarily rearranging the books in the case. I'd already been to visit Clio, but I had one more thing to do before taking the long train journey down to Cornwall.

'I've still got to write up my notes on this morning's lecture – Lagrange multipliers – but otherwise I'm free. You wanna play some *Goldeneye 007* for old times' sake?'

The more time I've spent with Ji, the more I've become convinced that he's going to be something big in business. He loves his maths, but he loves computer games even more, a combination of interests that will take him far.

'Actually, I could do with your help,' I said.

Fifteen minutes later we were hovering outside Louis' house on Mortimer Road. We'd approached with caution as I wasn't sure if the police would still be there, but I was relieved to find that they weren't. It suggested that Louis' house wasn't being treated as a crime scene. The only evidence of anything untoward was a small scrap of police tape, flapping on the gatepost.

I'd confided in Ji on the walk over there that I suspected the film of Aldous might have been recorded covertly in Louis' bathroom. I also explained that, in the absence of any proof, I wanted to take a look around said bathroom. I'd decided against directly confronting Louis, who I assumed had already left, and was hoping that one of his flatmates would be there to let me in. Ji's job was to loiter on the street, to keep watch, a role that he seemed to relish. In truth, I just wanted his company. I was nervous about returning to Louis' house on my own.

'I'm going to try the front door first,' I said. 'You stay out here.'

'"Trust in God but tie your camel,"' Ji said, cracking his

knuckles as he looked up and down the road. It was a new one on me. His lexicon of proverbs was expanding.

'And if no one's at home, we try round the back,' I added.

I remembered the wall in the courtyard, where I'd talked to Clio. It might be possible to climb over it from the street that ran parallel to Louis' road.

'Round the back,' Ji repeated. He seemed even more nervous than I was.

I felt Ji's watchful eyes on me as I approached the front door and rang the bell. A shadow moved behind the frosted glass and the door opened a fraction. For a brief moment, I wondered if it would be Clio again, but it was a man, older than me by a few years. I recognised him as one of Louis' flatmates. Unshaven, posh, wearing a holey woollen jumper and tartan pyjama trousers that were too short for him.

'Yeah?' he asked, glancing over at Ji, who was standing by the gate and now wearing a camouflage baseball cap. It was an oddly reassuring sight, in a videogame sort of way.

'I'm a friend of Louis',' I said. 'Came to the party last night. I think I might have left my bag here. Black, small rucksack?'

He looked at me, contemplating whether to believe my story. It wasn't great, thought up on the walk over here, but it seemed to do the trick. He ushered me in, glanced up and down the street, and closed the door behind us.

'When did the police leave?' I asked. He eyed me again with suspicion. 'I gave a statement,' I added. 'Two actually. I was… one of the last to see him alive.'

There was no need to go into detail, explain that I was, in fact, the last person on earth to see Lecter alive, but I needed to offer up something to reassure him that I was OK, a friend of Louis'.

'I know who you are,' he said, going back into his room beside the kitchen. His words unnerved me. We'd never met, been formally introduced. 'The feds left about an hour ago,' he added, over his shoulder. 'Take a look around for your bag. Haven't seen anything.'

'Is Louis still here?' I asked, but either the man didn't hear me or had lost interest.

It was odd to be back at the scene of the party. The scene of Lecter's death. I peered out of the closed French windows. Someone had left a bunch of flowers, placed on one of the speakers, which were still outside. Not exactly a mass outpouring of grief. Maybe more flowers would follow, now that the police had gone.

I walked up the stairs, glancing above me. The bathroom door stood open. At least it wasn't locked. I didn't know who else was in the house. The place felt deserted, abandoned in a hurry, piles of half-empty beer and wine bottles everywhere, the flotsam and jetsam of a student party that had run aground in the most brutal manner. I walked past Louis' room on the first floor. The door was closed. Should I knock? In case he was still there? He would have heard my voice, come out to say hello. Besides, Professor Beale had said he'd been suspended with immediate effect. If they'd found traces of class A drugs in his bathroom drawer, he might even have been arrested.

I kept walking up the stairs to the second floor, scenes from last night flashing past. Lecter and Clio dancing together; Angela Hayes and her rose-petal dress; the screams when Lecter's body slammed into the speakers. Outside the bathroom I paused for a second, took a deep breath and stepped inside.

39

May 1998

The first thing I noticed was that the drawer beneath the sideboard was hanging open. I also saw that the window on the far side was closed, the curtain becalmed, hanging still. Unlike my mind, which was in turmoil. Had I thrown Lecter a pill? Done anything at all that might have encouraged him to jump? I shut down the repetitive thoughts as fast as they arrived. I was sure I had done nothing to hasten his death. Learnt my lesson from what happened on the quayside in Newlyn. I had checked myself, stopped manhandling him around the bathroom. *I'm not a violent man.* I can't let myself think otherwise. My only 'crime' was to have locked Lecter in the bathroom, denied him a safe escape from whatever drug-induced demons were chasing him. Left him with only one, fatal way out.

I looked at the Indian cupboard, tried to imagine the naked bodies of Aldous and his lover. If the rotten.com footage had been filmed in there, where exactly were they having sex? On the floor? By the sink? And where was the camera? I turned to the back wall and felt around the fittings of a towel rail like a plumber. What exactly was I searching for – a hidden camera? The idea seemed increasingly absurd, like something out of the James Bond movie that Ji had ripped last week. I glanced up at the central light. This was a dowdy bathroom in rundown student digs, not the set of *Tomorrow Never Dies*.

I began to relax, happier now that it seemed unlikely I had been covertly filmed. And then I looked across at the shower cubicle in the corner. The sides were opaque with limescale, but the door was open. I walked over and peered up at the chrome showerhead. Rather than pointing downwards, it had been angled into the centre of the room – at the area in front of the Indian cupboard. I put one foot inside the shower and stepped up to take a closer look. There were six black rubber water outlets in a circle and a smaller outlet in the middle. It was this one that interested me. The outlet was covered in a thin layer of glass. Like a lens.

'Careful, it can come on unexpectedly,' a familiar voice said behind me.

I spun around. Louis was standing in the middle of the bathroom, rolling a cigarette. His eyes weren't orange any more. They were coal-black and no less disconcerting.

'I didn't know you were here. I was looking for my bag,' I said, adrenaline surging through me.

'In the shower?' he asked, a wry smile on his lips.

Which way was this heading? I hoped his smile would linger and that we'd be affable with each other, as we had been before; that he'd somehow make light of me snooping around his house. But that was too much to ask. His smile fell away, broke into a sneer.

'What the fuck are you doing?' he said, closing the bathroom door behind him. 'Come to kick the dying embers?

Like an arsonist? They always return to the scene of their crime. So I'm told.'

What did he mean? I swallowed, glancing at the closed window. This time it was me who was trapped. There was no way out.

'I know about Aldous,' I said, flexing my fingers. I wasn't expecting Louis to turn violent – his physique was frail, birdlike – but my body clearly thought otherwise.

'I'm sorry?' he said, feigning ignorance. But I'd caught a flicker pass across the dark pools of his eyes, like the flash of the kingfisher in Grantchester, so quick that you questioned whether you'd seen anything at all.

'I know you made a film about him,' I said, gaining confidence. '*A Life in the Day of...*, like the one you're making with me.'

'He was very pleased with it,' Louis said, eyes still focused on mine. All the charming bonhomie, the director's relaxed chatter, had gone.

'So why did he take his life?' I asked. I wasn't going to mention the rotten.com footage. Not yet. I still had no proof that Louis was behind it.

'You seem to be implying that my film and his tragic death are in some way connected. As I say, he was delighted with our little movie. "Chuffed to bits" – I think that's how he put it in his quaint Northern accent.' Louis lit his roll-up and inhaled.

'With all of it?' This time it was my turn to hold his gaze.

He turned away, said nothing. I decided to reveal my hand.

'I've seen the footage,' I said. 'Of Aldous with another man. It was posted on rotten.com. I'm sure you're familiar with the website.'

'I'm surprised *you* are. Didn't have you down as a rubbernecking pervert. That had nothing to do with me.'

I knew he was lying. 'But you're aware of the footage,' I said evenly.

He hesitated again, interrogating me with those dark eyes, trying to fathom how much I really knew. It seemed my mentioning the footage had caught him off guard. So I doubled down.

'It was filmed in here, wasn't it?' I said, looking around the bathroom.

'Here?' He laughed.

His games were beginning to annoy me now. He was a terrible actor. No wonder he stayed behind the camera.

'I recognised the cupboard,' I said, gesturing at it. 'The Indian mirrorwork. You filmed it from a hidden camera in the shower.' I nodded at the cubicle. 'I saw the glass lens – in the showerhead.' Did he secretly film his flatmates – his guests – in the shower too? I wouldn't put it past him, a man who had a camcorder that could see through people's clothes. 'And I think you also filmed me in here last night.'

I was on a roll now, fuelled by adrenaline. I had nothing to lose. He'd caught me red-handed, poking around his bathroom. 'Taking drugs – never a good look for an aspiring medic. Except that I didn't, did I? I resisted the urge to compromise myself on camera. Unlike poor Aldous. What did you do it for – the money? Aldous wanted to be a lawyer, had an important job interview. Did you blackmail him? Were you trying to blackmail me too? Is that what you're really doing here with your shitty little films? It didn't work though, did it? We all went off script last night. Improvised big time. I kept my nose clean and somebody died.'

I was breathing hard. I'd said too much, more than I meant to, pouring out barely formed thoughts. If even half of what I'd said was right, I was in trouble. In the presence of a dangerous man. On my own. Thank God the window was closed.

'Have you finished?' Louis asked, turning to push in the open drawer.

'I'm going to the police,' I said, thinking fast.

'Shame – you've just missed them.' He ran the tap and cleaned a smudge from the sink with his forefinger.

'I gather you didn't clear up quite enough,' I said, watching as he finished at the sink. 'Traces of class As found in the drawer.'

He turned to face me, leaning back against the sideboard. 'You think you're so smart, don't you? A fucking know-it-all.'

His tone scared me.

'For the record,' he continued, 'traces of cocaine were found in the drawer here, but there was insufficient evidence to link it back to me. Anyone could have left cocaine in there.'

'But it was locked.'

'Not when the police found it.'

Louis must have unlocked it before they arrived, hidden the key.

'They were more interested in our local drug dealer, who I was delighted to tell them about. An obnoxious little thundercunt who's been hanging around outside student parties in recent weeks, pushing dodgy drugs – MDMA cut with ket, that kind of thing. Lethal shit – you can't feel pain and it causes violent hallucinations. Accidental deaths.'

I remembered seeing the hooded figure lurking in the shadows when I arrived at the party.

'The police knew all about him, were only too pleased to

arrest him,' Louis continued. 'When the toxicology report comes through, I have no doubt they'll be able to link whatever drugs are found in Brandon's body with the crap that the dealer was pushing last night.'

'You think that's what made him jump?'

'Jump? That would be convenient,' he said.

Again, I didn't like the sudden change of tone.

'You must have caught it all on camera,' I said.

'Oh yes, I caught it alright. He didn't jump, though.' He smirked. 'Would you like to see what really happened?'

40

Adam steps off the train and for a second he expects to see Tania waiting on the platform, Tilly in her arms, Freddie rushing up to him. It's a scene that has played out many times in recent years, but not today. Instead, he watches as the elderly man in front of him is met by a young family.

'If I'd known grandchildren were this much fun, I'd have had them first,' the old gent says as Adam helps him with his luggage. Two small children run towards him from the far end of the platform, hesitating as they watch their grandfather step down from the train and steady himself, breathing in the spring evening air. 'I wasn't there for my own son,' he adds, nodding down the platform.

A couple are waiting at the far end – the man's son and daughter-in-law, presumably. Adam smiles as the children accompany the elderly man along the platform, one skipping, the other dragging a suitcase twice his size behind him. He turns away, eyes brimming. He hasn't phoned Tania to tell her that he's here in Wiltshire. Even if he had rung, he fears there wouldn't have been a reception committee. Nor has he revealed that he's been suspended from his job. He needs to talk to Tania in person. There's something else he must tell her too, a secret that he should have shared years ago, when they first met. Now, there's no excuse. No time left.

He stands on the platform, watching the happy family unit escort their grandfather into a battered old Land Rover. And then he notices the cameras. One on either platform. The station wasn't big enough to warrant CCTV – at least that's what the locals were told last year when someone decorated the shelter with graffiti. Now there are two cameras. Adam turns away, tells himself it's a coincidence, and walks down the platform, wishing he could throw off his paranoia. It's corroding him from the inside, like acid.

On the far side of the water meadow, a narrowboat makes its way along the Kennet and Avon Canal. In front of it, a pair of swans begin a low, unlikely take-off. The canal runs parallel with the railway, but it was here first, according to Crispin, Tania's father. For a while, it had the run of the valley – until the railway took over. It's been fighting back in recent years and is more popular than ever, as Crispin never ceases to tell Adam. He owns a boat further along the canal and takes the family on trips down to Devizes, up to Newbury.

Adam sets off along the towpath with a heavy heart, his head full of memories. In his hand, a bunch of freesias, bought on Paddington station. It's a half-mile walk to her parents' house, which is set back from the canal, outside the village. Ahead of him, a solitary tern hovers and plunges into the water. Cows graze on the far shore. And high above, red kites soar on the evening thermals. Adam came here for weekends when he and Tania were first married, only too pleased to be spoilt by her parents and to catch up on sleep. Happy, simple days. He should have told her his secret then, but he was terrified of losing her, the life they had created together. The longer he left it, the harder it became. And now he's about to pay the price.

'There should be no secrets in a marriage,' Crispin had said, on a walk together before the wedding, which was held in a big marquee on the back lawn after a service at the village church. Adam's suggestion of Cornwall had been shot down by Crispin – a pint of Proper Job in the Swordy wasn't quite what he had in mind for the biggest day of his daughter's life. Theirs was an uneasy relationship at the best of times. When Adam first met Tania, Crispin was wary, suspicious of a first-gen, state-school-educated medic, even if he had been to Cambridge (wrong college, apparently). Going into paediatrics only compounded the problem. It was a female specialty, a far cry from the alpha-male world of brain surgery, where women still number less than 10 per cent.

He is five hundred yards from the house when he notices the security cameras at the gates, perched on each pillar like birds of prey. There never used to be cameras at the property. Has Adam missed something? Have Tania's parents recently been burgled? At least the gates are open. He walks through them, glancing up at the cameras as he heads across the gravel courtyard towards the handsome farmhouse with its local limestone walls, Welsh slate roof and wooden sash windows. Crispin's pride and joy. To one side, the red-brick stable block where they always stay. To the other, more outbuildings, where Crispin keeps his vintage cars. Is everyone out for a walk? It's very quiet. Too quiet. Their own car is here, which is a relief. Tania could have decided to head back to London and not told him. For a second he feels like an intruder, which is weird, given how many times he's been here. But today he's unwanted by Tania, an uninvited guest.

'Daddy!' a voice cries out behind him.

Adam wheels around to see Freddie running across the paddock, a red bucket at his side. He ducks under the wooden fenceposts and sprints over, sloshing water everywhere.

'Hello, monkey,' Adam says, scooping Freddie up in his arms. 'Been out for a walk?'

'Catching crayfish with Mummy and Tilly.'

'Did you get any?' Adam says, peering into the bucket.

No crayfish. Just a few inches of murky water. They usually catch big American beasts – the ones that have been eating the native variety, much to Crispin's dismay.

Adam shakes his head in disappointment, but Freddie seems far from bothered.

'Grandpa's setting up the Scalextric,' Freddie says, sliding off Adam to the ground. 'He's got a new chicane.' In Freddie's world, Grandpa's Scalextric track trumps almost everything, except perhaps fish finger sandwiches, and he starts to hop up and down in excitement.

'That's good,' Adam says.

But he's not really engaged. Tania is walking across the paddock, Tilly in a papoose on her back. She looks up at him. Adam waves, but she doesn't wave back as she unfastens the paddock gate.

'How's Mummy?' he asks.

'Sad,' Freddie says, whooshing the water around the bucket.

Adam's heart sinks. 'Still sad? I wonder why,' he says.

'Hmmm. Missing Daddy?' Freddie tilts his head to one side. 'I don't know.'

'These should cheer her up, don't you think?' Adam says,

showing Freddie the bunch of freesias. They are Tania's favourite flower – she wore them in her hair at their wedding, a day when she looked so radiant and happy. So beautiful.

'Maybe,' he mutters, as Freddie runs back over to Tania. He's got a lot of energy today.

Maybe not. It's going to take a lot more than flowers.

'Daddy's here! Daddy's here!' Freddie shouts.

'I can see that,' Tania says, holding Freddie's hand as she walks up to Adam. 'This is a surprise.'

Not a *nice* surprise. Not missing him that much.

'I wasn't sure my texts were sending,' Adam says, glancing down at Freddie. They've become good at talking in code in front of him. 'Wasn't getting many replies.'

'I turned my phone off. Someone sent me this weird random photo. Quite upsetting actually.'

'Can Daddy cook us our tea?' Freddie says, wrapping himself around Adam's legs. 'I like it when Daddy cooks.'

Not helpful. Not helpful at all. Tania gives him a weary look, starts to rock Tilly, who is stirring on her back.

'Why don't you go and help Grandpa set up the Scalextric and I'll join you in a minute,' Adam says, bending down to Freddie. 'I just need to have a quick word with Mummy.' And then he whispers into his ear, 'To make her less sad.' If only that were true.

Tania looks on as Adam kisses Freddie's forehead.

'What did you say to him?' she asks, as Freddie rushes over to the outbuildings, leaving the bucket at their feet.

'Don't slam the—' she calls after their son. But it's too late. They both wince as the door swings shut, shaking the glass in the pretty fanlight above it. It's a smaller version of the one above the house's front door and a miracle it doesn't shatter.

'We need to talk,' Adam says, turning back to Tania. 'I bought you these.'

'I'm not sure there's much to say.' She brushes back a strand of hair as she takes the flowers from Adam's outstretched hand and smells them.

He looks around the courtyard, out across the shady paddock, bathed in filtered sunlight. Two ponies hang their heads over the fence. Life must be so simple as a pony.

'The photo Clio sent you is the least of my problems right now,' he says.

Tania smirks. 'Glad it's such a non-issue for you.'

'Nothing happened. I promise you. And if you'll just give me a chance to explain...'

Tania starts to walk away. 'I think it's best for everyone if you go back to London,' she says. 'Thank you for the flowers.'

'Tania, please!' Adam calls out. If Tilly wakes, so be it. 'Someone's trying to destroy my life. Our life. It's not just the photo you were sent of Clio. I've been suspended from work. Stephen Goddard asked to meet me this morning for a coffee. Wanted to tell me in person.'

Tania stops and turns to face Adam, her mouth open in shock. 'Suspended?'

Adam nods, pressing his lips together. He's not sure he can talk.

'What for?' she asks, her voice full of dread.

Adam takes a deep breath, looks around for strength, barely able to bring himself to say the words. 'Inappropriate texts – and photos – have been sent from my phone to... a female teenage patient of mine. I don't know which one. All I know is that I didn't send them. Of course I bloody didn't. I would never do anything like that. Just like I'd never cheat on you. Not in a million years. You know that?' Tears start to well up in Adam's eyes as Tania looks at him blankly. 'Don't you, Tania? You must believe me. If *you* don't believe me…'

Tania says nothing. Instead she walks over to Adam and wraps him in a tired hug. They stay like that for a long while.

'Who's doing this to us?' she eventually asks, still holding him.

His face is pressed against Tania's shoulder, close to Tilly, their beautiful, sleep-defying daughter. He knows the answer, knows who is doing this to them. And he needs to be strong.

'I love you, Tania,' he says. 'I love our family, Tilly and Freddie. I would never do anything to lose what we've got together, the life we have. I know it's not easy right now for you. I get that. And we'll sort it, I promise. But you must believe me. You must trust me.'

'I do,' Tania whispers, her own eyes wet with tears too now. 'You're a shambles – overweight, a little too comfortable with me being a stay-at-home mum, and you fart like a hippo in bed – but you're not a… I know you didn't send the texts.'

'Thank you. You fart too, by the way.'

'Don't wake our angel,' she adds, looking over her shoulder at Tilly.

'Sorry.' He feels stronger now. 'There's something I need to tell you,' he says, glancing at the security cameras. 'Something I should have told you when we first met, but I never did. And that was a mistake. An unforgivable mistake.'

'Is it about Clio?' she asks.

Her question takes him by surprise. Is that why Tania was

so convinced that something went on between them at their house?

'No. Not about Clio. It's about a friend of hers. A former friend.' He takes a breath. 'You know that film I showed you – highlights of my time at Cambridge?'

She nods. He played it for her when they were very drunk once, soon after they started dating. He'd been trying to impress and nearly told her the truth, but even his beer-sodden brain had balked at the idea.

'There's another version – with a different ending,' he says. 'Very different.'

'How do you mean?' He can hear the anxiety rising in her voice.

'The person who made it was this guy called Louis. I'm not sure I've mentioned him before.' Adam's being disingenuous. He knows he hasn't mentioned him. He's never wanted Louis, not even his name, to be anywhere near Tania, to contaminate the air between them, their life together. 'I came to an arrangement with him that the other version would never be shown to anyone.'

'You're scaring me, Adam.'

'I'm scaring myself.'

'What sort of "arrangement"? What other ending?'

There's no turning back now. There are some secrets so dark that it's not an act of love to share them. They contaminate the confidant, implicate them in the crimes of the confessor. But it's time to tell Tania. She knows that Adam was present at a party at Cambridge where a student died, is aware that he gave evidence at the inquest. He told her early in their relationship. Told Crispin too, who was none too impressed. Medics drank like sailors in his day, but they never took drugs. Another of the many reasons why he distrusts Adam. But he's not told Tania the full story, what Louis filmed that night at the party.

All this time he's kept his silence, fearful of what Louis might do, where he might post the video, the damage it would cause to his career. To his marriage. To his life. But now the twenty-four years is up and Adam is frightened. For too long he's been in denial about the play's ending. Marlowe pointedly refused to grant Faustus forgiveness, let him repent, even though Faustus realised, too late, the error of his ways. There was no last-minute let-off. No exit clause in the contract he'd signed with his own blood. He was dragged down to hell by demons, kicking and screaming, condemned to eternal damnation.

This is the time.

41

I entered Louis' room full of dread. I'd gone to his house because I suspected the film of Aldous having sex might have been recorded covertly in Louis' bathroom. But Louis had turned the tables and was about to show me how Lecter – Brandon – had really died. What did Louis know that he wasn't telling me? I wished Ji was in there with me, but he was still keeping guard on the street outside.

Louis' room was like a shrine to cinema. Thick, dark red velvet curtains half drawn, an anglepoise on his desk spilling an insipid pool of light. Film posters adorned every wall. Cameras old and new lined the bookshelves: camcorders jostling with Brownies in battered leather cases and Rolleiflexes. Propped up on the mantelpiece was an old clapperboard for *Angel Heart*, complete with shooting date (11.06.86) and director (Alan Parker). Beside it, a well-thumbed paperback of *Falling Angel* by William Hjortsberg. And in the far corner, blocking what little light there was from the bay window, a vintage cinema projector, two metres tall, hunched like a stooping figure.

There was no evidence of Louis packing up, of leaving. Perhaps he hadn't been suspended after all. If the police were focused on the drug dealer, Louis might already be in the clear. But I wasn't thinking about him. What concerned me was the large TV screen attached to the wall. And the film that had started to play.

'It's not a final edit, but I thought you'd like to see it,' Louis said.

His tone was back to how it used to be, friendly, genial, but I wasn't falling for that. Not after our exchange upstairs in the bathroom. He hadn't been troubled by any of my accusations, which made me nervous. I'd shown him all my cards. What hand was he about to play? I watched the film, chest tight as a vice: me in my room, cycling to lectures, having lunch with Clio, punting to Grantchester. Of course he'd secretly filmed us. And then I was at the party, talking to Clio. So far, so innocent. Just like the film of Aldous's student life.

I glanced across at Louis, who was watching the footage unmoved, a rollie at his lips. What was he playing at? I could barely breathe. I'd just accused him of blackmailing Aldous, of possibly causing his death, and here he was showing me a jolly little film about my dull student life. And then the tone changed as I saw myself hauling Lecter up the stairs. He put up much more resistance than I remembered and it wasn't a pretty sight. I winced. It was like a wildlife programme, a lion dragging a stricken animal to its den. But it was nothing compared to what followed.

I watched, aghast, as I pushed Lecter across the bathroom. I was right: there was a wide-angle camera in the shower, to judge from where the footage had been filmed. The quality wasn't great – grainy, badly lit, on a par with the sex scene with Aldous – but my actions were clear enough. And the terror on Lecter's face was palpable as he stumbled backwards. Towards the open window. A second later, he'd fallen. Dropped out of sight. Disappeared. The curtain billowed and I was through the bathroom door, locking it behind me.

My whole body froze. I needed to get away from there, away from Louis.

'I didn't push him out the window,' I whispered, desperately trying to recall the exact sequence of events.

The curtain billowed again on the screen, accompanied by sinister music, which didn't help. I'd pushed Lecter backwards and then caught him, settled him down against the wall. I was sure of it. And then I'd lifted him up by his lapels and shoved him again when he'd become abusive, rude about Clio. *You don't have to ask, you know. Not with her.* But I'd stopped well short of the window, hadn't I? Checked myself. Turned and left him there. Walked away.

'I am not a violent man,' I said, as much as to myself as to Louis.

My brain continued to spin like a dervish. I would know if I'd killed a man. Wouldn't I? I would have risen this morning plagued with guilt of a whole different order, felt it in my bones, in the very marrow. You would just *know*, however drunk you might have been, if you were responsible for having taken another human being's life? I was shocked and sorry for Lecter's death, of course I was. And I was worried that I might have been involved in some tangential way – the missing pill, locking the bathroom door – but that was it. This film, though... this film suggested otherwise. I should never have agreed to it. But I wasn't just guilty of naivety. I was guilty of murder.

The footage cut to the mayhem of downstairs, the screams as everyone ran inside from the courtyard. How long had passed between my exit from the bathroom and Lecter's body smacking into the speakers? There'd been an interval, I was sure of it, as I made my way down two flights of stairs, but not in this film. And now I was watching a shot, taken from above, a high window, of Lecter's twisted, distorted body, his eyes staring up into the night sky. The film faded to black.

We both stood there in silence as the credits rolled.

'I might change the typeface,' Louis eventually said, walking away from the screen into the middle of the room. 'Maybe sans serif?'

'What?'

'On the credits.'

I glanced at the screen. I couldn't care less about the fucking typeface. 'I didn't push him,' I said. 'I swear I didn't. I'm not that sort of person.'

I sounded desperate, pathetic. The protests of a guilty man.

Louis tilted his head to one side in consideration. 'Someone watching that might decide otherwise,' he said, nodding at the screen. 'It looked pretty conclusive to me. I haven't shown it to the police,' he added. 'Not yet.'

'What do you want from me?' I asked. 'What's this all about? This whole *A Life in the Day of…* charade? You held a party for Aldous and then you invited me here to another party last night. Did you know Lecter was going to—'

'Be pushed out of a second-storey window by a mild-mannered medic like you?' he interrupted, laughing. 'No, I didn't. It was a surprising turn of events.' His eyes were fixed on mine. Was he lying? Had he assumed that I'd get riled up by Lecter? 'An unexpected bonus.'

'A bonus? Jesus, Louis, a man's died.'

'A tragedy, of course it was. For both of you. But it opened up... other possibilities. A chance to upgrade.'

I shook my head in disbelief. Who was this man? I also couldn't shake off the feeling he was holding something back.

'What had you been expecting?' I asked. 'That you'd take me upstairs and I'd snort some coke on camera – was that it? Just like you lured Aldous up there. How did you manage to arrange that, by the way? Got the other guy into the bathroom first, said that Aldous was into him – once you'd made sure Grace was too drunk to notice? She's distraught, by the way. Utterly devastated. Her life is over, destroyed. What kind of a monster are you?'

Louis laughed again and I turned away in disgust, glancing at the posters around the walls. I had already clocked Robert De Niro and Mickey Rourke in *Angel Heart* in the corner, but I'd not taken too much notice of the others. Now they struck me, their common theme: *Rosemary's Baby*; *The Witches of Eastwick*; *Prince of Darkness*; *The Day of the Beast*; *The Prophecy*; *The Omen*.

The aesthetics of evil in modern cinema.

'I'm not a monster,' he said. 'Aldous's death had nothing to do with me. He was a conflicted, troubled soul with a secret he couldn't have kept from Grace forever. He killed himself because he wasn't prepared to live the life he was meant to lead. I like to think that my films invoke a higher truth.'

I was out of words, spent. I no longer knew how to respond, what to do, in the presence of this man's malevolence. I'd never met someone like him before. *He's not just a bad person. He's evil.* Was I now no better than him?

'It's money, isn't it?' I asked quietly. It's easy to forget that Louis has been cut off by his parents. Nothing about his student lifestyle suggests poverty. 'That's what you want. That's what you asked Aldous for, on the eve of his job interview, knowing what a dim view the big law firms would make of the video. And when he couldn't pay, you posted it.'

It was a while before Louis replied. When he did, his tone was strangely reflective.

'You're right – I was going to ask you for money. Taking class A drugs on camera wouldn't have done your prospects as a medic any good. A police caution can really change the tone of a CV. It's the same for student lawyers, teachers, accountants. They all usually pay up. Can't afford to ruin their careers before they've even begun. For the record, I think it was his love for Grace rather than a good job offer that made Aldous jump. He couldn't bear the thought of her seeing the video of him with someone else. Touching, really. I assumed he would pay up, but he chose a different route.' Louis smirked. 'Events took an unexpected turn with you too. And now I want something else. Something more valuable than money. Less nugatory. More ambitious.'

I had no desire to know what he wanted. Instead, I went on the attack. 'What's to stop me walking out of here right now and into the nearest police station?' I said. 'Telling them what you did to Aldous, how you blackmailed him, what you did to me and all the others?'

'Be my guest,' he said, gesturing as if to usher me out of the door. 'There's no proof that I filmed Aldous and his friend. Or asked him for money. He's the only one who knew and he's... no longer with us, sadly. As for the others, they can't afford to say anything. They wouldn't be so stupid. They know what I'd do. That's how these things tend to work. As for proof of my involvement with you, all you have is a film.' He nodded at the screen. 'Unfortunately, a film that says more about you than me. I'm sure the police would be delighted to talk to you.'

I closed my eyes, biting back a sudden wave of emotion. In my heart, in my soul, I was sure that I hadn't killed Lecter. But what if I was wrong? What if alcohol had redacted my memories, blacked out the crucial moments? What if, God forbid, I *had* pushed him out of the window? Already the idea had lost some of its absurdity. My medical career would definitely be over, just as Louis said. Mum would never survive the shock. And I would be a murderer, condemned to a lifetime of remorse, torn apart by guilt for having taken a person's life.

'So what *do* you want?' I asked.

42

Louis paused before answering my question, wandering around his room like a don lost in thought. He picked up a framed photo from the mantelpiece. I hadn't noticed it before. Two young boys in shorts, squinting in the sunshine.

'You're an only child, aren't you?' Louis said.

I managed a nod. Jesus, how did he know so much about me?

'It does something to a person. Seems to give them a particularly intense relationship with their parents, wouldn't you say? I mean, look at Clio.' Louis raised his eyebrows, let his words settle.

'Gabe made my childhood bearable – and he would have enjoyed last night,' he continued, placing the photo back on the mantelpiece. I assumed it was of him and Gabe. 'He used to be a massive cinema fan, but he's lost all interest in films now. Back in the day, he'd have come dressed as Charlie Chaplin. We used to make films together when we were younger, on holiday in Cornwall. Tried to re-create scenes from our favourite Chaplin films. *Modern Times* cracked us up every time. He could do that funny

thing with the spanners and the ears perfectly. You know
it?'

I shook my head.

'He was quite the comic, a born actor, always clowning
around. Made me cry with laughter. Not so much now.'

'What do you want?' I repeated, no longer interested in
his brother's depression. I couldn't get the footage he'd just
shown me out of my head.

'What do I want? That's an interesting question. When you
make a film of someone's life, you try to convey the essence of
that person – to capture their soul, as some cultures believe,'
he said. 'I thought I'd done that with you – until last night,
when you revealed a very different Adam.'

I tried to interrupt, to protest my innocence again, but he
held up his hand to silence me and I obeyed. Why didn't I
ignore him? Was a voice in my head already telling me that I
had another side? A darker, violent Adam?

'So all I want, in return for not doing anything with this
film, for not handing it over to the police, for not posting it on
the World Wide Web, is the opportunity to have another go at
capturing your soul, to make another one.'

'Another film?' I didn't understand.

He nodded. 'But not now. One day in the future. When
you've established your medical career, become the good
doctor that you dream of being. A dream that would be
shattered if the truth about last night's death were ever to be
made public.'

Another shiver of fear ran through me. I tried to focus on
Louis' offer, rather than last night's events, but he still wasn't
making any sense. From where I was standing, a second film

seemed a small price to pay compared with what he must have asked Aldous to cough up. Maybe he knew he wouldn't have got anywhere if he'd demanded money from me. I've barely enough to live on.

'And when do you envisage making this other film?' I asked, feeling strangely better already.

He turned to me. 'Twenty-four years from now has a nice ring to it, don't you think?'

'Twenty-four?' I asked, but I already knew why. I'd said it enough times on stage. *For the vain pleasure of four and twenty years hath Faustus lost eternal joy and felicity.*

And just as it was for Doctor Faustus, it seemed too far ahead to be of any concern to me right then. I mean, where would we both be in twenty-four years? Louis might be dead, to judge by his sickly demeanour and smoking habit. I could be too, for all I knew. Run over by a bus. But if we were both still alive, what harm would it do to have another film made of my life? It might be more interesting by then. My career would have had a chance to flourish. Louis' too. He could be a famous director. Even if he was, I would be more assertive next time, make it very clear what I did and didn't want to be filmed. No parties, for a start. And definitely no hidden cameras. It all seemed faintly ridiculous, a pretentious student artifice. In short, it was a massive let-off.

'And you won't go to the police?' I asked. I couldn't believe I was saying such words.

'If you don't, I won't. You might wake up tomorrow and decide to confess to pushing a man to his death, of course, and choose to give up your vaulting medical ambitions forever. In which case, I would understand and cooperate fully. But I don't think you will. You've got too much to lose. And what would be the point? The police are well on their way to telling the coroner that it was an unfortunate accident, death caused by drugs supplied by a dealer they've been wanting to bang up for years. The inquest will be a formality. No one will ever know.'

'And that's all you want from me?' I repeated, for my own sake rather than his. 'To be in another of your films? Twenty-four years from now? No money?'

He shook his head. 'No money. But maybe drop your inquiries into Aldous's death. Stop bothering poor Grace in her hour of mourning. Very insensitive to doorstep her like that.' So it *was* Louis I'd seen in the quad below Grace's window. 'If you continue to ask awkward questions, or mention our conversation to anyone, I will have no option but to publish the footage.'

'On rotten.com?'

'Wherever.' He waved his hand dismissively in the air. 'I'm sure there will be better video websites in the future. No film is complete without an audience.'

'Is that a threat?'

'It's just the terms of our deal.'

I stared at him, not sure whether to laugh or cry. And then I remembered his words at the ADC Theatre, when we first met. *One day I'd like to shoot the film. A modern take on the original Faustian pact.* He'd approached me at the bar as I was staring unsubtly at Clio.

'Oh come on, Adam,' he said, sensing my confusion. 'I'm not asking you to sign it with your own blood. That was good, by the way. How you cut your arm on stage. Very realistic.'

It had taken a lot of practice to get the moment right when

Faustus signed the deal with his own blood. 'Faustus wanted power and knowledge,' I said. 'And he turned to magic and necromancy to get it. I'm just a modest medic.'

Louis laughed. 'I didn't know such a thing existed. And let's be honest here: if your full-body dissection classes aren't necromancy, I don't know what is. Instead of summoning the dead to ask them questions, you cut open their cadavers.'

No wonder Louis was so keen to film my anatomy class. It was hubris that did for Faustus in the end. Am I arrogant? By nature, medical students are confident people. Some of us even get off on the thought of playing God, enjoy the power of making life-and-death decisions for our patients. But do we, like Faustus, fly too close to the sun?

'And if we are being honest, isn't immortality the ultimate goal of modern medicine?' Louis continued, getting into his stride. 'I think Faustus would have approved of that.'

He had a point, at least about Faustus, who rejected medicine because it couldn't yet *make men to live eternally.* If the NHS offered immortality, Faustus would have been a fully signed-up medic.

'Is Clio involved in all this?' I asked, keen to change the subject. The thought of her possible role in a blackmail sting was troubling me more than Louis' left-field musings on Marlowe. She'd invited me to lunch – was that at Louis' request? But then she'd argued with him outside the restaurant. She'd also tried to warn me off the party, told me not to attend. Did she know what Louis was up to? *Bad things always happen at his parties.*

'Clio?' he replied with disbelief. 'You really don't know her, do you? Has she ever told you about her parents? What happened?'

What did he mean? 'She told me about her father,' I said. 'How he used to abuse her mother, lock her in the wine cellar.'

'Clio killed him,' he said bluntly.

I turned away, stunned by his words. Her father had sounded like a monster but Clio wouldn't kill him. She wasn't a murderer. I'd assumed he'd eaten and drunk himself to death, ignored his doctor's warnings. Louis was lying, knocking Clio off the pedestal I'd put her on. And relishing every moment of my shocked reaction. She wouldn't harm anyone. And hadn't she once adored her father?

But the more I thought about it, the more it began to make hideous sense. *I've done some terrible things in my life* – didn't she tell me that herself? What if Louis did know something truly shocking about Clio's past and had blackmailed her into helping him blackmail others? It's what he did, after all. It might explain her behaviour. Maybe she had known about Aldous and that's why she and Louis had argued, particularly when Aldous subsequently jumped to his death from King's College Chapel. She had seemed genuinely upset in the punt. And when she heard that I was to be Louis' next blackmail victim, she had tried to warn me. Christ, she'd told me enough times not to attend Louis' party. The thought was a comfort of sorts. Unfortunately, I couldn't ask her about the footage of Lecter.

I couldn't ask anyone.

43

Tilly stirs, as if she's listened to every word of her father's soliloquy and now thinks it's time for the interval drinks.

'Is she awake?' Tania asks, glancing over her shoulder at Tilly.

Adam can't tell from Tania's tone how his story about Lecter has gone down with her. He checks Tilly on her back and shakes his head. Her eyes have closed again. In a bid to keep Tilly asleep, they looped around the apple orchard adjacent to the pony paddock as Adam finally confessed to his wife the strange deal he'd once struck with Louis in order to keep the film of Lecter's death a secret. At their wedding, they retreated here for a quickie between dances. It's felt special ever since, at least for Adam it has, and he was hoping the romantic resonance of the place might have softened the blow of what he's just told her. They're still in the orchard now, standing beneath one of the oldest apple trees, a Bedwyn Beauty apparently, another of Crispin's pride and joys.

'He blackmailed you,' Tania eventually says.

'You could say that,' Adam replies. 'Except that I didn't push anyone. That's one thing my conscience is clear on. I know I didn't push Lecter out of that window.'

In truth, there have been many times when he's wondered, when he's woken in the dead of night, dripping with sweat, Lecter's face falling away from him into the darkness. Of course there have. And he's duly exhumed the notion of his own guilt, turned it in his hands and buried it again, repelled by the stench of moral decay. But he's shocked by how easy it's been to convince himself that he's not a murderer. And over the years the probability of his innocence has hardened into a certainty of sorts, become fact in the absence of any legal challenge – of any challenge at all apart from his own waning conscience. What's consistently troubled Adam more is that he never went to the police about Aldous's death. Aldous threw himself off King's College Chapel because of the film Louis had made of him, and he, Adam Pound, brought up by hard-working, honest parents always to do the right thing, had done nothing. Failed to do right by Aldous's grieving girlfriend, Grace. Let Louis walk free to blackmail others, to destroy more lives. He'd put his own medical ambitions before all else, telling himself that such selfishness was acceptable, because becoming a doctor was all about helping others, wasn't it?

'I don't know what to say.' Tania's voice is quiet, numbed.

'It's OK. You're not married to a psychopath.'

She turns away, ducking under a branch as she walks down another line of trees.

'What? Do you think you might be?' Adam calls after her, troubled by her silence. He sees Lecter's face again, falling away. And the man from Newlyn, head smashing against the cobbles. A well-worn mental routine kicks in – he's not a violent man – and the images fade.

She walks on. 'I'm just so sad that you were never able to

tell me this. It feels like a betrayal. A fundamental breakdown in trust. You should have told me about Clio too. That our son was returned to us in the park by a murderer.'

Tania's words cut him to the quick, a stark reminder of Louis' claim that Clio had killed her own father. In his mind, the crime itself has gradually paled into insignificance. He'd even convinced himself that it was forgivable, if it meant that Clio's feelings for him at Cambridge were genuine, unable to flourish because of the hold Louis had had on her.

'There shouldn't be *any* secrets between us, Adam,' Tania continues. 'None at all.'

Adam draws level with her. 'That's what your dad said. Before we got married.'

'He said it to me too. And he was right.'

Adam is aware he's still not being completely transparent and knows there'll never be a better opportunity to be honest with his wife. Nothing can be worse than what he's just told her about his pact with Louis, what happened to Lecter.

'There's more,' he says.

'Seriously?' she asks, turning to him. 'I'm not sure I can cope with anything else.'

'Something that happened in the year before I went to Cambridge,' he says.

For the next few minutes, as they circle the orchard, he tells her about the incident in Newlyn, how he had only intervened to save Tom, how, even now, he can't shake off the guilt at not having made sure the young man who'd slipped was taken to hospital.

'I should have known about all this,' Tania says, once he's finished.

'I'm sorry.'

'Not sorry enough to tell me.'

'I didn't want to lose you.'

She stops to look at him, her head framed by apple blossom. He's never seen her look so beautiful. 'Why would you lose me if it was an accident in Newlyn?' she asks. 'If you're innocent of Lecter's death?'

They stare at each other, but all Adam can see is Lecter's crumpled body. He closes his eyes.

'The footage from the party – it looked terrible,' he says. 'Awful. Anyone watching it would think that I'd pushed him out the window. I couldn't take the risk. At first, it was about losing my medical career. Then, when we met, it was about losing you.'

Adam sighs as Tania turns away. The jury's still out.

'Can I see it?' she asks, walking on. 'The footage?'

He hesitates, surprised by her request, by his own instinct to refuse. The thought of not showing it to anyone has become so ingrained, such a part of who he is. It's almost as if, by keeping the film hidden, he's hoped that it might eventually cease to exist. But now he's told her everything, she deserves to see it.

'Adam?' she asks, accusingly.

'Of course you can,' he says. 'It's in London. In the loft.'

'All that time.' Her voice tails off. 'Just sitting there, inches above our heads. Above our marital bed. And you think what happened with... the photo of Clio, that was also—'

'I think Louis has started to make the second film,' he says, interrupting her. 'Just as we agreed. Yesterday was twenty-four years to the day since the party.'

'But would someone really do that? After all these years? You might say you will, when you're a student, but life moves on. We go our separate ways, grow up, become different people. And anyway, why not make a nice film?'

'Because Louis's not a nice person,' Adam says. 'He's evil.'

'Evil?' She seems genuinely surprised by his choice of words.

Adam nods. 'Evil.'

'And you think he sent the texts to your teenage client?' she asks.

'Maybe someone connected to him.'

'Clio?'

Adam hesitates before he answers. He's tried so hard to preserve Clio's innocence in all this, to keep her pure and untainted, but he realises that the time has come to let go of the Clio of his memories and accept her for who she really is. To stop excusing her behaviour. She must have known what she was doing at his house in her underwear, the damage the photo would cause, the pain. Just as she knew what she was doing in Grantchester all those years ago. She and Louis had worked as a team then and they are again now.

'They fell out badly at uni after having been very close,' he says. 'And she said yesterday that she's lost touch with him. But it's too much of a coincidence, her turning up like that after twenty-four years.'

'And in her next-to-nothings.'

Adam looks across at her. Is that the hint of a smile settling on her lips? 'Next-to-nothings' is one of her favourite expressions. When she's being coquettish. 'You get it now?' he asks. 'What happened?'

She sets off again, back towards the house. 'I'm trying.'

44

'I get that Louis might be behind what's been going on,' Tania says, as they approach her parents' house. 'But it sounds more like a student prank that's got out of control, rather than anything more sinister. Louis's just playing with you, messing around.'

'You don't know Louis,' Adam says, disappointed that Tania's still not onside.

'No disrespect, but who would actually watch a film about you? About us? Our boring lives?' Tania asks. 'Why would anyone *want* to?'

'Schadenfreude?' Adam says. 'Watching other people's careers implode can be quite cathartic.'

Tania shakes her head in slow disbelief. 'This is why you've been so weird about that camera appearing at the end of our street, isn't it?'

Adam doesn't answer. They are back at the gates to the main house and he looks around furtively.

'When did your dad get these new security cameras installed?'

'Don't ask,' Tania says. 'They've caused a bit of a domestic. Someone dropped a leaflet through their door a couple of weeks back. Offered a discount and free installation. It coincided with a burglary in the village, so Dad went for it. One watches the front door, the other the courtyard and outbuildings. You know he loves a good gadget. He's installed an indoor security system too – cameras and monitors in the kitchen and sitting room. All the cameras are monitored via an app on his phone.'

Adam turns away, a sudden nausea rising. *Someone dropped a leaflet through their door.* If Louis is making a film of his life now, he'd expect Adam to come down here. His in-laws are an integral part of their family life, particularly as his own mum lives so far away. It's like a second home to them. So Louis would need cameras in place. On location. All part of pre-production. Just as Louis knew he would need a camera in their street in Greenwich. Adam glances at the house, across to the orchard, over to the canal. Up to the sky.

'Did you hear that?' he asks.

'What?'

'A buzzing noise.'

They both stand still, straining to listen. In the distance a roar of an appeal from the village cricket field. Pre-season practice, maybe an early fixture. Crispin will know. He likes to go down and watch.

Tania shakes her head, eyes creasing with genuine concern as she looks at him. 'Are you OK, Adam?'

'I thought I heard something,' he says. 'You know, a drone.'

Tania's eyes linger on his before looking upwards. She scans the empty expanse of the Wiltshire sky and then turns to Adam again.

'I can't hear anything,' she says.

'That's because you don't want to hear anything. You think I'm being paranoid.'

'I do actually, Adam. A bit vain too, if I'm honest. Thinking that someone might want to film you with a drone, with security cameras. That you're the star of some elaborate reality show. It's all too far-fetched. Sophisticated.'

'So why's there a drone hovering above your parents' house?'

Tania looks again into the sky. 'One's been flying over the village a lot recently – there've been letters in the parish magazine about it.' She goes quiet for a second. 'I really can't see or hear anything.'

'There, listen,' Adam says. The sky is still clear, but he can hear the distinctive whine of a drone's tiny propellers.

'Where is it?' Tania asks.

Adam looks around, but he can't spot it. The noise is louder now, closer.

'I think Louis might be filming us,' he whispers, trying to disguise the fear in his voice. 'Right here, right now.'

It had been his first thought when he arrived, saw the new cameras on the gates, but he'd dismissed it. Now he can feel the zoom lens on him, sense Louis at work. Just as he had done in Grantchester Meadows all those years ago. At the restaurant too. But how's he doing it?

'Oh come on, Adam. Please...'

'What if he's somehow managed to hack into your dad's security cameras?' he asks, ignoring her scepticism. He's not mad, or paranoid or suffering from scopophobia. He's right. He *is* being watched.

'Adam, you're being ridiculous now—'

'It's been happening for weeks, months,' he interrupts. It

feels good to be finally talking to Tania about his fears, even if she won't entertain them. 'The sudden sensation that I'm being filmed. Today, as I was leaving the hospital, I could sense the CCTV camera above the door coming on, springing into life. And earlier at the café in Greenwich, with Stephen Goddard. I even went to see a psychiatrist at the hospital about it.'

'A psychiatrist?' she says. 'When?'

The sound of the drone has faded. Maybe he did imagine it.

'The other day,' Adam says. 'I haven't always felt this way.'

After Adam left Cambridge, he almost managed to forget about his strange pact with Louis, particularly when he couldn't find any trace of him or Clio online. Almost. Lecter's and Aldous's deaths had continued to trouble him more, particularly his own possible role in them. But this year has been different. The deal, Louis' second film, has entered his consciousness again, hovering in the wings like an actor awaiting his cue.

'I keep thinking I've seen Louis,' Adam continues. 'Yesterday, in the park – that man in the leather jacket?'

'Oh God, Adam.' She shakes her head.

It's all coming out now. 'When you start looking, you see cameras everywhere. That's the problem. It's not just people's mobile phones. There are cameras on train platforms, in our hospitals, on the streets. Above us.' He glances around again, but there's no sign of the drone. 'In the theatre. Last summer, at the Minack, when I took Freddie to see *Dandy Lion* with Mum, I thought the security cameras were watching me then. I think I'm being filmed all the time, Tania.'

They walk through the open gates. He knows what his wife

will say, now that he's explained everything. She'll switch to GP mode, reassure him that there is help available for his sort of condition. That there's been a marked rise in anxiety levels in society since the pandemic and he is right to have sought help. But she doesn't say any of those things.

'It just sounds so self-centred,' Tania says. 'Egotistical. But if you really think this guy Louis is filming you, you need to do something about it. Go to the police.'

'I can't. It's too risky. I would have to tell them why he might be filming me. Our pact. What happened at the party with Lecter.'

They walk on in silence. He feels flat, let down by Tania. Why doesn't she believe him?

'I'm not making this up, you know,' he says.

'How about your friend Ji?' Tania says, ignoring him. 'He's in the tech world. Can't he tell you if someone's able to hack into security cameras? It sounds so unlikely, even just saying it.'

'You really don't believe me, do you?'

'Talk to Ji,' she says, exasperated. 'He'll put your mind at rest. He knew Louis too, presumably?'

'Knew of him, but they never actually met,' Adam says. Or did they? Not as far as he knows. Contacting Ji is a good shout. Last Adam heard, he'd invested in a spyware company. Adam has never told Ji what really happened at the party. He needs to tell him now.

45

Ji was standing at the front door when I left Louis' room, talking to the flatmate who'd let me in. He sounded animated, asking where I was.

'It's OK, Ji,' I said, coming down the stairs. 'We're leaving.'

I walked past the flatmate without saying anything. I knew Louis was watching from the landing above, could feel his gaze burning into my back as we left the house.

'I was getting worried,' Ji said, taking off his camouflage cap. 'You were in there for ever.'

'Was I?' I asked.

I wasn't thinking straight, my mind still trying to process what Louis had just said, what I had seen in the film. If I was certain that I hadn't pushed Lecter to his death, why didn't I want to go straight to the police to tell them about Louis? It was clear, from what he'd said, that Aldous and I weren't Louis' only blackmail victims. His activities were more widespread. He'd spoken of undergraduate teachers and accountants, as if he'd blackmailed them as well, knowing that he could ruin their nascent careers. Clio too was clearly in his thrall. Why didn't I want to tell Ji what I'd just seen either? Because I had seemed so aggressive in the footage, so angry, pushing Lecter around in the seconds before he disappeared? Any jury that saw that film would find me guilty. The last look on Lecter's face was one of pure fear.

'Did you find a hidden camera then?' Ji asked.

'No,' I said quickly, in case I changed my mind.

I realised, in that one simple exchange, that lying will need to become a habit. In a few months' time, I'll have to stand up at a coroner's inquest and describe my last moments with Lecter. If I don't mention the film, Louis won't either. I'm already trapped in a web of deceit. A lifetime of lies. And if I see Grace again, I'll have to lie to her too.

'What took you so long?' Ji asked.

'Just saying my goodbyes to Louis.'

Another lie. I didn't say goodbye to him. I didn't say anything. I just walked away with a copy of the video wrapped up in a plastic bag. We have one copy each. He said that he'll post me the finished version – without the shocking ending – and might see me around in Cornwall. I can't think of anything worse. Cornwall is my retreat, where I go to get away from all this, from people like Louis.

'Thanks for waiting,' I said to Ji. 'And sorry I took so long.'

'Rome wasn't built in a day,' Ji said.

I smiled. A day. Twenty-four hours. Twenty-four years.

I've decided I'm not going to dwell on Louis' curious deal. I'm going to treat it as playful, a whimsy, even though I know that's naive, given it's Louis, someone who's prepared to blackmail his fellow students and let them die if they can't pay up.

We walked back to the college in silence. Ji knew I wasn't

telling him everything, that I was holding something back, but he's not the sort to pry. I'm going to miss him, his proverbs, the offers to play *Tomb Raider III* at 4 a.m.

'Do the police suspect foul play?' he asked later, watching me as I stacked my two suitcases in the corner of my room, ready for a painfully early departure in the morning.

'I don't think so,' I said, a chill passing through me. Had Ji somehow managed to overhear my conversation with Louis? Gone round the back, over the wall, to see if I was alright? 'Actually, that's not quite true,' I said. 'Turns out a local drug dealer might have sold him some dodgy gear.'

'Which made him jump out the window?'

I nodded, thinking of Louis' film again. The curtain billowing with accusation.

'I've just been looking at rotten.com,' Ji said. 'In case, you know, someone posted footage of the guy at the party falling out of the window.'

I shook my head in mock despair at Ji's ghoulishness. In truth, my heart was racing. What if Louis hadn't kept to his side of the bargain and had already posted the film he'd just shown me?

'You're one sick bastard, Ji,' I said, failing to sound casual. 'Anything doing?'

'No live footage. Maybe one day, when we all have mobile phones with cameras.'

God help us. Ji has a mobile phone, of course. A Nokia 5110 with interchangeable coloured covers. No camera, but Ji says it won't be long.

'There's one photograph that's just been posted that I did wonder about,' he continued.

My heart stopped. 'What is it?'

'You wanna see?' he asked, with his usual conspiratorial smile.

Thirty seconds later, I was looking at the same vertical shot that Louis had inserted into his film. Lecter's body, sprawled awkwardly on the brick courtyard, staring upwards. I was shocked all over again by his open, vacant eyes.

'Is that the guy who died?' Ji asked. 'Those look like speakers and you said—'

'I don't recognise him,' I said, interrupting Ji. 'Jesus, who puts this sort of horrendous stuff on the World Wide Web? It's awful, so insensitive.'

I know who posted it, of course. Louis. He's sending me a message. That there's a lot more material that he could publish – enough to end my medical ambitions; my life. He knows it. I know it. I have no choice but to drop my inquiries into Aldous's death, however much it upsets me. And I won't tell anyone of our Faustian pact, that he can film my life again in twenty-four years' time in exchange for him not going public with the footage of me and Lecter. If I tip off the police, tell them that Louis tried to blackmail Aldous, he'll know it was me and will release the film. It's a brutal, troubling agreement, one that makes me feel as if I'm a silent accessory to Aldous's death.

46

'There's one other thing I need to tell you,' Adam says. He pulls out the two cards, one with 'S' on it, the other with 'O', and shows them to Tania.

'I'm not sure I can take much more of this,' Tania replies, as they hover outside her parents' front door on the gravel. By some miracle, Tilly has remained asleep and Freddie is still helping to set up the Scalextric with his grandfather.

'I found this on the dresser, in our kitchen' – he holds up the 'S' card – 'after Clio had gone. And this one was left on my desk at work.' He shows her the 'O' card. 'Might they be Freddie's? When he was learning the alphabet?'

Tania shakes her head. 'Never seen them before. Do they mean something?'

'They could stand for any number of things.' He tries to recall all the acronyms he had to learn at medical school. 'Second opinion... systolic output...'

'Sphincter of Oddi.'

'You haven't forgotten much,' he says. The sphincter of Oddi is the smooth muscle that allows bile and pancreatic juice to flow into the intestine.

'You never remembered much,' she says.

She's right. She always knew more than he did. It's the first moment of lightness between them for a while.

'Salpingo-oophorectomy?'

He cocks his head for an explanation.

'The removal of one ovary and a fallopian tube.'

'Of course.'

He'd forgotten the rivalry that existed between them in their early days of dating, the flirty competition.

'I think they might have been left by Clio,' he says.

'Clio? Did she visit your office? The hospital?'

Adam hates how her name causes Tania such instant anguish, resents the damage Clio has already done to their marriage. 'I don't know. Maybe she was trying to send me a message of some kind, without Louis knowing.'

'She could have just left you a note.'

'Not if Louis was filming her. Filming me. He would have seen.'

'So she leaves playing cards around the place with letters on them? Adam, I thought we'd just been through this.'

'She might be in trouble, Tania.'

'And you think these' – she points at the cards – 'are part of some kind of Mayday distress call? S-O... We'd better keep our eyes peeled for another "S", hadn't we? They look like cards from a nursery, Adam. From your Day Care Unit at work. You must have accidentally brought one home. And I really couldn't care less if Clio's in trouble. I'm sorry, but she's not my problem. Not our problem.'

'I just don't understand what happened in the park, that's all,' he says. 'She had the chance to take Freddie, but she chose not to.'

'Because he's not her son, that's why. Jesus.'

He's thought about it a lot in the past few hours: why Clio brought Freddie back to them in the park. It doesn't make any sense, not in the light of her sending the semi-nude photos. Why didn't she take him?

'What if it was a dry run?' he asks, thinking aloud.

'A dry run? Hear yourself, Adam. You've got to stop this.'

Adam stops and listens. The drone has returned. And this time they both see it, hovering high above the railway line, five hundred yards from the house. Is it really watching them?

'You need to visit Ji,' Tania says, eyes still fixed on the drone. 'It looks exactly like the neighbour's drone. The one that's been buzzing the village.'

Adam pulls out his iPhone, weighing it in his hand. 'I'll buy us some burner phones too, before I go.'

Tania shakes her head.

'Daddy?'

They both turn to see a tearful Freddie by the front door of the house.

'What is it, monkey?' Adam asks.

'I can't find my Ferrari.'

If he could only hear himself. At least it's the Scalextric version, Freddie's pride and joy.

'I'm sure it'll turn up,' Adam says. 'Not in the garage?'

Freddie shakes his head, fighting back the tears. Crispin keeps the whole Scalextric set immaculately, knows what pleasure it gives his grandson. The extensive track, laid out in the garage, was built in the Ferrari's honour. The idea of the car going missing is unthinkable. Freddie keeps it in London with him, sleeps with it by his bedside, but a deal was brokered for it to be parked up safely by Grandpa whenever he comes to stay – locked up along with the real vintage cars in the outbuildings.

'I'll come in and have a look in a sec,' Adam says, turning to Tania.

'I found this,' Freddie says. 'Where my Ferrari was.'

Adam and Tania stare in horror at Freddie's outstretched hand. He's holding another playing card, this time the letter 'U'.

'Oh my God,' Tania says, rushing over to take the card from Freddie as if it's contaminated. She twists it in her fingers, staring at it in disbelief. 'It's a "U". S-O-U...'

'L,' Adam finishes. 'Now do you believe me?'

'We'll find it, darling,' Tania says, scooping Freddie up in her arms. He buries his head in her shoulder. 'Call the police,' she mouths to Adam. 'Right now.'

'I'm going to see Grandpa,' Freddie says, sliding out of Tania's embrace and running off, tears flowing.

'She's been here, hasn't she?' Tania asks. 'In Mum and Dad's house.'

Adam nods, trying to work out the implications. Tania's voice is freighted with anger. Clio's broken into the garage and found the one thing that Freddie would miss. How did she know? She must have been listening. Watching them. The thought of her stalking through the premises, keeping to the shadows, chills him to the bone.

'I think it was a message,' he says. 'A warning. If she can take the car, she can take Freddie.'

'Are you going to call the police or am I?' Tania asks.

'Freddie might be less safe if we ring them. We all might. Louis will lash out if he's cornered. Like a wild animal.'

'Looks like I'm calling them then.' Tania pulls out her phone.

'You don't know who we're dealing with here,' Adam says. 'Don't know what he's capable of doing if we go to the police. He will escalate things, believe me.' He thinks back to Louis in his dimly lit student room, his parchment-dry skin. Over time he's mutated in his memory into something almost reptilian.

'She's been on our private property, Adam. Stolen something.'

'I just need time to find out what he's really up to and work out how to stop him. How to keep you and Freddie and Tilly safe. We need to get those new security cameras turned off – and stay inside if you hear the drone again.'

47

Newlyn,
May 1998

It was early afternoon by the time I arrived here in Newlyn, my suitcases bulging with textbooks and lecture notes as I stepped off the bus. The train from London had taken an age, crawling through Redruth, Cambourne and St Erth before it finally reached Penzance, where the smell of the sea lifted my spirits. The Swordy looked busy, drinkers spilling out onto the street, but I took the back route to Mum's, unable to face making an appearance in the pub, having to explain to everyone why I'm home; to accept what's happened, that my studies at Cambridge have been suspended. I also didn't want to greet Mum smelling of beer – a reminder of the bad old days.

'Mum?' I called out, lowering my head and stepping through the tiny wooden doorway of the Nook. The smell of furniture polish hit me first, followed by something roasting in the oven. The polish was a good sign. Mum's only house proud when she's feeling well.

Mum appeared at the top of the old granite stairs that lead up from the front door and smiled down at me. She looked older than she did when I last saw her a few weeks ago, but there was a spark in her eyes. Tears too.

'You OK?' I asked, watching as she turned and stepped carefully back up the stairs. It was good to see her taking her time. Falls are what tend to do it in the end for the elderly.

'I'm alright,' she said, but I knew at once that she wasn't.

'What is it?' I asked, giving her frail little body a gentle hug in the sitting room.

'Got your books for reading week, then,' she said, looking at my suitcase.

'Absolutely,' I said, surprised by her comment. 'A lot to pack in.'

I was suddenly conscious of how strong Mum's Cornish accent is and how mine has already begun to fade. I felt ashamed, as if I'd betrayed her in some way.

'I've cooked us a roast lunch,' she said.

'I can smell it.'

Normally she'd get me to sit down at the window table with her, clasp my hands, ask me to tell her all about life at Cambridge. But not this afternoon. She was keeping herself busy, checking the already-laid table, adjusting a framed photo of Dad above the fireplace.

'What is it, Mum?' I asked, following her through to the cramped kitchen.

She stood at the sink. Maybe it was because she'd prepared herself for not seeing me for another month.

'I told Bernard that you're down for reading week,' she said, her back to me.

Bernard's been a good friend to her, even if he is the local know-it-all at the Swordy and won't let any of us forget that he once appeared on *Mastermind* (specialist subject: the Spanish Armada).

'Oh yeah,' I said casually.

'He said Cambridge doesn't have a reading week. Terms are so short you don't need one.'

I stared at the kitchen's lino floor, traced its familiar patterns. Mum and Dad moved into the Nook when they were first married – it had once belonged to her mum, before she went into a home – and I've never known anywhere else. I once tried to describe the Nook to Ji: its paper-thin wooden walls; the dank cupboard in the basement where the coal is kept; the old Davy Descender fire escape harness above the window in Mum's bedroom, last tested circa 1955; and of course my bedroom in the attic, too small to stand up in. 'The place used to be a net loft,' I'd added, but Ji was still none the wiser. The Nook has to be seen to be believed.

'*Do* you have a reading week?' Mum asked, her face etched with concern.

I shook my head, calculating how much I should tell her. How much her nerves could stand.

'What's happened?' she asked. 'Bernard said that people sometimes get "sent down", whatever that means, but not someone like you. Not my son. You haven't been sent down, have you, Adam? Tell me you haven't.'

'I haven't, Mum,' I said, taking a breath. 'Something happened, at a student party, and I've been told to stay away for a while, until it's all sorted.'

'A party?'

I'd already said too much.

'Something happened at a party,' I repeated quietly.

It was a while before she spoke.

'Bernard said Cambridge was in his newspaper today. Front page. I didn't read it – his choice of papers is worse than his taste in women – but he told me what it said.'

I closed my eyes. I did glance at the newsstand on the station in Cambridge when I left this morning, but they'd already sold out of papers. Now I knew why.

'Someone died at a party I was at. I tried to revive him, but he was already dead.'

'When Bernard mentioned the newspaper article,' she continued, seemingly oblivious to what I'd just said, 'I didn't think anything of it, until I told him about your reading week.'

'The college thinks it's best for me to keep away while they establish exactly what happened.' Mum's arms began to tremble. 'Away from the journalists.' It was a lie, but I didn't want Mum to worry any more than she was already.

'They said it was a "Cambridge drugs orgy",' she continued. 'According to Bernard, that's how he died. I thought those days were behind you.'

'I don't take drugs any more, Mum. And being away from Cambridge is just a temporary thing.'

She's so nervous about drugs, has seen heroin mess up too many young people's lives. It's only recently that I've realised how much pain I caused her by going off the rails after Dad died, even if I did avoid heroin. It was the constant worry that I might succumb that upset her. And she was in enough pain as it was, grieving for Dad.

'Thank goodness your father isn't here to see this,' she said. 'A small mercy.'

'Please, Mum.'

'You did so well to get there. So well! And now you've thrown it all away.'

'I haven't thrown anything away.'

'He would have been so proud of you – Adam Pound getting to Cambridge, to study medicine! I was so proud. The whole town was. How you managed to turn your life around. I thought Newlyn had the drugs problem, not Cambridge.'

Bloody Bernard. At least it sounded as if it was only conjecture, just Bernard putting two and two together. My name and photo weren't actually in the paper – at least I hope they weren't.

'I'm going upstairs,' I said. 'I'll just take my bags up to my room.'

'How long will you be staying?'

'I don't know. My director of studies has given me plenty of work. Lots of books.'

'So I can tell people you *are* here to read? Tell Bernard.'

I couldn't care less what she tells Bernard. He was always jealous of Dad, his painting, the profiles of him in the local paper: the artist fisherman. 'You can tell them that, yes, Mum.'

I picked up my suitcase and was about to go upstairs when I looked at Mum again, her tiny frame in the tiny kitchen. I put the case down and went over to her. She turned, eyes red with crying, and we hugged.

'It's going to be OK, Mum,' I said. 'I'll be back at Cambridge before that roast dinner is ready.'

I nodded at the old kitchen range, with its battered enamel lids and low-down tap for hot water. It's never had much heat at the best of times and looked more on its last legs than ever.

'Don't throw away this chance, Adam. Promise me you won't?'

I thought of Lecter, Louis. The compromising footage, the deal. 'I promise.'

48

Adam stands outside the building in Mayfair, looking up at the impressive matrix of Portland stone and glass. A CCTV camera above the main doors eyes him back, glinting in the spring sunshine. Is Louis watching him now? Did he track him on his journey over from Maze Hill, pick him out in the Monday morning commuter crowd? Surely someone like Ji wouldn't allow his local cameras to be hacked. Adam checks the street sign again to make sure that he's at the right address. Ashburton Place. Ji has definitely gone up in the world.

Adam called his old friend last night, when he got back from Wiltshire, on a cheap, pay-as-you-go phone that he'd bought in Marlborough, asking if he could meet. He's left his iPhone at the house, won't use it unless he has to. Tania's doing the same.

'OK, no problem,' Ji said. 'I've moved house – what's this new number?'

'I'll explain when we meet. Where are you living these days then?'

Ji gave him the address. 'One of my games came good,' he added, chuckling.

It must have done for him to be living in this corner of

London, overlooking Green Park. Adam can't even begin to think how much the place must cost to rent. He takes a deep breath and walks into the airy reception, tracked by a bank of cameras. Glancing up at them, he explains to the concierge who he has come to see and is shown to a lift, which raises him silently up the side of the building.

Adam has stayed in touch with Ji over the years, but he's not seen him as much as he'd have liked. Guilt seems to be a recurring theme of their friendship. Ji went back to live in China after he completed his degree at Cambridge, via an MBA at Harvard. Adam promised to visit him in Shenzhen but never quite managed to. And then Ji returned to live as a non-dom in London six years ago, drawn like many Chinese entrepreneurs by the opportunity to invest in the capital's booming tech start-up sector. They soon rekindled their friendship, and when Freddie was born Adam asked Ji if he would be his 'odd father' – Ji was not religious, as far as Adam knew. Ji was delighted, gifting Freddie something wholly inappropriate: one of his company's new virtual reality headsets for babies.

A couple of years later, Ji invited Adam and Tania to his London wedding. When the invite arrived by personal courier, Adam began to suspect Ji's various tech businesses were booming. The wedding was held at Hakkasan, round the corner from Ji's new home, and neither he nor Tania had ever been to anything so lavish in their lives. The champagne flowed all night and the food – Peking duck with Prunier caviar, Wagyu beef dim sum – was to die for. The guestlist was impressive too: an A-list of techpreneurs from mainland China, including Zhang Zhidong, co-founder of Tencent, one of the largest gaming companies in the world.

'Welcome,' Ji says, ushering Adam into his apartment on the third floor. The space is vast, all marble worktops and stone-slab flooring, inlaid kitchen cabinets and buttermilk leather sofas. But it's the enormous TV screen in the main living area that Adam's eyes and ears are drawn to. It dominates the entire apartment and some sort of computer game is in progress – just as Adam would have expected. The noise of bullets ricochets across hidden, surround-sound speakers.

'Phang Phang's beta-testing,' Ji says, nodding in his wife's direction.

Adam hadn't noticed the diminutive figure on the huge sofa, eyes glued to the screen. There's a large explosion, so loud that Adam ducks, and the figure throws down the console in mock anger.

'She's my harshest critic,' Ji says, as she comes over.

'I'm sorry, so nice to see you again, Adam,' Phang Phang says, smiling as she smooths back her hair.

'You too.' Adam shakes her hand. He's only met her a few times and has forgotten how open she is, how enthusiastic her smile.

'Tea?' Ji asks Adam.

'Thank you,' Adam says. 'If you're having one.'

'Where there's tea, there's hope.' Ji puts an arm around Adam. 'Come.'

Adam didn't go into details on the phone. He just said that he was in trouble and needed Ji's advice. He smiles at Phang Phang and follows Ji into a side office, where he's ushered over to a corner sofa while Ji sits down behind a big desk. On the wall behind him is a framed quotation: 'Keep your eye on the donut, not the hole.'

'Definitely not Confucius,' Adam says.

Ji smiles, turning to look at the quote. 'David Lynch. Very good advice.'

A moment of silence as the two friends look at each other. The years have definitely been kinder to Ji than to Adam.

'So, Adam, how can I help?' Ji asks. 'Tania and the kids well, I hope?'

'They're good.' Adam feels a pang of sadness, wishes he were back down in Wiltshire with them.

'And the doctor's life?' Ji asks. 'Still doing no harm?'

'It's not great, actually,' Adam says. 'In fact, I think someone's trying to harm *me*. Destroy my life.'

49

Ji doesn't react or seem surprised. He's never been one for extravagant displays of emotion. Over the years, he's become more measured, wiser, cultured too, feeding his unashamed Anglophilia. His passion for gaming remains undimmed, but these days he balances it with trips to West End theatres and the English National Opera, often inviting Adam and Tania to join him. They go when they can, but the arrival of children has made things trickier.

'And are they succeeding?' Ji asks. 'Is your life being destroyed?'

Adam glances out of the window, takes comfort from the fertile park spread out below. There are no cameras down there, not as far as he knows. He will walk back that way, stick to London's wide-open spaces.

'I've been accused of sending inappropriate texts – words and images – to one of my female teenage patients. It doesn't get much worse for a paediatrician.'

'Did you mean to send them to someone else?' Ji asks, chuckling.

'I didn't send any images,' Adam says, protesting. 'Someone must have hacked my phone.'

'Have you been through your old texts? Are they showing up in your history?'

'There's nothing.' Adam shakes his head. It was the first thing he checked after he left Stephen Goddard at the café in Greenwich.

'So someone's spoofed your number. Easy enough to do. The question is not how but why. Why would someone do this?'

Adam spent the train journey up from Wiltshire last night considering how much to confide in Ji. Tania's right. Whatever's happening to him, the threat feels more hi-tech than medical, more in Ji's wheelhouse than his own. He needs his friend's advice, his expertise, but he has never told him about the deal he struck with Louis. There were times at Cambridge when he came close to confiding in Ji, but the moment always passed. Months passed. And now here they are, twenty-four years later.

'Do you remember Louis?' Adam asks, as Phang Phang brings in two cups of tea. 'The guy who made that film of me.'

Adam had shown Ji the final, sanitised edit in his college room, once Louis had finished working on it and posted it to him. It didn't include Lecter's death, of course, but it had still been a tough watch, knowing how things had really ended. Ji thought it was great but joked that it would never make it onto rotten.com. 'You need a bit of death in there,' he'd said. 'Some blood and guts.' If only he'd known.

'He held that party, right?' Ji asks. 'Where the American guy died.'

Adam nods. He was hoping not to linger on Lecter's death, but it was the most traumatic thing to have happened at university during their time there. Not easily forgotten.

'I remember we went to Louis' house and I waited outside while you checked for a hidden camera in his bathroom,' Ji says, smiling.

Ji truly does have the memory of an elephant. Whenever they meet up, he reminds Adam of some anecdote or indiscretion from uni that has long since been erased from his own brain. The time they got so drunk together at the Eagle that Ji had to carry Adam home. The night Ji tried to leap the Cam in a supermarket trolley at 2 a.m. and went headfirst into the river.

'You thought the redhead who jumped off King's College Chapel had been secretly filmed by Louis having sex and taking drugs,' he continues.

'You don't forget much, do you?' Adam says, smiling, but hearing the details again makes him nervous. Sad.

'How could anyone forget these things? Actually, I've been thinking about them again only recently – we finally bought that spyware company I was telling you about.'

'The rival to Pegasus.'

Adam has read all about the Israeli spyware that's used by governments around the world to hack into the smartphones of journalists, opposition leaders and activists. Ji once tried to explain how it worked. 'Jailbreaking – a malicious remote exploit,' he said. But it wasn't the spyware's ability to read texts and track calls that had caught Adam's eye. It could access and operate a handset's camera and microphone *without the user knowing*.

'I also remember you thought there was a connection with the redhead's death and the student who died at the party, but you didn't want to discuss that with me.'

Adam shifts his position on the plush sofa. How much does Ji know?

'And after we left Louis' house that day, I never asked,' Ji continues, more serious now. 'Except once. When I found a photo of the dead party student on rotten.com. I showed it to you, but you said it wasn't the same person. Later I checked, when his photo appeared in the newspapers. It was the same person.'

'But you didn't challenge me,' Adam says, sipping his tea.

'I told myself that you had made a mistake. But I knew it was something else. That there had to be a good reason why you didn't want to talk about the party.'

Without warning, tears begin to well up in Adam's eyes. He has never cried in front of Ji, has seldom shown any emotion at all. Theirs isn't that kind of friendship.

'But maybe you want to talk about it now?' Ji continues, his voice softer.

'I've only just told Tania about it,' Adam says, getting a grip. 'All this time I've never told anyone.'

'"If you would wish another to keep your secret, first keep it yourself."'

'You're right,' Adam says. 'I didn't tell you everything about the party. Or Louis. Or the redhead.' The term seems so wrong now, offensive. 'He was called Aldous. Had a lovely girlfriend called Grace.'

'Aldous and Grace,' Ji repeats.

It feels better to hear their names. 'And what I'm going to tell you now has to remain between the two of us.'

Ji nods his head solemnly.

'There was a hidden camera in Louis' bathroom,' Adam

continues. 'He tried to blackmail Aldous, with tragic consequences. And then he secretly filmed me.'

'Having gay sex and taking drugs?' Ji asks, a familiar, mischievous smile dancing across his lips.

'Not exactly.'

Adam tells him the whole story, the film's shocking ending. His Faustian deal with Louis. Clio's reappearance in his life twenty-four years later, semi-naked in his kitchen. The failed abduction of Freddie in the park. The sexting allegations. The mysterious alphabet cards. And his fear that Louis' camera has started to roll for a second time.

'I didn't push him out of the window,' Adam adds. 'In case you were wondering.'

Ji holds up his hands in mock protest. 'Please, I don't doubt you for a second, Adam. I heard it all at the inquest, remember? But even if you did—'

'No one deserves to die,' Adam interrupts. Not even Lecter. Ji had been a good friend, went along to both days of the inquest with Adam to offer moral support.

'In my world, the bad guys always die. I personally insist on it,' Ji says, nodding at a framed poster on the wall for one of his most successful videogames.

'But if Louis' film of me in the bathroom was ever made public...'

'It might be a problem.' Ji shrugs. 'Depending on the quality of the footage. Nobody trusts film any more. We can do too much with deepfakes these days. But the second film he is making... This could be more of a problem. A much bigger problem.'

'It's not exactly going to be a montage of my finest

moments,' Adam says, worried by Ji's sudden shift in tone. 'More a study of a middle-aged man's life imploding.'

But Ji isn't listening. 'Are you certain that you're being filmed?' he asks.

'I know for sure that someone was filming me from the garden when Clio visited. And yesterday, when I was down at Tania's parents, there was a drone flying nearby. I can't be 100 per cent certain, of course. And Tania thinks I'm being paranoid. I've just got this feeling, that's all. Tania's dad recently had new security cameras fitted too. Could they have been hacked? Could the security cameras at work? The one on our street? You know better than me how these things work, Ji. Maybe I am just being paranoid.'

It's a while before his friend replies and when he does, his voice is even more serious.

'You're safe here. This place is swept regularly. But you might not be so safe out there.' He gestures to the window. 'These cameras you mention, it's possible – possible but not easy – to hack into all of them. Most domestic security cameras are operated by unsecured Wi-Fi with unencrypted passwords, which makes them vulnerable to what we call "man-in-the-middle" attacks. And a search engine like Shodan allows someone to scan for vulnerabilities in the security of any domestic device connected to the internet. Throw in a packet sniffer, and they're in. State-owned CCTV is more tricky, but it's doable.' He flips open his laptop and starts to type. 'Have you ever heard of a place online called the red room?'

Adam shakes his head. It doesn't sound good.

50

I bent down towards the toddler, a three-year-old called Zac.

'High five?' I asked, smiling.

Zac grinned and high-fived me back.

'We'll be in touch,' Doctor Ruan Pender said, showing Zac and his mother to the door.

'Thank you,' the mother said.

I high-fived Zac one more time.

'You've made a new friend,' his mother added, turning to me.

I waved at the boy as they left Doctor Pender's consulting room.

'So, what do you think, Doctor Pound?' Doctor Pender asked, once Zac and his mother had left.

I blew out my cheeks and bit on my bottom lip. 'Cerebral palsy?' I offered. 'Spastic diplegia, at a guess. To judge by the contractures of ankles and feet, scissoring, late motor milestones – his mum said he only started to walk a few months ago.'

Doctor Pender nodded in agreement. 'Sadly, I think you're right. Be careful not to overdo the high fives – you're their doctor, not their daddy.'

I turned away to the window, looked out across Truro's rooftops. I did try to shut myself away in my old attic bedroom in Newlyn to read my medical textbooks and lecture notes, but it only lasted a day. It's been unbearable to see Mum so sad at my being at home with her when I should be up at Cambridge. So yesterday evening I decided to phone Doctor Pender at the Treliske Hospital in Truro. I didn't go into details, just said I was down in Newlyn for a few days and could do with coming in for a chat. He's been something of a mentor to me ever since I first contacted him about gaining medical work experience at the Treliske. A first-gen medic like me, he was also state educated and is now a consultant paediatrician. His brusque manner belies a huge heart and he's one of the main reasons I want to specialise in paediatrics, proof that men can make good paediatricians too. He's always prepared to go the extra mile, to wage war on NHS bureaucracy on behalf of his patients.

'So, how's it going?' he asked as he typed up his notes on Zac. 'I don't remember having the time to come home for a few days during my first year at medical school, let alone hang around our local hospital.'

I told him what I told Mum, that I'd been present at a party where a student had died. I was the last person to see him alive and had tried to save him, but there was now an ongoing police investigation and my college had sent me home to sit it out until the media storm settled.

This time it was his turn to blow out his cheeks.

'You really don't want to screw this up, you know,' he said, sitting back, arms behind his head as he swivelled in his chair.

'I'm trying not to.'

'Good. You've got a great career ahead of you if you want

it. Paediatrics, whatever. Personally, I think you're trying to specialise way too early. But do you really want it? That's what you've got to ask yourself. Do you really *want* to be a doctor? Is this the life for you?' He swivelled back and forth in his chair, gesturing at his office. 'Because if it isn't, I'd suggest you don't go back to Cambridge. Don't piss away taxpayers' time and money. It costs a lot to train a doctor.'

'It *is* what I want to do,' I said, looking him in the eye.

Doctor Pender's in his forties, happily married with a young family. Lives on the north coast at St Agnes, cycles to work, saves lives, surfs at weekends. What's not to like? His is a life worth living. And I want to be sitting where he is one day.

'Then why the fuck are you going to parties where people are jumping out of windows and killing themselves?' he said, standing up. 'Did no one tell you about fitness to practise? The need for medical students to be whiter than white, cleaner than clean? We partied in my day, of course we bloody did, harder than other students – we were medics, that's what you did – but no one touched drugs, and no one ever died. Not as far as I remember.'

I was warned about all that. We all were. Professor Beale couldn't have been clearer about the need to behave, but did any of us actually read the GMC's fitness-to-practise guidelines for students that he handed out in freshers' week?

'Patients trust us with their lives,' Doctor Pender continued. 'We have to justify their confidence in us – in everything that we do.'

'I get it,' I said. 'I was just in the wrong place at the wrong time. If things had worked out differently, I could have been the hero, saved a man's life, but he was dead by the time I reached him.'

'So what do you want from me?' he asked, sitting back down again. He'd said his piece. It was strange hearing him speak like that. The voice of authority, the establishment. I'd always had him down as a bit of a rebel. A street-fighter.

'To be here for a while,' I said. 'Do whatever needs doing. Volunteer my services again, for what they're worth. Prove to my director of studies, to myself, to you, to my mum and late dad, that I'm serious about wanting to become a doctor.'

'Fair enough,' he said, turning to the notes on his desk. He had other patients to see. 'A & E can always do with some help. They're understaffed right now – who isn't? I'll talk to them, liaise with the work-experience coordinator. Come back tonight – say 8 p.m.? Nights are currently pretty lively.'

51

'Red rooms are pretty much the darkest places on the internet,' Ji says, without any emotion, 'where viewers pay big money to watch live streams of people being tortured and killed. Viewers can also interact, determine the victim's fate, by bidding with bitcoins or other crypto-currencies.'

'On the dark web?' Adam asks, glancing around Ji's minimal, pared-down office. Adam's got too much clutter in his life.

'The dark web,' Ji repeats. 'Successor to sites like rotten. com.' He pours two glasses of Talisker malt whisky into expensive, heavy-bottomed glasses and passes one to Adam. Even by Ji's standards, it's early for a drink, which worries Adam. 'Some say they owe their name to the eighties horror movie *Videodrome*, which featured a red torture room,' Ji continues. 'Others believe it's a variation of "red rum" – "murder" backwards.'

'Sounds like an urban myth to me.'

Adam has heard a bit about the dark web, that it's not all bad: the unsearchable underbelly of the internet, a place for whistleblowers as well as paedophiles, drug dealers and gun runners. But he's never subscribed to the more outlandish conspiracy theories.

'That is the general view,' Ji says. 'And so far there's no actual proof that red rooms exist. Every day, rumours pop up on 4chan and Reddit forums. But they're just elaborate hoaxes. "Seven captured Islamic State fighters to be tortured and executed live on air – you decide how they die." That one rears its ugly head every few months. It's like the stories of living dolls, gladiator fights to the death, hitmen for hire. People believe that the deeper you dig on the dark web, the more depraved things get. And right at the bottom are the red rooms.'

'But it's not like that?' Adam asks.

'If you'd asked me a month ago, I would have said no, it's not like that. These things don't actually exist – there's no demand for them, no public appetite.'

'But now?' Adam takes a nervous sip of his whisky.

'But now... now there's some evidence that red rooms might actually be a reality.'

'What sort of evidence?'

Ji sits back, sips on his own whisky. 'The problem with the dark web, from a purely technical rather than moral point of view, is that Tor, the browser that most people use to access it, runs too slowly to live-stream anything. It's the same with other dark-web browsers – they all run their traffic through multiple servers to avoid detection and conceal their IP addresses. Typically, to resolve a request of one megabyte takes between eight and ten seconds, meaning live-streaming is out of the question. Impossible. You couldn't even watch snails having sex.' Ji smiles at his own analogy. 'But now there's a new browser on the block, which can live-stream at commercially acceptable speeds.'

'How do you know this?' Adam asks, fearful of where this might be heading.

'I keep my ear to the ground.'

'For business or pleasure?' Adam remembers his friend's fondness for rotten.com, which has long since closed.

'Purely professional these days.' Ji grins. 'While we have no formal presence on the dark web, we need to keep in touch with what's happening, follow the latest trends. My team has been revisiting how to combine reality-TV shows with gaming elements. Exploring ways to encourage greater user engagement.'

'Not really my bag,' Adam says. He can't think of anything worse. He dislikes reality-TV shows even more than videogames.

'But it is a lot of people's "bag" – and potentially very lucrative,' Ji says. 'We noticed viewers were paying serious money to influence contestants' choices on screen. That's when we came across a particular site on the dark web.'

'What site was it?' Adam asks, dreading the answer.

Ji stands up and looks out of his window, across Green Park, swilling the whisky around his glass.

'I don't want to worry you, Adam. I might be wrong about this, and it might have nothing to do with what may be happening to you.'

Adam swallows. 'You're worrying me more by not telling me.'

'We only had access for a few minutes until we were thrown off the site. It was a red room of sorts, I suppose. Call it a "red life". From what we could tell, someone's everyday existence was being covertly filmed. An office worker in Warsaw. Married with one child. Warsaw has a lot of CCTV cameras – more than almost every other city in Europe. The game had been running for a while, we thought. Maybe several weeks.'

'A game?' It doesn't sound much fun.

'People were bidding in real time to make certain things happen in this man's life.'

'What sort of things?'

'We weren't on the site long enough, but top of the list was a car crash with life-changing injuries.' He pauses. 'No one had bid for that yet. Too expensive. Further down, things were more tame: a prostitute honeytrap; kidnapping his child; emptying his bank account; an arson attack on his home.'

In which warped world are any of these events tame?

Ji turns away from the window to face Adam. 'But there was one thing that makes me worry for you,' he says.

Adam holds Ji's gaze, searching his friend's eyes for reassurance. 'And what's that?' The whole damn thing is making Adam worried.

'The prize at the end.' Ji takes a breath. 'Have you heard of NFTs? Non-fungible tokens?'

'Sort of – I don't really understand them.' But they've piqued Adam's interest, one of those Generation Z trends that he feels he should know about, that keeps popping up in the news. And in his spam folder. 'I heard about the artist who sold an NFT for $70 million.'

'An NFT is a digital certificate of ownership that's recorded on a shared ledger, a blockchain like Ethereum,' Ji says. 'And you're right, they're currently big in the art world, as a way for collectors to own original digital images. They're big in my world too – play-to-earn blockchain games are all the rage right now. NFTs can be used to represent in-game assets – swag, weaponry – and give them real-world value.'

'How does this relate to me?' Adam asks, struggling to follow his friend. Always a challenge when Ji's talking about gaming and swag and guns, however much he tries to keep things simple.

It's a while before Ji answers. 'Because the ultimate prize for this particular red room game we came across was the man's life. Whoever bid the most for him to die won an NFT for the man's soul.'

'His soul?' Adam sits up.

'In many ways, it's the perfect fit – every human soul is unique,' Ji says. 'And an NFT offers proof of that uniqueness.'

Adam closes his eyes, panic rising. It sounds like just the sort of twisted thing Louis would be into. His first instinct is to ring Tania, check that she and Freddie and Tilly are OK.

'Do you really think that's what might be happening to me?' he asks.

'I don't know, Adam. As I say, I could be completely wrong. But if I'm right, there's only one way to make the game stop.' Ji looks at his friend. 'The victim has to stop performing for the audience. He must leave the stage, disappear. Go dark.'

52

I watched in awe as the junior doctor in A & E listened calmly to the patient's description of what had happened to her.

'She took a bite out of my back, a bloody great chunk,' the woman said. 'Maybe she was hungry, I dunno. We'd just had a Maccy D, so I can't see why she was. Thing is, you don't just bite your best mate, however hungry you are. Ex best mate. Bitch. Wanna see?'

The woman was drunk – the smell of alcohol was overpowering – and already pulling up her blood-soaked top to show us her bite wound. The teeth marks were impressive, but her attacker had decided to abandon rather than close the deal, as it were. There was no actual chunk of flesh missing.

'We'll get this cleaned up by the nurse, give you some co-amoxiclav to stop any infection, and have you on your way,' the doctor said. 'Take her over, will you Adam?'

'Sure,' I said, excited to be doing something. Up until now, I had just been an observer.

'That it?' the woman said. 'Aren't you going to take some skin off my fat arse and fill the hole in my back?'

'That won't be necessary,' the doctor said. I could see she was stifling a smile. 'Your back – and your arse – seem fine to me.'

Last night was my fourth night of work experience in Minors in the Emergency Department. Doctor Pender did put in a word for me, as promised, and I've been loving every second. The trauma of Cambridge – Lecter's death, Louis' blackmail – seems a world away, but I also know that I'll have to return there sooner rather than later if I'm ever to be in this environment as a doctor rather than as a volunteer. After each shift I've been getting home at dawn, sleeping for a few hours and then turning to my medical books. Doctor Beale is doing what he can to supplement the lectures and classes I've been missing. Yesterday he also said that he might have some good news for me soon.

So far it had been relatively quiet in Minors, unlike Majors and Resus, which had both been frantic. In addition to bitten backs, we'd had a patient presenting with paper cuts, two unconscious drunks – 'frequent flyers', according to the ambulance paramedic, who dropped them off every night – and a sweet-smelling toddler who'd swigged from a bottle of perfume. I was tasked with keeping him entertained while he waited to be seen by a doctor, but he did all the entertaining. Ethanol, the same alcohol used for distilled spirits, can make up as much as 90 per cent of a scent. Fortunately, he'd only consumed a small amount, but enough for him to stumble and slur his words while beaming cutely at everyone, which had the whole department in inappropriate giggles.

I was about to escort the woman with the bite wound over to a nurse when the on-duty registrar, an Australian, popped her head into our curtained-off cubicle. 'We're down to three hours fifty,' she said. 'Do I hear cheering? Deafening applause? This time last week, we were five hours forty.'

'Want me to change it on the board?' I asked. This was my other big responsibility of the evening: updating the waiting time for patients to be seen.

'Would you?' the registrar said. She's a good friend of Doctor Pender's – they go surfing together – and knew that he'd arranged for me to volunteer in A&E.

'No worries,' I replied.

If she'd asked me to clean the floor with my tongue, I would have obliged. I'm always just so happy to be there, in amongst those people. When I was asked in my Cambridge interview why I wanted to become a doctor, I tried to avoid the clichéd answer, that I wanted to help others, and opted instead to talk about Dad and his death, and Mum and her ongoing problems. But the truth is that nothing tops watching people get patched up and sent on their way again. That and the sense of responsibility, the fact that people trust doctors with their lives. A sixth-year medic who came to talk to us at Cambridge said that doctors are the maintenance people, the caretakers of humanity, and that, better still, no one remembers their names. Which is just as it should be. Doctors don't do it for the glory; they do it for the species.

The mood in the Emergency Department changed when the call came through that the air ambulance was about to land. It had taken off from the helipad at the front of the hospital 45 minutes earlier and was now returning with its human cargo: a man in his mid-twenties who had fallen – possibly jumped – from the cliffs at Porthcurno, below the Minack Theatre.

'Adam, mate,' the registrar said, calling across the room, 'get yourself over to Resus.'

I checked with my junior doctor, who watched enviously as I followed the registrar into the Resuscitation Unit. I shouldn't have been allowed in there, for legal as well as practical reasons.

'This one could get interesting,' the registrar continued. 'Paramedics found him on the rocks, no pulse. An angler pulled him out of the sea unconscious. Not so easy round there – do you know it?'

I knew it well, had passed that stretch of coastline many times when I was on the gill-netter. I went to the window and watched as the helicopter blades spun down in the floodlights. And then I was standing in the corner of Resus, listening to the senior doctor brief his team. He'd already done a pre-brief, but the patient's condition had deteriorated on board the helicopter. I tried to make myself as inconspicuous as possible, standing in a corner. No one asked me to leave.

'This patient's intubated and hypotensive. Possible anaphylaxis,' the senior doctor said. 'There's swelling around the lips and face. Pulse is erratic, and he's hypothermic. OK, let's get him hooked up,' he added with more urgency as the patient was wheeled in.

I watched as his vital signs were checked: systolic blood pressure, body temperature, respiration rate, oxygen saturation.

'This patient's way too cold,' the senior doctor said, looking up at the screen.

'Core body temperature twenty-six,' a team member confirmed.

'Twenty-six?' The senior doctor looked up to double-check.

Even I knew that wasn't good. Core temperature is normally thirty-seven degrees Celsius. Hypothermia can kick in at thirty-five degrees, amnesia at thirty-three degrees, loss of consciousness at twenty-eight degrees. Profound hypothermia and death occur at twenty-one degrees and below. The man had clearly spent a long time in the water. Had he fallen or jumped? Tried to take his own life but changed his mind, hauling himself out of the sea? The only plus side is that a low body temperature can reduce inflammation of the brain in the event of cardiac arrest. In rare cases, people can survive up to thirty minutes with no heartbeat and recover without any brain damage if their body has been kept cold.

For the next five minutes, the team battled to save the patient's life, gently warming him. I couldn't see his face – there were too many people crowded around his body – but then he went into cardiac arrest and the decision was taken to defibrillate. He had already been defibrillated once, at the base of the cliffs, but a steady pulse was proving elusive. It wasn't clear what might have triggered the latest arrest, but the emerging consensus was that he could have had an acute allergic reaction to something while in the water, in addition to suffering from extreme hypothermia. There were no signs of any jellyfish stings, which can cause anaphylaxis.

'Clear!' one of the medics said.

Everyone stood back as the paddles were applied to his chest. And then, for the first time, I saw the man's swollen face as his body bucked upwards with the shock of 3,000 volts. I'd have recognised that jet-black hair anywhere.

It was Louis.

53

Adam walks up Maze Hill towards his house, head down as he passes the camera, Ji's words still ringing in his ears. It's been impossible to avoid being filmed on his way back from town. Going dark won't be easy, if that's what he needs to do. London has even more CCTV than Warsaw.

Adam pushed Ji further, asked him if he really thought that his life is being live-streamed for a bunch of sick gamers, but Ji wouldn't be drawn. He's going to ask his team to do some further research and get back to Adam. In the meantime, he urged Adam to stay away from cameras as much as possible, just in case. '"Dig your well before you're thirsty,"' he said as Adam left. This time it was Confucius.

Adam stops outside his house, glancing up and down the street as he unlocks the front door.

'Adam? Adam? Oh yes, it is you. I almost didn't recognise you under that curious hat.'

He bows his head in defeat. For one joyful moment, he thought he might be able to slip in without being spotted by his neighbour, Lynda. Some chance. Louis doesn't need to hack into London's CCTV network to keep an eye on him. He just needs to talk to Lynda. She's a one-person surveillance unit, trained to spot neighbourhood activity at a thousand yards.

'Hello, Lynda,' Adam says with as much enthusiasm as he can muster, which isn't a lot.

'Tania and the children still with her parents?' Lynda asks.

'Just been down with them, actually.'

'Ah, that's nice. Not at the hospital today, then?'

Adam manages a thin smile. 'Working from home this morning,' he lies. 'You wouldn't believe how much paperwork doctors have these days. Even our paperwork's got paperwork.'

He resents having to explain himself to Lynda, but he hasn't got much choice. The last time he saw her, he was bundling Clio out of the door and into a taxi. He's about to go inside, hoping he's said enough – Tania's always telling him to be more friendly to her – when she produces a small parcel from the porch.

'I've got this for you,' she says, holding it up triumphantly. She's not done with him yet.

'I'll come over.' Adam walks across to her front door, just in case she tries to bring it round to his house, invite herself in, have a good snoop, expect a cup of tea over a chat about his marriage. He has no idea what the package might be. They're not expecting anything, not as far as he knows.

He thanks Lynda and takes the lightweight parcel, managing another smile as he turns to go. Lynda's shot her last bolt and he's escaped unharmed. Resisting a little skip, he heads back to his house.

'She was here again today,' Lynda calls after him.

Adam stops, his back still towards her. 'Who was?' he asks.

She's enjoying this, got him on a string. 'That pretty university friend of Tania's.'

'Really?' Adam says, spinning around. His blood runs cold. 'Do you know what she wanted?'

He realises it's a stupid question.

'You tell me,' she says, raising her eyebrows. 'Rang your doorbell, but I told her you were up at the hospital. At least that's where I thought you'd be on a Monday morning. And then she gave me the parcel.'

'She delivered it?' Adam can't disguise his surprise. Lynda's a sadist at heart. Cruel. Why didn't she tell him that straight away?

'Wouldn't fit through the letterbox, so she asked if I'd take it in.'

Adam walks back round to his house, checking the street before he goes inside. He's glad he missed Clio, fears what he might have said or done. Has someone bid for her to try to seduce him again? Is that what's happening here? Because if it is, they're wasting their bloody bitcoins.

He places the parcel on the kitchen table and looks around. He might not have as long as he thought. A quick search on Google before he'll call Tania, fill her in on what Ji said. Only then will he open the parcel. Walking over to the windows, he scans the moss-infested lawn, Freddie's sagging mini goalposts, the broken footpath fence. No one's out there, but he still draws the curtains, glancing at his watch. It's not even lunchtime. Let Lynda think what she likes. He's not going to give anyone the satisfaction of watching him unwrap it, particularly as he has an idea what it is.

He pulls out a packet of Elastoplast from a drawer – Tania calls it 'Adam's drawer', as it's the only untidy place in the kitchen – and flicks open his laptop on the kitchen counter. Covering the camera with a plaster, just to be sure, he types in 'Adam Pound' and 'paediatrician', searching for news. Nothing. The press hasn't got hold of the story of his text messages yet.

He checks his work email but can't seem to log on. He tries again. Access denied. He's been locked out of the system. A rush of panic. Snapping shut the computer, he pours himself some fresh orange juice, glances at his iPhone on the sideboard. It won't harm to check for messages one last time. He gets out another plaster and sticks it over the camera lens of the phone. There are three increasingly urgent text messages from his boss, Stephen Goddard. *The Sun* is about to break the story and can he ring him ASAP? They're running it tomorrow.

The room starts to spin and for a second Adam thinks he's going to black out. He's also got a voicemail. It's a journalist from *The Sun*, offering him a right of reply: 'We've interviewed a teenage girl who's made a number of sexual allegations about your behaviour towards her in a recent consultation. She's also shown us the explicit texts and photos you sent her afterwards. Perhaps you'd care to give us a call back with your response before 6 p.m. Cheers.'

Cheers? They're not down the bloody pub, having a cosy chat over a pint. He writes the journalist's details on a scrap of paper. Louis must have paid the teenager. It's the only explanation. He turns off the iPhone and flings it across the room.

54

May 1998

Nobody seemed to mind that I hung around the Emergency Department in a daze. The waiting time went back up to over four hours, which I duly recorded on the whiteboard, and Cornwall's sick, inebriated and injured continued to be dropped off by ambulance, taxi and helicopter. I tried to do what I could to help, but the sight of Louis on the trolley had completely thrown me. There is only one major hospital, one proper Emergency Department, for the whole of Cornwall, so it wasn't a complete coincidence that he'd been brought there, but it was still a shock.

Louis did once talk about having a holiday home in Polzeath and spending time there with his younger brother Gabe, making films together. He mentioned the Minack too, come to think of it, but I had assumed he was still in Cambridge. Perhaps he was sent down after all and sought refuge in Cornwall, just like I have, so maybe it shouldn't be such a surprise that our paths have crossed, however strange the circumstances. The more I've thought about it, the more I've been wondering if he tried to take his own life, if he's not so confident and assured as he seemed at Cambridge. Cut off by his own family, thrown out of university.

'I told you that case would be interesting,' the registrar said in a rare quiet moment.

It was the first time I'd talked to her since Louis had been brought in by helicopter.

'How is he, anyway?' I asked.

'Alive – though I'm not sure if he wants to be.'

'You think it was suicide?'

'It might explain the lack of ID on him,' she said. 'It's a miracle he's not dead. His body temperature was ludicrously low and his heart kept stopping, which is never good.'

'What caused the anaphylaxis, do you think?' I asked, trying again to imagine Louis on the rocks below the Minack Theatre.

'We suspect he might have had a very rare allergic reaction to the sodium chloride in seawater. A form of aquagenic-induced urticaria. He already suffers from atopic dermatitis and in some cases sodium chloride can be a factor in allergic immune reactions. His body temperature made no sense at all. No bloody sense. We're warming him up slowly.'

'Will he survive?' I asked.

I tried to keep the tone of my question as neutral as possible, but a lot was hanging on her answer. Potentially my entire future medical career. If Louis died, a cloud would be lifted from my life. There would be no danger of the film of Lecter's death being released, now or in twenty-four years' time. I would be free of my strange bond forever.

'He should do,' she said.

'Where is he now?' Again, I tried to keep my question casual, matter-of-fact.

'Critical Care – second floor, Trelawny Wing. Ever been up there?'

'Once, I think.' It was when I volunteered at the hospital last summer. I glanced around us. 'I think I might know him, actually,' I said. Louis' face had been distorted, but I was certain it was him. 'From uni.'

'You sure? That could be helpful,' the registrar said, looking across at me. 'As we have no clue who the guy is.' We were walking down the corridor towards the canteen. 'There's no ID on him, no relatives have visited. What makes you think you might know him?'

'I may be wrong,' I said. 'His face was...'

'Swollen. That was the anaphylaxis.'

'I'm sure I've seen him around at uni.' I didn't want to tell her how I knew Louis. I was already in denial, determined to expunge him from my memory.

'You should definitely go up there, take a look,' she said. 'They'd appreciate a visit, any help you can give with a positive ID.'

'Is he conscious?' I asked, convinced that my questions were beginning to sound suspicious.

'Not as far as I know. Hey, why are you still here anyway? Shouldn't you have gone home hours ago?'

'Couldn't tear myself away,' I said, pleased to be talking about something else. 'Been an interesting evening.'

'One way of putting it. I had no idea it was so late.'

Ten minutes later, I was on the second floor, talking to a nurse at the Critical Care Ward reception. I explained that I'd been in the Emergency Department on work experience when Louis was brought in and that I thought I might know who he was.

'That would be super useful,' she said, leading me down the corridor. 'He's in here.'

'Has his body temperature risen?' I asked.

'Very slowly,' she said, turning to me. 'Cold as a penguin's arse, he was. At least the swelling around his face and neck has gone down. And his heart rate's stabilised.'

The nurse held open the door and I stepped inside. I expected her to follow me, but a colleague called out to her from the far end of the corridor.

'Won't be a minute,' she said. 'I'll leave you to it. Call me if there's a problem.'

I turned and faced Louis as the door slowly closed. The room was dimly lit, an eerie blue colour. The ECG monitor winked and glowed in the corner, behind the bed. Louis was still intubated and had a drip in his arm and an array of electrodes attached to his torso and limbs. I checked the door again and moved to stand beside Louis. The nurse was right: the swelling around his mouth had subsided. He looked like the Louis I'd last seen in his house, when he showed me the footage of Lecter. His lips were back to being puckered, almost feminine.

It was strange to be in Louis' company again. And this time he was the vulnerable one. I held all the cards. He was at death's door, in the hands of doctors. In my hands. I could quietly disconnect the oxygen, set myself free from our perverse pact and the ongoing threat of a jail sentence, and help him to succeed in what he had seemingly attempted at the Minack.

Without warning, a light flashed on the ECG monitor and an alarm sounded. It was Louis' heart rate, starting to accelerate. Had he become aware of my presence? Felt threatened? Sensed the dark thoughts that were swarming through my head? His eyes burst open and he stared upwards.

His heart had suddenly stopped. I watched his pulse flatline across the screen again, just as I had done in the Emergency Department. If I reached out and turned off the cardiac monitor, silenced the alarm… the nurse would not come. It would only take a second. His heartbeat might return or, more likely, his condition would deteriorate rapidly. I could slip out of the door, leave Louis to die in silent agony, and tell the nurse on my way out that I was sorry, I didn't recognise him.

But I did none of these things. Instead, I rushed to the door and called down the corridor at the top of my voice. 'Nurse! Nurse!' I couldn't do anything else, couldn't stay silent. My response was instinctive. It was in my DNA to do everything I could to help this man, just like it had been with Lecter. The nurse hadn't heard the alarm and came quickly. What seemed like seconds later, the cardiac arrest team arrived too, flooding into the room with their trolley and defibrillator. For the second time that night, I watched as Louis was once again brought back from the brink of death.

'You saved his life,' the nurse said later. 'Saved my arse too. I was talking to my boyfriend – he works in the canteen. We're having a baby.'

I left as dawn broke, having saved a man's life. Louis' life. Oh, the irony. I told the nurse his name, hoping that, by some strange moral alchemy, it might one day help to save my life too, but I had a horrible feeling that it wouldn't.

55

Adam stares at the package on the sideboard, stalking around the kitchen as if it's an unexploded bomb. Why did Clio feel the need to deliver it herself? He doesn't want to dwell on what *The Sun* might say in its story tomorrow. Stephen Goddard's phone went straight to answerphone when Adam rang him just now. He left a message, asked him to call back on the landline, said his mobile's playing up.

He still hasn't rung Tania, warned her of the media tsunami that's about to break over their lives. Is he afraid that their marriage won't survive? Hanging on to the hug she gave him, he starts to open the package. What was going through Clio's mind when she wrapped it? She seems so determined to destroy his life. For a brief, intense period twenty-four years ago he had genuinely thought there was something between them, felt a love for her that he'd never felt for anyone before. And he was sure she'd felt something back, however fleetingly. But he'd been wrong.

He rips apart the final layer of cardboard and stares at the contents. As he suspected, it's the missing Scalextric car, wrapped up in tissue paper. The red Ferrari, Freddie's pride and joy. He's about to ring Tania when the front doorbell rings. It's probably Lynda, wanting to talk more about Clio. He walks over to the door to open it and then hears voices outside. Peering through the spyhole, he sees a man and a woman. The man has two cameras slung round his neck. Press. Adam freezes. Should he front up to them, explain that the text messages are fakes? That his phone must have been hacked? They'll never believe him. He also doesn't trust himself to keep his cool. Instead, he backs away from the door and tiptoes upstairs, from where he can look down onto the front doorstep. Four reporters now – and Lynda, calling to them from next door. Careful not to be seen, Adam watches as they are drawn like magnetic filings across to her porch, from where she addresses them. She'll be loving every second of it. She'll also tell them that he's definitely inside the house.

Moving quickly, he packs a rucksack in their bedroom, stuffing in random clothes. He hesitates, pulls out a sleeping bag from a top cupboard, and stuffs that in too. Who knows where he might have to sleep tonight? Down in the kitchen, he replaces the Scalextric car in its box and adds it carefully to his bag. It had been his plan to stay here, but the arrival of the press has changed everything. He has no intention of appearing on his doorstep, a shamed middle-aged man hounded out of his job by a sex scandal. He's not a bloody Tory politician.

Two minutes later, he's about to slip out of the kitchen door into the garden when he hears a noise in the hallway. The letterbox flap. And a voice so loud and clear, he thinks that someone is inside the house.

'Doctor Pound, are you a paedophile? One of your teenage patients, a seventeen-year-old girl, says you touched her breasts and sent her intimate photos of yourself. Have you got anything to say?'

Adam stands there, frozen to the spot.

'Doctor Pound, we know you're in there. Are you a paedophile? Why did you send her intimate photos of yourself?'

Adam can't bear to hear any more. He closes the kitchen door, slips on the rucksack and takes his bike out of the garden shed. Grabbing his helmet, a snood and a pair of sports sunglasses tucked inside it, he lifts the bike over the broken fence at the end of the lawn, hoping that Lynda is still holding court out front. The footpath takes him down to the station car park, but it's too narrow and uneven to cycle. Instead, he pushes his bike along, running beside it like a triathlete on a dismount, his heart humming. *Doctor Pound, are you a paedophile?*

At the car park, he glances to the left, where the camera is still staring up the road from its pole. It will have tracked the journalists arriving at his house and be waiting for him to appear on the doorstep to make a tearful statement. What other local security cameras have been hacked to feed the live coverage? The house on the far side of Lynda's, one of the biggest on the road, is bristling with CCTV.

It's too risky to board the train with his bike – the platform has cameras, as do the trains – so he pulls on the snood to cover as much of his face as possible, and puts on his sunglasses and helmet. Cutting back up past the station, he takes care not to be seen as he turns down onto Trafalgar Road. ANPR cameras, speed cameras and junction cameras track his progress across London, but he does what he can to keep his face down. With a bit of luck, Louis still thinks

Adam's holed up in his house in Maze Hill, being hounded by the press. Lynda will be making them all mugs of tea by now, checking that they have the right spelling of her name ('it's Lynda with a "y"'). He almost feels sorry for the journalists. Almost.

It takes him an hour to reach Paddington station. Since the arrival of Freddie and Tilly, he's hardly got out on the bike and is not as fit as he once was. If he were, he would consider cycling the ninety miles on to Tania's parents in Wiltshire, but he knows his limits. And the bike is single speed, no gears. Instead, he will take his chances, board the next train to Newbury, and cycle the fifteen final miles from there. First, though, he needs to speak to Tania.

56

Adam tucks himself into a doorway on a side street that runs down next to Paddington station. There are no cameras around, as far as he can see. The next train to Newbury leaves in twenty minutes and he needs to be with his family, to protect them from Clio. What might she do next? He also needs to shield them from the breaking story. Tania can't deal with the press on her own if they turn up at her parents' front door, firing questions through the letterbox. *Is your husband a paedophile?*

He called the journalist back from a payphone outside Paddington, withholding the number, and left a message on his voicemail. He denied all the allegations, told the journalist he wouldn't be available for further comment, said that his phone had clearly been the subject of a malicious spoofing attack, and explained that there were no texts in his phone history to any patient and that he never texts patients anyway, on principle. He hopes he said enough to give the newspaper pause for thought.

He looks up and down the street and pulls out his burner phone. After five rings, Tania answers.

'Sorry, just talking to Mum.'

'Are you outside?' He doesn't want to risk their conversation being overheard.

'I am now. Tilly's actually asleep for the first time in her life. A miracle. Have you seen Ji? How was it? What did he say?'

Adam bites his lip. Tania sounds like her old self. Full of life, optimistic. And now he's about to bring her crashing back down to earth.

'The press has got hold of the story... about the alleged texts,' he says.

Silence.

'Are you there?'

'I'm here.' All the energy has gone, her voice sounds deflated, as if she's been punctured. 'What do we do now?' she asks.

At least it's a 'we'. 'I've left a voicemail,' Adam says. 'Told the journalist my phone must have been hacked. They were at the house – four of them, talking to Lynda. I'm at Paddington.'

'Shouldn't you consult a lawyer?' she asks.

He knows she's right.

'There's something else...' He pauses, loath to scare Tania any more than he has done already. 'I've got the Scalextric Ferrari. It was dropped off at the house this morning, when I wasn't there.'

'The car? Who dropped it off?'

'Clio. She left it with Lynda.'

'Clio?' Adam can hear the anger erupting in Tania's voice. 'So it was her. She's been here at the house. That's it, I'm calling the police. I'm sorry, Adam, but this has gone too far.

And I don't care about some weird deal you struck more than twenty years ago at university. That woman has broken into my parents' property, walked around half naked in our house, tried to take Freddie from the park.'

Or did she find him? Adam closes his eyes, remembers the sight of Clio walking down the hill towards him, Freddie in her arms. In that moment, she looked like a regular mum with her son in the park, natural, at ease. *I never, ever want to be a mother.*

'Going to the police won't help,' he says, trying to keep his voice calm, measured. 'What can they do? There's no proof that Clio's done anything wrong, or threatening or illegal.'

'But Freddie's car was in a locked-up garage! She broke in and stole it.'

'And your dad's security camera would have been switched off first, before Clio went inside.'

'I can't believe this is happening,' Tania says. 'Freddie? Freddie!'

Adam listens as she calls out to their precious son, wants him nearby. She's understandably scared, protective. Adam is too.

'Where are your parents?' he asks.

'Freddie was cutting radishes in the vegetable patch with Granny, weren't you Freddie?' Tania says. Adam can picture him by his mother's side, nodding his head like a donkey. 'It's Daddy on the phone. You can talk to him in a second.'

'Tell your parents that a story's about to run,' Adam says, wishing he was with them now. 'But don't go into details – I'll do that. It's not for you to break that sort of news. Just say it's an article about the hospital and that the tabloids are targeting senior consultants.'

'You need to get down here now,' she says. 'And don't be surprised if the police are here too.'

Underneath her anger, he can hear the fear too. He needs to be there.

'I'm coming.'

57

May 1998

I was happy to be back at the Treliske again today, after being given the previous two days off. Stuck at home, I did try to study my lecture notes on the functional architecture of the body, but it was difficult to concentrate. Ditto with my textbooks on histology and homeostasis. I nearly went out for a sail in Dad's old National 12 dinghy, which we still keep at the sailing club in Marazion, but Mum was hovering like a nagging conscience downstairs, so I stayed at my desk. I couldn't shake off the image of Louis in his blue-lit hospital room, the sight of his body arcing with electricity. What happened to him on the cliffs beneath the Minack? Did he really try to take his own life? It seems so unlike Louis. His brother Gabe is meant to be the one with depression.

At least the hospital now knew who he was. And I consider my identification of him as a test of sorts, likewise when he went into cardiac arrest again and I called for help. It was a chance for me to reset my moral compass after the Lecter affair. Some days my conscience is clear. On others, I visualise myself pushing Lecter out of the open window, terror in his eyes.

I arrived early for my shift at the hospital this morning

– Doctor Pender had arranged for me to spend some time in Paediatrics – so I decided to head up to the Trelawny Wing on the second floor, to see if Louis had regained consciousness. I wasn't sure what I was going to say, but I wanted to have a moment with him when the tables were turned. To remind him that we are all occasionally vulnerable, our lives resting in the hands of others, as had been the case the other night.

It was the same young woman on duty, the one who was expecting a baby.

'How's he doing?' I asked. 'That patient with hypothermia who was brought in the other night?'

'He's gone,' she said.

'Gone? But—'

'Don't ask. It's all been kicking off around here. We've had security and everyone involved. He just got up first thing and walked out.'

'But that's impossible. He was so unwell.'

For a second, I imagined Louis walking down the corridor, trailing tubes and electrodes behind him like flailing entrails.

'Tell me about it,' the nurse said. 'We tried to stop him, but he discharged himself – against medical advice, of course. At least he signed the forms. He was beginning to get on my tits. Tried to light up in his room.'

'Can I see it?' I asked. 'His room?'

She gave me a curious look. 'I think it's still being cleaned,' she said. 'But sure.'

I walked down the corridor and popped my head into the room. I don't know why. Maybe I just needed to see the empty bed to believe that Louis had really gone. It seemed so unlikely. Sure enough, the room was deserted, a bucket and mop propped up in one corner. I went over to the bed, looked at the bedside cupboard, and pulled on a half-open drawer. Inside was a copy of the Bible, face down.

'Was he like this at uni, then?' the nurse asked from the doorway.

I snapped the drawer shut and turned around. 'I didn't really know him,' I replied.

'He creeped me out, to be honest,' she said.

Downstairs in the Paediatrics Ward I was greeted by Doctor Pender, who promptly informed me that Mum had just called and wanted me to ring her back. 'You can use the office phone,' he said.

'Everything alright?' I asked when Mum picked up after one ring. She must have been waiting by the phone.

'Your tutor called,' Mum said. 'A Professor Beale.' I knew from her upbeat tone of voice that it was good news. 'I'm afraid I was a bit nosy,' she continued. 'He sounded like such a nice man. They want you to return to college and resume your studies immediately.'

58

Adam pulls up on his bike and looks down on Tania's parents' house. The fast train got him as far as Newbury, from where he's completed the journey by road, taking quiet back lanes via Inkpen and Shalbourne. The scene below him now is one of bucolic tranquillity. Colourful narrowboats animate the landscape. A column of poplars march across the water meadow, their silver leaves shimmering in the evening sunshine. Children's laughter carries up through the folds of the valley from the village playground. And above it all, a clear sky, cross-hatched with fading contrails. For a few moments, Adam enjoys the scene, inhaling its simple beauty. The dark web feels a million miles away from this peaceful corner of England, Ji's theories of red rooms and bitcoin bids seemingly more fanciful by the second.

A pheasant, startled by something, rises up into the evening sky, breaking Adam's reverie. He texts Tania on her burner phone, asks her to walk away from the house and head into the back garden. It takes a few minutes and then he sees her tiny figure on the lawn. She's out of sight of the cameras at the front of the property, and the ones inside.

'You OK?' he asks when Tania picks up.

'Where are you?' She looks around her. 'You sound weirdly close.'

'I am,' he says, checking the sky for drones. 'Up on the hill behind you. To the left. I'm about to come down. I could meet you in the back garden – away from the cameras?'

She glances up in his direction and he steps out from under the trees, waves at her. She waves back. He steps back into the shadows again.

'That might not be such a good idea. Dad's furious,' Tania says. 'I tried ringing you.'

'Furious? With me? You didn't tell him?' Adam was preparing himself on the train to tell his father-in-law about the sexting allegations. Crispin is steeped in the medical world, fourth generation. He will take the sex allegations badly, see them as a stain on the family profession, par for the course for a son-in-law who attended the sort of parties at university where students took drugs and died.

'One of his old colleagues beat me to it,' Tania says. 'He'd heard on the grapevine that the papers were running a story about you tomorrow and rang Dad. To warn him.'

And no doubt confirm what Crispin has always suspected about his first-gen medic son-in-law. Adam shakes his head in despair. Relations with Crispin are better than they used to be, but there's always been an underlying tension. Crispin might be retired, but he's still well connected, lunches with other retired surgeons, sits on boards, keeps his stethoscope to the ground. The medical establishment will close ranks and spit him out.

'Let me talk to him,' Adam says. 'This is my problem, not yours. I'll come down now. He should have heard it from me first anyway.'

'It's really best if you don't see him, Adam. Not at the moment. Trust me. I've tried talking to him, told him you're innocent, that your phone was hacked, but he's not listening. Freddie's in tears.' She sniffs. 'And this is *our* problem.'

Adam closes his eyes, grateful for her support. It can't be easy having a father who disapproves of her choice of husband, but she's always been loyal to Adam. Tania's relationship with her mother is much closer. Adam gets on well with her as well.

'The police have been here too,' Tania says.

'You rang them?'

'I had to, Adam.'

'What did they say? What did you tell them?'

'What I told Mum and Dad. That a woman broke into their house and stole Freddie's Ferrari.'

'And what did the police say?'

'That if it had been a real Ferrari, they might be more interested.'

Adam shakes his head. She shouldn't have called them. 'Did you tell them who Clio is?'

'I explained that she'd also tried to take our son from the park. And that she's an old flame of yours from university.'

Oh God. That would have made them see Tania's concerns as jealousy, as her suspecting that her husband was having a fling with an old flame. 'Did you mention the photo she sent?'

'It was humiliating enough as it was, Adam. They were as good as laughing at me, said I was wasting police time.'

'I'm sorry.' At least she didn't mention his pact with Louis. They wouldn't have believed her anyway.

'And it just confirmed Dad's worst fears about you,' Tania adds.

'Thanks for that.' In truth, Crispin couldn't think much less of him.

'Where will you go now?' she asks.

Adam scans the surrounding woodland, tears welling. Crispin has a sulphurous temper on him. Poor Freddie. He hates it when he hears people shouting. Adam has no desire to give Louis the satisfaction of watching their family fall apart, fracture along ancient fault lines of class and petty snobbism.

'I'll stay up here, in the woods. I brought a sleeping bag, just in case.'

'Don't be stupid, Adam. Why not go to a pub or something? Until Dad's cooled down.'

'I'd rather be close to you and the kids.' He doesn't say that he needs to keep an eye on the house, in case Clio returns.

Adam looks again at the fields, the trees, the sky. A pair of red kites swoop and soar, adjusting their tails like ailerons as they cry out to each other. In the far distance a military helicopter. At least there are no drones.

'Maybe you could come up here?' he says. 'It's a beautiful evening. Bring Freddie and Tilly? It would be good to see them. To see you.'

'Have you got Freddie's Ferrari?' she asks, ignoring his question.

'In my bag.'

'Thank God for that.'

'He's still upset?'

'Beside himself.' She sighs. 'I can't bring him, Adam. The questions will never stop. He'll want to know why his father has turned into Bear Grylls and now lives in the woods.'

59

Adam stands in the gloaming, watching the sun slip below the Wiltshire skyline as he hugs himself for warmth. How has his life come to this? He should have been at the hospital today, helping south London's children and teenagers. And he should be with his family now, enjoying dinner with his own children, playing Scalextric with Freddie, reading him a story, rocking Tilly to sleep (some chance), making love to Tania (more of a chance: sleeping in her old bedroom always seems to do it for them, a reminder of their corridor-creeping days). But it hasn't worked out like that. Instead, he's preparing to spend a cold May night on a hillside. And he's about to be shamed in the tabloid press for inappropriate sexual behaviour at work. He's not sure if it could get much worse.

He turns on his burner phone to check for messages. Tania's been unable to get away from the house and come up to see him. Tilly has given her hell all evening. And Freddie's still inconsolable about the car, which is upsetting, given it's in Adam's rucksack. He'll try to drop it down later, after dark, give it to Tania. There's one message: a voicemail from Ji. Adam stares at his phone, paralysed by a sudden sense of foreboding. For some reason, he knows it's going to be bad, a point of no return. What would happen if he just deletes the message? Might this nightmare end and everything go back to normal? Glancing around, he presses play and listens.

'Call me as soon as you get this message,' Ji says. 'It's urgent.'

Adam stares at the phone. He doesn't like the tone of Ji's voice. Taking a deep breath, he rings back his old friend.

'It's me,' he says.

'Where are you?' Ji asks, his voice almost unrecognisable with worry.

'Is it safe to talk?'

'This is your burner phone, right? We should be OK for a while.'

'I'm out of sight on a hillside overlooking Tania's parents' house in Wiltshire. Have you found anything?'

'You need to be very careful, Adam. Stay away from everyone, all cameras, any devices that can be hacked. I mean it.'

Adam's mouth dries. 'You're scaring me, Ji. Please, just tell me what's happened.'

'My team... we've found a site on the dark web that appears to be live-streaming your life. I'm sorry.'

'Shit.' Adam involuntarily looks around him again, checking the sky, the woodland. It's far worse than he imagined. Far worse.

'It appears to be a play-to-earn blockchain game, with real-time bidding,' Ji continues.

'For what?' Adam can barely bring himself to ask.

'Where's Tania?' Ji says, ignoring the question.

'At her parents'.' Why won't Ji tell him what people are bidding for?

'She needs to turn off the baby monitor,' Ji says. 'The audience is currently watching your two children asleep.'

Adam's stomach twists so violently, he thinks he's going to be sick. He can just about cope with the thought of himself as a target, but not his family. Not Freddie and Tilly.

'What the—'

'Send her a text, Adam. Right now.'

'OK.'

Fingers shaking, Adam manages to send Tania a message.

Call me from the garden. Urgent.

'What the hell's going on here, Ji?' he asks. 'I thought you said if I went dark, everything would be OK.'

'The audience can't see *you*, so they've switched to filming your family, to keep viewers interested and to draw you back in front of the cameras, centre stage. It's not just the baby monitor. Tania needs to turn off everything in that house, Adam. If Louis is using Shodan, he will find and access any domestic device that's connected to the internet. Everything must be disconnected – home-security software, computers, TVs, radios, smart thermostats. But she needs to turn them off subtly, not let on that we know they're watching. It's our only advantage.'

'Oh, Christ,' Adam says. 'Tania's dad loves his gadgets.'

'And if anyone sees or hears the drone again,' Ji continues, 'they must stay indoors, keep away from the windows. We need to starve your audience of content. Bore them so rigid they'd prefer to watch paint dry. It's the only way this game is going to stop.'

Adam paces up and down between the trees, glancing over

to the house as he waits for Tania to call. He feels so helpless up there on the hillside. The thought of people on the dark web watching his children as they sleep is too painful to contemplate. He should contact the police again, the cyber-crime unit, show them the site on the dark web that's live-streaming his life, but they won't be interested. Not after Tania's already been told off for wasting police time. As for the sexting allegation, it's still a matter for the General Medical Council. At best, the police might ask why someone would want to film Adam and his family, question whether they are in real and imminent danger, but all he'd be able to tell them is what Tania's already said. If they were to ask him about a possible motive, would he reveal his strange pact with Louis twenty-four years earlier? He would not. He can't say anything to anyone. The police would dismiss the deal – his soul in exchange for twenty-four years of his life – as a pretentious student prank, and Louis would release the film of him pushing Lecter to his death.

He turns in despair to look down at the house, running his hands through his hair. Only he can sort this problem. Dusk is falling, but he spots the reassuring figure of his wife, walking away from the back of the house.

'Everything OK?' she asks, when she calls on her burner phone. 'Sorry, I haven't been able to come up yet. Freddie's been—'

'You need to turn off the baby monitor,' Adam says, interrupting her, shocked by the alarm in his own voice.

'What? Why?'

Adam takes a deep breath. Tania has stopped in her tracks. He should be down there to comfort her.

'Adam? Tell me what's happening.'

Adam's instinct is to shield Tania from the news, but she needs to be aware of the very real danger they're now all in. So he tries to explain what Ji has just told him, that his life is being live-streamed on the dark web as a form of depraved entertainment. It sounds even more unreal saying it out aloud. When he's finished – he didn't mention red rooms, or that people were currently bidding for bad things to happen to them – Tania stays quiet for a while.

'How do we stop the game?' she says.

'By turning everything off in the house that's connected to the internet. Starting with the baby monitor.'

The monitor was given to them by Crispin after Tilly was born, to try and give his daughter a break, some peace of mind. It's state of the art, with a microphone and camera, allowing parents to see and listen to their child from another room. From another house, if necessary, as it uses the internet. Which means it's hackable.

'Are they really watching the kids?' she asks.

Adam can hardly bring himself to reply. 'I think so, yes.'

'Adam, I'm scared.'

'It's OK. I'm coming down now. I'll meet you at the back of the lawn. But first you need to—'

'I spoke to Mum,' she says. 'After what you said earlier about your fear of being filmed.'

At last his wife is onside and has switched to hyper-efficiency mode. It's her way of coping in a crisis.

'She's already turned off the security cameras. Mum's never liked them. I didn't think about the baby monitor. I'm so sorry. Freddie was tired and Tilly fell asleep after a feed, so I put them to bed. I know it's early but...'

'It's OK, it's not your fault.' Adam's mind is whirring as

fast as Tania is talking. They are both on edge. 'You've done well. You need to trip the main fuse in the house first. It's in a cupboard by the front door. Then turn off the monitor in the kids' room and switch everything on again at the mains. They mustn't suspect that we know they're watching us.'

'OK,' she says.

It's good to be talking practicalities. It makes Adam sound calmer. Tania too.

'Dad might get to the fuse box before me,' she continues. 'He's a bit obsessed with electricity. Watches their energy consumption on an app.'

'Do what you can,' Adam says. Christ, is there a piece of home technology that Crispin doesn't have? 'Just say the baby monitor was playing up earlier and you think that's what might have tripped the main circuit. And see if you can get your mum to turn off the Wi-Fi. There might be other devices connected to it. I'll see you in ten minutes. Everything's going to be OK, Tania. We have to deprive these people of what they want. I've got to go. Ji's on the other line.'

Adam hangs up and connects to Ji as he makes his way down across the fields towards the house, stumbling as he runs. He's left his rucksack hidden in the woods, but he's carrying the box with Freddie's car in it.

'Where are you?' Ji asks.

'Heading down to Tania's parents' house.'

He's out of breath, finding it hard to speak. It must be the adrenaline. He thought he was relatively fit, but he's only jogged five hundred yards and he's already knackered. The house ahead is illuminated in the twilight, floodlit front and back. Too well illuminated. Adam tries not to think that it looks like a filmset as he aims for a cluster of Scots pines at the far end of the lawn. It *is* a filmset. Tania has gone back inside, but she'll meet him there once she's turned off the monitor.

'Be careful,' Ji says. 'I'm looking at the screen now and they've got multiple cameras, as I feared, not just the baby monitor.'

'How's that even possible?' Adam asks. 'Tania's about to disconnect the monitor. Her mum's already turned off the security cameras, indoors and out. Tania's trying to shut down the Wi-Fi too.'

'Does anyone have smartphones?'

'Tania's using a burner I gave her – it's not a smartphone. But her parents both have iPhones.'

'The iPhones have been hacked – get them turned them off.'

By Pegasus – or a rival. Shit. What if Louis is using Ji's spyware? What if it was Ji who personally sold it to him? Adam dismisses the thought as quickly as it arrived. Ji's an old friend, loyal to the core.

'One's providing a reasonable audio feed, the other must be in the kitchen,' Ji continues. 'It's not a great picture from the camera, but it's live. Figures moving in and out of shot. Voyeuristic. That's all these people care about. No live stream, no bids.'

'Is anyone actually bidding?' Adam asks, shocked by the mere thought of it.

He remembers what Ji said about the other game he'd come across in Warsaw, the options on offer to destroy an innocent man's life. How much would someone actually pay to arrange for an arson attack on his home? The kidnapping of his child? A near-fatal car crash?

'I'm coming down to join you,' Ji says.

'Is that a yes, then? Someone's bidding?' Adam asks, trying to ignore what Ji's just said, that things are so serious he's planning to drive from London.

'They're bidding now, but no one's reached the reserve yet.'

The reserve? 'On what, Ji? For Christ's sake, you've got to tell me.'

It's a while before Ji answers. 'On your soul, Adam,' he says. 'The game ends tonight.'

60

Adam closes his eyes, trying not to dwell on what Ji's just told him, the urgency in his friend's voice, the hatred Adam feels right now for Louis. Because of him and their foolish deal, his obsession with Clio, the student play he once performed in when he should have been studying, his life is due to end tonight.

Ah, Faustus,
Now hast thou but one bare hour to live,
And then thou must be damn'd perpetually!

'You must keep away from the house,' Ji continues, 'however much you want to protect them. Nothing can happen to you – to your family – if they can't see anything. These people bid to watch. Watch to bid. That's how it works. Now please tell me where you are and I will come to join you.'

Adam gives him his location, thinking again about the deadline.

'My driver will bring me down,' Ji says, hanging up.

Seconds later, the house ahead plunges into darkness. Tania's tripped the mains. Adam sighs with relief. It's ironic, but the property seems so much safer in the dark, without the lights. Without the security cameras. Unplugged. His family seem safer too. No one can see Freddie and Tilly asleep any more. He stands still, breathing in the night air. It's a big, clear sky, spray-painted with stars. After a minute, the lights come on again as Tania appears outside the back door. She looks around and heads across the lawn towards him.

They hug in silence in the shadow of the pine trees, holding each other tightly.

'I've turned the monitor off,' Tania says. 'And Mum will switch off the Wi-Fi when they go to bed. She's been wanting to do that for years, thinks it fries their brains while they're asleep. They just had an argument about it.' She looks hopeful. 'That's good, right? If Louis is listening, he'll put the Wi-Fi going off down to a domestic.' Her voice drops. 'Were they really watching our babies?'

'I think so,' Adam says. 'I'm so sorry. I've got the car for Freddie.'

He pulls back and gives her the box.

'He'll be so happy.' Tania wipes away a tear. 'I know it's not right, a child being fixated on one thing, and maybe I should be tougher on him, but he just loves this stupid bloody car.'

'It's OK. And hey, at least it's a Ferrari. It could have been worse. A Trabant or something.'

Tania humours him with a smile, which fades quickly when a twig snaps in the woods behind them.

'Just a deer,' Adam says, catching sight of a muntjac snuffling for food. 'Ji's on his way down from London to help – he's managed to get onto the site where they're showing the live stream.'

'I can't believe it,' she says, shaking her head. 'It's so

horrible. But if the monitor's off, can't you come into the house now?'

'Your parents' smartphones are still on. One's transmitting audio, the other video. We need them turned off.'

'Mum's will be easy. She hardly uses it.' Adam hopes that's the one in the kitchen, transmitting video. 'I'll do Dad's when they go to bed. He lives on his.'

'Do it subtly. Remember, they can't suspect we know they're watching us.'

'Then you can come in? I don't want to be left on my own, Adam. I'm sleeping in the children's bedroom tonight.'

'That sounds good. And Ji's here to help. He knows about this world. I'll go back up, see what he says, and come down again when I can, I promise. Leave your burner phone on, and put the key by the back door, under the usual pot, in case you're asleep. And can we turn off those outdoor security lights?'

He glances in the direction of the house, which is still illuminating the darkening sky.

'I'll try to switch them to motion only,' she says, 'but Dad might notice.'

'Ji's bringing his laptop, so we can check that we've starved these people of their viewing. It's going to be OK, I promise. We'll be watching the house from up there.'

Tania shakes her head again in disbelief. 'What about the press?' she asks. 'Is the story running tomorrow? Are we going to be hounded by journalists too?'

'I've denied it,' Adam says. 'I'm not sure what else I can do.'

'You could have hired a lawyer, threatened them with legal action. Like a big person.'

She's right. Her father would have fought fire with fire,

issued writs in all directions if he'd been accused of sending inappropriate texts. Maybe it's a legacy of Adam's different background. His life as a successful London doctor, happily married with two children, has always seemed a bonus for the boy from Newlyn, who, like Faustus, is *of parents base of stock.*

'Actually, I think Dad believes you,' Tania says, opening the box to look at Freddie's car. 'Mum told me tonight that something similar once happened to him, soon after they got married. A female colleague made up all these bullying allegations about him. Sexism, sexual harassment, you name it. Went to the papers with her story.'

'What happened?' Adam watches as Tania puts the Ferrari carefully back in its box.

'Dad hired a lawyer, hit back hard, and the paper pulled the story. That was the end of it. Apart from the fact that he now hates all journalists.'

It wouldn't surprise Adam if Crispin had been a sexual bully at work. There were very few women in most surgical disciplines when he was practising, and it's not that much better now. There's still a lot of prejudice.

'I guess the only difference is that he hadn't made a stupid deal at university with a man intent on destroying his life,' he says. 'I'm happy to talk to your dad, but I can't tell him why all this is really happening.'

'I understand that,' Tania says. 'At least I think I do. I just want this all to end, Adam. I better get back. They'll be wondering where I've gone.'

'He knows not to answer the door, though – your dad – if journalists come knocking tomorrow?'

'I've tried to tell him, but he's—'

'Wait, did you hear that?' Adam asks, holding up a hand.

They both stand still and listen. It's the telltale whine of a small drone somewhere high above them. Tania looks at him with unvarnished fear in her eyes.

'Quick, you need to get back inside,' Adam says. 'Make sure all the curtains are drawn. Turn their phones off as soon as you can. And those lights. I'll call you once Ji's arrived.'

He kisses her and they both head off in opposite directions.

61

Cambridgeshire in the winter is a bleak place, cold, north-easterly winds blowing in uninterrupted from Russia. And Huntingdon's town hall is no exception. It's where I've spent the last two days, attending the coroner's inquest into Lecter's death. Out of respect, I'll call him by his real name here: Brandon.

There was a pre-inquest review hearing back in June, at the end of the Easter term, where the coroner outlined the evidence that would be considered, and we already knew that the police had arrested and charged a man with the possession and supply of a controlled drug. Plus the toxicology report following the post mortem had confirmed the presence of LSD and Ecstasy in Brandon's body. So there was a feeling that the inquest would be a formality in terms of its findings but an important part of the healing process for Brandon's friends and family, who had flown over from America. It was a chance for them to better understand the circumstances of their son's tragic death in Britain.

I was one of the first to give evidence in person and more nervous than I've been in my life. There was a jury, at the request of the senior coroner, a lot of press, and various interested parties, mainly Brandon's family, who were to be allowed to put questions to the witnesses, under the guidance of the coroner. Ji came along to give me moral support and we listened, spellbound, as Louis' witness statement was read out. The coroner had granted Louis an exemption not to appear, based on chronic ill health – I hadn't seen or heard from him since our paths crossed in the Treliske, and he wasn't expected to resume his PhD at Cambridge. Louis kept to the agreed script – no mention of his own drugs stash in the bathroom drawer or of the footage he'd filmed in the bathroom – but every sentence was a challenge to my conscience. Had I given Brandon the Ecstasy pill that killed him? Had I pushed him out of the window, as Louis seemed sure I had?

And then it was Clio's turn. I hadn't seen her in the town hall and I held my breath, eyes fixed on the witness box, waiting for her to appear, but her statement was also read out. She was now apparently living in France with her mother, having completed her degree in the summer, and the coroner had granted her an exemption too. Did she really kill her own father or was Louis lying about that too? I never had the chance to ask her before she left Cambridge, before she gave me the feather on the doorstep of her room, before she kissed me, told me to be careful.

Her statement described how Brandon had been pestering her in an increasingly aggressive manner throughout the evening of the party and thanked me by name for my intervention. Maybe it was because she knew his family would hear it, but she put Brandon's behaviour that night solely down to the drugs he'd taken, adding that he was normally a gent.

And then it was my go, my legs turning to jelly as I walked up to the witness box. Ji caught my eye and gave me a nod of reassurance as I was asked to swear an oath on the Holy Bible. I was given the choice of a secular affirmation, but for some reason I sought comfort in my lapsed Christian faith.

'I swear by Almighty God that the evidence I shall give shall be the truth, the whole truth and nothing but the truth,' I said, worried that my faltering voice would betray me.

I read out my witness statement, which I'd spent weeks preparing, and the coroner asked me various questions. My guiding principle, for what it's worth, was not to tell any overt lies in anything that I wrote or said. Whether that was 'the whole truth' was not something I wished to dwell on. Unless the coroner specifically asked, it didn't seem necessary, even under oath, for me to tell him about the secret film footage. Louis had made no mention of it and he was the only other person who knew of its existence.

It was all going well until the coroner asked his final question.

'As we've heard today, you were the last person to see him alive, Mr Pound. Would you say that Brandon was under the influence of hallucinogenic drugs?'

'Yes, I would,' I said, happy to steer the conversation into medical waters. 'He was totally gone. You could see it in his eyes. Pupils dilated. Evidence of nystagmus too – rapid involuntary movements of the eyeballs.'

'You're a medical student?'

'Yes, sir. Second year.'

'So you know of what you speak.' He smiled. 'As you are aware, we're not here to apportion blame for Brandon's tragic death. I just wish to be clear on this important point. Because of his incapacitated state, you thought it was the safest course of action, as a medical student, to take him upstairs and lock him in the bathroom for a while.'

'I did, yes. I decided it was best for everyone at the party. For him and for Clio, the student he was harassing. As I said in my statement, he was sitting on the floor when I left him, propped up against the wall, drifting in and out of consciousness.' I recalled the fear in his eyes in the film footage. 'I thought it was a safe place to leave him to recover. I would have checked on him again in a few minutes, but he...'

My voice faltered.

'Thank you, Mr Pound.' The coroner nodded. 'Is there anything else you wish to add that might be of interest or significance to the jury?'

I didn't wish to add anything. Instead, I looked across at the jury and then glanced to the back of the hall, where Ji was sitting. But it wasn't Ji I saw, it was Clio. Was it really her? She was standing by the door, a scarf wrapped around her head that partially obscured her face.

'Mr Pound?'

I turned from Clio to the coroner. Why was she there?

'Nothing else to add, sir.'

And, mercifully, no interested parties or jury members wanted to ask me any questions either. After I'd sat down, I was desperate to find Clio and talk to her – I missed her terribly over the summer in Cornwall – but I also wanted to hear the other witness statements from people who'd been at the party, check that nothing would contradict the clear narrative that was emerging. I kept swivelling round to look for Clio, but I couldn't see her anywhere. I started to doubt that she'd ever been in the hall. Why would she risk the coroner's ire if she'd said that she couldn't travel from France?

Over the next hour, I relived the night of the party in more detail than I wanted to, but none of the other witnesses said anything to challenge my own account. The toxicologist who'd confirmed the presence of Ecstasy and LSD in Brandon's body said that the levels of MDMA and the nature of the adulterants found in the Ecstasy sample matched the batch seized from the local dealer who'd been arrested. She also said that it was well known that the hallucinogenic properties of LSD sometimes convinced people that they could fly. 'In extreme cases, it can distort their perception of reality to the point where they make misjudgements about their personal safety,' she said. 'It can also induce profound suicidal ideation. Jumping off buildings, out of windows – it's rare but not uncommon.'

'That went well,' Ji said when the inquest broke for lunch.

'Did you see her?' I asked, frantically looking for Clio.

'You OK?' Ji said as I hurried outside and paced around, searching for her.

I never found Clio. This afternoon, the coroner returned a verdict of drug-related misadventure. I'm in the clear.

At least for twenty-four years I am.

62

Adam doesn't want to dwell on how little time it's taken for Ji to arrive from London. Not because his driver must have pushed 100 mph all the way, but because it means that this whole live-streaming business is serious. Ji's not normally a man in a hurry.

Ji's driver rings Adam when they are fifteen minutes away and asks for directions. Adam is keen not to attract any attention to his hiding place in the woods, so he tells the driver to meet just up from what used to be a pub in the nearby hamlet. It's a ten-minute walk from there back to the woods.

Adam reaches the rendezvous point early and climbs over the wooden fence, waiting in the corner of a field. A flock of sheep huddle under a tree nearby, eyeing him suspiciously. There's no traffic on the lane, but he's not taking any chances. Five minutes later, at 9 p.m., a black Mercedes E-Class sweeps up the hill and stops. The driver opens the rear door and Ji steps out. At least, Adam assumes it's Ji. He wasn't quite sure how Ji, urban to the core, would dress for a cold night out on a hillside in Wiltshire – in recent years, he's only ever seen him in a suit – but he wasn't expecting full combat fatigues, a black balaclava and camouflage baseball cap. He looks like a character from one of his company's third-person shooter games, except that he's got a laptop bag slung over one shoulder, rather than a gun, and a small rucksack on his back.

'Thank you for coming, Ji,' Adam says, climbing over the fence to shake his hand. He glances again at his friend's attire. 'I feel... a little underdressed.'

Ji ignores him and barks something in Mandarin to his driver. The car drives off.

'We haven't got long,' Ji says, scanning the area. 'Where can we see the house?'

Ten minutes later, they are hunkered down on the edge of the woods, looking across to Tania's parents' property in the darkness below. The moon has only just risen, casting a faint light across the landscape. Tania has successfully managed to turn off the house's outdoor security lights and it's hard to make out its shape.

Ji isn't in the mood for small talk and Adam no longer finds his friend's balaclava and fatigues funny. They're chilling, another reminder of how dangerous Ji must think things have become. He hardly exchanged a word on the walk up there, except to say that he'd watched the live streaming in the car, until the baby monitor went off. Tania's mum's iPhone has dropped too, which just leaves an audio feed from her dad's phone. It sounds like good news to Adam, but Ji isn't celebrating.

'There's nothing else they could hack into?' Adam asks, staring across at the house again. 'The Wi-Fi will drop when they go to bed.'

Ji pulls out his laptop. 'It depends,' he says. 'Your father-in-law sounds like a man of many gadgets.'

'But there are no images right now?' Adam asks hopefully, trying to see what Ji is looking at on his laptop.

'Not moving ones. Just a holding shot of you with a woman in her panties.'

Ji angles the laptop for Adam to see. The screen has been dimmed to avoid attracting attention in the dark, but there's Clio, in his kitchen, in all her glory.

'Oh, God,' Adam says, turning away, trying not to dwell on the memory. 'We heard a drone earlier, about an hour ago,' he adds, keen to change the subject.

'That could be an issue,' Ji says, tapping at the keyboard. 'The bidding tailed off when the baby-monitor feed went down, but it looks like there's more activity now.'

Adam leans over again and Ji stops typing, his fingers hovering over the keyboard.

'What is it?' Adam asks, looking from Ji to the computer screen and back again.

'The reserve's just been met,' Ji says, closing the laptop.

Adam can feel his skin prickle, the hairs on his neck begin to rise, like Faustus when the clock struck midnight.

O, it strikes, it strikes! Now, body, turn to air,
Or Lucifer will bear thee quick to hell.

And yet it still doesn't feel real, as if all this is happening to someone else, in a parallel universe.

'What exactly does that mean?' he asks, suddenly angry. 'I'm here on a hillside with you. Tania's safe with the kids and her parents down there, in relative darkness. Nobody's watching any more. And I'm really struggling to understand how that world' – he points to the laptop – 'that fucked-up

314

online world, is related to any of this.' He gestures at the landscape around them.

'Want a drink?' Ji asks, pulling out a silver hip flask. 'Talisker?'

'Do I need it?' Is it a final drink, like a last meal on death row?

Ji hands him the flask. 'According to my technical team, this site is well run,' he says, tapping the closed laptop. 'It has a lot of resources behind it, not your ordinary bunch of cyber terrorists. Which is why I'm here tonight, when I'm meant to be at *The Marriage of Figaro* with Phang Phang. I'm really worried, Adam. Worried for you. For your family.'

Adam takes a swig, the whisky warming the back of his throat. 'So what do we do?'

'Have you read *The Art of War* by Sun Tzu?'

Adam shakes his head, takes another slug of whisky and hands the flask back to Ji.

'They teach it at Sandhurst,' Ji says. 'Tzu was a great Chinese military tactician. Born in 544, seven years after Confucius. He said many wise words, including these: "Appear strong when you are weak, weak when you are strong."'

'I don't feel very strong right now,' Adam says.

'All the more reason to appear so.'

Like a big person, as Tania would say.

Ji pulls his rucksack onto his lap. 'I brought us this,' he says, lifting out an old Sony Handycam. 'Nightshot – infrared vision.'

'The one that sees through clothes,' Adam says, remembering that Louis used an identical Handycam at uni.

For the second time today, small seeds of doubt have taken root in his paranoid mind. First, the discovery that Louis might be using spyware that's similar to Ji's. And now the Handycam, the same model that Louis used to film women at that fateful party in his house.

'I purchased it recently on eBay,' Ji says.

'For looking at women's underwear?'

Adam remembers now how excited the young student Ji had been when he came across the camera's nightshot facility on rotten.com. There's nothing suspicious about Louis having had one too. He's just being paranoid.

'What is this?' Ji says, grinning for the first time this evening. 'You take me for some kind of pervert?'

Adam did once, when Ji was addicted to rotten.com. He's changed a lot since uni. They both have.

'As it happens, my team is creating a retro remake of a 1990s game,' Ji continues. 'I wanted to remind myself of the technology at the time.'

'I'll believe you,' Adam says, watching as Ji turns on the camera and looks down at the house.

The half moon has passed behind a cloud, throwing the valley into darkness. What seems like a second later, the property's outdoor security lights come on.

'What's happening?' he asks.

Ji doesn't answer. Crispin must have opened the curtains, noticed the lights were off. Or someone's outside and has triggered them.

'What is it, Ji?'

'Is that your father-in-law?' he asks. 'With a shotgun?'

A shotgun? Is he looking for Adam?

Ji passes over the Handycam. Adam takes it, his hand beginning to shake with cold and fear.

'That's him,' he says, looking at Crispin through the

infrared lens. He's waving a shotgun in the air like a deranged farmer. 'What the hell's he doing?'

Ji flicks open the laptop and logs into the site again.

'We're back live,' Ji says. 'And your father-in-law is centre stage.'

Ji shows Adam the screen. It's an aerial shot looking down on Crispin, who is standing on the lawn and pointing a gun up towards the camera.

'There must be a drone out there.'

'Why can't we hear it?' Adam asks, checking the wind. It's coming from behind them, a gusting northerly. No wonder.

'There's no audio on the live stream, but it looks as if he's shouting. And about to shoot down the drone.'

'He's a good shot,' Adam says, remembering the one and only time Crispin took him shooting. It wasn't really Adam's thing. 'Do you?' Crispin had asked. 'Do you shoot?'

'I'm afraid they're going to love this,' Ji says. 'A real-life, third-person shooter. And videos of drones being shot down? They tend to go viral.'

The sound of a single shot echoes across the valley. Adam looks at the screen. There's a dizzying image of spiralling trees as the drone spins and falls to the ground. But the onboard camera's still operational, its lens pointing at an awkward angle from where it's crashed into the undergrowth. The house is partly in view. They both watch as Crispin walks back inside.

'Bloody hell,' Adam says. 'He's lost it.'

'Everyone's logging on,' Ji says, still looking at the screen. 'They're already showing the shooting as a replay.'

The screen is now split into two: a looped replay on one side, the live feed from the downed drone on the other.

Adam watches the flash from Crispin's gun and the spiralling footage. It's dramatic, no question. Compelling viewing. If you're into that kind of thing.

'We're in the endgame now,' Ji says, glancing at his watch. '9.30 p.m.'

'I need to ring Tania.' Adam reaches for his burner phone. 'She's waiting for me to go back down.'

'I must advise against that,' Ji says, glancing across at him.

'But I need to check that everyone's OK. Crispin has a temper on him. If he's blasting drones out of the night sky—'

Ji shakes his head again. 'I know this isn't easy, Adam, but you mustn't do anything that could let the viewers know you're here.'

Adam closes his eyes. This is all so wrong. He should be down there with his family, and yet that's exactly where they want him to be.

'We have no idea what other equipment they might have hacked in the house,' Ji adds. 'Do we know why he chose to shoot down the drone?'

'I'm guessing he thought it belonged to a prying journalist. He hates journalists.'

'He doesn't know about the live streaming?'

Adam shakes his head. 'We didn't want to worry them.'

'In that case, we must sit it out. Either they will get bored or they'll play a trump card.'

63

One hour later, at 10.30 p.m., the only shot on Ji's screen is the skewed angle of the house from the crashed drone, and the image is beginning to break up. Low battery, according to Ji. The audio from Tania's dad's iPhone has dropped too. If it wasn't for Ji's continued sense of urgency, Adam might have begun to relax a little. It's not late, but everyone seems to have gone to bed. There aren't many online viewers now either. Tania is tucked up in the children's room. Ji let him check his phone and she'd texted twice. Once to ask where he was; the second time to announce that she was going to bed. After a discussion, Ji let him text her back and explain what had happened, that the audience was dwindling, and why he was still not with them. That it's safer if he remains out on the hillside, doesn't get drawn onto the stage. She hasn't replied.

'Looks like the drone camera has finally died,' Ji says, watching the flickering laptop screen.

Adam is on the Handycam – they are taking it in turns to keep an eye on the house.

'And they've stopped showing the crash replays.' Ji glances up at the night sky, patting his arms for warmth. '"The day is for honest men, the night for thieves,"' he says.

Adam smiles. 'Confucius?'

'Euripides.'

'You still having lessons from that tutor in Shenzhen?' Adam asks. Ji's growing reservoir of sayings never ceases to surprise him.

'That was a long time ago. These days I'm the one giving the lessons.'

'Seriously?' In truth, it doesn't surprise Adam. Ji speaks better English than he does these days, drawing on an extensive vocabulary as well as a deep well of quotations, of course.

'Some of my English programmers have a lot to learn about their own language. They're very naive. Uneducated. So I send a company email every Friday, with my quote of the week. Mostly they are English ones, occasionally Chinese. Sometimes Greek. I try to avoid feelgood bromides. Last week's was from *The Art of War*, actually. "In the midst of chaos, there's always opportunity."'

Another gust of suspicion blows through his thoughts. 'They're lucky to have such a well-read boss,' Adam says. Ji is an old friend, on his side. Always has been.

'I think they see me as a father figure,' Ji says. 'We're not that old, are we? You and I, Adam?'

'Would you like to be a father?' Adam asks. If Tania were there, she'd have nudged him, stopped him from being so insensitive.

Ji smiles awkwardly. 'We've tried. No dice.'

'Sorry. I shouldn't have asked.' He regrets the question already, his earlier suspicion.

'OK, no problem,' Ji says, taking a swig from the hip flask. It's the one linguistic tic left over from his university days.

Ji checks his laptop again. 'No one's going to keep watching this stuff...'

Adam doesn't like the way Ji's voice has suddenly tailed off.

'What's up?' he asks.

The whole laptop screen is now black except for two small shards of light cutting through the darkness like tiny headlights. Is it a vehicle driving across the Wiltshire landscape? They both glance around but can't see or hear any traffic.

'I'm not sure,' Ji says. 'Looks like a new camera's just come on. Maybe another drone, flying very high.'

Instinctively, they both stare up at the night sky. Nothing. A winking plane in the distance. A passing satellite. Adam takes the laptop from Ji and lifts it up closer to get a better look.

'Careful,' Ji says, angling down the lid to shield the glowing light.

But Adam's not listening. Instead, he stares at the screen, the grainy darkness. The image is not an aerial drone shot, it's much closer to home. Human shapes have begun to form, like figures emerging in the mist, lit up dimly by the two small beams of light. Tilly in her cot and next to her Freddie in his bed. And lying across a mattress on the floor is his wife, fast asleep.

It takes a moment to work out where the beams of light are coming from, where the camera must be. And when he realises, Adam knows he only has himself to blame. His stomach contracts into a tangled knot. He feels a fool for having been played so easily. Louis – and Clio – must have put money on him bringing the Scalextric car down to Freddie.

Adam closes his eyes. He's too soft a touch, always has been as a father. Louis would have had plenty of opportunity to insert a small camera inside the car, between the time when Clio took it from the outbuildings and when she delivered it to their home in Greenwich. The technical know-how too, if he was already installing hidden cameras in showerheads when he was at uni. The Ferrari car is like a miniature Trojan horse. Adam gave it to Tania, who duly placed it by Freddie's bed, ready for when he wakes in the morning. And now live images of their sleeping children are being broadcast once again across the dark web.

64

'Come on, Tania, wake up,' Adam mutters, phone pressed to his ear as he paces backwards and forwards under the trees. 'Wake up.'

He's just explained to Ji where the live images are coming from, how the camera got there, that this particular Scalextric model, the Ferrari 412P, has working front and back lights. It's the feature that Freddie likes most about the car, particularly when his grandpa turns off the garage lights and plunges the track into darkness.

'Once Tania's asleep, there's no waking her,' he continues, smacking his hand against the trunk of a tree. 'It's on silent and her parents' phones are both switched off. I'm going down there, to take away the car.'

'That's exactly what they want you to do,' Ji says, looking up at him from where he's sitting on the ground. He's still glued to his laptop. 'To protect your family.'

'Too bad. They know we're watching?'

'We must assume so. Maybe they managed to listen in to you and Tania talking earlier. Intercepted your texts. I don't know. Or they became suspicious when the baby monitor was turned off.'

Adam looks across at Ji for a second. Is his friend bluffing? Did *he* tell Louis that they were watching?

'I can't just stay up here, Ji, not with those images going out live on the dark web. Not of my sleeping family. It's a violation.' Adam paces around like a wild animal, his suspicions about Ji giving way to raw anger.

'I understand,' Ji says. 'If Phang Phang were down there, I'd feel the same. If my children were there...'

A moment later, they both spot a van on the main road. The driver kills the headlights as it turns into the lane leading down to Tania's parents' house.

'That's not normal,' Adam says, looking at the van through the Handycam. 'It's still going, pulling up outside the gates.' Far enough away not to trigger the security lights.

'A new feed's come up,' Ji says. 'From the van's dashcam.'

The screen is filled with the front of the house. Who's in that van? Is it Louis? Clio? Someone else?

'I'm going down there,' Adam says again. 'Call me on the burner if anything changes.'

'The bidding's started again,' Ji says.

'What for?'

'I'm not sure yet.'

'I can't stay up here any longer, Ji. I have to go down.'

'Be careful.' Ji holds up his hand to shake. 'I will try to help from here if I can.'

Adam shakes Ji's hand and disappears down the hill, running across the field. He's got no option but to trust Ji. For once, he wishes Tilly were unable to sleep, in need of a midnight feed. But she's clearly out for the count and Tania will be too. She's so tired and an uninterrupted night is a rare event.

When he's still a good eight hundred yards from the house, Adam feels his phone begin to vibrate. Has Tania woken up?

It's Ji.

'Tell me,' Adam says, slowing to a breathless jog.

'I'm afraid it's Freddie.'

Adam's stomach lurches. 'How do you mean?'

'It's why the car camera came on. Someone's just bid for him. Reserve met.'

'Jesus.' Adam starts to run again, faster than he's ever run in his life, heart jumping out of his chest as he tries to talk to Ji. 'The van? Has it moved?'

'I can't hear you.'

Adam slows to repeat himself. 'Has the van moved?'

'Someone's just got out,' Ji says. 'Looks like—'

'Who? Who does it look like, Ji?'

'That woman in your kitchen.'

Clio. 'Tell me what she's doing.'

'Running around to the outbuildings. Where Tania and the kids are sleeping.'

Adam looks up. 'Why hasn't she triggered the security lights?'

'Easily overridden.'

'We need to wake them up. Warn them.' He starts to yell and shout as he sprints towards the house, as if it's on fire. 'Hey! Hey! Get away from there.' He tries to call out Clio's name too, but it sticks in his throat. 'I know it's you!' he bellows. 'Get away from my son. Get away from my fucking family, do you hear?'

It's difficult to run and shout and talk on the phone. 'Are you still there, Ji?' he asks, slowing, out of breath. 'What's happening now? I'm nearly at the house.'

'She's dropped out of sight. There's no camera by the door. She's in the bedroom.'

Jesus. Another burst of adrenaline. 'Hey! Hey! Tania, wake up!' he shouts. 'Tania! Anyone! Please wake up! What's happening, Ji?' he says into the phone, barely able to speak as he tries to keep running. 'I need to know what's happening to my son.'

'She's taken him. Lifted him up in his sleep. I think your daughter is awake.'

'Awake? Tilly! Please, Tilly! Make a fucking noise. Cry! Tania! Wake up!' He is still shouting at the top of his voice. 'Please start crying, Tilly. Please wake your mummy.' Words he never thought he'd say.

He's still five hundred yards from the house, tears streaming down his own face. And then in the distance he sees Clio, Freddie asleep on her shoulder as she walks quickly through the front gates.

'She's gone round the far side of the van, I can't see her,' Ji says. 'She's in a blind spot. Off camera. I think she's just put Freddie in the back.'

'Freddie! Wake up! You've got to wake up!' Adam shouts. He's nearly at the side of the house now, running across the lawn.

But he's too late. He hears the van first, and then sees it turn round and speed away down the drive, just as he reaches the gravel courtyard. He runs round to the outbuildings where Tania is sleeping. The door is open, key in the lock. Somehow Clio must have had a key. And then he checks under the flowerpot. Nothing. They were listening when he asked Tania to leave a key out. Has Louis managed to hack into his burner phone? The only person who knows his

number, other than Tania, is Ji. It must be her phone that's
been hacked.

He pushes open the door and runs down the corridor to
the children's room.

'Tania! Tania!'

Breathless, he bursts into the room.

'What is it?' Tania says, sitting up on the mattress, confused,
eyes heavy with sleep.

Tilly starts to cry from her cot. Too late.

'They've taken Freddie. Where are the keys? To our car?'

'Oh my God, oh my God,' Tania says, looking across at
Freddie's empty bed.

'It's OK. I'm going to get him back. They've just left. I need
the car keys.'

'Over there,' she says, pointing to the back of the door,
running a hand through her hair. 'In my jeans. Who took
him?'

He rummages for the keys in her jeans pocket and hovers
by the door, gesticulating at her as he speaks. 'Ring the police,
tell them that Freddie's been taken.' He can't bring himself to
tell Tania who by. 'Tell them everything. That he was driven
away in a dark blue Transit van. I'll call you with the number
plate. I'm going after him.'

He's about to leave when he stops, turns, and picks up the
red Ferrari. He runs out the door and hurls the car as far as
he can into the undergrowth as he sprints around to their car.

65

Clio could have gone two ways: to Marlborough, or down towards the Salisbury road. Adam will call Ji to find out, hopes he's been watching the dashcam, memorising the turns. Freddie will be terrified when he wakes up, if he's not done so already, and will wonder where he is and why the strange woman from the park has taken him again.

Adam jumps into the car, their old Touran, keys the ignition and wheelspins towards the gates, throwing gravel up behind him. He's never liked gravel. A second later, as he passes through the gates, headlights on full beam, he jams on the brakes, bringing the car to a juddering halt. Standing in the middle of the road in his pyjamas, a young black puppy in his arms, headlights dazzling his sleepy eyes, is Freddie.

'What are you doing here, monkey?' Adam says, getting out of the car and rushing round to him. He stopped the car just a foot from his son.

'She gave me a puppy,' Freddie says. 'The nice lady from the park. She said she would.'

Adam puts a hand to his mouth to stifle a gasp. He's not

sure if he's about to throw up or cry. Kneeling down, he hugs them both.

'He's called Louis,' Freddie says.

'No, he's not, monkey,' Adam says. 'He's not called Louis.'

'Yes, he is. The lady said his name was Louis.'

Adam bites his lip. 'Let's go and find Mummy, tell her you're OK, shall we?'

Adam scoops up Freddie and the dog, cradling them both in his big arms, and jogs round to the outbuilding, confused and frightened and relieved all at the same time.

'He's here,' he calls out. 'It's OK, he's here. Freddie's safe.'

He walks into the corridor, where Tania is on the phone, talking frantically. Her eyes widen at the sight of Freddie. He listens as she makes her excuses, apologising profusely to the police for wasting their time again, and hangs up.

'What the—'

'Don't ask.' Adam shakes his head as he passes Freddie and the puppy over to Tania. 'I have no idea what's going on either. Are your parents awake?'

'Not yet.'

Thank God. Crispin would be shooting people by now if he was up.

'And who's this little monster?' Tania turns to her son, somehow managing to sound normal.

She hugs Freddie, kisses his head, smooths his hair like he's a newborn. The puppy follows suit, licking Freddie's face.

'He's called Louis,' Freddie says.

'No, he's not,' Adam repeats, running a hand through his own hair. 'He's not bloody called Louis.'

Tania gives him a look as Freddie begins to cry.

'Yes, he is,' Freddie whimpers. 'That's what the nice lady said his name was.'

'I'm going after whoever was in that van,' Adam says, turning to leave.

'Was it Clio?' Tania asks. '"The nice lady"?' she adds through gritted teeth.

'Her and maybe someone else,' Adam says. 'Ji will know more, where the car's heading. He's still up on the hillside, watching the... the live feed. This can't go on any longer. It has to end. And I'm the only one who can make it stop.'

'Where are you going, Daddy?' Freddie asks as Adam heads for the door.

'I'll be home in a bit, monkey, I promise,' he says.

He walks back into the room and kisses Freddie. And then he kisses Tania.

'I'm so sorry,' he says. 'I need to do this.' Bring the final curtain down.

He's about to turn and leave for the second time when something catches his eye on Freddie's pillow. Walking over, he picks it up, twists it in his hand. Another card, this time the letter 'L'. And then he sees something else on the pillow.

A brown-patterned feather. Just like the one in his memory box, given to him by Clio at Cambridge. *It's from a barn owl. Symbol of protection. Owls will do anything to protect their young.*

66

Adam jumps back into the car and sets off down the drive. Clipping the mobile phone into the holder on the dashboard, he calls Ji.

'Freddie's OK,' he says, checking the rearview mirror. 'He's back with us.'

'That's not possible,' Ji says. 'He's in the van. And I thought you'd be following by now. They've got a camera on the tailgate as well as the dashcam.'

'Clio didn't take Freddie. She left him outside the gates and brought him a puppy.'

'A puppy?'

'Long story.'

'On the live feed everyone thinks that Freddie's still in the van, that he's been kidnapped. They're now bidding on what to do with him.'

'Well let the sick fucks continue to think that,' Adam says, shaking his head. Who are these people? 'For whatever reason, Clio's gone off script,' he continues. 'Freddie's fine. Safe. And I've chucked the Ferrari into the bushes. As long as they don't have any other devices in the house, we have an advantage.'

'You need to turn left at the end of the drive, and head up

to the Salisbury road, then turn right towards Burbage. Take the first left at the roundabout to Collingbourne Ducis.'

How does Ji know how to pronounce it 'doo-cis'? Even locals get it wrong. He pushes the thought away. 'Am I right to be going after her, Ji?' Adam asks. Should he have stayed back at the house, with Tania and the kids?

'It keeps Freddie safe,' Ji says. 'They would expect you to follow the van if everyone thinks your five-year-old son's in it. Several people have already asked why you aren't following him. I think they're expecting a car chase. It would explain the cameras at the back and front of the van. Every game has a good car chase.'

'This isn't a game, Ji.'

'It is for these people.'

'Where is she now?' Adam asks.

'Tidworth.'

'I'll catch her up.'

'I don't understand why she didn't take Freddie,' Ji says.

'Me neither, Ji.'

'Very unorthodox gameplay.'

'One way of putting it.'

'There's something else you should know,' Ji says.

'Go on.'

It's been reassuring to have Ji watching over him on his laptop, but Adam doesn't like the new tone of voice.

'Someone's just bid on a car crash,' Ji says.

Adam's hands tighten on the steering wheel. That's all he needs. 'Fatal?' he asks, glancing in his mirrors again.

'Life-changing injuries.' Just like the live stream of the man in Warsaw.

'Where's this game heading, Ji?'

'Hard to tell. But the risk is now too high for you to continue to follow Clio in the van.'

'I have to finish this. For my family. Are you certain there are no live images coming from the house – of Tania and the kids?'

'Nothing. They liked your father-in-law taking out the drone with a shotgun, but they've lost interest in them. You're centre stage now.'

Just where Louis wants him. At least his family is safe.

'And there's no live stream from my car?'

'Not that I can see. Just dash- and rear cams on the van. She's driving fast. High audience approval. I'm going down to be with Tania in the house.'

Adam has to trust his friend. He's got no option. Putting his foot down too, he turns onto the Fair Mile, accelerating up the old Roman road. It's a shortcut that will gain him five minutes on Clio and bring him out in Collingbourne Ducis.

It's not until Adam joins the A303, on the other side of Tidworth, that he finally catches sight of the van, half a mile in front of him, heading west. There aren't many other cars on the road and its familiar profile is briefly lit up in the darkness by a passing car. Adam knows this stretch of road well as it's the one he takes when they go to Cornwall. Where's Clio heading?

Glancing at the time – 11 p.m. – he phones Ji and asks if he's with Tania yet. He doesn't want to risk calling on her burner.

Ji passes Tania his phone.

'How are the kids?' he asks.

'They're fine. We might have to keep the puppy,' she says. 'He's adorable. Where are you?'

'Approaching Stonehenge.'

'You should turn around. Come home.'

'I can't. If I do, they'll come after me. I need to make this stop.' Or at least draw them away from his family.

'Ji's taking good care of us,' Tania says.

Adam should be reassured that Ji is with his family, but he still can't shake off an unfathomable feeling of doubt.

'He also says that's exactly what they want you to do: follow the van,' she adds.

'I know.'

'As soon as you've got the number plate, we need to ring the police again.'

'And tell them what? That someone dropped off a cute little puppy for our son in a van in the middle of the night? It's not exactly going to trigger police roadblocks and stingers.'

'Someone? It was Clio, Adam. You're always making excuses for her. She broke into my parents' house in the middle of the night and took Freddie out of his own bed – abducted him, for God's sake, while I was asleep two feet away. It was totally traumatising for Freddie, not to mention a criminal offence. I would never have forgiven myself – or her – if we hadn't found him. If we call the police, we can show them Ji's laptop, the live feed, tell them about the incident in the park, the photo she sent, tonight's attempted kidnapping.'

She's got a point. Maybe that's what needs to happen. He's trying to do too much on his own. 'OK, I'll call you when I've got the number plate. And if the police come out to the house, let Ji explain to them about the live feed. Get him to show them the site on the dark web. I don't think they'll do anything, there's not enough evidence of criminal activity, but it's worth a try.'

'Promise me you'll turn round as soon as you've got the number plate?'

Adam taps the steering wheel. 'If I do, they'll follow me back to you and realise that Freddie's not in the van. I don't think Clio's told Louis that she hasn't got him with her. I also think I'm the real prize here. Freddie's attempted abduction was a sideshow.'

'Is that what you call it – a sideshow? I've never been so scared in my life, Adam, for those few minutes he was missing.'

'Me too,' Adam says. 'But I think it was just to lure me back into the frame.'

'So why can't you step out of the frame now?'

'This will never end until I meet Louis again.'

Tania falls silent. 'Call me with the number plate as soon as you've caught up with her,' she says.

'I promise.'

'And then let the police take over. They can stop the van, talk to Clio, to Louis. They can put an end to all this.'

'OK,' Adam says. 'Call you back in a minute. I can see the van up ahead.' He doesn't add that Clio is driving like a woman possessed.

'Be careful, Adam. There are two little people here who need their daddy back.'

'I love you,' he says, welling up.

He reaches forward and ends the call, not wanting to dwell on his family, what he's put them through. He needs to think straight, keep his head clear.

Clio is pulling away from him. He puts his foot down,

checking the rearview mirror for police. There are speed cameras on the A303 and he knows where they all are, but that's the least of his problems right now.

Up ahead, a set of temporary traffic lights turns red after Clio passes them. They are still red when Adam draws up. He taps the steering wheel impatiently. Strange. The lights look more temporary than usual, flimsy foldaway units, and there's no sign of any roadworks. No sign of traffic lights on the other side of the road either. They change to green and Adam pulls away. Further down the road, Clio is already approaching the Countess Roundabout at speed. More traffic lights, but they are a permanent, familiar fixture and remain on green as she accelerates through the junction and heads on to Stonehenge. Adam does the same, driving up to the roundabout at 80 mph, worried that he'll lose Clio. He begins to slow, in case the lights change. They remain green, so he keeps going.

It's too late when he sees the red Toyota pickup to his right. There's no time to brake or to alter course. Instead, he braces himself as the pickup rams into the side of the Touran, just behind the driver's seat. Did it jump the lights? Weren't the lights showing green, his right of way? Adam sees his family in the kitchen, like a portrait painting: Tilly on Tania's lap, Freddie holding the puppy, all of them staring impassively at him. As the car begins to roll, the night air ripped apart by the sound of twisting metal, Adam's last thought is of the Ferrari, spinning in the air before it lands in the undergrowth.

67

Adam doesn't know where he is when he wakes. There's a howling wind, gusting from all directions, and waves crashing. Or is it his head throbbing with pain? He can smell the ocean, the ionised air. The sea feels close, threatening. Everywhere is pitch black. And then he realises.

He tries to remove the tight blindfold from his eyes, but his hands don't move. They are tied behind his back. Panic rises like a racing tide. A strong blast of wind, the roar of another wave. Instinctively, he turns to look at the sea, but his head is bound too.

Is he in a neck brace? Had an accident?

It's coming back now.

A roundabout. Green traffic lights. A pickup truck approaching at speed from the right. The injustice of it.

He attempts to shake a leg. Nothing. Both ankles are constricted, bound in what feels like coarse, heavy-duty tape. His torso too. He tries to shake his shoulders, arch his back, kick his feet, terrified now. Is he paralysed?

'Hello?' he shouts out, his ears pumping like pistons with blood. 'Hello?'

He doesn't expect a response, his voice lost in the din of the roiling sea, but the reply is almost instant.

'You're awake.'

A familiar voice, close but distant.

'Where am I?' Adam asks, eyes bulging with fear beneath the blindfold.

His voice works, but it could be in his head. The other voice too. What if he's still unconscious, strapped into his car seat, the paramedics trying to talk to him? It feels like he's on a chair of some sort, with a high back.

'Am I dead?' he asks, his mouth parched with fear.

Is this what death feels like? He checks his body again for pain. His lower back aches and his head and neck are on fire. It feels like there's a bandage around his forehead rather than tape, in addition to the blindfold. His chest is painful too when he breathes in, a sign of fractured ribs. Otherwise he's OK, intact. Just sitting in the middle of a raging storm.

'Dead? Not yet.'

A hint of mirth. It's Louis. Adam knows it's him, but he's in denial, doesn't want to make the connection, link the words to the person. At some subconscious level, his brain understands what that voice means, the existential threat it represents.

The date is expired. This is the time.

The inky blackness in front of his eyes is chased away by a bright light – artificial, strong enough to be visible through his blindfold.

How can he be sure that he's alive? He's conscious, aware of himself, his own thoughts, the terror that's stealing through his body. And he can feel his limbs, even flex them a little. They don't appear to be taped up in the same way as his torso, just secured at the wrists and ankles.

'Where am I?' he repeats. His voice sounds distant, detached, as if someone else is speaking the words.

'On stage. You were in the theatre when I first saw you, trying not to undress Mephistopheles with your salivating, student eyes. And now here you are, at the end of our acquaintance, treading the boards once again.'

On stage?

The blindfold is ripped from his face, leaving the bandage in place, which continues to restrict any head movement. Adam opens his eyes and flinches. In front of him, standing close, too close, is a figure in a Greek mask. It takes a second for Adam to realise that it's Louis. The mask is porcelain-white with a tragic, open mouth, through which Adam can see Louis' distinctive lips, twitching like a sphincter. His eyes blink at him out of two drooping, mournful sockets.

Adam's own frightened eyes flick from side to side, trying to take in his circumstances, assess them for danger, but they're struggling to work after being blindfolded so tightly.

Slowly, his surroundings become clearer. He is on a cliff edge at night, his back to the sea, the wind swirling around him in anger. 'Lifeboat weather', his dad used to call it. He's been bound up in silver duct tape, as he suspected. The whole cliff face seems to shudder as a huge wave – a 'walloper' – crashes behind him on the rocks far below, throwing up plumes of spray. He wishes his dad was alive, was here now to help him, wherever he is.

Then Adam realises, blinking his eyes to sharpen their focus. He's on the outdoor stage of the Minack Theatre. Behind Louis, rows of familiar seating carved out of the granite cliff rise steeply upwards, the names of plays written on the concrete seats like tombstones: *The Tempest*, 1932;

Elektra, 1960: *Doctor Faustus*, 1967. He thinks again of his dad, how he used to bring him here as a child, telling him the story of when the theatre was built by hand as he sketched the rugged coastline. He always had his sketchbook.

To Adam's right, a camera on a tripod. In front of him, a big white station clock, propped up on a front-row seat. A single gantry spotlight casts him in a pale pool of yellow from its position below the control room, a small hut overlooking the stage. And to his left, on top of a stone plinth close to the cliff edge, an open laptop, its distinctive glow lighting up a handgun beside it. The spotlight must have been what he saw earlier, when he was blindfolded, but the beam is less bright now. Sufficient to illuminate him but not so strong as to attract the attention of any boats out at sea. Adam passed this point so many times in his year on the gill-netter.

He closes his eyes, wishes he were with his mum at the Nook in Newlyn, warming himself against the wonky range – so close and yet so far. Instead, he's further down the Cornish coast, four miles from Land's End, on the very edge of Britain, overlooking the mouth of the English Channel. His dad called the Minack the eighth wonder of the world, chiselled out of the rocks in the 1930s by its founder Rowena Cade, who brought sand up from the beach far below to mix the concrete herself. Louis must have broken into the outdoor theatre complex, fired up one of the spotlights, hacked into the security cameras. Maybe they *had* been watching him last year, when he was here with his mum and Freddie.

'Where is my family?' he asks, trying to stay calm, think rationally.

Another huge wave thumps into the rocks. He remembers

it now, the zawn, a fissure in the granite far below, where the angry, protesting sea is funnelled and trapped. He wants to turn around, see how close he is to the ninety-foot drop. The theatre's vertiginous setting used to scare him as a child, add to the drama playing out on the stage.

'Freddie's here,' Louis says.

Adam breaks into a cold sweat. He tries to lash out, but the tape bites into his wrists and ankles.

'What have you done with him?' Adam asks. 'If you so much as—'

'Please, I know we're on stage, but cut the histrionics,' Louis says, dismissing Adam with a flick of his hand. 'He's fine. Clio's looking after him. Positively spoiling him, by all accounts. You know what she's like. She gave him a puppy, of all things.'

Another shard of memory glints in the darkness of Adam's mind. Clio took Freddie away in her van. Except that she didn't. She left him at his grandparents', and the puppy too. Away from the cameras. Ji had been watching the live feed and he was convinced that Clio had gone round to the back of the van with Freddie and put him inside, which means that Louis would have assumed the same. But Adam had found Freddie seconds later, hadn't he? Nearly run him over outside the gates, in a camera blind spot. Is that what really happened? He's sure it is. He held his son in his own arms, took him back to Tania.

'Where is he?' Adam asks, almost shouting to be heard above the waves.

'Up in the car park with Clio and the puppy,' Louis says.

Adam remembers the car park at the top of the cliffs, beyond the visitor centre and café.

'Waiting for his cue, apparently,' Louis says, 'like the seasoned young actor he is. Chip off the old block.'

For the first time, Adam feels a glimmer of hope. Louis definitely thinks that Clio abducted Freddie. The online audience thinks so too – the audience that he assumes is watching him now. And Louis might not think to question whether Clio actually has Freddie with her, if she has only recently arrived by van and hasn't yet come down to see him. He stops himself. Too many ifs.

'And what is his cue?' Adam asks.

'That depends on the audience.' Louis walks over to check the laptop. 'What fate they choose for him. Yours, of course, has already been decided.'

Adam closes his eyes, fearing the worst. How will this perverted performance end? He prays that his son is still with Tania and not in the back of the van in the car park.

'What is my fate?' he asks.

'I suppose it's only fair that you should know,' Louis says, walking back to Adam, his mask at once emotionless and chilling, like a demented gargoyle, forcing him to focus on Louis' words.

'Does the name Duncan MacDougall mean anything to you?' Louis asks.

'No,' Adam says, trying not to let his thoughts run off to dark places.

'He was a doctor from Massachusetts. Published a scientific study in 1907 that claimed to have measured the weight of the human soul.'

It's coming back to Adam now. He remembers Louis mentioning MacDougall once at uni, when he was filming him on his way to the Anatomy Building. Louis kept asking him where Adam thought the seat of the human soul was located. *The Mesopotamians thought it was in the liver. Descartes, the pineal gland.* It troubled him then and it troubles him even more now.

'Twenty-one grams,' Louis says. '"The weight of a stack of five nickels. The weight of a hummingbird. A chocolate bar." They made a film about it once. MacDougall's study was selective in its reporting, to say the least, but it was still an interesting experiment. He placed a tuberculosis patient, about to die in his deathbed, on a giant set of industrial beam scales. At the precise moment of death, he lost three quarters of an ounce – 21.3 grams.'

'What's all this got to do with me?' Adam asks, but he already suspects the answer.

'What's about to happen here tonight is not really my doing. It's been decided by your audience – without whom no film is complete. You know I've always believed that.' Louis nods at the camera. 'And you also can't have forgotten that in exchange for me keeping quiet about what really happened in the bathroom at that party, you agreed to me making another film that would capture your soul on celluloid. As the great Al Pacino himself once said, "The camera can film my face, but until it captures my soul, you don't have a movie." Now is the time to honour our deal. I appreciate we agreed twenty-four years, which was all very Faustian in an undergraduate sort of way, but I have moved with the times, and have no plans to drag you down to hell. It's so... sixteenth century.'

Adam can still remember how it felt to be manhandled off stage by a group of demons at the end of *Doctor Faustus*. The director had asked him if he was OK with a few bruises and Adam had happily agreed, keen to impress Clio with his commitment. *Ugly hell, gape not! Come not, Lucifer!* If only he were in a play now.

'We live in the digital age, which is why I have gone for something more contemporary,' Louis continues. 'I've decided to mint an NFT of your soul and sell it to the highest bidder. Your life seems to have caught the imagination. Perhaps it's the personal history between us, our Faustian backstory, the finality of it. People have started to bid serious money over the last few days, as they've watched your life fall apart. So I've had to take it seriously too. I don't know if you're familiar with the process, but you need a lot of bureaucratic details to mint an NFT on a blockchain.'

'You're out of your mind.'

'It's all about certifying the ownership and properties of the asset that an NFT's associated with – in this case a human soul,' he says, ignoring Adam as he walks around the stage in the shadowy windswept gloom. Only Adam is spotlit. 'I know your date of birth, your name, where you were born, your parents' names, but I don't know the weight of your soul. And this level of detail really matters on public blockchains, in the world of Web 3.0.'

'I don't know what you're talking about,' Adam says, desperately trying to remember what Ji told him about NFTs.

Louis holds up a hand like a lecturer challenged by an impatient student. 'You're sitting on a chair. And that chair is on a finely calibrated, digital platform scale.'

Adam tries in vain to move his feet, feel for the platform.

'More often used in slaughterhouses for weighing animal carcasses,' Louis continues. 'A bed really wasn't practical. Not out here in the furthest reaches of Cornwall. When you die, which you're about to do, by the way' – he glances at the clock – 'in just over fifteen minutes, from a single dum-dum bullet to the head – spoiler alert! – we'll measure your weight loss, taking into account the mass of the bullet, of course, all of which will be watched by your adoring audience, one of whom has paid a lot of money for the privilege to take your life. To own your soul.'

Louis pauses, as if he can sense the nausea rising in Adam's throat. Adam wretches, his torso straining against the duct tape. Another monstrous wave crashes out of sight, sluicing into the zawn.

'You're a popular man,' Louis continues. 'The bidding's gone sky high. NFTs are more fashionable than I thought. Not so niche, after all.'

'Am I online now?' Adam asks, glancing at the camera lens.

He spits out some bile, tries not to dwell on what he's just heard. A single shot to the head. Dum-dum bullets are designed to expand upon impact rather than pass through the body. An A & E surgeon who worked in a Cape Town hospital once told Adam all about them, the internal trauma they cause. Adam can only guess at Louis' gruesome logic: that he doesn't want to lose a few grams of brain matter that might distort the final weigh-in.

'When are any of our lives not online?' Louis says. 'Tonight, my own camera here is providing the close-up. And the CCTV up there below the control room is kindly providing a locked-off wider shot. We've been filming you for the last few months. On and off. As per our deal. But let's be honest, your life wasn't the most compelling watch – a bickering marriage, unbearable children, no social life to speak of, obsessed with your job, presumably because it was a respite from your depressed wife. Bit of a bath-time dodger too, if we're honest, preferred the fun bits of parenting at weekends rather than the diurnal slog, despite your reputation for being a hands-on dad. So I started to curate your day-to-day existence. Bring back an old flame, throw in a sexual misconduct claim at work, abduct the son and you begin to see what a man's made of, observe the real person, capture their soul. I'm afraid no one would have bid for it if I hadn't... spiced things up a little.'

Adam would do anything to have that life back now. It wasn't so bad, was it? Even the bickering was low-level sniping, fuelled by nothing more than parental tiredness. He loves Tania more than ever, the life they had together. Freddie and Tilly too. And he got back for bath time when he could, didn't he? Left work early? He knows he's trying to distract himself, desperate to not dwell on Louis' repeated references to his soul and the online bidding.

'Why is my body bound so tightly?' he asks.

'Apologies,' Louis says. 'MacDougall chose patients who were at death's door, unconscious and with little or no muscular movement. The weighing scales he used were sensitive – not as good as these, of course, but pretty accurate – and he didn't want people to thrash about, convulse, skew the readings. You're still very much of this world, which is why we've had to restrain you.' Louis comes over, his white mask close to Adam's face. 'You'll need to stay very calm. Can you do that for me?'

'What about Freddie?' Adam asks.

He can't turn away from Louis. He could spit on his mask, but he doesn't want to do anything to antagonise him, not while there's still a possibility that Freddie is here. Instead, he closes his eyes.

'Freddie? Your love for him is almost affecting – or must be, I imagine, if you like children. It was actually the audience's decision to abduct him, not mine. One of the hazards of an interactive medium. But it was Clio's idea to use a puppy. Which is uncanny. MacDougall didn't believe animals had souls, so he repeated his weight experiment with canines. Sure enough, there was no loss of weight when they died. I'm tempted to replicate the experiment with Freddie's puppy, but I'm not a monster. I love animals, despise all cruelty to our fellow creatures, particularly experiments on dogs. It's humans I have a problem with.'

'You're crazy,' Adam says.

He thinks again of Freddie. What has his precious son done in his short life to deserve this? Adam pushes the thought away, tries to hold on to what he believes to be the truth. That Clio disobeyed instructions to abduct Freddie, who is safe with Tania and her parents. But what if Clio went back for Freddie and the puppy, after his car crash, and brought them to Cornwall? Is Freddie up there in the car park with her?

He can't go there. He needs to think. Keep a clear head. What would Ji do in this position? What would Sun Tzu do? And whose side is Ji really on? Someone must have seen the car crash, rung the police. Unless the traffic was briefly kept away from the roundabout by the temporary lights.

'Can I have a drink of water?' Adam asks.

'I was going to offer you something stronger, given the circumstances.'

Louis looks up the cliffside again and shouts above the roar of the waves. 'Clio? Come down and give this man a drink.'

Clio. Adam hasn't seen her since she came to their house and tried to destroy his marriage. Now she could be his only hope. He thinks of the feather she left on Freddie's pillow, the one she gave him at Cambridge.

'The bidding is truly remarkable,' Louis says, looking down at his laptop and then at the clock. 'And still ten minutes to go. People are prepared to bid to watch the most extraordinary things on the dark web. There was a lot of disappointment when you resisted Clio's advances at your house. A lot of disappointment.' Louis leans down closer to look at the laptop, the glow from the screen illuminating his white mask. 'But maybe we can put that right tonight,' he adds, starting to type. 'Someone calling themselves @SunTzu544 has just made an irresistible offer to watch you two get it together. How sweet. Sometimes I think the internet was invented for sex. A little light distraction before the final act.'

@SunTzu544. It's Ji, has to be. His friend has betrayed him. The one person who could help him. Why else would he pay money to see Adam with Clio? Adam should have gone with his gut instinct, challenged Ji when he first began to suspect him on the hillside in Wiltshire. He must be in league with Clio. Did she drive back to Tania's parents and take Freddie? Last time Adam spoke with Tania, Ji had come down off the hill and was with her and the children in the house. What if Clio has kidnapped Freddie at Ji's request? He said he couldn't have children. Stop. He must stay focused.

'Ah, Clio,' Louis says, gazing up at the steep banks of seating, 'how is the little brat?'

Adam wants to tell Louis that his son's never once been a brat in his short life, but he bites his lip, waiting for Clio to appear. And when she does, near the top of the cliff, where the bench seats are covered in grass, his heart misses a beat. All he can see in the dark is the occasional flash of a white mask zigzagging down towards them through the ghostly seating.

68

It's as if time has stood still and Adam is back at uni, playing the part of Faustus again. Clio is dressed in the same black leather outfit she wore as a punkish, menacing Mephistopheles twenty-four years ago. Her mask, which is identical to Louis', seems to amplify her sexual power, the frozen, tragic face a warning to all men, like a siren call.

'Freddie's asleep in the van – with the puppy,' Clio says in her familiar husky drawl.

Is Ji in the van too with Freddie? Adam spots a silver hip flask in Clio's hand.

'How cute,' Louis says. 'We've just received an offer we can't refuse – for you and Adam here to do what you should have done at his house. What he's wanted to do his whole life. We haven't got long – eight minutes – but you wouldn't deny a condemned man his final wish, would you?'

Adam flinches at the words and looks across at Clio. It's impossible to gauge her reaction behind the mask. Seconds later it becomes clear. She walks over to Adam and runs her hand through his hair, above the bandage. And then she sits astride him on his lap, forces his legs apart and slides a hand down between them. His last hope has gone. She must have gone back for Freddie, who will be up there in the car park now, smacking his small hands against the side of the van, pleading to be let out. Her loyalty is to Louis, to Ji. They are all in this together, united against him.

'How am I going to fuck him if he's wrapped up like a silver mummy?' she says, calling out to Louis.

There's no tenderness in her actions, the way she's kneading him, and he feels nothing in return. She's just going through the motions, acting for the camera like she's always done. Unblinking. He's been such a fool.

'You'll find a way,' Louis says. 'Think of it as unwrapping a present. And you know what they say about a hanged man. Angel lust, they call it.'

Still sitting on his lap, Clio pushes her mask up on her head, takes a swig from the hip flask and kisses his mouth, filling it with warm whisky.

'He's only got one bullet,' she whispers in his ear as he swallows the burning drink.

At the same time, he feels something cold and smooth placed in his left hand, behind his back. She swings off him, tousling his hair again before she replaces her mask and sashays away to the far side of the plinth like the whore Louis wants her to be.

She's given him a knife. A knife to cut himself free. He can hardly breathe. Clio wants to help him. He tries not to sob with relief. Does that also mean Freddie is safe and not in the van? He's wrong about Ji too. He must have known that Clio represented Adam's only chance to escape. By bidding online as @SunTzu544 – 544, the date of the Chinese tactician's birth – Ji engineered a way for Clio to get close to Adam and slip him a knife. His weird, wise, dear friend Ji. *In the midst of chaos, there's always opportunity.* How could Adam have ever doubted him?

'I think @SunTzu544 was expecting more than a half-hearted handjob,' Louis says.

'They'll have to bid a bit higher then, won't they?' Clio replies, looking at the laptop on the plinth. She rests a hand on Louis' shoulder as she leans closer to the screen. Christ, what hideous hold must he have on her? Adam starts to cut away at the tape on his left wrist with the knife as Clio and Louis peer at the laptop together to his left. Below them, another surge of water fights its way into the zawn, sending a thunderous shudder through the very foundations of the headland.

'One moment,' Louis says, turning to take a call on his mobile, a hand pressed to his other ear to shield out the noise of the sea.

Adam and Clio both watch as Louis turns away from them. Clio glances over at Adam, but he's unable to read her expression through the mask. Is it fear? Something's wrong. Louis' body language changes as he checks the handset. Maybe the signal's dropped.

A gust of wind brings snatches of Louis' conversation. 'Are you sure?... They can't have gone far... Keep looking.'

Adam glances again at Clio, still to his left. He can't nod, but he moves his eyes from her to the plinth next to her. To the gun. Clio looks at it too. Is she about to reach out and take it?

Louis comes off the phone and turns to Clio.

'Freddie and the puppy appear to have gone walkabout,' he shouts above another blast of wind.

'But I left them sleeping in the van,' Clio says.

Adam wishes he could see her face, read her emotions. He

prays that she's lying. She glances across at Adam, who keeps working at the tape binding his wrist. He's nearly released his left hand. What if she did have Freddie and the puppy in the van and has set them free? They could be out there now, wandering through the darkness on the treacherous, windblown cliffs.

'Damon says the van's unlocked,' Louis says to Clio, who backs away from him. 'Did you leave it unlocked?'

Who's Damon? Louis must have had help to arrange tonight. He couldn't have done all this on his own. Maybe Damon was the driver of the red pickup, the go-to man for whenever there's an online bid for a life-changing car accident.

'Of course I didn't,' Clio says.

Louis' phone rings again and he turns away to take it, protecting himself from the wind. The conversation is brief. Clio looks at Adam. Even with the mask, he can see her eyes widening with terror.

Louis is still to Adam's left, on the far side of the plinth with Clio, close to the cliff edge and just within Adam's sightline. 'He's been back to the van, says there's no sign of anyone having been in there,' he says to Clio.

'That's impossible,' Clio says, her voice faltering. She can no longer act the part. She stares at Louis, holding his gaze. Adam's left hand is finally free.

Louis shakes his head in disappointment. 'I gave you a second chance,' he says. 'After you failed to take the kid from the park. My mistake, obviously. It's quite touching, in a way – your loyalty to him.' He gestures across at Adam. 'I always suspected that there was a connection, that he was different from the others. That you weren't playing to the cameras that day when you romped in Grantchester Meadows like young lovers. And when you had the chance twenty-four years later, you tellingly failed to seduce him at his house, didn't consummate your relationship.'

'Because I respect him,' Clio says. 'His marriage, his family.'

'Is that what it is between you? Respect? Doesn't sound like much fun. I thought it might have been something more interesting. Kinky sex perhaps or maybe even love.'

'You wouldn't know what love is,' Clio says, almost spitting the words out.

'But I thought that's what *we* had.' Louis' voice is dripping with sarcasm.

'Love? Us?' Clio laughs, shaking her head. 'Sure, I wanted to love him at Cambridge, but you never let me.' She nods at Adam. 'You were jealous of him, his innate goodness, his desire to help others as a medic. His innocence. Traits you've never possessed.'

'You could have left me,' Louis says.

Adam blinks. *I wanted to love him at Cambridge.* Does that mean she did? Was he right to have believed that they had something? For years, he's told himself that he was deluded, a naive first-year medical student who was punching way above his weight with a sophisticated third-year from France.

Clio stares at the ground and then back at Louis. 'Could I?'

Louis turns to Adam. 'Did she ever explain how she killed her father?'

Adam flinches. He looks across at Clio, wishing he could see her face beneath the mask. He's always wanted to know more about the circumstances of her father's death, whether she really did murder him, as Louis had once claimed.

'She locked him in the sauna,' Louis continues, almost laughing.

Adam stops, transfixed. He needs to concentrate on the knife – it's easier to use with one hand free – but he can't take his eyes off Clio.

'Please,' she says.

'Do you know what happens to the human body at 110 degrees Celsius?' Louis asks. 'It's not pretty. Your skin starts to slough off in great chunks, your internal organs begin to cook. If you're lucky, you've already died of a heart attack, or dehydration, but Clio's father was still alive as his body bled from the inside out. And she watched it all through the sauna window as he begged for his life. Then she watched him die. The smell must have been horrendous.'

'He made my mother's life a living hell,' Clio says, shouting now. 'But I didn't mean to kill him. And I didn't watch him die. The door jammed—'

'And she could have tried harder to let him out,' Louis continues, interrupting her. 'No one else was around to help him – her mother was away. Fortunately, the police believed it was an accident. Indeed the door was found to be faulty. They also believed Clio's story that she wasn't present at the family home in France at the time. That she was with her new boyfriend from Cambridge, who was happy to verify her alibi. No prizes for guessing who that was.'

Adam turns away. It's all beginning to make sense.

'He abused her day and night,' Clio says, her voice raging with passion now. 'Day and night for twenty years! For the "crime" of being a mother who loved her daughter.'

Adam has almost released his other hand, but his mind is spinning. No wonder Clio did Louis' bidding, helped him to blackmail people like Adam, just as he'd suspected. He had the ultimate *kompromat* on her.

Another few seconds and both hands will be free.

Adam remembers his conversation with Clio about children, all those years ago in Grantchester Meadows. *I never, ever want to be a mother.* Now he knows why. Her life suddenly strikes him as so sad. Has she been doing Louis' bidding ever since? Have they been living together all this time?

'Of course you could have left me,' Louis says, arms outstretched in mock innocence. 'Any time you liked. And I wouldn't have told anyone that you took revenge on your own father.'

'And you know all about family revenge.'

Adam glances across at Louis. What does she mean?

'At least I serve it cold,' Louis says, checking on Adam. 'Rather than at 110 degrees.' And then his tone changes, the first hint of panic in his voice, a hitch in his carefully laid plan. 'Now tell me what the fuck you've done with the child. People have paid good money. Money that was to have been shared between us.'

But Clio doesn't answer. Instead, she lunges towards the plinth. Adam braces himself, wide eyed, as he watches her pick up the gun and throw it to him.

'Screw you, Louis!' she shouts. 'Screw fucking you!'

Louis pulls out a second handgun from his jacket and fires at her, just as she jumps off the cliff into the darkness. The gun she threw seems to hover in the air for an eternity before Adam reaches out with his hands, both now free, and catches it.

The wind pauses – the whole world takes a breath – as Adam and Louis point their guns at each other. Clio has gone, lost into the raging sea far below. Was she shot? It's immaterial now. She will never survive the fall. Even if she avoided the cliff edge and landed in the zawn, the waves will lift and throw her onto the rocks like a rag doll.

'Well this wasn't in the script, but I like it,' Louis says. They are still pointing their guns at each other. 'In a Tarantino sort of way.'

He's only got one bullet. Did Clio mean the gun in Adam's hand? Or the one Louis is holding? If it's Louis' gun, then Louis is bluffing, knows he's out of bullets.

'Who are you?' Adam says, trying to stop his arms from shaking, to stop thinking about Clio, her selfless bravery. What had she meant about family revenge? He's holding the gun in both hands, but it's surprisingly heavy.

'Me? You know who I am. Deep down.' Louis pauses. 'I'm the older brother.'

'The older brother?' Adam doesn't understand.

'Newlyn, North Pier. Where Gabe's life changed forever. Where you changed it forever.'

Adam's stomach tightens.

'Someone smashed his head against the cobbles. A bright young local boy, apparently, off to Cambridge to study medicine. Pride of the town. Toast of the Swordfish.'

69

Adam tries to process what Louis has just told him, the magnitude of his words. All the old fears about that night on the North Pier come tumbling back. Clio did once mention that Louis had a younger brother called Gabe, the prodigal son, who was unwell. Depression, she thought. And now it transpires that Gabe was the person who'd slipped and fallen. It couldn't be any worse.

'I thought he was fine,' Adam says, remembering how he'd watched him being helped to the car.

'He was – for a while,' Louis says. 'But the brain's a funny thing, as you will know, particularly when it's suffered a traumatic injury. And my brother's brain started to do funny things. Not at first, but it gradually became obvious that all was not well. A week later he had his first seizure. Other symptoms followed: loss of balance, slurred words, blurred vision, irritability. And a deep, dark depression that enveloped him like a sea fog.'

Adam winces, his nightmare confirmed. His nurse friend at the Treliske had been right to have a go at him. As an aspiring medic, he should have known that head injuries were serious, made sure that the guy was brought in for a check-up.

'He was my best friend, despite our differences,' Louis continues. 'Despite my parents telling me one day that they wished I'd been the one to have the brain injury. They didn't like me or my life choices – the feeling was mutual. The consultant said early on that Gabe's poor quality of life was unlikely to improve. He even hinted at a shorter life expectancy. And he was right. Gabe soon had full-blown epilepsy, suffering regular seizures that were resistant to treatment. And he was depressed or angry most of the time, no longer himself.'

Louis' voice is low, slow, weighed down with sadness. Adam wonders if there are tears behind his mask.

'What upset me most was that he'd lost his spirit, the spark that made him my cheeky younger brother,' he continues. 'He was the one who used to do handstands on his surfboard, be the first to somersault off the harbour wall, pull all the prettiest girls at the Mariners with his irresistible smile and foppish blonde hair. I was the older brother, but it was me who was the weak one. Always sickly, allergic to everything. Gabe was the fit and sporty type. I thought he was invincible – he once walked away from a horrific motorbike crash – but that night in Newlyn he lost what made him Gabe.' Louis swallows, struggling with his emotions. 'He lost his soul. And I vowed to find the person who had taken it. Going to the police was out of the question, given what his friends had done to your mate. And my parents thought that he'd just slipped on wet cobbles. So I took matters into my own hands.'

'He did slip,' Adam says.

Louis holds up his other hand to silence him. 'At the time, I was trying to decide between Oxford and Cambridge for my PhD. First World problem, I know, but the choice was made for me when I discovered where the bright boy from Newlyn was going to study medicine. And when I heard about a student production of *Doctor Faustus*, a play that had always intrigued me, it became clear what I needed to do. I wouldn't blackmail you for money, as I'd done with all the others. I'd take away your soul, just like you'd taken my brother's. Just like Lucifer took Faustus's. I told Gabe what I was planning and he didn't disapprove. It gave him something to live for, you see, the thought of you dying in twenty-four years' time.'

Adam thinks he might be sick.

'I wavered in the early days. I even tried to take my own life once – at this very spot, as you might recall – but I owed it to Gabe to see it through,' Louis continues. 'And then he succeeded where I'd failed and killed himself a couple of months ago, unable to cope with the seizures or the depression any more. He'd lost the ability to speak but I took the timing of his suicide as his way of telling me to go through with the plan, stick to our *Doctor Faustus* script.'

Adam sits there stunned by what he's just heard, the guilt washing through him as he tries to keep the gun pointing at Louis. A man he once pushed in a brawl went on to suffer post-traumatic epilepsy and depression and eventually killed himself. Never mind that he slipped, or that Adam's friend Tom has also never been quite the same since. At least Tom's still alive. It's the calculated nature of Louis' plan, like a complex game of 3D chess, that's so unsettling, the realisation that Adam was a marked man, his fate predetermined, from the day he arrived at Cambridge. That nothing in his first year of being a medical student was down to chance or free will. He only auditioned for *Doctor Faustus* because Clio persuaded him to. The altercation with Lecter at the party must have been a set-up as well, Louis knowing that Adam had lost control once before, on a harbour wall in Cornwall, and would readily lose control again...

'Were you there?' Adam asks. 'In Newlyn that night?'

'Unfortunately not. I might have been able to keep my little brother out of trouble. And sadly there was no CCTV footage. But I heard all about it. According to Gabe's friends, you were like a firework that just needed to be lit, a temper primed to explode. It wasn't difficult to trigger you again at the party – and to make sure it was captured on film this time. Clio knew what to do, who to flirt with on the dance floor, which buttons of yours to press. She's a pro, had done it all before. I just had to make sure the bathroom window was open and the hidden cameras were rolling.'

Adam thinks again of Lecter dancing with Clio, of the billowing curtain, how easily he had been played by Louis. Had Clio nearly confessed to him, revealed the master plan? *Be careful, Adam*, she'd said, on the last day they'd talked in Cambridge. She'd known then exactly what Louis had in store for Adam in the future, warned him of the dangers of his past. And she's just sacrificed her life tonight trying to protect him.

'I'm sorry about your brother, truly I am, but he slipped as I was trying to get to Tom, who couldn't swim—'

'Please, it's almost time,' Louis says, interrupting him. 'Spare me the bleating.' He glances across at the clock. 'Do you know why 3 a.m. is called the witching hour?'

Adam tries to shake his restricted head, still aiming the gun at Louis' chest. He feels another wave of sadness for Clio. He owes it to her to survive – to kill Louis.

'Because it's the exact opposite of 3 p.m.,' Louis continues, having to shout again. The sea and the wind have resumed their bid to tear down the cliffs of Cornwall. 'The time they crucified Christ.'

'You'll never get away with this,' Adam says, shouting too now.

'Shall we go to hell together, then?'

Adam remembers there was no redemption for Faustus. It was brutal to the end. 'How do you mean?'

'We're almost out of time. It's nearly 3 a.m.'

His gun is still trained on Louis' chest, but Adam's arms are growing weaker by the second.

'You and I will never know, but at least those out there will discover how much your soul weighs,' Louis says, nodding at the camera and then the industrial scales Adam's sitting on.

'Why did you shoot Clio if you loved her?' Adam asks.

Louis doesn't answer. His hand is beginning to shake too. The sight of his trembling gun – the first sign of weakness – gives Adam hope. *Appear strong when you are weak, weak when you are strong.*

'And who else have you destroyed with your wretched films?' he asks. 'How many?'

'Three,' Louis says, holding up three fingers.

There must be more people than that. Other innocent students like him and Aldous. Didn't Louis study Classics at Oxford before switching to Cambridge for his PhD? And how many people has he preyed on since then? He glances at the clock and back at Adam. Adam looks too, realises what's happening. He tightens his finger around the trigger, heart pounding.

'Two.'

Is there a safety catch? Too late to check. He offers up a

prayer, begs that Clio was right about the bullet. His whole body is shaking now. Please God, let there have been only one bullet in Louis' gun.

'One.'

Adam closes his eyes as he squeezes the trigger. The crack of the gun is louder than he expects and knocks his body backwards against the chair. Or was it a second bullet from Louis' gun? He waits for the shock of pain, the agony to spread like ignited petrol, but he feels nothing. Mentally he checks himself from head to toe, and then slowly, very slowly, he opens his eyes. Louis' body is on the ground in front of him, blood leaching from his head onto the stone stage.

Adam can barely believe that he is alive, out of danger. He checks his body again, but all he can feel is relief coursing through his tired limbs. He's survived. Clio had been right. One bullet. He's going to live, see his family again. And then a phone starts to ring nearby...

Adam hadn't noticed that Louis had placed it on the plinth, beside the laptop. He looks around, panic returning. A solitary figure appears at the top of the cliff, a handset to his ear as he zigzags down towards the stage, just as Clio had done. Is it Damon? Adam still has the gun in his hands. Was it only loaded with one bullet too? Damon might not know. Unless he was the one who prepared them. Should Adam sit still, pretend to be dead? Or bluff with the gun? Damon is closer now, six rows from the stage. But then he stops in his tracks. Above the sound of the storm, a police siren. Several sirens, rising and falling on the wind.

Damon stares at Louis' body. Glancing at Adam, he turns, runs back up the pathway and disappears. Adam punches out a sigh of relief. His eyes flit from the empty seats, to Louis, to the darkness all around. He starts to cry, slowly at first and then big, heaving sobs, his torso pulling at the duct tape. Clio died to save him, to save Freddie, his family, his marriage. He needs to free himself, ring Tania with the handset on the plinth, tell her he's OK, that he loves her and always will. Theirs is a relationship tempered to endure. It would never have worked with Clio at Cambridge, no matter what she said. Their time together there was too ephemeral, too fleeting. Clio must have understood that as well, deep down. And later she saw how much he loved Tania, his children. Twice she refused to abduct Freddie. She respected him, the family life he had made, just as she said.

Heavy rain starts to streak in from the Channel as he pulls at the duct tape wrapped around his aching ribs. And then he stops, hit by a sudden spasm of agony. Maybe he has been shot. His head begins to throb again too. He looks around the stage, at the carnage of the final act, Louis' dead body, the camera, the laptop, the clock. Louis tried to kill him, to take his soul, but he failed. And Adam has escaped Faustus's fate, slipped the noose of twenty-four years.

'*Stand still, you ever-moving spheres of heaven,*' he whispers, rivulets of water running down his face. '*That time may cease, and midnight never come.*'

But his voice is lost in the roar of the diabolical sea.

70

'Go gently,' Tania says as Freddie climbs up onto Adam's hospital bed to hug him. 'Daddy's a bit sore.'

It's weird being back in the Treliske after so many years, this time as a patient, but at least Adam's being well looked after, like a long-lost friend.

'He's really naughty, Daddy,' Freddie says, driving a toy car – not the Ferrari – over Adam's bandaged head.

'Ow,' Adam moans, but he manages to grin at his son.

'Freddie!' Tania says. 'Be careful.'

'It's OK.' Adam smiles at Tania.

His voice is croaky and he still feels weak, five days on from the dramatic events at the Minack. Today is the first time he's felt strong enough to entertain Freddie, to talk to Tania. He needs to tell her about Louis, who he really was. Tell her everything.

'Who's being naughty? Is it Ji?'

Adam nods towards Ji, who is on his own in the corner of the hospital room, rocking Tilly to sleep in the pram. He has a new job if he wants one. For the past five days, he's been living and working out of a hotel in Truro, coming into the hospital whenever he can to help Tania, keep an eye on Adam.

'Ji can be very naughty,' Adam says. But he's loyal too. He can't believe he ever doubted his old friend.

'Louis, silly,' Freddie says.

Adam closes his eyes, hit by a wave of exhaustion. Now's not the time for a family argument, but the puppy's not going to be called Louis. Not in a thousand years.

'Everything alright in here?' Doctor Pender asks, popping his greying head around the door. He's to retire soon, spend more time walking the coast path at St Agnes with his grandchildren.

'All good,' Tania says.

Adam nods. It's great to see Doctor Pender again. He feels bad he hasn't been in touch more.

'Keep an eye on him,' Doctor Pender says, gesturing at Adam. 'Doctors make the very worst patients.'

Adam wasn't actually shot by Louis, but the car crash had left him more injured than he'd realised at the Minack. Whiplash, deep lacerations on one side of his head, two broken ribs and a bruised and contused spleen. It could have been worse; he could be dead, like poor Clio. There was no sign of her when the police, paramedics and HM Coastguard crew arrived on the Minack's windswept stage, battling against the rain and wind. He watched as they carried Louis' body up between the steep rows of seats, already composing the letter he plans to write to Clio's mother in France. He'll explain how she turned against Louis and sacrificed herself to save Adam. He won't mention that he knows how Clio's father died.

The doctors say Adam should be out of hospital in a few days. He gave a short statement to the police in the Minack car park, before the ambulance brought him here at dawn, but he'll give a fuller one as soon as he's able. The police were baffled, to put it mildly, by the scene they came across on the cliffs. He expects more searching questions in the days ahead about the exact nature of the deal he struck with Louis at university. So far, though, Louis' obsession with filming has worked in his favour. The police found Adam on the Minack stage with a gun, sitting on a chair next to Louis' dead body, which didn't look good, but the live stream, recorded by Ji and subsequently shared with the authorities, clearly showed that Louis had been trying to shoot Adam too. It also captured Louis firing his gun at Clio as she leapt over the cliff edge. Her body has yet to be found.

'How are you feeling?' Tania asks, resting a hand on his arm.

'I've felt better,' he says. It's suddenly very painful to speak.

Tania had apparently not been able to watch the live feed that night, but she saw enough to identify the Minack and call the police. Ji watched it all from the front passenger seat, keeping her informed without going into too many details as they were all driven in his car through the night to Cornwall. Miraculously, Tilly, Freddie and the puppy had slept for most of the journey – a testament to the smooth driving skills of Ji's chauffeur. Tania wasn't going to let anyone leave her side and Freddie had insisted that the puppy come too.

'Clio died saving your life,' Tania says. 'I'll always be grateful to her for that.'

'Me too.'

Tania was saddened but not surprised to hear of the hold that Louis had exerted on Clio. In the wake of the pandemic, a lot of women had tried to escape coercive relationships, according to her former GP colleagues. It also seemed to repeat down the generations. Clio's mother had been drawn to a controlling man. In turn, Clio had been drawn to Louis. As for Clio's father's gruesome demise, Tania wasn't quite so sad. Female solidarity and all that.

Taking Tania's hand in his, Adam runs his finger over her wedding ring.

'Nothing happened in Greenwich, you know,' he says. 'She was at our house under sufferance. For Louis' cameras.'

'I just feel so sorry for her, poor woman.' Tania shudders. 'And I'm not sure I ever want a sauna again.'

Adam smiles, drawing strength to continue. 'She didn't want to take Freddie either,' he says. 'Or ruin my career. Still no word on the sexting story?'

The Sun hasn't published anything, according to Doctor Pender. Nor has any other paper. Crispin has been trying to find out what happened.

'I think the story's been pulled,' Tania says.

Adam tries to speak, explain what might have happened, but he's too tired. If Louis had initially asked Clio to befriend Adam's teenage patient, give her some money, maybe later she asked the girl to withdraw her allegations too.

Tania wipes at her eyes and turns to the window.

'You OK?' he whispers.

Ji's mobile phone starts to ring. He checks on Tilly in the pram, gives the thumbs up to Tania and steps outside the room to take the call.

'How many people's lives do you think Louis destroyed?' she asks. 'How many marriages?'

Adam shakes his head. He dreads to think what Louis' crude blackmailing of student doctors and lawyers – the means by which he funded himself at university – had morphed into over the years. Deadly NFTs and more bidding in red rooms, presumably. The police will get to the bottom of it, find out what he did, where he went next, after dropping out of Cambridge. They have already arrested Damon, the driver of the red pickup and the only other person who appeared to be working for Louis. No doubt because Louis had blackmailed him too. And they have discovered where Louis lived, in a remote farmhouse on West Penwith's bleak moorland, near Gurnard's Head. Clio seems to have stayed there too, in between long periods with her mother in France, coming over to Britain when she was needed for one of Louis' stings. It didn't sound like much of a relationship.

'Sorry to interrupt, but I need to get back to London now,' Ji says, coming into the room.

OK, no problem, Adam says to himself, mimicking one of his friend's less literary catchphrases. He smiles at Ji as Tania moves to one side.

'Of course, Ji. And, you know… thank you for everything. For being here, for being such a good friend.' Another stab of guilt.

'That was my office… about the film Louis made of you at Cambridge. The student party scenes.'

'Any news?' Adam asks, his body tensing.

Louis had made it available on the site – for a fee, of course. Thanks to @SunTzu544's deep pockets, Ji was able to take a look. He recorded it too and sent it to his company's FX team for analysis. They also managed to take the original film offline. Adam could have lent them his old video copy from home, if he'd known.

Ji glances at Tania and then at Adam.

'It's OK, Tania knows everything,' Adam says.

Ji smiles nervously. 'Given it was made almost twenty-five years ago, they said the editing of the bathroom scene was pretty good,' he says. 'Good enough to convince a lay person. A jury. It took my team a while, but they eventually found something. It had been edited – heavily, as it turns out.'

'You mean...?'

Adam feels a huge weight lifting, as if he's floating up from his bed. All the years of worry, the nightmares – Lecter's terrified eyes staring back at him – start to slip away like melting ice. For so long he's carried the burden of not knowing, alternating between a gut feeling of innocence and the most profound sense of guilt. What if he had been too drunk to check his anger in the bathroom, to remember his actions afterwards?

Ji glances around the room in case a nurse or doctor has walked in. 'I mean that you didn't push anyone out of a second-floor window,' he says.

Tania stifles a sob. Adam can feel tears welling too, but something still troubles him. If Adam didn't push Lecter out of the window, who did? Or did Lecter jump, fuelled by LSD and MDMA, as the coroner concluded? *I just had to leave the bathroom window open.* It sounds too random, too unpredictable to be a part of Louis' carefully crafted plan. He couldn't have known for certain that Lecter would jump.

Adam thinks back to the party, trying to picture those seconds after he left Lecter in the locked bathroom and before his broken body was discovered in the courtyard. Louis strode past him on the stairs when the screaming started. Where had he been? In the bathroom? Did he slip in and push Lecter out of the window after Adam had locked the door and gone back downstairs? It's the only explanation. Adam had left the bathroom key in the door. He adds it to his growing list of things he must tell the police.

'Thank you,' Adam manages to call out after Ji, as he heads for the door.

'Thank you, Ji,' Tania adds. 'For everything.'

'Someone better come and get the puppy,' Ji says, pausing in the doorway. His driver has been looking after it in the car park. 'A dog is for life, not just for Christmas.'

'I'll be down in a sec,' Tania says, smiling through her tears.

'It's going to be OK.' Adam smiles back, squeezing her hand. He feels stronger already.

'I know it is,' she says. 'But I just can't help feeling that if you'd gone to the police at the time—'

'Please,' he says, interrupting her. He knows justice might have been served for Aldous, and God knows how many other lives would have been spared. 'But the film... You heard Ji. It was well made. Any jury would have been convinced by it. It was too much of a risk. I'd been seen by everyone at that party manhandling the guy up the stairs. Pushing him out of a window would have seemed very plausible.'

Adam's thought it through so many times, every possible permutation. Now he can let go, see Aldous right, and all the other victims of Louis' blackmail too – he's sure there are many.

'Will you show Louis' film to the police?' Tania asks.

Adam nods. He doesn't want to carry any other secrets through his life.

'She kissed me,' he says, remembering how Clio had slipped a shot of whisky from her mouth into his. 'At the Minack. Just before she gave me the knife.'

'It's OK,' Tania says. 'I don't need to know the details. Ji told me what he was doing by bidding, that he sensed Clio might want to get a message to you.'

'The kiss was for the cameras. For Louis.'

Tania goes over to the pram. Freddie is on the floor, happily pushing his car around. 'Are you going to come down with me to get the puppy?' she asks him.

'Louis!' Freddie says, jumping up.

'Say goodbye to Daddy. We'll be back soon.'

They're staying with Adam's mum at the Nook in Newlyn. She's eighty-five now, but more mobile than she used to be, and plans to visit Adam this evening. It will be good to catch up. When he's out of here, he'll join them over in Newlyn, treat them to a meal at Mackerel Sky, a delicious fish tapas bar on the bridge.

'Bye-bye, Daddy,' Freddie says, driving his car over Adam's legs.

Tania keeps the door open with one foot as she holds Freddie's hand and manoeuvres the pram.

'Extraordinary,' Adam says. 'You seem to manage perfectly well without me.'

Tania smiles wryly. 'Bye,' she says, blowing him a kiss. And then she hesitates in the doorway. 'Who do you think he was – Louis?'

'Louis!' Freddie repeats from outside in the corridor. The driver has come up to find Freddie, take him back down to retrieve the puppy.

'There's something else I need to tell you.' Adam can't put it off any longer.

'That sounds ominously familiar.'

It's true. He's had a lot to get off his chest. He takes a deep breath.

'You remember I told you about what happened on the pier in Newlyn once, with Tom and that group of posh students?'

She nods.

'The one who slipped when I pushed him…' He hesitates, composing himself. 'It turns out that he was called Gabe and he was Louis' younger brother.'

Tania's eyes widen in shock. They widen even more when Adam tells her what happened to Gabe, the seizures and depression, how he took his own life almost twenty-four years later, prompting Louis to go through with his Faustian plan. Tania leaves the pram in the corridor and comes back over to the bed, where she sits down and takes Adam's hand. It's a while before she speaks.

'You need to tell the police.' Her voice is quiet, measured. Without anger.

'I know – I'll tell them everything. When I give my full statement.'

'It's the only way you'll ever get any peace of mind, Adam. The only way any of us will.'

'Tom's never fully recovered. It doesn't make it any better, but—'

'You should have gone to the police at the time,' Tania interrupts. It's become something of a refrain of hers.

'I know.'

'You were trying to save Tom. On your own. He might have drowned. It was a brave thing you did, given how many of them there were. The police would have believed you, understood how Gabe slipped when you tried to break free and get to Tom. The courts would have believed you too, if it had come to that. And the police will now. I'm sure they will.'

She sighs. 'God, what a twisted bastard Louis was. He gave me the creeps. What you've told me about him.'

'Chuck some salt over your shoulder and you'll be fine,' Adam says, trying to lighten the mood.

They smile at each other. He's glad he's told her about Gabe.

She leans over the bed and kisses him. 'I love you,' she whispers.

'I love you too, more than you know,' he whispers back, 'but you're hurting my ribs.'

Adam lies there in the empty hospital room, already looking forward to Tania's next visit. It was a room like this where he visited Louis, twenty-four years earlier. Slowly, he reaches over to the drawer and pulls it open. A copy of the Bible is inside. He closes the drawer again and lies back, staring at the ceiling. And then he sits up, very gingerly, and slides his legs out of bed.

He stands at the window, looking down on the car park. There's Ji and his driver, handing over the puppy to Freddie. Tania has Tilly in her arms now, the pram next to her. He'll never be able to thank Ji enough for his help. Without his intervention – @SunTzu544's intervention – he'd never have survived. And to think he mistrusted him.

He watches as Ji kisses Tania goodbye, squeezes Tilly's foot and shakes Freddie's hand with an exaggerated bow. He would have made a good father. Adam's about to turn away when he notices a security camera overlooking the car park. He waits for the surge of anxiety as the camera angles its gaze down on his precious family. But the camera doesn't move. Instead, its gaze remains averted, as if it's looking the other way.

A knock on his door. He turns to see a nurse.

'You shouldn't be out of your bed, Doctor Pound,' she says, smiling.

'Just waving goodbye to the family.' Adam nods at the window.

'Special delivery,' she says, holding out an envelope. She turns to leave. 'Best to rest as much as you can.'

'I'll try.' Adam looks at the typed address on the envelope: 'Doctor Adam Pound, Treliske Hospital, Truro, Cornwall, UK'. Maybe they will move back to Cornwall one day and he'll work here. And then he sees the French stamp and postmark. Swallowing hard, he opens the envelope and stares.

No letter or documents. Just a single feather, brown and striped.

He takes it out and looks at the envelope again, opens the door, but the nurse has gone, the corridor deserted.

Is it from Clio? Is there any possible way she could still be alive? The storm was raging at the Minack that night, the chances minimal of anyone surviving a fall into such a violent sea. Who else could have sent the feather? Clio's mother? She used to give feathers to Clio. But how would she know what had happened or where to send it?

He turns to the window just in time to see Tania and Freddie wave Ji's car off, the dog at Freddie's side. Instinctively, Adam raises his hand too, waving the feather. Whoever it's from, the feather did its job. He and his family were protected. They are all safe. And maybe Clio is too, having finally outwitted Louis to live her own life of freedom. Of *liberté*. And she wanted to let him know. He hopes so, with all his heart.

He will need a debrief with Ji about everything, feather included, when he's feeling better. Maybe Adam will take him to dinner at Hakkasan as a thank you. He looks again at the dog as it tugs on its lead, almost pulling Freddie over. Why did Clio tell Freddie it was called Louis? And then something strange happens. The dog appears to look up at Adam's window. Adam stares back at the black creature. It's only a puppy, but it seems to have stepped out of its boisterous world and continues to look up at him.

Adam blinks, his mouth drying. Something glints in the dog's eyes, catching the afternoon sun. He remembers the tap on his shoulder at the fancy-dress party, spinning round to see Louis and his horrific orange irises. Are the dog's eyes glowing up at him now? Adam peers closer, cupping his hand against the window. He shakes his head. Of course they're not. Such things are the stuff of movies, Louis' films. And he's not in one of those any more. It's time for the credits to roll, for the epilogue, for the chorus to speak a final time.

Faustus is gone.

Acknowledgements

Dr Andy Beale; Conor Beale; The Boathouse, Portscatho; *Dark Salt Clear* by Lamorna Ash; Peter and Sue Evans; The General Medical Council & Medical Schools Council (*Professional Behaviour and Fitness to Practise*: *Guidance for Medical Schools and Their Students*); Alex Goldsmith; *Dr Faustus*, adapted and directed for BBC Radio 3 by Emma Harding; Mark and Susanne Hatwood; Laura Palmer, Peyton Stableford, Lucy Ridout, Bethan Jones, Anne Rieley and all at Head of Zeus; Mick and Jo; Immerse Education (*Why Become a Doctor?*); The Infographics Show (*Worst Ways to Die*); Will Francis, Kirsty Gordon and the team at Janklow & Nesbit; Ji Ma in Shenzhen; Mansfield College, Oxford; Marlborough LitFest; Lana Mawlood; Cameron Mclennan; The Minack Theatre, Porthcurno; Rob Pender; The Royal Literary Fund; J.P.Sheerin; Felix, Maya, Jago and, most of all, Hilary.

About the Author

J.S. MONROE read English at Cambridge, worked as a foreign correspondent in Delhi, and was Weekend editor of the *Daily Telegraph* in London before becoming a full-time writer. His psychological thriller *Find Me* became a bestseller in 2017, and has since been translated into 14 languages. Writing under the name Jon Stock, he is also the author of five spy thrillers. He is currently the Royal Literary Fund Writing Fellow at Mansfield College, Oxford, and lives in Wiltshire with his wife, Hilary Stock, a fine art photographer. They have three children.